TH

TICKET

Dave Bonestroo

To Hazel, Arbor, and Beth for providing the legacy.

To my extended family who provided the stories.

To my family for the inspiration.

Contents

A TICKET

We have all had one, a simple piece of paper with numbers printed on it. It could be as innocuous as a parking garage ticket tossed away and blowing along a city street or a ticket stub to a baseball game dropped when exiting the stadium. Maybe a grocery store or restaurant receipt stuck in a pocket.

It could be as worthless as a betting ticket for a horse that came in last place or perhaps a lottery ticket worth millions of dollars. All printed on the same paper, same ink. Each destined for a different use, and each of much different value to the holder. The following is a story about the last item, a small thin slip of printed paper, a lottery ticket, and how it impacted the lives it touched.

THAT MORNING

Jack drank from a glass of orange juice as he sat at the old, small Formica-topped kitchen table and checked lottery results as he had done every Sunday morning for the past two and a half years. His phone displayed last night's winning numbers: 5-7-12-24-49-04. He read them mindlessly, without focus, the first time through. Then his mind registered recognition and clicked into gear; those numbers were familiar. He reread them, this time out loud: 5-7-12-24-49-04. Then again. Then again, for a third time.

They were the right numbers. He knew it, yet was not ready to accept it. He thought his mind must be playing tricks on him, punishing him with an inability to focus for his partying the night before. His brain and body seemed to freeze as his excitement level spiked. He opened his iPhone Notes app and read the numbers recorded there. He carefully wrote them down on a piece of paper. Then he looked back at the lottery results link. He stared at the numbers on the phone and then on the notepaper, carefully looking back and forth, reading them out loud one by one, right to left, then left to right. He fully expected one or the other to change and not match. His heart was now palpitating. He found it hard to breathe. Adrenaline coursed through his body, overwhelming remaining hangover symptoms.

He leapt out of the chair, jostling the table and knocking over his glass of orange juice, and pumped his arm like a pitcher who'd just thrown a perfect game in the World Series and yelled, "Oh my God, we're rich, rich, we hit the lottery, yes, yes, yes!" How rich, he wondered? He read the news article stated that the single winning ticket was worth $685 million and was purchased in the Los Angeles area.

He thought he was going to stop breathing. "Oh my God," he repeated. "I can't believe this. Where's the ticket? Where's Amelia?!" Looking for a towel, he quickly cleaned up the spilled orange juice from the table and the floor.

SITUATION

Amelia and Jack had individually made their ways west to Los Angeles on different paths, searching for a good life in the warm southern California sun. They discovered that LA was a competitive town in terms of finding opportunities and achieving success. They both worked hard to make ends meet. Now a couple, they were optimistic about their future. Perhaps more importantly, they were in love and did not need a lot to be happy: just each other.

Jack had proposed to Amelia over beer and pizza on the patio at a quaint Laguna Beach bar while celebrating the second anniversary of their first date. As he stared intently at her face. She asked if he was thinking about how much he loved her. He replied, "Yes. Every time I look at your face." He had not purchased the engagement ring yet but knew it was the right time to ask the question. She happily accepted. He had given her the engagement ring two weeks later. The diamond was small. Their love was real.

On the morning that Jack read those fateful lottery numbers, the wedding was three weeks away. They both were excited to commit to each other and make their way through life together. They were not extraordinary people. They were just like most of us are, were, or will be: two kids figuring it out together, living one day at a time.

This is their story.

AMELIA

Amelia grew up with her older brother, Henrik, on Wilcox Street in Stillwater, Minnesota. When she was eight years old, her parents were killed by a drunk driver in a head-on automobile accident. Amelia's grandparents on her mother's side, Kate and Gerald Oster, moved into the Stillwater house to raise their two grandchildren.

Gerald and Kate were both microbiologists who researched sterilization indicators at the nearby 3M campus. Kate quit her job to be at home for her grandchildren. They used some of the settlement from the drunk driver's insurance policy and some of her parents' life insurance policies to help with finances.

Losing their parents was extremely hard on both children, but hardest on Amelia. Kate and Gerald were kind, but at their age, they did not have energy to deal with day-to-day conflicts and emotions typical of young children. As a result, Amelia and Henrik's upbringing was loving but "old-fashioned" and strict.

Amelia felt constrained under their parentage. She did not often have access to the newest games and toys as the other kids at school did. She did not like being prohibited from watching cool TV programs and streaming shows. Her clothes, never the most expensive or fashionable, were always purchased at big-box discount chains. She respected Gerald and Kate's rules but disliked restrictions. Being eight years older and a sophomore in high school with a part-time job, Henrik avoided the constraints and had money to buy things he wanted.

Sadly, Grandpa Gerald passed away from a heart attack when Amelia was fifteen, after which Grandma Kate became more dedicated to her church and the circle of support from friends she had within the congregation. Kate turned inward emotionally. She had already lost her daughter and son-in-law, and now she could only cling to memories of the man she loved. She struggled to be present for Amelia.

By this time, her brother had graduated from the University of Minnesota with a degree in journalism. He moved to California in search of a career writing TV commercials and short stories. Amelia felt even more isolated at home. She turned her full focus toward school and friends. She enjoyed math, science, and working with algorithms of computer programming and application design. These were built on order, logic, and understandable rules, concepts that made sense to her.

Amelia was a relatively attractive girl with brunette hair and blue eyes, though she had never been called beautiful. At 5'10", she had a strong, lean, muscular frame. She was a good athlete, with better-than-average speed and balance, which allowed her to earn three letters for the Stillwater High Ponies in basketball and volleyball three times and twice in track, as a high jumper and hurdler. She loved to compete. Between school, athletics, and friends, Amelia was always busy and fully engaged in the small river town's social life.

When friends described Amelia, they used words like *levelheaded, introverted, quiet, uncertain, follower, loyal, unassuming, smart,* and *honest.*

Following high school, she graduated from the University of Wisconsin, Madison, with a dual degree in graphic arts and computer science. She initially intended to live in the Twin Cities and work for a local firm. However, the Twin Cities wasn't far enough from Stillwater to prevent Grandma Kate from continually trying to insert herself into Amelia's daily life. Although she loved her grandmother, it was frustrating and hard to be around her for long periods of time. Kate always wanted an accounting of Amelia's day and frequently offered unsolicited opinions about whether Amelia was doing right or wrong things. Amelia knew Kate loved and cared for her, yet she felt smothered at a time when she wanted to be carefree and explore what life had to offer.

Henrik, located in Los Angeles, was barely surviving by writing copy for TV shows and commercials while living with five other would-be writers and actors, all waiting for their big breaks. During one phone conversation, he told Amelia that LA had ample opportunities for her skillset. If it didn't work out in LA, she could always head up north to Silicon Valley, where she could easily find work with a tech firm like Facebook or Google.

Although she felt loyalty to Grandma Kate for raising her, Amelia knew she would be miserable staying in cold, dark Minnesota for another winter. She announced that she was moving to LA.

Kate was heartbroken, saying, "Meels, I really would rather you stayed here with me. I count on you to help me. I would be so lonely if you left me. I know I'm selfish, but you are such a large part of my life. I need you here."

After several weeks of conversation and increased frustration on Amelia's part, Kate finally told Amelia that she understood and that Amelia should enjoy her life. "I get it," she said. "I was once young, too. But I will miss you terribly."

Amelia headed west.

WEST COAST FRIEND

Amelia sent out job applications before leaving for LA and secured a part-time position at West Coast Advertising. She did simple ad layouts for the print side of the business. It was menial work for someone of her skills, but it paid the bills. She slept on the couch at Henrik's house until she found a small efficiency apartment of her own. Her earnings provided enough to cover rent with just enough left over for food and living expenses. After six months, she was rewarded with a raise and a full-time position on the business's more lucrative website side.

Eventually, Amelia rented an apartment with Kim Robinson who worked three cubicles away at West Coast. Kim came to LA from Phoenix, Arizona, to attend UCLA and play volleyball for the Bruins while studying for an art history degree. Her goal had been to play on the pro beach volleyball circuit, but as a junior, she'd badly torn her ACL when she jumped and landed on a teammate's foot. Kim could no longer play at the highly competitive level required. She'd turned her focus to her education and changed her field of study to earn a degree in web design. She had been with West Coast for about a year before Amelia arrived. The two became close friends.

Amelia was happy in the California sun, excited about being alive, and looking forward to the next phase of her life.

JACK

Sheboygan, Wisconsin, is a town proud of its old-world German, Dutch, and Irish heritage. Located on the western shores of Lake Michigan, it's known for its relationship to the Kohler Company.

Jack grew up on Ontario Avenue with two older brothers and three younger sisters. Helmut and Alice Lemke's children grew up in the small house sharing bedrooms, and had typical experiences of being kids from the wrong side of the tracks in a small town. They grew up tough and learned to defend themselves. There were the usual arguments and fights over space and material things. Jack's older brothers weren't afraid to rough him up if they wanted something he had.

Jack was smart enough to compete well in class. He was tough enough to play linebacker on the Sheboygan North Vikings football squad and, at six feet tall, he was quick enough to be the backup point guard on North High's State Championship basketball team. In the spring, he played on the golf team and enjoyed the courses at Kohler Golf where he caddied summers to earn money for college. Girls called him attractive. He was popular with schoolmates and got along well with his friends. When people described Jack, they used words like *confident, outspoken, extroverted, rule-bender, self-centered,* and *tough.*

At Marquette University, Jack studied business and marketing. He worked hard enough to earn a 3.2 GPA. Like so many growing up in small towns, Jack had plans and dreamed of getting away from home as soon as feasible. Although he would miss his friends and to a lesser extent his family, he could not wait to put Sheboygan in his rearview mirror.

After he graduated Jack sent his resume to Silicon Valley and LA marketing firms. After a trip to LA, he received two offers. Jack accepted an entry-level position at Ventura Marketing, selling web and print-based advertising for local businesses. He worked hard, and within two years had earned two promotions and his own small inner office as a sign of appreciation for his efforts. Jack was willing to work hard to get ahead, but he saw life on a California beach as his true calling. He worked for the weekend: sun, sand, beer, parties, and most importantly, California girls.

To afford a decent apartment in a safe location, Jack had a roommate. Bill Klancher, an attorney who had grown up in the LA area near San Clemente. They'd met when Jack sold him on a marketing piece for a local "Best Dressed" article in *LA Today* magazine. Bill liked the idea of having a local designer dress him and then be photographed for the spread. The article's success led to a closer friendship; Bill eventually invited Jack to share his two-bedroom apartment. He felt that the layout would provide free publicity in the marketplace as Bill had just started working with a law firm specializing in entertainment law. The firm provided representation for Hollywood talent and local professional athletes.

Bill was a tall, prototypical southern California surfer with sun-bleached blond hair and natural athletic skills. He preferred working smart versus working hard. Bill avoided being judged by performance related to the annual hourly billing requirements set by the firm. He was focused on networking and marketing to bring in work vs. actually doing it. He had been successful at it so far.

BUMP, SET, LOVE

One of the more frequent weekend recreational excursions the roommates made together was a trip to Laguna Beach, where Bill taught Jack to surf. It took several trips before Jack became proficient enough to say that he was competent on the shortboard. Bill also knew the city's ins and outs, local places to go where two young bachelors could mingle with new girls and old friends.

One Saturday afternoon in June, nearly a year after Jack landed his first job in LA, Bill and Jack loaded their surfboards and headed to Laguna. After a couple of hours on the surf, they came ashore to rest and catch some sun to warm up and check out girls.

The beach featured sand volleyball courts where locals showed off skills they may or may not have. One court emptied as they watched. Two girls sitting on towels nearby got up and carried a ball onto the court. They began to warm up, bumping the ball back and forth. Bill watched for a moment. Then he asked Jack if he played volleyball.

Jack replied that he was not a player and hated the game.

Bill responded, "Good, sounds perfect," and pulled him to his feet, then pushed him toward the court where Amelia and Kim warmed. Bill asked the girls if they could play too.

Kim looked at Amelia and wryly smiled as she raised her eyebrows and said, "Sure," thinking that Bill was about as hot as they came. They introduced themselves, and the boys joined the warmups. It quickly became evident that the girls and Bill knew what they were doing on the sand court and that Jack, although athletic, was totally clueless. Two other couples walked onto the court's opposing side; a game ensued. The opposition had clearly played before. It didn't take long for them to expose Jack's lack of volleyball skill. Kim, Amelia, and Bill made the game competitive. Eventually, with the opposing team focused on hitting the ball to Jack, his carries, missed spikes, missed hits, and serves into the net or deep over the backline contributed to a loss.

After the match, Bill thanked the girls and asked if he and Jack could come sit with them on the beach. Kim agreed, and the boys moved surfboards and gear, settling on their towels next to the girls.

Jack did not like to lose at anything and was embarrassed by his performance, but Amelia seemed to go out of her way to comfort his ego and tell him not to worry. She told him it was only a game, and she and Kim had both played for years at a high level. Soon they were laughing about his execution.

Kim's attention was laser-focused on Bill; Jack was happy to pair up with Amelia. The way she'd moved on the volleyball court, so smooth and fluid, was alluring. Her quick smile and the way she listened closely as he talked and told stories about his life, and how she laughed at his often-weak attempts to be humorous made him feel like they had known each other for a very long time. Amelia casually touched his arm and shoulder, conveying physical attraction and familiarity. Her slight touches were like electric shocks. He enjoyed it and casually touched her in return. He wanted to spend the afternoon looking at her smile. She let him lead the conversation and focused on learning about him. Bill also found Amelia attractive; however, Kim was working hard to keep him focused on her, which he didn't mind.

Bill and Jack planned to go to a party hosted by an acquaintance of Bill's in Long Beach that evening. The boys asked if the girls were interested in coming along. After a brief whispered discussion, a check on Amelia's Apple watch, and Kim's giggling, the girls agreed. Before Bill and Jack packed their belongings, they had the girls' phone numbers and an address where they'd be waiting to be picked up.

As Bill drove back to their apartment, Bill asked Jack, "What do you think of the girls?"

Jack replied, "They are pretty cool and attractive." After a pause, he continued, "Amelia is awesome. She makes me feel so relaxed and listened to all the dumb things I said to impress her. I haven't met anyone quite like her before. I plan to spend the whole evening with her."

Bill was about to comment that he felt the same way about Amelia, and that perhaps there should be some type of contest to see who would be her escort that night. But he thought better of it and decided to let Jack have his way.

TWO AND A HALF YEARS LATER

Two and a half years later, Jack and Amelia were on their way to yet another party. It seemed like someone in their crowd hosted a get-together just about every Saturday night. As they drove, they reminisced, looking back to their first date: that magical evening when they shared their first kiss. Amelia reminded Jack how they left Bill and Kim at the party, purchased two bottles of prosecco and snacks, and driven back to Laguna Beach, wrapping themselves in a blanket, holding each other to keep warm. They talked until just before daybreak, when they fell asleep in each other's arms. Jack recalled how strange it was to wake up on the beach; a little kid was staring at them when they woke, with his dog sniffing their feet.

It was now exactly three weeks until their wedding day. They loved each other, and were excited about getting married. They talked about wedding plans, circling back to an ongoing disagreement whether Jack's family should pick up and drive out with Grandma Kate, as she was reluctant to fly. Jack mused that perhaps it would be simpler if they just drove to Vegas and eloped. It would be easy. She reminded him that they had invested too much money in the wedding to pull out of their plans now.

Amelia sighed and sank back deeper into the seat of their old Toyota Camry. She looked forward to getting a new car after they had paid for the wedding. She thought back to the second Saturday night they had been together. That night, while picking up caramel corn and beef jerky at the local 7-Eleven, he asked for her birthday information. She wondered aloud why he needed that information right then, and he'd asked her to trust him. She replied May 24, and then he said, "Mine is July 12, so our lucky lottery number is 5-7-12-24…well, we need two more numbers."

Amelia thought for a moment, then said, "My basketball jersey number in high school was 4."

Jack replied, "My football jersey number in high school was 49. That works. So, our special lottery numbers are 5-7-12-24-49-4!"

That was the first time they played the lottery.

"We should buy some beer to celebrate our impending good fortune," Jack said. "You know, it's only a matter of when we win, not if! Someday our occupations will be 'retired lottery winners'" He picked up a six-pack. "By this time tomorrow, we could be rich!"

"So what are we going to do with all of the money we win?" she asked.

"We are going to live the perfect life. No work, all play, travel, we will have the best of everything, houses, cars, parties with the other rich and famous people who will want to be with us."

"That sounds like a wonderful dream, doesn't it?"

"Yeah, the perfect life for you and me."

They continued this lottery ticket purchase ritual every Saturday and Tuesday night for the last two and a half years. If they weren't able to pick up the ticket together, they would agree about who would pick up the ticket that night. They always played the same numbers. They kept up the banter as to how they knew that they would win.

On the way to a party that night, they stopped into the 7-Eleven right off the Pacific Coast Highway. Amelia asked Jack, "Do you need anything more than cheese puffs and potato chips?"

Jack said, "I'm getting a couple of Diet Cokes, too."

Jack paid for the items and was ready to leave the store when she looked at him and made a quizzical face, asking, "Jack, do you remember what day of the week it is?" He looked confused. She said, "It's Saturday night. You know, lottery night!" He slapped his forehead in a display of false contrition. She handed him two dollars.

Jack said, "Right, one winning lotto ticket coming up." He filled out the form and handed the clerk the bill.

The cashier rolled her eyes and handed the printed lottery ticket to Amelia.

PARTY NIGHT YET AGAIN

Snacks, drinks, and lotto ticket procured, they parked two hundred yards down the street from the party location, entered the house, and were confronted by the party's activity and noise.

Kim was already there, chatting with a couple of other women in the kitchen while Bill stood with other men at the bar catching the NBA finals on the big screen TV.

Amelia slid into the girls' group in the living room and listened as Kim lamented that although she was quite infatuated with Bill, it seemed that even after nearly three years, being friends with benefits was as close as she could get to him.

"He has a constantly roving eye," she said. "He's always looking for something better, someone who has more money, or a sexy female newcomer trying to break into the Hollywood rat race." Kim pointed at Amelia and proclaimed that Amelia was lucky: she had a great guy who would never hurt her, and they were getting married in a few weeks. Some of the girls encouraged Kim to look for a different guy who would treat her with more respect and attention. Kim nodded in agreement, but said sadly that her heart was telling her that Bill was the man she desired.

At the bar, the guys talked hoops, work, and of course, girls. Jack partied hard and enjoyed the Dos Equis beer on tap and snacks, but Bill was quiet, monitoring the room to see who came and went. He always watched Amelia and wondered what might have been. He found that he was still attracted to her.

As the evening wore on, Jack overconsumed the Dos Equis. The guys kidded him with those time-worn lines about getting married and how stifling life will be with only one woman for the rest of his life. Jack laughed and responded that they should all be so lucky. The basketball game ended with the LA Lakers winning, and it was time to head home. Jack handed Amelia the keys and said that he could not drive. Amelia also felt a bit lightheaded, so she pulled out her phone and called an Uber.

THAT MORNING PART II

Waking up late the morning after the party, Jack shielded his eyes from the bright morning sun and groaned, thinking that he would have to stop drinking and partying so much. Amelia started to move beside him. She rolled out of bed and slipped into a pair of jogging shorts and a top. Once they were married, she thought, they might not spend quite as much time at parties, and they would not drink so much. Perhaps they would start spending more time with other married couples they knew, with more wholesome activities and evenings of relaxed and meaningful conversation.

Jack said, "My head is throbbing. I don't even remember how we got home."

Amelia reminded him about the Uber ride and how their driver incessantly talked about basketball the whole way home. Jack nodded.

As she put on her running shoes and socks, she reminded him that the car was still where they parked it before the party last night and that he had promised to pick it up this morning. She took a big drink of water to hydrate and stretched. She was meeting Kim for a run to clear her head and get her body moving. Jack said he would chill out a while longer and try drinking some orange juice. Amelia grabbed the extra set of keys, locked the door behind her, headed out the door and, unbeknownst to Jack, into Kim's car.

Jack lay in bed for fifteen minutes more, lamenting his aching head and all the Dos Equis he'd drunk the night before. He finally got out of bed and walked into the kitchen, poured a glass of orange juice and grabbed his phone to review the day's headline. He always went to the sports page first. The Brewers had lost again. "What bums," he said wishing that they had more hitting power and were not already slowly fading out of the division championship hunt. At least Aaron Rodgers and the Green Bay Packers would be good this year.

He checked the national headlines and scanned the top two stories related to several political issues coming out of Washington, DC. Then he looked for the lottery results.

WHERE IS THE TICKET?

Jack cleaned up the spilled orange juice with one hand and called Amelia's number with the other. After connecting to her phone, he heard its ringtone coming from the bedroom. There it was, sitting on her bedside table. Why hadn't she taken her phone with her?

Damn, where was that ticket? He looked in his wallet: not there. He looked in the pants pocket of the jeans where he had left them last night on the floor: nothing. He looked in the kitchen and bathroom. He dumped out Amelia's purse on the kitchen counter and checked in all the little pockets within. Nothing. He concluded it must still be in the car. Maybe he'd put it in the sun visor. But the car was still at the party house. No bueno. Now what?

He hit the Uber app on his phone, requested a car, then quickly dressed, brushed his teeth and hair, and grabbed the car keys from the hook on the kitchen wall as the Uber pulled up. Jack jumped in, his mind reeling bad-luck scenarios. He imagined they had left the car doors unlocked, that someone had gone in and taken the ticket. What if someone had stolen the car? What if it simply wasn't there?

"Please hurry," he said to the driver.

As soon they turned onto the street where they left the vehicle. Jack saw his worst-case scenario had come true. The car was gone. He immediately thought that someone had stolen it. He said, "Oh no, we parked the car right here."

The Uber driver looked back at him and then out the car's right-side window at the signage on their side of the road. He said, "Well, this is a no-parking zone seven a.m. to five p.m. every day. I'm guessing it got towed."

"No!" said Jack. "Where would it have been towed to?"

The driver said, "I think there's a police website where you can find that out."

"I can't believe it," Jack groaned.

The driver said, "You know what? I just remembered that my cousin had her car towed a couple of months ago. She said she found out where it was towed to by asking at the local police station. I bet the cops might be able to help locate which impound lot it might be at."

Jack considered this and said, "Sounds like it would be worth the effort."

The driver looked up the nearest cop shop's address while Jack tried calling Amelia again. As he waited, his mind raced. Where was she? Why wasn't she home yet? Her phone went directly to voicemail. He left a message pleading for her to call him as soon as possible—it was important.

Amelia often took her longest runs on Sundays, but Jack didn't know that Amelia and Kim had planned to run and then enjoy a buffet breakfast afterward, so she would not be home for a long time.

The driver headed toward the police station. He looked in the rearview mirror and asked, "Everything okay?"

"Yeah," Jack replied. "I'm looking for an important document, and I think it's in the car, so I'm just a bit stressed out. I don't know who would steal the old Camry, so I think you're right. It probably was towed."

At the police station, Jack asked the driver if he would wait. It was quiet inside, as there was not much activity this Sunday morning. Jack approached the on-duty officer at the front desk and asked if he would help locate his towed car.

The officer asked for the license plate number and Jack's drivers' license. He tapped the information into the database and told Jack, "Yeah, it's over at Swanny Mac Towing." Grabbing a pen and a yellow sticky note, he jotted down the address and handed it to Jack.

Jack was relieved that he knew where the car was but remained concerned about the security of its contents. He thanked the officer and rushed back to the Uber. Twenty minutes later, they were at Swanny Mac Towing. Jack confirmed payment to the Uber driver, gave him an excellent rating, and included a $30 tip for his patience.

Once inside, he got in line behind two other people complaining about having their cars towed. The clerk was immune to their comments; she had heard them all before. Jack called Amelia again. Still no answer. For God's sake, where was she?

When Jack's turn arrived, the clerk seemed to take forever to pull up the information on the car and said, "I'll need your driver's license, and the fee will be, let's see, $125 towing plus storage at $100 comes to $225 including tax." Jack paid with a credit card and was shown into the impound lot, where he found his car. The back windows were one-quarter open. Someone could have easily unlocked the doors, he thought. He quickly unlocked the front door, slid inside, and started frantically searching for the ticket.

He looked under the sun visor but found only two old parking lot ticket stubs. He looked on the floor, in the center console, and in the glove box, and found nothing but hamburger wrappers and half a pack of cough drops.

His mind kept telling him bad stories. The ticket was lost. Did the store keep purchase records? Did the ticket machine track tickets? Would he show up on the store video? Could he prove that he'd bought the ticket? He felt the pressure of the situation building. Where was that goddamn ticket?

Jack tried to recollect memories from last night, but the alcohol had blurred them, and he could not bring them into focus. Amelia must know. He tried calling her again, nothing. Damn! Where was she? The suspense was about to cause his heart to fail. The ride home was only twenty minutes, but it seemed more like an hour. He pulled into the apartment parking lot, hopped out of the car, and dashed up the stairs.

The front door was unlocked. Praise the Lord. She must be back! He burst in; Amelia sat at the kitchen table. He exclaimed, "Amelia, where's the damn..." and stopped.

Amelia held the lottery ticket up in her hand and smiled at him. She excitedly finished his sentence: "Lottery ticket!"

Jumping up, she ran to Jack and jumped into his outstretched arms, wrapping her legs around his waist. They spun around. Then he set her down, and they danced around the room, hugging and shouting, "We won! We won! We're rich!"

They stopped and looked into each other's faces, screamed again, continued dancing, then hugged tightly again.

Winded, they finally flopped on to the futon. Jack asked, "Where was the damn ticket? I spent all this time looking for it. I looked all over, they towed the car, and oh my God, I'm so happy right now."

"It was in the back pocket of the shorts I wore last night. They were in the laundry. This is so fantastic. I just can't believe it." After another hug, Amelia asked, "Okay, what do we do now? What do we do with the ticket? Where do we turn it in? When do we get the money? What do we do with the money?"

"Slow down, slow down, Amelia. Let's just take this slow and make sure we make no mistakes. First, let's double-check that ticket."

Amelia still held it in her hand. "Okay," she said. "You look at it online, and I'll read it off. Ready? 5-7-12-24-49-4."

"Yep, it's a match! It's a winner!" Jack said. "Can you believe it? Best wedding present ever. Okay, we need to get advice on the money and stuff; first, let's look at the lottery website."

The California Mega Millions website gave redemption information about taking an annual payment versus a single cash payment. The state would withhold income taxes from all payouts.

Amelia said, "We don't know enough about this. Who can help us with money questions? I remember hearing that people come out of the woodwork asking for money if you win the lottery, and many winners end up unhappy."

"Girl, that's not going to happen to us. We are set for life. We'll get married and have a magical life with no worries. No more work, all play. We are going to party most days and every night." Then, doing his best Tony the Tiger imitation, he said, "It's gonna be Greeeaaaat!"

ADVICE

After thinking it over for a few minutes, Jack said, "You know, maybe we should talk to Bill and get his advice."

"Yeah, sure, that seems like a good idea," said Amelia. "Give him a call and ask him to come over."

"It is Sunday morning. We might want to give him a bit more time to wake up and get his head functioning. He had a lot to drink last night, and you know what a night owl he is."

Amelia handed Jack his phone, saying, "Hell no, call him now. This is important. Friends help each other out."

Amelia considered where to put the ticket for safekeeping. Did one tape it under the table, put it in the freezer, in the sock drawer? One thing was for sure, she thought- they would keep it safe until they brought it to the lottery office.

A groggy voice answered Jack's call to Bill. "Yeah, hello."

"Hey, Bill. Jack here. I didn't wake you up, did I?"

"No, of course not," Bill replied. "Well, yeah, you did. What's wrong? Are you in jail?"

"Nothing is wrong. Everything is perfect," said Jack.

"Great. Oh man, what a night. You should have stayed a little longer. A couple of scorching hot girls showed up just after you left." Jack heard a woman's voice in the background. "Just a minute," Bill said, and Jack could tell that he muted the phone. When Bill came back on the line, he said,

"Hey, sorry about that, man, had to solve a minor domestic issue there. So hey, what's so urgent early on a Sunday morning?"

"First of all, it's not that early, and second of all, I don't want to talk about it over the phone. How long would it take for you to get here? It's vital."

"Seriously, are you in trouble?" queried Bill.

"Surprisingly, no, not this time. Quite the opposite. You need to get here. It's a once-in-a-lifetime thing."

"Okay, okay, I'll be there in an hour. I gotta get something to eat."

"What do you want? We'll have it waiting for you when you get here." Bill told him, and Jack replied, "Done."

Jack hung up, then turned to Amelia, saying, "I gotta go out and get some breakfast burritos. Do you want anything?"

"No, no, I think I'm too nervous to eat more right now. Plus, I ate earlier with Kim."

Jack grabbed the car keys and left.

Amelia sat down on the IKEA futon. The implications of what was transpiring was starting to settle in. Her life had just been flipped upside down. Nothing that seemed important last night at the party mattered much anymore. She remembered the conversation she'd had with Kim, fretting over the cost of her wedding dress and the upcoming nuptials, her stress over the fact that they had maxed out their credit cards paying for it all. She thought about the issues that were bothering her at work and figured that they would be surprised when she called in tomorrow morning and quit. She could get a new car now and not have to rely on that little old Camry. "I can't believe that this is actually happening," she said out loud.

Meanwhile, Jack drove away from the apartment with his head spinning. He was confident by now that they had indeed won the lottery, but the next steps were unclear. Keeping the ticket safe was a given of course, but what came after that? He would not need to work anymore. He could tell off his boss and get away with it. A new car, a house in the hills, or better yet on the beach, parties, travel, golf, the possibilities were endless. He could hardly stand the excitement. He could not turn off his brain. It was hard to focus when one's head was reeling and spinning.

He went through the drive-through at McDonald's, ordered a large assortment of breakfast food without any concern about cost, and headed toward home. He pulled in and carried the food up to the apartment. Amelia had showered and came out of the bathroom drying her hair.

Jack said, "I've got food." They both sat down, and Jack began to eat. "Man, Meels, I'm sorry, I forgot that you said that you have already eaten. I bought way too much. I just was not thinking. I guess I'm just a wee bit distracted."

"That's okay. I don't know if either of us is thinking clearly right now. The money is both wonderful and confusing." As he ate breakfast out of the bag in relative silence, they were excited and lost in their thoughts.

There was a knock at the door. Bill had arrived. The friends shook hands and clapped each other on the back. Amelia hugged Bill, and Jack said, "Come on in and sit down. I have lots of food."

Bill looked in the bag and said, "Yeah, looks like you have enough here to feed an army." He grabbed two sausage burritos and an apple pie and sat down.

Amelia asked, "Would you like an orange juice?" and Bill nodded. She poured a glass.

"So, what's on fire?" Bill asked.

Jack said, "Us. We're on fire," and showed Bill the winning ticket. "We bought this last night. We played the same numbers we always do and, Bill, this little ticket, this little scrap of worthless paper which I am holding in my hand, is worth $685 million."

Bill stared at the ticket and then at his friends. He opened and closed his mouth several times, then said, "Are you kidding me? You've got to be kidding me! You're not just jacking a guy around on a Sunday morning?"

Jack showed him the iPad, which displayed the winning numbers. Bill looked back and forth, comparing. Finally, he said, "Unbelievable. You two knuckleheads just hit the lottery." He looked back up and said, "This is incredible. What are you going to do?"

Jack pulled out his wallet and handed Bill a dollar saying, "Well, first things first. You are now on retainer as our attorney, and we're going to figure it out together. We know that we need to keep the ticket safe and make tax decisions. We know that sometimes people plan out any number of things before they come forward with the ticket. We know that winning a lottery can change people's lives for better or worse. We can see where this could be both a blessing and a challenge."

Bill said, "Let me think about this for a minute." He entered notes into his phone's app. After several minutes he said, "Okay, here are my thoughts. First, you're right. We have to get this ticket somewhere safe. We have a safe in my office, and it's fireproof. We can lock the ticket up there. I will see if I can get my assistant into the office this morning. We'll photocopy the ticket, she'll notarize the deposit, and we'll provide you a receipt as she logs it in. Second, who bought the ticket?"

Jack said, "Well, I did." He looked at Amelia and saw a concerned expression appear on her face. At that moment, he realized there might be a legal means to keep or control the entire prize for himself. He also realized that his fiancé would likely turn and walk out the door if he said those words out loud. But he was not sure of the legalities and thought it might just be a moot point anyway. Quickly, he concluded that he was not ready to make that call, at least not right then. He said, "We have always played these numbers together, as a team. It's our thing, and we're going to get married; I guess we sort of both own it."

Amelia could not believe that Jack had even hesitated with that answer. Her antennae went way up, and she became wary. "Of course, we both own it. There is no question about that. I gave you the money to buy the ticket."

Bill didn't want to see Amelia lose out on her share of the winnings. He also wanted time to make sure that there was no legal precedent for that in the law. He said, "Hmmm, I may have to do a bit of research on that. But for right now, let's say you each own half, right? We'll have to check on the payout. If I remember right, you can get either a one-time lump sum payment or so much a year for thirty years or so. We'll have to talk to an accountant to get advice on the best option for your situation. I know of a guy who might be able to help. After that, you should probably make decisions about how to respond to relatives, friends, and, I'm guessing, the many others who will come to you with their hands out looking for money. Of course, my fees will be in the millions."

He laughed, then continued, "I'm just ballparking it, but even if the combined income tax rate is at fifty percent tax for easy math, that means about $342.5 million. If both you live to one hundred, well, that's enough to spend over $4 million a year, assuming no growth at all, so your money worries are over. That means you can quit your jobs and buy a great house, travel, live la vida loca." He grinned. "Hey, guys, this is huge and so great. I'm happy for you. However, I admit I'm also very jealous. Let's get this ticket somewhere safe, then go out and celebrate. Then I'm going to return the wedding present I bought for you two, because frankly you just won't need it anymore!"

At Bill's law office, they met his assistant who drove in at his request. They documented the ticket and locked it in the large, fireproof document storage vault. Jack wondered for a moment whether he could trust Bill with the ticket. He let the thought pass. Bill handed the assistant a hundred dollar bill for her efforts. As they walked out of the building, Bill told them that he would put the tip on the legal fees account. Jack just nodded and smiled. "No problem. Today, everything is going to be Greeeaaaat!"

The three of them went to their favorite bar and restaurant on the beach. Sitting at an umbrella-covered table on the outside deck, they celebrated amongst themselves. They were careful not to tell anyone else of their good fortune; however, it was apparent to any patron they were celebrating something big, far into the evening. Over the mild protests of Amelia and Bill, Jack bought several rounds for the bar patrons. Jack had always loved a party and could not see missing an opportunity to have one now.

MONDAY, MONDAY

They all woke up the next morning at Jack and Amelia's apartment to sunlight streaming through thin drapes. All felt lingering effects from the previous night's celebration. Bill groaned as he got up off the futon and called out that he had to get into work as he had to bill quite a few hours that week.

Jack had barely opened his eyes when he came out of the bedroom. Yawning, he said, "Bill, call into the office and tell them you have a client meeting. We will buy your hours for all of today and this week and going forward until we don't need your advice and assistance anymore. You are our consigliere, you know, like Robert Duvall in *The Godfather*. Your first assignment, counselor, is to get in touch with that accountant you mentioned. Then, please call the lottery office on our behalf and talk to someone about the process of claiming the money. By the way buddy, that was a fun night."

Bill quickly agreed; he knew that he would undoubtedly be distracted and not be much value to others at the office today anyway.

Jack returned to the bedroom where Amelia was still under the covers. "Let's get up and get moving. When we get some food in our stomachs, we'll all feel better."

Bill drove them all to the small café just down the street, and they quietly ate enough to quiet the hunger pangs in their stomachs and allow their thoughts to sharpen. No one was in the mood or condition to make idle chit-chat.

After finishing their meal, Jack looked at their reflections in the window glass and chuckled. "We are a real mess," he said. "I'm kind of surprised that they even served us. Time to go. Bill, if you could drop us at the apartment and make an appointment with the accountant for eleven, we can meet up with you later at his office."

Bill replied, "I'll take care of it."

Bill took secret pleasure watching Amelia in the rearview mirror as he drove them back to the apartment.

Jack and Amelia each showered and got cleaned up, ready to go.

Amelia said, "This still all seems surreal. I'm already stressed and nervous after waiting just an hour this morning for events to unfold."

"Yeah, I know what you mean," Jack said. He brought up the LA Times website on his phone and saw a small article identifying the 7-Eleven where they had bought the ticket as the location where it was sold. The article reported that the shop's owner, Kim Lee Park, was excited to collect $100,000 for his part in selling the winning ticket. "There you go," Jack said, pointing out the article to Amelia. "We're in the news."

"Hey, we both better call into work and tell them we won't be in today," she said.

They both called into their workplaces to inform their employers that they would not be into work. Amelia's boss, Connie, did not sound happy, as Amelia performed an essential daily project quality control role.

Jake's boss, JP, was similarly non-plussed and growled, "Okay, but I better you see you in here early tomorrow."

"Let's go," Amelia said. "We don't want to be late for this meeting." They left the apartment and drove to the accountant's address on Wilshire Boulevard.

Bill was waiting for them in the lobby of Best, Gustafson, and Wessel's accounting firm. The accountant, Leo Wessel, ushered them into his large and well-appointed office. Leo had a busy schedule and had never heard of Bill, although he had worked for the firm before. However, Bill was persistent in getting a meeting this morning. He would not tell him what was at issue but assured him that it would be worth his time. After introductions, Leo asked what he could do for them.

Bill described the situation. Jack and Amelia could barely control their excitement as both made comments filling in mundane facts as to where they bought the ticket and where it was now and that they were engaged to be married in a couple of weeks.

Leo pursed his lips and said, "Good to know. Let's slow it down and relax. I know everyone is excited. Hell, to be honest, I am too. First of all, congratulations. So very happy for you two. Now give me a minute here." He typed into his computer and brought up the California Lottery website, browsing the information available on payouts. Then he turned to Amelia and Jack and said, "So who owns the ticket?"

Jack answered, "Well, technically, I bought the ticket. Bill is going to check into the legalities to make sure there aren't any issues." He paused thinking about what to say next. "But we agreed that each of us owns half, at least for now. We are getting married, so wouldn't we share it?" Jack looked at Amelia and nodding his head, said, "Right?"

"Yes," she replied, looking flustered about his response. "That's what I thought we decided. I never really considered any other possibility. Jack, don't you think that's right?"

Jack opened his mouth to speak, but Bill interrupted, "Let's think this through. Leo, is there an advantage one way or the other? You know, in terms of payouts or taxes."

"Not at this level of income. The combined overall tax impact is going to be the same together or apart." He held up his hand and continued, "I did not hear Jack's reply."

Jack looked at Amelia again and back to Leo and said, "Yeah, we should plan on us both sharing this equally. Unless, of course, there is a legal reason not to."

Bill quickly jumped in and said, "I agree. It seems to me that legally it may be prudent to approach this as a fifty-fifty split to keep it financially clean until you guys get married. You know, each of you might have different ideas on what to do with your winnings, and an even split might keep disagreements to a minimum."

"What do you mean by disagreements?" asked Amelia.

"Well, let's say that you wanted to give some money to your family. Or Jack wanted to buy an airplane and a place in the Bahamas. You don't have to agree on those types of decisions right now. Once you get married, then you can decide how to deal with it together. We can get something written up to protect both of you now on the ticket split and a pre-nuptial agreement for when you get married."

"Well, that does make some sense," said Jack, and Amelia concurred with a nod.

After reviewing payout information on the website, Leo explained that they had two choices regarding how to take the money. He laid out the lump sum and annual payment options, and Jack and Amelia agreed that the yearly payment program would make the most sense for them. Further, Leo advised that they should have Bill contact lottery staff and tell them that he represented the winning ticket holders. "That way," said Leo, "you can set up a time to deliver the ticket to them for verification. They can make whatever announcements that they want to make. I had one previous winner, admittedly for a much smaller amount, as my client, and I know that they'll want to announce the winner of such a large amount as soon as possible and show you two off. The website is already stating that this is the largest individual lottery win ever. I'm sure they'll want to make the most of the publicity with two good-looking young kids like you. You'll be the lottery poster children for a couple of years to come."

Thinking of his media contacts, Bill added, "We'll have a chance to get you two on some TV talk shows if you want to. I think it could be fun, maybe even go out to New York to do a morning show."

"Now that does sound like fun," said Amelia. "I've always wanted to go to New York City! Getting to be on TV would be cool, too."

The meeting ended and Bill headed to his office where he worked his way through the hierarchy of the California lottery bureaucracy until he got the person who had authority to respond to his statement that he was an attorney who represented the owners of the winning lottery ticket. Joe Doyle was executive director for the California State Lottery and had been waiting for this call. He expected more than one call, in fact, crackpots and forgers almost always showed up about this time. With this much money on the line, Joe was wary of all claims until he had a chance to examine and document the ticket physically. He asked Bill if he could bring the ticket over immediately to the office for an examination.

Bill thought about it and said, "I want my clients to be there and would not be comfortable moving the ticket from my firm's vault without their presence. I can't promise that I can get them there today, but I can have them there tomorrow morning. We have some financial and legal issues to nail down. How about ten a.m.?"

Joe said that would work. He told Bill that his clients should bring two forms of ID. They would make a thorough physical ticket examination, which could take some time. If all checked out, the California Lottery Office would make the public announcement about four p.m. so that there would be time to make the evening news cycle. Joe also said, "After that, it usually takes a few days to deal legalities, and then the money will become available as a lump sum or an annual payout depending on the winner's preference."

"We covered that in a meeting this morning, and they would be taking the annual payout, and they will be sharing the prize evenly as two separate winners. Also, Joe, are there any legalities which the California Lottery sets out regarding two winners in terms of which one actually made the purchase? And what if, as in this case, the other gave the purchaser cash to buy the ticket?"

Joe said, "The California Lottery does not deal with any legalities as to ownership. We simply pay the person or persons who present a valid lottery ticket. How it got to us is not our concern unless the courts step in and direct us otherwise. We hear about those types of issues from time to time with divorces or guardianship disputes, and once there was even a robbery. In your situation, we will pay whoever provides the ticket and requests payment. I will see you at ten a.m. Ask your clients to wear something nice, as they will be taking a lot of pictures."

Bill promised to have them looking presentable by morning.

Next, Bill called Jack and repeated what Joe said. Jack and Amelia were on their way to the First Premier Trust Bank office to open separate accounts to receive funds. They agreed that it might be a good idea to have Leo there, too. All was ready for the big day.

As they left the bank, Amelia said she was suddenly starving and proposed that they stop and pick up a meal at In-N-Out Burger, her favorite fast-food eatery.

Jack said, "Wait a minute. We just won millions of dollars in the lottery. We can eat anywhere in the valley, and you want to go to a burger place?"

She replied, "I don't feel any different right now. I didn't think that we would act differently just because we could afford it. Now that I said that out loud, it sounds a bit foolish, doesn't it? But we still will be able to be like ordinary people, won't we? You know, like eat at a fast-food place or have pizza or get ice cream. I want our lives to be better, but do they have to be that different?"

Jack responded, "Baby, we are going to lead a very different life. We can eat at Rpublique every night if we want to. Nothing but the best for us. We can mingle with the rich and famous, buy a big house in the Hollywood Hills, and invite our movie star neighbors over to party. We can travel, buy our own plane, see the world. No more work, just play and enjoy our lives."

"I get it, and that seems all well and good. It just seems that we are who we are. Money doesn't change our values, does it? But, I guess we will find out! But for right now, we are going to get that burger, because I want it! If you want to eat at a chic highbrow restaurant, you go right ahead but I want an animal-style burger with large fries and a chocolate shake. I'm famished." They proceeded to the burger shop.

After eating Amelia suggested that they check back in with their respective offices and relax when they got home. Amelia wasn't sure why she had recommended checking into work other than it just felt right. She commented that for something so wonderful, she was nevertheless feeling more than a bit stressed.

WORK

Upon arriving home and at Amelia's urging, Jack called his office and asked for his boss.

Mr. JP Hass came on the phone in his typically gruff manner, saying, "Hope you'll be in tomorrow. I can't stand goldbrickers."

Jack said, "Boss, I'm going to need some time off."

"What? Why? How long? I've got a business to run here."

Jack responded that it might be two weeks or more. Jack wasn't quite sure that he wanted to sever all ties until he actually had the lottery money in his hands.

"You're kidding," said JP. "In this economy, I need feet on the ground and voices on the phone, selling. I can't do that for you, Jack. Plus, didn't you ask for time to go on a honeymoon in a couple of weeks?"

Jack replied, "Yes, I did. However, I have something life-changing going on, and it will take up my time. I don't think that I'm going to accomplish much or represent the firm well until it's all squared away."

"Jack, what about your clients? We just can't let them languish. We need sales."

"JP, can I have at least this week? Maybe we can touch base on Friday and see what the lay of the land looks like then?"

JP grumbled, "Jack, I just don't like it. Do you actually want your job? You're not the best producer we have, you know."

Jack ignored the cut. "Boss, I work hard for you, but, this is the best I can do right now. Call me if you have any situations arise which need my input. Thanks, bye." Then he hung up. He smiled as he visualized JP's face and bald head turning red, steam coming out of his ears, his considerable bulk trying to get up out of his swivel chair in an effort to yell at him through the phone.

Jack grinned, saying to Amelia, "I wanted to tell JP where to stick it. But I don't want to burn that bridge until the money is in the bank."

Amelia nodded. She genuinely liked the people she worked with every day yet understood that she didn't need to work anymore.

She dialed her supervisor, Connie Glidden. When Connie picked up, she said, "Hey, Connie, it's me, Amelia."

"Oh, hi, Amelia, glad you called! The Godfrey Toy website you're working on just turned white-hot. They're launching a new toy next week, and they want their website up and running *tout suite*. Can you get it finished up by tomorrow night?"

"Connie, I don't think I can. I've had something personal arise, and it's overwhelming. Can't you put Kim or someone else on it?"

"No," replied Connie. "She's pushing hard to get the Hardman project complete by the deadline. You didn't ask me for time off, and right now we are crazy busy. We need you. Don't you value your job?"

"Connie, you know I do, and I don't want to let you down, but I just can't do it."

"You mean you won't do it."

Amelia, a bit exasperated, sharpened her tone. "No, Connie," she said. "I can't. Sorry, I will talk to you later, bye." She broke off the connection. Tears came to her eyes. Amelia put her hands on her head and began to cry.

Connie was quite upset and called Kim into her office. "Hey," she said, "What's going on with your buddy, Amelia? She just said that she couldn't come into work on the Godfrey site."

Kim shrugged her shoulders and said, "I don't know. I just saw her Saturday night, and everything seemed okay. Maybe she's having issues with the wedding or Jack."

"Well, I'm pissed off," said Connie. "What are we going to do?"

"I'm totally booked. Can you find a temp or contractor?"

"Doubt it. Crap. Hey, why don't you give Amelia a call in a while and see what's going on? Maybe she could get it done later in the week if whatever is going on blows over."

Kim said that she would and went back to her desk. She finished what she was doing, saved the work, and called Amelia.

Amelia answered with her usual upbeat energy when she saw Kim's name on the caller ID. "Hey, Kim! How are you?"

"I'm fine, Meels. Are you okay?"

"Yeah, Kim, I'm great."

"Well, hey, I just came from Connie's office, and she's more than a bit steamed. She's worried and angry at the same time. She asked that I give you a call to get the skinny on what's going on."

"Kim," said Amelia, "I can't talk about it yet, but something wonderful has happened. It's all good, and it's more important to me than getting Godfrey Toys' website design done. Anyway, that project is close to done. You could finish it up in about two hours."

"I don't have two hours to spare."

Amelia thought for a moment. She had nothing to do for the rest of the day, and she knew she could get the project finished. She said, "Hey, tell you what. I'll come in tonight and finish it up. But don't let Connie assign any more work to me, because I won't be there to do it."

Kim said, "Are you sure you're okay? You're not pregnant? Or sick? Or are there are issues with Jack and the wedding? Skipping work just doesn't sound like you."

"I know," said Amelia, "but I can't go into it just yet. It's all good. I'll let you know what is going on when I'm able, and then you'll understand, okay?"

"Okay, I'll butt out and let Connie know," said Kim. "Keep in touch and let me know if you need anything."

"Thanks, girlfriend. Will do," said Amelia and hung up.

Then she said, "Jack, I need to go to work for a while."

Jack looked at her like she was crazy. "What? You don't have to work anymore!"

"That's correct, I don't have to, but I want to. I just feel that it is the right thing to do. Connie hired me and promoted me, and I don't want to let her down. That's not who I am."

"That just doesn't make any sense to me," said Jack. "Do you think that *they'd* worry about *you* if they didn't have enough work for you? No, they would lay you off in a second! Just stay here with me. We could have some champagne and talk about our future."

Amelia thought about her choices for a few moments, then said, "No, Jack, I've got to do this. It's the right thing to do. I'll be back in three or four hours. I owe this to them. I would hope someone in the same position would treat me the same way if the roles were reversed. I wish that you would support my decision on this."

"Are you kidding me, Amelia? Fine, suit yourself," he said. "But I think it is stupid. You owe them nothing."

"It's not all about you, Jack." Amelia grabbed the Camry keys and headed out the door, slamming it behind her.

An hour after she left, Jack's phone rang. Bill was on the line. "Jack, I have a couple of things to go over with you. Have you got a few minutes?"

"Sure."

"Is Amelia there?"

"No, that crazy girl just went into work. Can you believe it?"

"Yeah, actually, I can. That is who Amelia is, man. You know that she would never leave them hanging. She's too loyal."

"Well then, maybe you're nuts, too. What have you got for me?"

Bill said, "I've done some research related to the lottery ticket ownership question. There is not an exact comparable case with your fact pattern. You bought the ticket; she gave you the money. Perhaps the biggest issue is that you gave her the ticket, and she was holding it when the numbers were announced and afterward. Possession is a powerful factor within the law. My advice is that you need to consider your next step very carefully. First, obviously, you could destroy your relationship with Amelia. Second, you might end up with nothing, as she might well be able to prove that the ticket was all hers. I think that you drop any pretense of inferring that the ticket was yours and let her know that you agree that it is a fifty-fifty split."

Jack thought about what Bill said. "I can see what you mean. Okay, I'll do that. You understand that I was only looking out for legal issues, like if something were to happen between now and when we get married, or if a family member got involved."

Bill knew Jack was not telling the truth but let it pass. He had heard Jack lie before. He was relieved that he had protected Amelia so far without damaging the relationship he had with Jack. He said, "Glad we got that settled. Now let's get to the fun stuff. I have arranged for a limo to pick up you two at eight-thirty. First, you will come to my office to get the ticket. I will meet you there. Second, we will continue to the lottery office and arrive by ten, and make you rich and probably famous."

Bill also repeated the request from the lottery that Amelia and Jack "look pretty" for the inevitable photographs. "I know Amelia can do that, but it's going to be a real tall order for someone as ugly as you," Bill cracked.

"Screw you, Bill," Jack responded, laughing. "Mañana, amigo." He hung up.

In the apartment's silence, Jack found that he was still upset with Amelia for going to work. He spoke to the apartment walls: "Damn her. She did not have to do that. She didn't have to work. She could've stayed here and celebrated with me."

He popped open the champagne and poured himself a healthy glass. When he finished, he poured himself another.

By the time Amelia returned hours later, Jack was fast asleep on the futon. Amelia poured a small glass of the remaining bubbly, sat on a kitchen chair, watched Jack sleep and let her mind unwind. As she sipped, she came to realize that they should probably postpone the wedding. There was going to be a lot going on; change was surely coming, and they could now afford to get married anywhere and any way they wanted. Maybe they could have the ceremony on an exotic white sand beach in Tahiti or a mountainside wild-flower meadow in Switzerland. She made a mental note to talk to Jack about it in the morning. She started to think of all of the places that she had always wanted to go. With six random numbers and the risk of two dollars, all of those dreams could now come true. She went into the bedroom, crawled under the covers, and fell into an exhausted, deep sleep.

Before dawn, Jack came into the bedroom, laid down next to her, and held her close. He spoke softly, saying, "We have to be ready to go by eight-thirty…" And then he drifted off.

Fortunately, Jack and Amelia's circadian rhythm caused them both to awake up at about seven.

Awake, but still lying in bed holding Amelia in his arms, Jack said, "I'm sorry that I didn't stay awake for you last night. I was exhausted and I'm sorry that I was sore at you. I do respect your decisions."

Over breakfast, Amelia said, "Jack, while you were sleeping last night, I did some thinking. Compared to the lottery announcement, our wedding could only be an anticlimax, and that wouldn't be right. By the end of today, we'll be in a mad whirlwind which might well last a while. I propose that we postpone the wedding."

Jack was caught off guard. He had not thought much about the upcoming nuptials since it was determined that they had won. He considered the idea, sensing that it might not be a bad one, as he also felt a bit overwhelmed by recent developments. "What do we do about all of the arrangements, though?" he asked. "And some people probably already bought gifts and booked plane tickets."

"Yeah, I thought about that," said Amelia. "I think that we'll be able to afford to reimburse anyone who asks to be made whole. We'll have enough money to get married anywhere we want. We could even fly all the guests to be wherever we chose. Heck, we could also elope to Vegas right now, but I want to do what *we* want to do, *where* and *when* we want to do it. We don't have to conform to any preconceived notion or plan anymore. So, what I was thinking, is that after the ticket is confirmed, I'll get in touch with the church and photographer and—no, that's exactly *not* what I am going to do. I'm going to call a wedding planner and hire them to unplan the wedding. Would that be okay with you?"

Jack said quietly, "Yeah, I guess that makes sense." Then more forcefully, as if he clearly saw the obstacles in front of them, he said, "Yes, sure, let's reset the wedding plans after we have a chance to focus on all of our options. Just don't think that you're getting out of it. You're stuck with me."

She put her arms around him. "I'm happy to be stuck with you."

CONFIRMATION

The limo arrived right on time. Jack and Amelia rode in relative silence to Bill's office, nervous, each lost in their own thoughts.

Upon arrival, Bill gave Amelia a big hug, shook Jack's hand, and said, "Anybody here ready to have their lives changed?"

Jack and Amelia smiled and nodded. Jack took Amelia's hand and asked, "Ready for the first day of the rest of our lives?"

She smiled. "Absolutely."

Once inside, Bill and his assistant gained access to the vault and brought out the ticket. Jack was relieved that it was still there. With the amount of money involved, he didn't know if he could fully trust anyone. Bill held it out to them, saying, "Well, who wants it? I'm sure not going to take responsibility."

Jack said, "Amelia can take it. She's the most sensible one of the three of us."

Amelia took the ticket, put it in her purse, zipped the bag closed, and said, "On with the show. Let's do this."

The ride to the lottery office was also quiet, with more than a little nervous tension in the air. That is until Jack told Bill that they were going to delay the wedding. Then the conversation focused on the decision and possibilities for rescheduling. Hoping for an opportunity to postpone the marriage as long as possible, Bill said that he felt the reasoning was sound and that they should take their time and not rush anything. Take all the time they need.

They soon pulled up to the steel and glass building which housed the California Lottery offices. Leo Wessel met them outside the entry doors.

Inside the lobby, Bill asked for Joe Doyle. The receptionist at the front desk inquired if Mr. Doyle was expecting them. Bill nodded and said, "Yes, Mr. Doyle should be expecting us. We have a ten o'clock appointment."

Soon enough, Joe Doyle walked through the double glass doors and strode to the desk.

"Mr. Doyle," Bill said. "I'm Bill Hart. We spoke on the phone. This is Jack Lemke, this is Amelia Bauer, and this is Leo Wessel, our accountant."

They all shook hands and greeted each other, and Mr. Doyle said, "Let's go up to my office and talk."

Amelia reflexively gripped her purse to assure herself that the ticket was still with them and followed the group to the elevator. Once in his office, Joe introduced them to the lottery lawyer who was onsite to observe the transaction.

Joe said, "Let's get right to it, shall we? May I see the ticket?"

Amelia unzipped her purse and handed it over. Joe looked at the ticket intently and then turned it over, carefully examining the back and front. He held it up to the light from the window. He compared the numbers to a sheet on his desk. Finally, he handed a printed form to Amelia, pulled a pen out of his pocket and asked her to sign it, stating that it was an affidavit form declaring that the ticket was real and that she was the rightful recipient. Then looking at Jack, he said, "Oh, wait, you're both claiming this together, right?"

"Yes. That is correct. A fifty-fifty split," said Jack.

"Are you two married?" Joe asked.

"Not yet, but soon, I hope," replied Jack with a smile.

"Then you should both sign the document."

Amelia handed the affidavit and pen to Jack. He signed beneath her signature on each.

Joe asked Jack, "And where did you buy this ticket?"

Jack replied, "The 7-Eleven off the Pacific Coast Highway. Near Laguna."

Joe nodded. He used the scanner he had on his desk to make a scan of both sides of the ticket and the affidavit. Then he picked up the phone and dialed a number. "Steve, would you come to my office, please. Yes, now." He listened for a few seconds and then said, "Yeah, it's about what we talked about yesterday."

A minute later, an elderly gentleman entered the room. Joe held out the ticket to him and said, "Steve, would you please verify this ticket?"

Steve nodded, took the ticket, and left the room.

Joe said, "Sometimes we review the video footage of the sale. We always verify the bar codes and corresponding ticket number, the time stamp, and the paper stock. If they all match up, then you have a winner."

Amelia grabbed ahold of Jack's hand and squeezed it. Jack could tell that she was extremely nervous, and so was he. He kept wondering if he was imagining the last two days.

Amelia could not focus on anything except whether the ticket was real. Although they had every reason to be certain that the ticket was a winner, when $685 million and the promise of a beautiful, carefree life are at stake, there is always a reason to worry. Amelia's cautious nature led her to think that nothing was for certain.

Jack, however, was confident from the beginning that the ticket was a sure thing, and he was already imagining what he would do with the money. He saw himself in a bright red Ferrari, top-down, wind in his hair as he drove along the ocean highway taking curves at exhilarating speeds. He wished that Steve would hurry up.

Joe, Leo, and Bill made small talk while they waited. Joe asked Jack and Amelia where they grew up and about their lives here in California. Jack spoke for both of them, as Amelia was entirely too distracted to be present for the conversation. Her hands and legs trembled.

Ten minutes later, Steve returned and handed the ticket to Joe, murmuring words which no one else could hear. Steve smiled and winked at Amelia as he left. Her pulse began to race. It was about to become real.

Joe turned and faced the group. He said, "Congratulations. This ticket has been certified as authentic and is eligible for payment. I just love saying that!"

Jack and Amelia jumped to their feet and hugged each other. Bill joined in. In a way it was anticlimactic, but it was a great relief to have confirmation of the win.

When the hugging subsided, Jack asked, "Well, what happens next?"

Joe said, "First, congratulations again. This is the first time I'm going to hand over a check for anywhere close to this much money. We'll need you to fill out IRS forms, determine how you want to receive the money, and also sign a disclaimer that no one else has rights to this ticket, like an ex-spouse or dependents. We'll need your IDs and eventually, your bank account information. We don't issue paper checks; everything is all done by electronic ACH transfers these days. Lastly, we want to get some publicity when we present the check, take photos and give you a chance to talk to the media. We want to do that at about three this afternoon." Joe checked his watch. "So. After this, you will have what, about four to five hours to enjoy being *not* rich?!"

Jack said, "Well, let's get started!"

Joe opened a sealed manila folder and checked the contents. Then he motioned them over to a small conference table in his spacious yet spartan office. "Please, have a seat," he said, and the lucky couple settled into their chairs.

Leo and Bill sat on either side as they worked to fill out documents. Jack and Amelia gave Joe their driver's licenses and passports, and he scanned copies. They worked back and forth as Joe described the need for each document. Leo and Bill carefully reviewed the forms and the entries. Joe commented that they appeared to have all of their ducks in a row for a couple of young people. Jack nodded toward Bill and Leo, saying, "We have good advisors."

Soon it was all done. Joe said, "We will present you with one of those big cardboard checks this afternoon. It won't be worth anything, but most people keep them as souvenirs. The funds will become available and ready to be transferred to your accounts within the next 24 to 48 hours."

He continued, "I do have some advice. Perhaps you have been advised already, but here it is: after the announcement, do not go home. The press, along with every conman in the city, might be looking for you. Well, maybe not every single one, but plenty. So again, my advice is, don't go back to wherever you live for a week or so. Don't answer your phones unless you know who's calling. In fact, I suggest that you get new phones with new numbers. Also, set up new email addresses and be ready to keep a low profile with your friends for a while. Work through your advisors and use them as spokespersons if you need to. Good luck, although I think that you have already had plenty of good luck just to be sitting here."

Jack and Amelia both nodded in understanding.

Jack said, "I guess we have some things to do before the press conference. Gotta get back to the apartment and get clothes and personal things, then come back here."

Bill said, "If you want me to, I can book a nice hotel room for the week so no one will be able to track you down. You can reimburse the firm after the money comes in."

"Thanks, Bill, that sounds good," Amelia said.

Jack and Amelia held hands tightly as they walked out of the building toward the waiting limo. They got in and asked the driver to take them back to the apartment, then requested that he raise the privacy window so they could talk.

Jack pulled Amelia close, kissed her, and said, "Now that we're rich, what do you want to do?"

She laughed. "You know, we knew this was coming. I was waiting to feel exhilarated or something, yet I don't feel any different. I haven't changed. I guess it hasn't sunk in. Like it's all just on paper. I still find myself thinking about work and all these things that won't matter after this afternoon. It's very surreal, kind of like you're floating on wings above everything in a holding pattern, knowing that you're going to be leaving, yet this world is what you know and care about, and you want to see what is happening and stay connected."

"I think I understand what you're saying. But hey, I'm looking forward to whatever comes next. It's going to be Grrrrrreat!"

Back at the apartment, they quickly packed a week's worth of clothes. By the time they purchased their new cell phones, they only had an hour to get back to the lottery office. They were both famished, so the driver took them through the Carl's Jr. on the next block. This time, Amelia was pleased that there was no discussion about whether they should eat fast food.

As they drove back to the lottery office, Amelia said, "We've got to get in touch with our families and let them know what happened before they hear it on the news."

"Hey, yeah," Jack said. "That's an excellent point."

Using their old phones, they began the process. Amelia called her grandmother and left a message on the old voicemail/fax machine that Kate had kept using: "Grandma Kate, this is Amelia. I have some wonderful news to share. Jack and I won the lottery. Isn't that great? We're thrilled. We will be on TV this afternoon out here in LA. I'll try to call you later. Love you much. Bye." She left a similar message with her brother, Henrik.

Jack had to inform his family. Even before he dialed, he decided that he did not want to tell his mother how much money they'd won. He knew that she would find out soon enough, and then the calls would start. His goal was to let her know the news and that they would delay the wedding and then end the conversation as quickly as he could. He did not want to get into a long discussion with his mother. Her personality had always been a difficult one to handle, and she struggled with fentanyl addiction. Whenever she was able to talk her children into sending her money, too much of it ended up being used to purchase the drug. Her children were increasingly more reluctant to respond to requests for monetary or other assistance. Jack knew that the longer he was on the phone with her, the more difficult it would be to just say no to requests for money.

Jack reached his mother, and she was excited to hear the news. "How much did you win?" she asked.

"Well," Jack replied evasively, "you never get the full amount because of taxes and how they pay out the money. Plus, half of it is technically Amelia's, so I guess the best way to answer that is that I'm not sure, but I know that I won't have to work anymore. Isn't that amazing? I'll call you again once we get our heads around the whole thing. The announcement is this afternoon. It might get picked up on the news networks, so maybe there could be a blurb on the local news. Can you let everyone know to keep their eyes on the news tonight? Also, one more thing, Amelia and I have decided to delay the wedding for a while. We will be dealing with getting our lives settled here, and don't want to have to deal with wedding issues until we are ready. I would hate for everyone to find out about all of this second-hand."

She said she would. "We are excited, Mom." Before she could formulate another sentence, Jack quickly continued. "Stay safe. Think about you a lot." Then he quickly hung up.

"I feel bad about what I just did," said Jack. "I sensed where the conversation was going to go. I just didn't want to deal with it. I'm just not prepared."

Amelia nodded. "Yeah, I actually kind of hoped that Kate wouldn't answer the phone. I don't quite know what to say to her right now. It's not that I think that she would expect any money or anything like that. That's not who she is. It's just hard to tell someone in your family that you are now wealthy, knowing that they aren't. We're going to have to learn to deflect questions and to say no politely and firmly."

Jack stared out the window. "I'm glad we're not going home tonight." Then he turned his old phone off.

Amelia dialed Connie, who picked up the phone on the third ring.

"Connie, Amelia here. I just wanted to connect with you and let you know I came in last night and finished the Godfrey project."

"Yes, I saw that. Thank you very much, Amelia," Connie replied. "How are you doing? I hope you are recovering from whatever was going on."

Amelia replied, "Connie, I have never been better. I can now share a little. I have come into some money. The bottom line is that I don't have to work anymore. We're handling the details now. The reason I'm calling you is to tell you all this, and let you know that I won't be coming into work anymore."

"I don't know what to say. I'm stunned. Of course, I'm happy for you, but I still want you to be part of our team. We have so many projects lined up, and you leaving will leave us shorthanded."

"Yeah, I know," said Amelia. "Deep inside, I love what I do. I was excited to work on those projects with all the great people we have. You took a chance and hired me, and I am grateful for the opportunity. I'm conflicted as to how to handle this. I feel very guilty, but I want you to know that my life just changed in a big way. I'm embarking on a new journey, and I'm sorry, I don't think it can include working there."

"Would you consider working for the next two weeks until I can get someone good to replace you?" asked Connie. "I could pay you more."

Amelia laughed softly. "Oh, Connie, you do such a great job managing that place. You deserve more than they pay you. Please understand, I'm not laughing at your offer or at you. Money is simply not a motivator for me anymore. I'm going to have to pass. It's not that I don't want to work for you. I want you to know, Connie, that I'm so grateful that you trusted me and saw enough in me to give me a job and the chance to work doing something I love. That is very so important to me. Ventura Company was a big part of my life, and I will never forget the opportunity and my friends there. Hey, Connie, I have to go. A lot is going on here."

Connie said, "Amelia, I'm disappointed in the way you are leaving. However, I do care about you and wish you every success. So good luck, whatever you do."

Before she hung up, Amelia added, "One more thing, Connie. Whatever money the company owes me for the Godfrey project or in pay, would you give it to our team? Maybe a surprise gift, a party or a bonus or something. I would feel good about that."

"Okay, sure. This is all a bit of a shock. Be safe, and we will miss you." She paused, then said, "A lot."

"Thanks. And Connie? Don't say anything to Kim. I will talk to her later," said Amelia. "Vaya con Dios. I promise we will talk again." And then she disconnected.

Amelia teared up. "That was so very hard to do, Jack," she said, beginning to cry. "I felt a part of something there, and I enjoyed what I did. I was good at it."

He replied, "Yeah, I understand, Meels, but you don't have to work anymore, and there are so many other things we can do. The alignment of our stars has been changed forever."

THE BIG CARDBOARD CHECK

The limo pulled to the curb in front of the lottery building for the second time that day. The lucky couple got out.

They walked hand in hand through the doors. This time, the receptionist jumped out of her chair and rushed up to them excitedly, saying, "Mr. Doyle is expecting you! Please take the elevator directly to the third floor. He will meet you there."

They went to the elevator while the receptionist hurried back to her desk to notify Mr. Doyle that his important guests had just arrived. As the elevator opened to the third floor, Joe Doyle and Bill stood there, waiting for them.

Joe wore a big smile on his face. "Are you ready for this? We have our media room set up for the presentation. The reporters for the press and the TV stations will be waiting for us when we walk in. I expect that the room will be full. The plan is that I speak and then present you with that oversized check you always see in the photos, and shake your hands. Then we pose for pictures and video footage. How it shapes up after that is up to you. The size of the payout and the story behind the winners would make for good to great press.

You can walk out of the room or stay to answer questions. The reporters will typically shout comments and questions while we are being photographed, and you can answer them or not—don't feel obligated. There will be bright lights in your eyes, so it's a little hard to see who the voices are coming from. When done, we leave and go out the secure back entry door and then down the stairs right to street level. You won't be as likely to be bothered. You may get followed once you're outside, but you'll have a head start. Beyond that, I can't help you."

Bill stepped in and said, "You have a bungalow ready at the Beverly Hills Hotel. I prepaid for it for a week, and I have already checked you in. Here are your keycards. The limo driver will deliver your bags, so all you have to do is walk in and go to Bungalow 22."

Jack said, "Great, thanks, Bill, we appreciate it." Then he clapped him on the shoulder and gave him a man hug.

Bill thought: I'm doing most of this mainly for her, not for you, buddy.

But out loud he said, "Would it be okay if I was the contact for all of the feedback or inquires your lottery win gets? That way, I can screen you from the crazies."

"Sure," said Jack. Joe Doyle nodded.

"Well," he asked, "are you two ready?"

With nods from Amelia and Jack, they started moving. Joe Doyle led them into the press room. Bright TV floodlights came on and lit the podium. The human activity noise and the conversation in the room fell toward silence.

Joe went to the podium and spoke. "My name is Joe Doyle. As some of you may know, I am the executive director of the California Mega Millions Lottery. I want to thank you all for coming to this exciting presentation. As you may be aware, one individual California Lottery Mega Millions ticket was purchased on Saturday night. It is worth $685 million. I am very pleased to present the two lucky young people who purchased that ticket: Amelia Bauer and Jack Lemke." The press applauded lightly, and Joe motioned the couple forward. He said, "On behalf of the California Lottery Commission, I am very pleased to present to you this check for $685 million. Congratulations."

Together, Jack and Amelia accepted the oversized cardboard check. Cameras flashed, and they smiled at photographers while holding up the check.

One photographer called out, "What are you going to do with the money?"

Jack stepped toward the podium. Joe Doyle deftly stepped in and grabbed the bulky check, allowing Amelia to stand next to her fiancée. Jack leaned into the microphone and said, "We don't have any real solid plans right now. Possibly buy a car and maybe look for a house."

Someone in the crowd called out, "Are you two married?"

"No," said Jack.

Amelia chimed in, "We're engaged, and we were going to get married in a couple of weeks, but we might put it off until we get more situated."

"Will you marry me?" one older, overweight, balding male photographer called out. The crowd laughed.

Amelia said, "Maybe!" As she could not see well through the bright spotlights, she shielded her eyes against the glare and continued, "Are you young, single, and handsome?" The crowd laughed louder at her witty response.

"Are you going to keep working?" asked a woman holding up a small video camera.

Jack responded, "Nope, last Friday was my last day. And, JP, when you hear this, I won't be in tomorrow and will be a little late for, well…" He paused. "…the rest of my life. So, don't expect to see me around in the foreseeable future unless it's for an office party! I'll miss all you guys at work, but I don't need to do that anymore."

Someone called out, "How did you pick the numbers?"

Jack said, "We've been playing these same numbers for almost two and a half years, starting the very first week we met. They were mainly our birthdays. Kind of silly I know, but we got lucky, and here we are."

Amelia added, "We played the same numbers every Saturday and Tuesday night. We never missed a chance to play. It was kind of our commitment to each other, our thing." She thought for a moment and said, "I guess, right now, I'm so glad we did."

"How did you two meet?" the video camerawoman asked.

"Playing beach volleyball. I lost the game but won the girl," Jack said, smiling and squeezing Amelia around her waist.

Another reporter asked, "What are you going to spend the money on?"

"Well," said Amelia, "as Jack just said, I think new cars, maybe a house. We will figure it out."

Another asked, "Will you give money to your families?"

Jack hesitated, then said, "Hey, we just got the check a couple of minutes ago. We'll have to figure all of that out going forward."

Joe could tell that Jack was frustrated by the last question. Taking that as his cue, he stepped in and said, "Okay, I'm cutting it off here. I'm sure that these two kids have a lot to do. All you out there in the fourth estate, thanks for covering this event. Make sure that the California Lottery gets a lot of great free press on this award. Remember, Lottery proceeds fund California schools and education. Again, congratulations to Jack and Amelia, and best of luck in the future."

The reporters shouted more questions, Joe ushered them toward a single black door at the back guarded by two security officers. It opened directly into a stairwell with a staircase descending to the street where the limo awaited them.

They climbed inside. Bill put his head in the door and said, "Joe said that the California Lottery will transfer your money within forty-eight hours. I have your new phone numbers and will call if there is something important. You lucky kids go have a great evening."

Amelia thanked him; Jack shook his hand and said, "Thanks for all of your help, buddy. We'll be in touch."

The limo quickly pulled away into traffic.

They were relieved that the ceremony was over. Finally, Jack and Amelia were on their own, wealthy beyond their wildest dreams.

"What do you want to do?" asked Jack.

Amelia said, "You know what, let's get beer or wine, some cheese and crackers, and go to the beach and chill a while. If we go to the hotel, I'm afraid that we'll hole up and won't come back out the whole evening."

"I don't have a problem with not coming back out," said Jack with a wolf-ish grin.

Amelia slugged his shoulder and said, "You know what I mean."

An hour later they were on the beach, feet in the sand, looking out over the blue horizon. They ate and drank in silence for a while, then Amelia asked, "So, what's next?"

"First things first," he responded. "I think that we should each get a car and get rid of that little Camry. Any car we want, no limits. Then…I don't know. Maybe we get away for a while, maybe a trip to give us time to think and make plans."

Amelia thought for a moment, then shrugged. "I think that we should consider getting a house, but beyond that, I don't have any solid ideas either. It's hard, isn't it? When we were just working stiffs a week ago, we knew just what to do. We had a schedule and rhythm and knew what came next. Now that we have all the money in the world, we are baffled. Money changes everything, I guess. I'm sure it should make our life easy and less complicated. Rich people have it so easy. We'll certainly find out. You know, I just thought that maybe we each make a list of things we can do with the money that come to mind, then we can talk them over sometime."

"Sounds good to me," said Jack. "Make a list on your own, and we will compare. Until then, let's enjoy each other and try to stay normal. We have all the time in the world."

Amelia raised a closed fist, and Jack gave her a fist bump. "Done," Amelia said. She lay back in the soft sand. She let the sun's radiance bathe her face and body. She started thinking about things that she would love to do.

Jack sat back and watched kids playing volleyball. He noticed a beautiful girl on the court. He watched for a while, admiring her body and athleticism, then realized that it was the very same court where he had met Amelia over two years before. He thought about how coincidences and the patterns of life can certainly be thought-provoking. The events of the past two days were real but surreal at the same time. Maybe it was all a dream. He lay down and soon napped in the warm sun.

Their new phones both buzzed almost simultaneously, alerting them to incoming texts. Amelia reached out and picked up her phone, and read the message. The text was from Bill, with two weblinks and the words: "YOU ARE FAMOUS!!!!"

YOU ARE INVITED

The link to the *LA Times* was an article about them: it told the story of a young couple engaged to be married, who had struck it rich with the lottery. The report quoted the odds of winning with a single ticket and mentioned some of the information they'd shared during the Q&A session at the award ceremony. The accompanying photograph showed a young, happy, attractive couple holding a large cardboard check.

Amelia clicked on the second link. The same information was posted on the CNN website. She smiled and said, "Wow, that's pretty cool." She nudged Jack out of his sun-drenched nap and said, "Hey, check your phone. We're famous!"

Jack checked his phone and laughed. Now fully alert, he stood and said, "Awesome, I'm ready to go. How about you?"

He helped her to her feet. They picked up their belongings and trash, and hand in hand they walked toward the limo driver, who sat at a table at the beach restaurant awaiting them. He said, "Congratulations! I just saw your picture on the web. You could have said something."

"Thanks," said Jack, "We are trying to keep it all low-key. We'd like to get going now." He put down a fifty-dollar bill on the table to cover the driver's bill and tip. Then he tipped the driver $100. The now-famous couple headed toward Sunset Boulevard and their swank hotel.

The lobby of the Beverly Hills Hotel was simply opulent. It reflected the highest standards of wealth and class. The driver advised them of a side entrance which they entered and followed the signage to Bungalow 22. No one recognized them as they made their way. The room was well appointed and featured a grand piano and fireplaces both in the room and the private patio outside. Amelia wandered around the suite and confessed that she had never been in such a beautiful space and that she was uncomfortable and almost afraid to sit down. She viewed the grey marble bathroom and decided that the place was at least twice as lovely as the honeymoon suite they'd booked in Cabo.

Jack grabbed a bunch of grapes and ate them as he walked through the rooms. Then he took a handful of complimentary nuts from the bowl on the table and laughed He said, "These are complementary nuts, and they have not said anything nice to me yet. Man, I'm so funny today!" Amelia rolled her eyes and shook her head. He walked into the bedroom and sat on the bed. Amelia followed, sat down next to him and said, "This is an incredible place. I've only seen these types of rooms on those TV shows about the rich and famous."

"Kind of beats the pants off our apartment, huh?" said Jack. "Well, get used to it, babe, because for the rest of our lives, this is a baseline. We can have the best of everything. We have to get accustomed to the fact that this is where we belong from now on." He put his arm around her and kissed her deeply. Their romantic interlude was interrupted by a knock on the door. The bellman had arrived with their bags. Jack tipped him $50, which was all the money he had left in his wallet. After the bellman departed, Amelia said, "Hey, wasn't that was a pretty big tip just to deliver two bags?"

"Yeah, I guess. But we've got it, might as well flaunt it a bit."

Amelia frowned and turned away, yet said nothing. She realized that she would not have been as generous and wondered if she needed to rethink her values. Or maybe her values were fine. Perhaps she would need to work to control Jack's impulsiveness from now on.

By nine p.m., the story had quickly gone viral on the internet. The calls into the California Lottery were routed to Bill. Some clamored for promotional appearances. Within an hour, Jack got a call from Bill.

Bill said, *"Good Morning America* has offered to fly you out to New York City, interview you on the air, and put you up in a hotel for a few days. All you have to do is agree, and you'll both be on a plane tomorrow morning."

Jack told Amelia. Smiling ear to ear, Amelia exclaimed, "Oh my God!" and started jumping around the room. "New York City! Yes, wow, really freaking cool. This is going to be way fun!"

"Okay," Jack told Bill. "We're in!"

Before they went to bed that night, Amelia checked the *Star Tribune* website to see if the local Minnesota news sources were covering the announcement. It was one of the main stories. The article showed a picture of Jack and Amelia receiving the award and stated that Amelia was from Stillwater.

NEW YORK CITY

The next morning, the same driver limo was again on duty to take them to the airport. As he dropped them off at LAX's charter terminal, he said, "Travel safe, you two."

The private jet used by the network to shuttle staff and VIPs between Hollywood and New York City was warming up on the tarmac. A lovely stewardess met them at the base of the steps and told them to take any seat, as they would be the only passengers this morning. Jack found himself admiring the stewardess as she provided food and drinks. He wondered what it would be like to be with her. Amelia, meanwhile, enjoyed the view from the window.

A little over five hours later, they touched down in New York City. Once they'd deplaned at the JFK private terminal, they were met by a chauffeur who whisked them downtown to a hotel in Times Square.

They spent the remainder of the day wandering about the once seedy but now bustling area. Long blocks of buildings created concrete canyons. The noise from cars, trucks, and buses entwined with the sound of human activity was foreign to Jack and Amelia. Their previous experiences in Los Angeles and Minneapolis paled in comparison to the bustle of NYC. It was intimidating to be among so many people, all going somewhere fast. Jack and Amelia's concerns about safety in the city made them cautious. They ate dinner at an Olive Garden, filled up on breadsticks, then walked the streets as the city lights came on. When they slept, the city did not.

In the morning their phones rang with an early alarm. They rose and went through their morning routines before heading down to the lobby. Jack wanted to find a unique breakfast place for a genuine NYC breakfast. However, Amelia insisted on enjoying the free complimentary breakfast buffet as there was no reason to waste that money. Then they walked to the *Good Morning America* studio across Times Square where the producer met them in the lobby, hand extended.

"Welcome to the Big Apple," she said. "I'm so pleased to meet you two! I am Kristine Larson, an assistant producer here with *GMA*."

Guiding them into the elevator, she said, "I'll take you up to makeup. You're scheduled for the middle segment of the show. We will likely use your appearance as a teaser before you come on. During that time, you'll sit on our interview couch When the director points to you and the camera light comes on, just smile and wave at the camera. While on-camera, don't speak; your mic's will be off. Just wave and smile at the people out there in TV land! Got it?"

"Yes, thank you, Kristine," Amelia said. "No problem."

Kristine knocked on a door. "Coming in," she said, waving Jack and Amelia into the brightly lit makeup room. "Do what you need to and make them look stunning," she said.

"Will do. Shouldn't take much work," said the beautician, who then proceeded to deliver on her promise. When done, she took off her white jacket and said, "Follow me."

They rode the elevator down to the street-level interview studio and pointed to a small loveseat. "You two sit right there."

The stage staff moved quickly back and forth during a commercial break. A cameraman walked over from behind a camera and said in a heavy New York accent, "This'll be a piece of cake for you guys. The director will get your attention and then count down from five, and then the red light on my camera will come on. That's all there is to it."

Robin Roberts appeared from around the screened corner and said, "Welcome to New York City and congratulations on your good fortune! Thanks for coming and being on our show. I wanted to at least meet you before we put you on air. Please don't think me rude, but I have to get back. You'll be on in about ten minutes. See you then."

Jack and Amelia sat on the loveseat and watched the show on the monitor. Jack was getting nervous. "What if I say something stupid? We should never have done this."

Amelia said, "Jack, you're going to be fine. You handled the lottery office meeting with ease. Why is this different?"

"Well, because we are in New York City on national television with millions of people watching. Not quite the same animal, wouldn't you say?"

Amelia thought for a moment, then said, "You have a point, but you will still be fine, I think." She squeezed his hand, then smiled and winked.

Jack said, "You're better at these things. You don't get nervous."

"Oh Jack, of course I do. I just focus on being myself and think of the interviewer as someone I just met and am trying to get to know."

The director appeared and said, "Okay, kids on in five, four, three, two, one…you're on!"

At that moment, the red light came on the camera, and Jack and Amelia smiled broadly and waved silently for what seemed like at least a minute until the camera light went out. The director told them that they were clear and would be up again for the next segment. They had four minutes to wait.

Robin and Michael Strahan came around the corner. They all shook hands. Michael introduced himself. Jack could not get over how powerfully built the ex-NFL defensive player was. Jack was glad he never had to play football against someone with that kind of strength.

Robin said, "We will ask about how you won and what it means to you. If you get stuck, don't panic; just stop talking, and we will come in and smooth it over and then ask another question."

The director came back into the studio and said, "On in five, four, three, two, one," then pointed at them.

Robin began talking as the camera light went red, saying, "Some people have all the luck. We are sitting with two of those people right now."

The hosts asked Amelia and Jack the same questions they had previously answered at the lottery announcement. They came across as genuine and humble.

Michael asked if they were going to do any late-night television talk shows. Jack said that they had no other shows scheduled while they were in New York and that they appreciated the opportunity to appear on *GMA*.

Amelia said, "Maybe when we get back to LA, we could get on Jimmy Kimmel's show. I think he is so funny. I'm a big fan. I especially enjoy it when Jimmy and Matt Damon prank each other. Give us a call, Jimmy," she said, putting her hand to her head like a phone and smiling.

The rest of the interview seemed to go by in a flash. Once off-camera, the hosts shook their hands and congratulated them again, then disappeared around the set curtain to continue their work.

Kristine came up to them and said, "That's it for you. You did great. Thanks for coming. I will show you out. Enjoy your time in the Big Apple."

After the appearance, they were on their own. They decided to grab brunch at a sandwich shop before sightseeing. While they ate, Jack opened the banking app on his phone. His face lit up, and he showed Amelia the screen. It showed his account with a balance of over $5.7 million.

Quickly doing the math in his head, he said, "That's with the withholding tax already taken out."

Amelia checked her account just to confirm that she had received funds also. She had and grinned. They gave each other a congratulatory high five. It was a great start to an exciting day. It struck Amelia that she did not know how to act now that she was a multi-millionaire. They did not include an "instant millionaires" handbook with the lottery check. Should she dance around the restaurant or buy a jet plane?

She said, "So, now that we have money, what are we going to do? I don't feel any different than I did five minutes ago. I'm excited, but I'm still the same person. What should I do differently?"

Jack said, "I know the first thing I'm going to do. Finish up. I'm taking you shopping."

"For what? I have everything I need."

He said, "Perhaps that may be true, but now we are in a position to get everything we want!"

They left and caught a cab. Jack told the driver to take them to Tiffany's. Once there, Jack told the salesman that his fiancé required a much larger diamond engagement ring and perhaps a matching bracelet.

"Oh, Jack," she said, "what I have is fine."

"Not for a future wife of mine," he responded proudly.

The new diamond ring and bracelet were carefully selected. Jack provided his debit card for the purchase of just under $75,000.

"Jack," she said, "this is so wonderful. I wish I could thank you in some way."

"Babe, the rest of our lives are going to be wonderful. This is simply the first morning."

She said, "Then I need to do something for you."

"Well, what have you got in mind?" said Jack with a wolfish grin.

"Oh, not that. At least not now. I was thinking of a really nice piece of jewelry for you. Maybe a nice watch." Before they left, Jack wore an Atlas® 3-Hand watch.

The next stop was the Oakley Store in Times Square, where Jack picked up five pairs of sunglasses. Amelia picked up two. "Now we're styling," Amelia said.

"Okay, this a good start," said Jack. "Let's duck into this restaurant and do some reconnaissance on some activities befitting our first day of wealth. Maybe if we like the restaurant, we can buy it." Amelia laughed and passed through the door that Jack held open for her.

By late afternoon, they had taken a private helicopter tour above Manhattan, had a limousine tour of the island to see it from ground level, spent several thousand dollars on designer clothing and shoes, and took a private yacht ride on the Hudson River. Jack booked a room at the Soho Grand Hotel and asked the concierge to lay in three bottles of champagne, transfer their luggage, get tickets for a new hot play on Broadway, and get reservations for dinner at the Gramercy Tavern for that evening.

After the play, Jack asked the driver to raise the privacy screen on during the limo drive back to the hotel. He asked Amelia, "Do you feel more like a millionaire now?"

"Kind of. I am starting to understand how money can provide you experiences and material things that are not available to most people."

Jack asked, "Do you think that you would ever want to live here in the 'Big Apple'? We can afford to buy a penthouse here. We could fly back and forth whenever we wanted to."

She replied, "I think we need to get settled in LA first. I believe that an occasional visit to a nice hotel would suit me just fine. There are just too many people here."

Jack smiled and asked, "Have you ever wanted to make love in the back of a limousine? The driver can't hear or see us." Jack pushed the intercom button and asked the driver to take a "more scenic route" back to the hotel. It was a first for them both.

When they arrived back at the hotel, Jack tipped the driver handsomely and asked him to pick them up at nine a.m. The driver tipped his hat, nodded, and gave Jack a knowing smile.

The following day, the driver provided an exclusive private limousine tour of the popular sights: Central Park, including a carriage ride, Strawberry Fields, then Wall Street. They also visited the Saturday Night Live set at Rockefeller Center, went to the top of the Empire State Building, and visited the Museum of Natural History. They ended the tour at the World Trade Center Memorial and spent time reading the names carved into the marble walls. The limo returned them to their hotel later in the afternoon, they found a cozy pizza place for beer and a slice of deep-dish pizza just down the block from their hotel.

They took in the Broadway show, ate a late dinner and listened to a singer at the Greenwich Village Tavern. They were pleasantly surprised along with the other patrons when Van Morrison showed up close to midnight and did an impromptu set, before disappearing into the warm night. Jack celebrated by buying the bar patrons a round of drinks.

As they rode back to the hotel, Amelia answered a call from Bill.

He said, "Sorry to disturb you. I know it's late out east. The lottery office is getting lots of calls. Jack's family members keep calling since you guys changed your phone numbers. Anyway, the good news is that the *Jimmy Kimmel Live!* producers want you two on the show."

Amelia was thrilled. "When do they want us?"

"Tomorrow afternoon LA time, so you would have to catch an early flight."

"We can do that," Amelia said. "I'll let Jack know. Thanks, Bill, that is great news! I'm excited. Wow, Kimmel. Thanks so much, I owe you big time!"

Meanwhile back in LA, Bill called the show's producer, Steve Best. He had a favor to ask. Bill said, "I can deliver Amelia and Jack, but I would like to ask a favor."

"And what's that?" Steve asked, his voice revealing of trepidation.

"My firm has a client I'd like to get some air time on the same show."

"Oh? Who's that?"

"Londyn Bridges," Bill replied.

"Not sure I know of her. Where did she get that name? Is she English?"

"No, she's not, but you know of her," said Bill. "She was in that vampire flick that's so hot right now with the younger crowd. She was the one who ended up, well, in a state of being underdressed in several scenes."

"Oh yeah," said Steve. "Now I know who you mean. She's your client?"

"Yeah, one of many," said Bill. "You could have her on and promote the film with a clip and then a quick interview before going into your second music break. You make that happen, and the happy millionaire couple is exclusively yours for your viewers to enjoy."

"Let me talk to the team on this one. I'll get back to you."

"I'll make sure she's on her best behavior. She does have a wild, sexy side."

KIMMEL SHOW

During the flight home, Amelia asked Jack if he had been thinking about his "list."

He said, "I've thought about it, and although I have some ideas, I have not written anything down."

"Care to expand on that?"

Jack said, "Okay. I want to buy a nice car, something fast, a convertible. I'm thinking of a Ferrari or a Porsche. Audi makes a nice car, too. Of course, you should get whatever you want, too. Then we could look for a house, perhaps up in the Hollywood Hills or on the beach, maybe season tickets to the Lakers and a trip to somewhere exotic like Tahiti or Bora Bora. What are you thinking?"

Amelia considered what he'd said. He wasn't thinking long-term about how to put their money to work for their future. His were short-term self-gratifying material considerations. She had thought of those types of things too, but she was trying to get a vision of the bigger picture.

She slowly nodded and said, "Those ideas make sense and are all well and good; however, what should we do with the rest of the money? What about our future and our potential family-to-be? How will we make our lives and other lives different and better?" She noted that he hadn't said anything about their postponed wedding; however, she did not comment on that.

Jack said, "I wasn't thinking in those terms, but I promise that we'll talk further on the subject."

She smiled and nodded, and they turned back to the entertainment console on their first-class seats.

Upon landing, Amelia got the text message from Bill confirming the *Jimmy Kimmel Live!* booking and Amelia cried out, "Yes!" a bit too loudly for aircraft surroundings.

LONDYN BRIDGES

Londyn was motivated whenever she recalled the old Dionne Warwick song about Hollywood hopefuls who ended up parking cars. She was determined never to have to make an actual living parking cars, pumping gas, waitressing, or doing any other menial work.

Londyn Bridges was born Carol Krabbenhoft in Bonita Springs, Florida. She was an only child, and doted upon by her mother who was one of those stage moms who pushed Carol to compete in dance and beauty contests as a young girl. Carol won the title of Junior Miss Collier County when she was fourteen years old and knew at the very moment the judges put that little tiara on her head that she wanted to always be under bright lights and listen to applause of crowds. For hours, she practiced singing and dancing to music videos in front of the mirror.

Carol was easily the most attractive girl in Bonita Springs High School, home of the Bull Sharks. She was elected homecoming queen and voted the most popular girl in her senior year. She knew that she was going to Hollywood to be a star the moment she could figure out how to get out of hot, sticky, boring Southwest Florida with all of its old, wrinkled, slow-driving, retired people.

The boys at school seemed so immature compared to the men she met during her modeling and dance training, that she found she just didn't have time for them. She dated occasionally, but never got involved in a relationship that lasted.

Carol was a drama club member and had the female lead in the school play her junior and senior years. Write-ups in the local papers praised her acting.

Carol was also a good student, smart, with a quick mind and excellent memory. But she had no interest in a college education. She wanted fame and fortune, and four more years of school would only serve to delay that quest.

She did some modeling in high school for some companies, and from that work had a decent portfolio of photos. The local modeling agency was run by a fair and honest woman who saw Carol's potential and wanted to help her. Carol also saw the business's seedy side when men who should not have paid attention to a girl her age got far too close during talent contests. Her mother and agent had warned her to always be aware. She learned to be careful. She managed to avoid situations from which she could not safely exit. She also clearly saw and understood that men were attracted to her and that if they wanted something, tradeoffs were possible.

After high school graduation, Carol started working as an assistant to a real estate broker to earn money to advance career opportunities. The work was simple enough, allowing personal time to pursue her dreams. She won the Miss Collier County pageant. Then she won the Miss Florida Teen Contest.

Carol asked her local agent to see if they could get her placed in California with a LA modeling agency. The agent connected with The AMF Agency in LA (where Bill Hart worked) and sent her portfolio for review. The feedback was that there could be work if she was actually in LA and ready to go to rehearsals, castings, and photo pre-shoots. They said there was no shortage of attractive women already in LA. To compete, she had to physically be in the city. Carol used her beauty contest prize money to buy a used car and headed out to the City of Angels and Hollywood's bright lights.

After settling into a small efficiency in one of LA's seedier areas, she worked hard, making the rounds and trying to get work. She got some jobs, but not enough, or of the desired quality, to call it a real career. She followed the time-honored actress tradition of working as a waitress/hostess while she continued to model. On the advice of her agent, she changed her name. Her professional name became Londyn Bridges. She thought that it would make her seem more worldly and exotic, more foreign and cosmopolitan. Perhaps people would think she was from England. Plus, she'd always had a girl crush on Jeff Bridges and thought that in some way this might enable them to meet someday. Her new name would set her apart from other girls, and she certainly did not want to be a Carol.

On casting calls, she had skills and experience to tactfully fend off lecherous casting. She was usually quickly reminded that a thousand girls were just like her, all looking for a chance to become a star. As a result of her refusal to play such games, there were fewer callbacks.

At her agent's encouragement, she entered a well-known wet t-shirt dance contest at a beach bar and won. The photographer at the event invited her to pose for a studio shoot. He said that he could also take shots to sell to men's magazines. She declined both offers.

The photographer was professional, polite, and respectful, but said, "If you change your mind, here's my card. It pays well if you get selected."

Three months later, tired of working on her feet all day and getting hit on by overweight, middle-aged men, she asked her promotional agent at the Feldman Agency what he thought of the photographer's offer. After a discussion, they agreed that her career was going nowhere fast and that she needed something to give it a boost. Her agent made it clear that it was her decision. And what Londyn decided was that waitressing was too much like pumping gas. She gave the photographer a call and set up an appointment. They did some nice glamour photos and then she disrobed. The session resulted in her becoming a valentine and a popular centerfold as Miss February.

The video release led her to a casting call for a B-grade movie about vampires, where she caught the producer's eye. She spent a weekend in the Hollywood Hills with him and earned the leading role as the sexy vampire queen. He was nice enough, and they both understood what expectations were. During the film's shooting, she spent increasingly more time with him and actually grew to care about him. She thought the relationship was going somewhere. However, on the evening of the film wrap party he suggested that she would have more opportunities elsewhere and wished her good luck. She saw him leaving the party with his arm around the waist of a well-proportioned brunette who was one of the film's vampire victims. There goes the next starlet of the month, she thought.

Londyn clearly understood that LA draws in hopeful, talented people and spits them out. The only ones who are successful have exceedingly exceptional or unique talents, are just plain lucky, or have scratched and clawed their way to the top. She knew that her claws had to get sharper.

Although Bill's firm represented Londyn in LA, Bill and Londyn did not meet personally until after she'd become Miss February and the vampire film was wrapped. The firm sent several attorneys as representatives to a promotional party for the film's release. When Bill met Londyn, there was an immediate attraction. They talked and flirted. However, her head was on a swivel, constantly scanning the room for someone who could help move her career along. Bill understood and said, "I'll wait." She told him, "I'll be back, don't leave me. I have to say hello and be nice to one old guy after the next."

He watched as she smoothly moved in to schmooze each new target. After a few minutes, Londyn's mark would spot their own target, someone higher up in the Hollywood pecking order, and make excuses to cut the conversation off and move away. Bill observed that she would casually wave goodbye and walk toward the bar as if she ended the conversation because she needed a drink. Once she had scanned the room and found no people to whom she needed to pay attention, she looked around, located Bill and meandered back to him to continue their flirting.

At the end of the evening, Bill asked if he could take her home. She had not latched on to anyone else who could further her career, so she said that would be very nice. They slept together. In the morning as Bill was leaving to go to work, he asked if he could see her again.

Londyn said, "You're sweet. Sure, honey, give me a call sometime. I like you, and I don't mind having friends with special benefits at the agency."

They slept together several times over the next several weeks. However, they both knew that the relationship was not going to blossom into anything serious. And yet Bill liked her and casually inquired if there was something he could do to help her out.

She said, "Sure, Bill, get me some publicity. Get me slotted on a talk show or something. That type of exposure can do wonders for a gal's career."

JIMMY KIMMEL

Jack and Amelia sat in the green room with Bill before the show when Jimmy Kimmel entered and introduced himself. He told them both how happy he was for them. He made them laugh by asking if they would like to adopt him or maybe just one of his kids. He told them that he'd make sure to go easy on them. Jack replied that they'd done a few interviews and were getting used to them, so they should be fine.

Amelia gushed, thanking Jimmy for having them on and saying that she often caught the show and that he was a hilarious guy. She asked if Matt Damon was going to come on that night. Was he really always waiting in the green room and never getting on the show?

Jimmy just laughed and said, "You just never know with Matt."

Amelia said, "I love the interaction between you two! It makes me laugh so hard."

Jimmy smiled and said, "Me too. Matt is a great guy," and thanked her. He was about to leave when Londyn Bridges opened the door and strode into the room.

She was dressed to kill in a provocatively short, low-cut black party dress. Jack had difficulty keeping his eyes at the appropriate eye level. Her body filled out and spilled over the top of the dress most appealingly.

Jimmy looked at her, smiled, and said, "You must be Londyn."

Bill jumped up and said, "Jimmy, this is Londyn Bridges, and Londyn, this is, of course, Jimmy Kimmel."

They shook hands, and Londyn said she was delighted to make his acquaintance. She asked if he had caught her in the vampire film. He cracked a little smile and said, "No, not yet, but I'm sure that I will at some time."

Londyn gave him her most radiant smile and said, "Great, I'm sure that you'll enjoy it."

"I'm sure, too," Jimmy replied. "I've got to get on the set right now. If you need anything, just holler and the staff will be here to help you out."

Bill turned to Jack and Amelia and said, "Jack and Amelia, this is Londyn Bridges. She is a movie star on the rise and yet another satisfied client of our firm."

Jack shook her hand, and Londyn gave Amelia a small hug and said, "I heard about you two. You just got married and hit the lottery. Congratulations."

"Well, we did hit the lottery, but we are not yet married," said Jack. "We've put that on hold until we get this whole lottery thing figured out. There are just too many challenges and changes."

Londyn looked at Jack and smiled. "So right now, you're good-looking, rich, and single? Just my kind of guy." She grabbed his arm and gave little hug, making sure to press her body firmly against his. She teasingly said, "Let's go," pulling his arm a step or two toward the door.

They all laughed. Jack could not help noticing how beautiful and genuinely sexy she was. Her perfume made his head swim. He noted how his body reacted just by being close to her. She seemed to be in a different league than all of the other girls he had known.

Before long, Amelia and Jack heard Jimmy announce their names. The audience applauded. The runner led them to doors which slid open onto the stage. The spotlights were bright. They walked out to where Jimmy greeted them. He shook Jack's hand and gave Amelia a hug and kissed her cheek, and guided them over to seats next to his desk.

When they were seated, Jimmy said, "Well, the reason I brought you here was to ask for a loan or to be adopted. Either one or both is fine."

Jack and Amelia laughed, and Amelia assured him that they would be happy to oblige to either.

The audience applauded and laughed. Jimmy related what he understood of their story: they had dated for two and a half years and bought tickets every week using their birthdays as the lottery numbers. Then, a miracle: the numbers hit. Jack confirmed that was the case.

"Well, what was it like to learn that you had won?" asked Jimmy.

"It's kind of a crazy story," Jack said, "I was a bit, um, well, hungover." (The audience laughed and Jack grinned.) "I could not remember where the ticket was, and Amelia had gone out for a run. I searched everywhere in our place. Our car wasn't with us as we'd Ubered home from a party the night before, and so I went looking for the vehicle to hopefully find the ticket in it. The car had been towed. Once I got it out of the impound lot and I didn't find the ticket in the car, I was panicked and convinced that we'd lost it. I drove home. It turns out Amelia had it in the pocket of the shorts she wore the night before. I'm sorry, I didn't describe that very well, but the bottom line is that we were excited, and it got a little, like, cloak-and-dagger until it was confirmed."

Jimmy continued, "So, $685 million. Meaning, what, about half of that after taxes? What are you going to do with the money?"

"You mean besides lending it to you?" asked Amelia. The crowd laughed. "Well, we're still making plans. The best answer is nothing is certain yet."

Jimmy continued, "You aren't married, correct? So, is the money all in one account?"

Jack said, "Well, right now, she has her half, and I have mine." Then he smiled and laughed and squeezed Amelia's hand. "We will share it soon."

"Unless she marries me first?" said Jimmy.

"I do!" kidded Amelia.

Back in the green room, Londyn and Bill watched the interview. Londyn asked him, "So, how do you know those two?"

"I met Jack a couple of years back. He was my roommate, and we were together the day he met Amelia. We both liked her, but he swooped in and carried her away. I thought that she was a great girl, but since Jack is a friend, it was hands-off, and you know, I played the diligent wingman role."

Londyn looked at the green room monitor. "Well, I think that Jack is a pretty good-looking guy to be single and have that much money. She had better lock him up quick."

"Yeah, I agree," laughed Bill, looking at the screen and thinking Amelia looked good, too.

As the interview wrapped up, the same crew member who'd walked Jack and Amelia out reappeared and said, "Miss Bridges, you'll be on right after the break. Please follow me."

Londyn said goodbye to Bill with a kiss on his cheek and murmured, "I owe you a big favor," followed by a wink.

Amelia and Jack passed Londyn in the studio hall. Londyn gave them her most dazzling smile and hugged them both, saying, "Good luck."

Bill asked Jack and Amelia if they could watch Londyn's interview from the green room. They sat down and watched as Jimmy introduced her. Londyn slithered into the chair next to him, gave him a huge smile, and said in a sexy voice, "You're very cute."

The audience applauded, causing him to blush and raise his hand for them to stop. Jimmy shook his head, smiling, knowing a come-on when he heard one. "Well, my wife used to think so. Now, not so much. Thank you, though. You're cute too."

"Why, thank you. Do you like my dress?"

"Well, yes, I think it is very attractive. Audience, what do you think?" There was a roar of applause.

Londyn stood up and spun around 360 degrees, then took a bow. Again, the audience applauded.

Jimmy asked Londyn questions about the new movie she appeared in. Londyn graciously gave the director and producers credit for making the movie so lifelike and entertaining. He asked about her role; and she described how she was the vampire queen who hungered for blood, preferably from men. Somehow, several times in the movie, she managed to be without clothing or had her clothing rip and tear or come off in all the R-rated places. They ran the clip with black censor lines over her exposed body parts. The audience applauded.

She asked Jimmy, "So, how did you like my lines?

Jimmy laughed and said, "You spoke? I missed that, I guess." He commented that her part was a bit racy.

She replied, "Yes, but so were the…what were they called, Jimmy? Was it the 'Juggy Girls and the Girls on Trampolines' back when you were on *The Man Show* with Adam Carolla?"

Jimmy laughed and said, "Yeah, those were the days. I also understand that you are a social media influencer."

Turning to the audience, she replied, "Yes, I am. My Twitter handle is @ LondynBridges. I have over 300,000 followers. I comment on women's fashion trends, fitness and do some funny skits and fun, sexy dances from time to time. My fans love it, and I love my fans! So, join up or watch some of my videos on YouTube, please."

The applause sign lit up, encouraging the audience. "You should follow me, Jimmy. You could be enlightened," she said, flashing a bright smile at the camera.

Jimmy laughed, "Oh, yeah, I'll probably start tomorrow." He turned to the audience and said, "Londyn Bridges, ladies and gentlemen. We will be back with our musical guest, Alicia Keys, right after these words from our sponsors."

The crew member escorted Londyn offstage and back to the green room. She was angry and crying. "He hated me. I'm so embarrassed. I was trying to be cute, light, and funny, and he just made fun of me the whole time. What a disaster. Bill, you might have to help me do damage control on this one."

Bill responded, "Oh Londyn, I don't think it was that bad. He was teasing you a bit, but you came across as someone who had it all together. You got to talk about your influencing and came back at him with the *Man Show* response. You did just fine."

She said, "Do you really think so? It just seemed like he did not give me any respect at all. Like he was disappointed that I was on the show."

Bill said, "Really, you did fine." Turning to Jack and Amelia, he asked, "Don't you think so?" They both nodded. Jack wanted to give her a sympathetic hug but thought better of it. She looked so sad and vulnerable yet incredibly sexy as her mascara ran from her tears. Amelia sympathized.

Bill said, "I'll call you a cab. We can touch base again in the next day or so."

After Bill dropped the couple back at their hotel room and was driving home, he again found himself contemplating how lucky Jack was. He had a great girl and now all the money in the world. Bill knew he should have put up more of a fight two and a half years ago and asked Amelia for a date. Because now he would probably be the lucky guy with the *rich* girl. He shook his head and sighed. Dumb, dumb, dumb.

He wished he had followed his heart. Life just wasn't fair.

SATURDAY

The next morning Bill had barely sat down to check his email when his phone rang. It was Londyn.

She called to thank him for getting her on the Kimmel Show and apologize for being so upset. She told him that she watched a clip of her segment online, and although Jimmy could have been more supportive of her work, it wasn't as damaging as she'd originally thought. She continued to say that they should get together and have dinner sometime soon. After a few more minutes of conversation, she asked if he had Jack's phone number available, as she wanted to ask Jack a question about something he said in the green room. Bill asked what that was, and Londyn politely responded that it was personal and none of his business. Bill's intuition kicked in. He suspected that Londyn might be trying to get in touch with Jack for perhaps less-than-honest intentions.

He said, "Look Londyn, Jack's a good friend of mine, and I can't just give you his number. What I will do is talk to him and see what he says about talking with you."

She replied, "Well, I was just going to ask him a question, but if that's the way you want it, then let me know what he says."

"Tell you what. I'll ask if he wants to get together for lunch. Would that work?"

"Perfect," she cooed. "Let me know. Talk to you soon, sweetie."

Back at the Beverly Hills Hotel, room service breakfast was complete. The quiet room and the fact that there was nowhere they needed to go made Jack and Amelia realize that some of the initial buzz was over. They had to talk about what they needed to do next.

"How do you figure this all out?" asked Amelia, "There just seems like so many decisions to make, but then on the other hand, we don't have to do anything." Reaching over and stroking Jack's hair, she said, "Not that I would ever want to, but we could live in this hotel the rest of our lives and just be happy with each other."

They talked about where they might live and about a bucket list of fun ideas of things to do.

Jack said, "We also need to think about our friends and relatives. Do we stay in line with each other on what we may or may not do for them? Is there anyone in your family you wanted to do anything for?"

"Mine? Not really," she replied. "I mean, of course I will do something for Henrik and Grandma Kate, but besides that, I don't have any close family."

Jack replied, "Well, you know I have a bunch of family, and it seems to grow every time I check my phone. I know that they will keep trying to get in touch. I'm concerned that my mom's inability to control her addiction will hamper me from giving her money. I could route it through one of my siblings, but unfortunately, I don't trust them either."

Jack's phone rang. He looked at the caller ID and saw it was Bill. "Hey, dude. Kimmel was a lot of fun! Thanks for setting that up. What's going on?"

"My pleasure, my friend, my pleasure. Say, Jack, is Amelia in the room?"

"Yeah," replied Jack.

"Well," Bill said, "I have a bit of a dilemma here. I'm supposed to be looking out for you two, and we are friends, and... well, I have a sensitive situation that might be of interest to you, yet it's something that Amelia would be best off not knowing about right now. So why don't you give me a call when she's out of earshot."

"Oh, okay then," said Jack. "Thanks for the call. I'll catch you later."

"Okay, and say hi to that beautiful Amelia for me."

Amelia asked, "What was that about, Jack?

"Bill simply wanted to check in after the show. He said that he would call back later once we had a chance to settle in."

They sat down on the couch and looked at each other. Jack remarked that he was thinking about the wedding and wondered who they might need to get in touch with now that they were back in LA and what the next week might bring.

Amelia nodded and affirmed that she had been thinking along the same lines. She said, "I'm glad we put the wedding on hold. We have each other, and we don't need a piece of paper to be in love. Our situation is fluid, and things have changed so fast. The wedding planner should get all of the cancellations made. I posted a note on our webpage telling everybody we are on hold and we love all of them. I have the mailing list of all of the invitees. To ensure we catch everyone to be notified, I will hire Jacky, that administrative assistant at my work—sorry, ex-place of employment—to print up something nice and mail it out. Maybe we say something to the effect of we're excited by our big news, and we will get back to you all after we get our lives normalized. She can do it after hours, and I'll pay her for her time, so that should handle that one. You know Jack, another option has crossed my mind more than once is just to run off to Vegas and get married, then have a huge blowout party whenever we want to."

Jack nodded and said, "We could do anything we wanted to do. We could even fly to Bora Bora and get married on a beach. The possibilities are endless."

Then he said, "Hey, babe, I've been thinking a bit more about what we should do next. I know it isn't an overall plan. Still, we should find a house somewhere in the Hollywood Hills or on the beach where we could live and eventually raise a family. I also thought that we should travel to somewhere in Europe and maybe even look for another house somewhere like Italy, so we have another warm-weather base on the Continent to stage other travels. I don't plan on working a day job anymore. Our purpose is to enjoy our good fortune. Although, hey, you know, I was thinking about maybe producing movies. But mostly, I just want to enjoy the sunshine and take our days as they come, one by one."

Amelia replied, "That sounds like a great start. I hope that we have long lives in front of us. It seems like we should have a purpose. Something we want to accomplish now that we have the means to do it." She thought that there had to be more to her life after the initial excitement wore off. "Don't you think so?"

But he said nothing more. He was thinking about what Bill wanted on the phone. His silence was disappointing to Amelia.

Amelia sighed and said, "Well, I need to call my grandma and let her know what's going on. Do you mind if I do that now?"

He replied that he would give her privacy. Jack put on his sunglasses and his Green Bay Packers ballcap and went for a walk down Sunset Boulevard. He called Bill, asking what he wanted.

Bill answered, "Buddy, I'm not sure what the right thing is to do here."

"What do you mean?"

"Well, this is sensitive, since you and Amelia are engaged and all."

"What's going on, Bill? You can tell me anything, my friend."

"Okay, but don't go holding what I'm going to tell you against me. And you can never mention it to Amelia."

"I won't, pinky swear. Now you've got my interest peaked. What's up?"

"Well, remember when you were on *Jimmy Kimmel Live!*, and we were in the green room? You met Londyn Bridges?"

"Yeah, she was really hot. Hey, did you get a date with her?"

"Well, not exactly. That's not important. She wanted me to ask if you would like to meet her for lunch."

Jack stopped walking as if he had run head-on into an invisible wall. He remembered Londyn very well. He visualized her body straining against that tight dress, how she had smelled so alluring when she hugged him close, and how he'd stared at her when no one else was watching. He remembered her face and how struck he had been with her beauty and how she was so very, very sexy. Then he came back to the present and focused on the conversation. "Well, I don't know, I'm with Amelia, and…I don't know if it would be right."

"I can tell her that," said Bill. "She said that she was only looking to have lunch and get to know you. She said she thought that you were, well as she put it, 'an attractive guy.'"

"Lunch, huh?" Jack hesitated. "Maybe that's okay. I mean, two people should be able to meet, right? Maybe I'll become a movie producer, and I'll need actresses for my movies."

"Sure," said Bill. "You could just meet her for a simple lunch. I think she has an idea to discuss with you."

"Yeah, I think that would work," said Jack. "I just have to make sure I have the time free."

"What?" said Bill. "You mean a rich guy like you has a schedule?"

"Hah, you got me there. I just have to make sure that I don't have any conflicting schedule obligations with Amelia."

"Okay, I will let her know. And you stay out of trouble, all right, Jack?"

"For sure," Jack replied, laughing nervously.

Bill smiled and stretched his arms behind his head while leaning back in his office swivel chair. He thought that life doesn't always work out the way you want it to, and yet, this might just work out perfectly. Jack wouldn't even know what hit him.

CONNECTIONS MADE

Back in the hotel room, Amelia connected over the phone with Grandma Kate. Amelia described how the lottery was going to make a huge difference in her life. She told her grandma that with the lottery winnings, she could do virtually anything she wanted. Travel and see the world, have a big, lovely house, have a large family, adopt a bunch of kids, donate to charities, and make a real difference in the world. Amelia described how she was so excited, yet in some ways, although it had only been a few days since they'd won, she felt stymied and didn't know what to do next. She told her grandma that she and Jack were putting a hold on the wedding.

In response, Grandma commented that holding up the wedding was a shame, as she knew how much Amelia cared for Jack. Amelia replied that it was all right, as they had their whole lives ahead of them and her head started to spin when just trying to figure out what she should do tomorrow, much less next week. As she spilled out her feelings over the phone, she realized that work had given her life structure, and Jack was someone she loved and played with and relied upon for an escape from the stress of work and now that need had changed.

Her grandma's voice interrupted her thoughts.

"If you have some free time, Meels, dear, I have an idea," her grandmother said. "My health is not the best, and I don't know how much time I have left on this ticker of mine. I've always wanted to visit California and see the western United States. Why don't we take a road trip? You fly here, and we get a car. We travel west, hit the Badlands, Yellowstone, then on toward the Pacific Northwest. Then we can head south, maybe see the Golden Gate Bridge, and then LA. You could show me around there. Maybe I could stay in LA for a while and then, God save my soul, you put me on a plane back to Minnesota."

Kate had mellowed considerably over the past several years. Amelia thought that it was likely that after she and Henrik left and Kate did not have to worry about anyone but herself, she had become more relaxed and carefree. Grandma Kate would have been reluctant to take such a journey back when Amelia lived in Minnesota.

Amelia considered what her grandmother said. Could she manage maybe ten days with Kate in the confines of a car? She tried to imagine ten days with anyone except Jack in a car; it felt claustrophobic. It might not be comfortable, yet she owed Kate as much.

"Grandma, you've got a deal. Except I'm not going to promise that we can get you a place out here, but I'm not saying no to that either. Let's play that one by ear. But a road trip, now that sounds like a solid idea."

Grandma said, "I will plan the route if you book the hotels and plan the stops. There are two places we need to stop for sure: Spearfish, South Dakota—I hope that we can get tickets for the Passion Play there—and Yellowstone National Park. We will need to spend a night and most of a day there."

Amelia said, "You got it. I'm looking forward to it already."

Meanwhile out on Sunset Boulevard, Jack walked a few blocks farther, contemplating what he would do next. It might be uncomfortable if Amelia ever found out he met up with Londyn, but what the hell? Like that dating commercial said, "It's just lunch." He tapped in the number that Bill provided to call Londyn. She answered on the second ring, saying in a sweet voice, "This is Londyn."

Jack said, "Hi," and went on to say she might not remember him but that he was the lottery winner she met on the Kimmel show and that she had been in touch with his friend Bill.

She said, "Well, of course, I totally remember you. It's hard for a girl to forget a rich, handsome man, you know," and laughed. "I was just wondering if you would ever consider simply having lunch with me sometime. I would love to get to know you better, just as a friend, of course, and talk about what it was like to have your world changed in an instant. I even think that there is a story in it. Maybe it could become a movie or at least a made-for-TV special."

"I think that I would enjoy that very much," Jack replied.

"That that would be great. There's no rush. Could we talk in the next week or so to set a time and place to meet? I'm looking forward to knowing you much better."

He replied, "Yeah, same here. I'll look forward to giving you a call. Talk to you soon." Even before he hung up, his imagination already wandered far beyond just talking.

When Jack got back to the room, he found Amelia looking at Google Maps on her laptop. He asked, "So how is Grandma Kate?"

"She's fine. We're going on a road trip! We're going to drive from Minnesota to Seattle, then back down here to LA. I think we both want to reconnect, maybe put our relationship on a more adult, person-to-person level, versus a grand parent and child. It's certainly going to be a much different relationship paradigm. Until the lottery, I think she saw me as the little girl who still needed her support and protection. Now, I have means far beyond anything she could ever dream of. I've suddenly become the adult, and she has become the frail senior who needs to be looked after and can now depend on me for help and support. It's kind of heartwarming, and I have to admit I kind of like it. I might even put her up here in LA for a while. I could set her up in a small place."

Jack nodded and said, "You could set her up," but he was groaning inside, thinking that it would be a royal pain to have to deal with an old woman who probably should be in a nursing home or at least an independent living facility. He'd never met Grandma Kate, but tending to an old lady was not part of the vision he had for his new life.

Amelia continued, "Grandma said that she was going to plan a route, but knowing her, she hasn't traveled enough to know much about route planning, so I'm working on actually planning the trip. I think I will leave next week. I can get the rooms booked tonight, and I'm guessing that it'll take about a week to ten days to get back here. Jack, I'll miss you. Would you like to come along? Would that be okay?"

Jack pictured himself in a car with the two women and said, "It might be interesting, but I think I'll pass on this trip. I will miss you, too."

Just then, Jack's old phone rang. It was his mother.

Jack sighed, his head drooping in defeat. He hesitated, sighed again, then answered the phone. "Hey, Mom."

He heard his mother say, "I am so excited. You're a millionaire! I saw you and Emily on the TV set! You looked so handsome and Emily so beautiful. So, what are your plans now?"

Jack said, "First of all mom, her name is Amelia. My fiancé's name is Amelia. And we really do not have any set plans. We might look for a house and buy a car, and we don't have to work anymore. But beyond that, there's nothing big in the works."

Alice Lemke replied, "Yes, son, that is such great news. I know your brothers and sisters are excited to celebrate your good fortune with you."

"Well then, please let them know that I will be in touch when the time is right."

"Oh, Jack, they want to hear from you soon."

"I will do what I can when I can. So, how are you doing, Mom?" he asked.

"Well, Jack, now that you ask, I'm having a tough time. You know that I have not been feeling well recently and times are tough, as I can't work. I am in constant pain and would love to feel better. I simply can't afford to go to the doctor. I can't drive anymore since the auto insurance company said I wasn't insurable anymore, and I just don't understand why. So I need to take a cab just to get to the doctor, even if I could afford the appointments. In fact, I was actually wondering if, well, if you could send me a little money, just as a loan, mind you—I can pay you back as soon as I'm better."

Jack responded, "Man, this is difficult. How much are you looking to get?"

She said, "Well, maybe now that you have more than you need and I am the mother who went through ten hours of painful labor with you, changed your dirty diapers, raised you and kept you fed, and was there for you all the time, twenty-four seven, you know, I guess, maybe $250,000 would be good."

Jack's heart sank. Although Jack had known that this phone call was coming, hearing his mother's voice made him realize that saying no to her, now that he was a multi-millionaire, was going to be more challenging than he'd thought. He said, "That is way more than I feel comfortable giving you. I know you have bills, but aren't you on Medicare and Social Security?"

"Well, yes, dear, but you know how bills can pile up. Life has dealt me some lemons."

Yeah, Jack thought, when you spend your money on drugs, it can't go where it needs to keep the wolves at bay. He said, "Would you consider checking into a rehab center? You know, like what we talked about last summer."

She replied, "Oh, Jackie, I don't need to go there. I'm fine. I have everything under total control. I just hit a rough patch and could use a bit of help. I've never asked for anything from you before."

Jack felt pulled in two directions. He wanted to end this uncomfortable conversation. He also tried to help her, but deep down, he knew it would be a mistake. "Mom," he said, "I will send you a check for $10,000. Right now, I just think that $250,000 is way, way too much money."

"Well, I appreciate that, but I was just reading a story about one of those big old football players who bought his mama a new house and a car. So, I just thought that my son, who just won the lottery with his pretty fiancé, Emily, would be able to help me out too."

Now Jack felt anger welling up. He bit his tongue to hold back what he wanted to say. He said, "Mom, someone is at the door, and I have to go. I'll send you the check, and we can talk later. Bye." He disconnected the line and sat down heavily on the couch. He put his head in his hands and tried to relax and clear his mind.

Amelia asked, "What's wrong?

He said, "It's starting to happen. My family will be coming after the money hard. We have to be careful, and I know we will be. However, I can sense that it will be a constant flow of requests, and it's only just starting."

Amelia stood and held out her hand, saying, "Let's go get lunch and talk about what we want to do the rest of the day."

Jack sighed and agreed. He stood too, and gave her a hug and a long kiss. He said, "Maybe after lunch we can just lounge by the pool. Have some drinks, get some sun."

She responded with another kiss and said, "Perfect. We could even spend some one-on-one time a little later."

Jack grinned, saying, "You're on, lady."

There were a couple of entertainment beat reporters hanging around in the hotel lobby. Since Amelia and Jack were not sure who they were stalking and did not want to be bothered, they turned around and left by the hotel's rear service entrance. They snuck around the corner, ducked into a sandwich shop, and ordered a couple of submarine sandwiches and Cokes.

While sitting partially obscured in a back booth, Jack's new phone rang. He answered. Clive Bultena, the personal banker with whom they had set up Jack and Amelia's bank accounts, was on the line. He confirmed with Jack that his money's wire transfer had arrived and was on deposit in his account. He also said that there had been activity on the account from New York City, and he assumed that Jack made those charges. Clive stated that they already had their debit cards, and he now had both their credit cards and paper checks in hand and ready for use. Clive also told Jack that part of the bank's exceptional concierge service was to arrange special introductions and concierge access to car dealers, realtors, clothiers, jewelers, etc. Even though it was Saturday, he would like to bring Jack and Amelia's items right after lunch, personally. Jack said, "Could you bring the items to our hotel later this afternoon? We are at the Beverly Hills Hotel on Wilshire."

Clive said, "Certainly I will. Also, please let me know what I can do to be of service to you. You have this number; it's my cell phone, and you can call me *any time.*" He paused for effect and repeated, "I mean *any time* you need any service."

Jack could not help picturing the banker as a nervous small man with a pencil-thin mustache and slicked-back dark hair, anxiously pacing his office awaiting the client's beck and call.

"I have to give your fiancé a call next to let her know I will drop off her package, also."

Jack told Clive that she was right here with him and that he'd let her know. Then he thanked him kindly for his service and punched the disconnect icon.

He repeated what the banker said and continued, "Hey, later this afternoon, let's go buy new cars!"

She thought a moment and said, "Yeah, that sounds like fun."

"Great," he replied. They finished their sandwiches and headed back to the hotel and the pool and to spend the afternoon precisely as planned.

Later that afternoon, Jack focused on the actual purchase of a vehicle. Remembering his offer to help, he decided to see what Clive Bultena could do. He dialed the banker, who picked up immediately, saying, "Clive Bultena here. How may I be of service?"

"Jack Lemke here," said Jack. "Clive, you mentioned that we could work through the bank to purchase cars?" Jack told him they would like to visit an Audi dealer so that he could pick up an Audi R8 V10 Spyder and that Amelia was interested in a Q-5. He wondered if there was any specific procedure he needed to follow to get that special introduction that Clive mentioned when they last spoke.

"Well, Mr. Lemke, what color would you like?"

"Oh, well, I was thinking black for the Spyder, and, just a minute..." He called across the room to Amelia, "What color Q-5 were you thinking of?"

She called back, "White would be great."

"She wants a white one. But I'm curious—why do you need to know the color right now?" Jack asked.

"Well, sir, with your resources and our special connections, we can simply purchase the automobiles over the phone, assuming that the dealer has that color in stock. We will have the vehicles delivered to your hotel. You do not need to endure the hassle of having to go to the dealer. We get a flat five percent discount on the sticker price, and we will make all of the arrangements. You will only need to sign the purchase and title documents and execute an auto insurance application form when the cars arrive. I will let you know when the vehicles will be delivered. Will that be acceptable?"

"Wow, cool! That sounds great!" Jack replied.

"Good. We aim to please our clients."

Twenty minutes later, the banker called back and told him that everything was arranged. The vehicles would be delivered within the next two hours. Jack thanked him. He was beginning to appreciate the evidence that they had entered a whole different world. He asked Clive if he could connect him to a realtor, as he had also mentioned that service.

Clive replied, "Certainly. I will have her call you as soon as possible. By the way," he added, "I was just running some numbers, and we can pre-approve you two for a home mortgage of up to $15 million, should you find something to your liking. I can make a special introduction to an agent that we work closely with to serve our most important clients."

"Wow. Again, that's crazy," he said, thinking that they would never spend that kind of money on a house. "Okay, we will try to stay within our budget!"

Jack called out, "Hey Amelia, Clive says that the cars will be here in two hours or so. Do you want to take mine for a spin up the coast?" There was no reply. Jack listened more closely and heard the water in the shower running. Jack went into the bathroom. He decided to ask again in a more intimate setting. He undressed, entered the shower, and asked the question again.

She said, "That sounds wonderful." The warm water ran over them as they wrapped themselves in each other's arms.

HOUSE HUNTING

An hour later, Jack's phone rang again. A female voice identified herself as Ms. Harris, the real estate agent the banker referred. She started by saying, "I've heard about you two. Congratulations on the great news."

Jack couldn't help thinking, Yeah, great for us and your commission earnings. "Thanks," Jack said. "We are very excited, too. Say, Ms. Harris, we were going to head up toward Malibu on a drive in a while. Are there any houses on the beach or overlooking the ocean which you might like to show a struggling young couple?"

She replied, "I've already done research and have four specific homes in mind that could work out. I will text you the address of the first one. Just Google Map it, and you will be able to drive right to it. Once to the gate, give me a call, and I will let you in."

Jack replied, "Okay, great. See you at about when…at what, seven p.m.?"

"Sure, looking forward to seeing you then."

An hour later, the front desk called. They informed Jack that there was someone from the Audi dealer in the lobby. A dapper older gentleman and two young shuttle drivers were waiting at the concierge desk.

"Good afternoon," said the older gentleman in a heavy English accent, offering his hand. "My name is Clark Kent." Then he grinned. "No relation to the superhero, nor any comment required. My parents had an odd sense of humor, or they were oblivious to current culture. Some days I rather wished they had named me Sue, like in that old Johnny Cash song." He smiled, seeing that his last remark had gone over Jack and Amelia's young heads. "Anyhow, I have some documents for you to sign for your vehicles and insurance, if you please." He produced a folder with yellow "Sign Here" stickers, and they quickly went through the signing process. When complete, he handed them each their key fobs and a folder with the completed papers and said, "The vehicles are in the valet parking lot. The gas tanks are full. We thank you so much for your business, and if there is anything we can do, or if you have any questions or issues, please just let us know. You have my card."

He was about to turn and leave when Amelia said, "Mr. Kent, there is one thing I could use your help with."

"What's that, my dear?" he replied.

"I would like to have my car shipped to a Minnesota address. You see, I'm planning a road trip, and I'd like to fly there and then drive it back here to LA."

"Why, certainly, my dear," said Mr. Kent. "I can certainly manage that for you. Can you give me a name and address for the delivery?"

"Yes, of course," said Amelia, and she jotted Grandma Kate's name and address on a piece of hotel notepaper and handed it to him.

Mr. Kent said, "Consider it done. There may be a small shipping charge to deliver it there. We will work that out with the bank. Please enjoy your vehicles and the rest of the day." Then he walked out the door, whistling.

They found the Audi R8 in the lot. Jack was ecstatic, smiling ear to ear. He had dreamed of driving a car like this since he was a little kid, but never really thought that he would actually own one. Lifestyles of the rich and famous, baby, he thought. It was like getting the best Christmas present ever. He walked around it admiring its lines, and touched the hood's smooth finish before he popped it open and inspected the massive engine.

They climbed in. He started it up and enjoyed its throaty rumble. After syncing their phones to the Bluetooth system, they left the hotel parking lot.

Jack wanted to give the throttle some gas and test the vehicle's acceleration but thought better of it due to traffic and the posted 30 MPH speed limit.

He negotiated their way through town and took California Highway 1 toward Malibu. The car's top was down; the sky was blue and crystal clear. It was a beautiful late afternoon summer day. They listened to old Beach Boys tunes on Spotify and sang along at the top of their lungs. Owning a cool car—he could check that one off his bucket list. Life was getting good, Jack thought. You can keep your electric vehicles. Even though Jack was burning fossil fuel, this car was worth it.

About forty-five minutes later, they pulled up to a significant security gate. The address numbers which Ms. Harris had given him were displayed on the steel gate. Jack called her cell number, and the gate opened in front of them. They exited the car as Ms. Harris walked out the front door and came toward them. She was a woman who had once been quite attractive. With the platinum blond-dyed hair, too much makeup and perfume, and an outfit that was at least a size too small, she struck Jack as the prototypical real estate saleswoman. But they were not buying her. They were here to look at houses.

"Hello, Jack and Amelia. Please call me Sheila. I am just tickled pink to meet you. Congratulations on your good fortune. Putting some of your winnings into real estate is a solid investment."

The first home was on a clifftop overlooking the ocean. The view was spectacular, but the house was dated and would need work. In addition, the interior was broken up and did not flow. They knew this was not the right place within five minutes of arriving. The second house was on the beach; however, the lot was small with no place to gather or play outdoors, and the neighbors were jammed in within spitting distance.

Ms. Harris could tell that they were disappointed and said, "Well, I saved the best two for last. Follow me." They followed her pink Cadillac for ten minutes along the beach road until she pulled into a driveway, using a remote control to open the gate. They pulled forward and before long were looking through glass windows at crashing waves on the Pacific Ocean.

"My God, this is so beautiful," Amelia said.

"Nothing but the best for you, my dear," Jack replied.

Ms. Harris said, "A Hollywood power couple owns this property. I can't tell you the names due to my confidentiality agreement. They are moving back East for family reasons, and we were scheduled to go live on the market with this property next week. The house is 5,250 square feet with 120 linear feet of Pacific Ocean shoreline. The listing is priced at $12.5 million. Let me show it to you. Follow me."

They toured the two-story house and found it nothing less than stunning. The beachside pool and spa were private, shielded from neighbors by high walls and dense vegetation, with a living space elevated above any beach-comber's view. There were five bedrooms and a study with massive bookcases. With a walk-in freezer, two refrigerators, four sinks, two double ovens, and a full room-sized Wine Captain, the kitchen was made for people who had more skills and experience cooking and drinking than both of them felt they could ever hope to attain. The home also featured a fully-equipped gym, a theater with twenty seats, and a video game room for relaxing.

Ms. Harris sensed a likely sale and said, "Mind you, the price includes all of the furnishings and accessories except the two cars in the garage. It's a lot of money. However, I know that you two will grow into it. Celebrities and some very, very important people live in this neighborhood. They have all done very well for themselves, or at least their parents did, and they have good tax lawyers. When you have thoroughly explored the house, I have one last one just up the beach for you to take a look at, if you wish. It's a little smaller, older, and has less in terms of features. However, it's also less in terms of price."

Jack said, "Sheila, give us a minute." He pulled Amelia into the study off the entertainment room. He asked what she thought.

She said, "Jack, I love this house. I never dreamed that I would ever visit a place like this, let alone live in it. I'm just thinking of our little apartment. It is so dingy in comparison."

Jack replied, "I agree. I know it may seem compulsive, but this place is one in a million. I don't see a reason to visit the other place, do you? The banker said we could afford it. It's beautiful, we both love it, so let's do it! Maybe we can offer a lower price. I don't know. I've never bought a house before."

They hugged each other, and he lifted her off the ground and spun her around. She kissed his cheek. They held hands as they walked back into the living room.

"Do you think they would take $12 million for the house?" Jack asked.

Sheila thought about her answer and then responded, "I doubt it. And guys, I represent the seller. In my role as their agent, I cannot legally advise you on what to do. But off the record, let me say this: there are only so many homes right on the ocean here in LA. This house is not even on the market yet, and we priced it very competitively to comparable listings on Zillow and my firm's market valuation. If asked, I would advise my client not to take a lower offer on such a unique property until it had been on the market for at least two or three weeks. However, I will take an offer of $12 million to them if you want me to."

Jack looked at Amelia. She nodded her head, indicating that he should go ahead. "Okay, we'll take it! We'll offer at the full $12.5 million!"

"Great!" said Sheila. "I'll write up the offer right now. Why don't you two enjoy the pool area for a bit while I get this written up? How should I title it? Mr. and Mrs.?"

Jack said, "No, we are engaged, but not yet married, so I guess we'll own it equally together. Jointly, or whatever the proper legal real estate term is."

Sheila replied, "How much earnest money would you like to include with the offer. Typically, it's about ten percent down."

Amelia did the mental math and said, "So $625,000 each?"

"That would be correct," Sheila replied.

Both sat down on the couch and wrote out checks. Neither had ever even pretended to write such large a number on a check.

They handed the checks to Sheila, and she said, "Okay, if you just give me a little time, and I'll get this written up."

"Question," Jack said. "When could we move in?

Ms. Harris knew that the present owners had inflated their initial asking price so that they could lower it if they did not get any quick offers. She said, "I think I can talk the owners into accepting this offer. So, it might cost a bit extra, but we should be able to set up an expedited closing for as early as Monday afternoon, the day after tomorrow."

Jack nodded and took Amelia's hand. They walked through the glass doors to the wall overlooking the beach. The neighboring houses were amazing. Most were modern with clean lines, featuring glass and steel and impeccable landscaping with palm trees. The design focused one's attention on the deep blue Pacific Ocean and sunsets.

"How are we going to fit in here?" Amelia said. "We're like the Clampetts on that old television sitcom, *The Beverly Hillbillies*."

Jack said, "We just will. I believe that it's a time-proven fact that enough money can get you accepted anywhere."

Thanking Ms. Harris, they left the house. Even though Jack wanted to head north and see how the car could perform on the cliffside road, he followed the same route they came in on, back toward the hotel. Both were growing tired and reflected on changes the day brought. They did not talk much or sing at all.

Once back in the hotel room, Jack took out his old cell phone and saw that he had received 34 calls in the last four hours. He groaned and scrolled through them, listening to select messages. Some were from his sisters and brothers. The messages were congratulatory for the most part, even though two brothers flat out stated that he owed them for helping him grow up and survive his youth. Further, his mother had left three messages, each getting more insistent that he should take care of her like some of those basketball players did for their mommas. She said she needed help paying for food and healthcare, and she reminded him again that she could have died and had suffered great pain giving birth to Jack and had raised him well. She said she was entitled to a large payment and to please say hi to Emily.

Uncle Roy, a realtor, who Jack had met only once when he was very young, asked him to call as he had some excellent investment property opportunities that only he knew about and were guaranteed to make lots of money. And Aunt Sarah asked him straight out when he could write out a check for $45,000 to get her a new car. He glanced at the sources of the remainder of the calls, deleted them all without listening, then turned off the phone.

Amelia had only two messages: one from her brother and one from Kim. Before she returned the calls, she asked Jack if she could give their old Toyota Camry to Kim. It wasn't worth a lot, she said, and Kim could use the help.

Jack replied that he didn't mind and that she was right; Kim was deserving of help.

Next, Amelia called Henrik. "Hey, it's me," she said. "Sorry to call you late on a Saturday night. I have not had a chance to talk to you since we won the lottery."

"Hey, Amelia," he said. "Sorry, it's loud. We're just getting started over here. We're having a house party, and you will certainly be a topic of discussion. Wow, unbelievable! You hit the jackpot for what, $685 million?"

Amelia replied, "Yeah, it's crazy. We've played those numbers forever, kind of as a lark, never expecting to win, and now this happens. It's wonderful and starting to sink in. We just bought cars and are buying a house on the beach. I'm so fortunate."

Henrik said, "Hey, remember that $20 I lent you last winter when we had Christmas dinner together, and you needed to pick up some wine? Well, any chance you might be able to pay me back now? I think you might be flush enough where it wouldn't break you."

Amelia laughed. "Yeah, well, I'll see what I can do. I have to check my bank balance before spending the big bucks. Hey Henrik, next week I plan to pick up Grandma in Minnesota and take a roundabout road trip back out here. It's what she wants to do."

"That sounds interesting," he replied. "I'm glad you are doing it, not me. I love her and all, but I'm not sure I could handle that much time with her. You two know each other much better. Say, are you going to keep working?"

Amelia responded, "No, I've already resigned, although I know that I can't just lay around the rest of my life. Jack seems more content to take that track, though. I wanted to let you know that we postponed the wedding until we get more settled. I would like to do something to make your life easier, not sure what, but why don't you think about it? Do you need a car?"

"Hey, thanks, but I have the little Honda that gets me around, and I usually bike or walk to almost every place I go, so no, I'm good. We can talk after you get back from Minnesota."

"Okay, let's talk more in a while. Stay safe. I love you," said Amelia.

Jack's phone buzzed with a text. Jack looked at it, clenched his fist, and said, "Yesss! We just bought ourselves a house."

Amelia stood up, gave him a high five, and hugged him. "This is just so cool, Jack! Imagine us living in that beach house in Malibu. I wonder if we could ask to access the house and move our stuff into the garage at least. I want to get what we need out of the apartment and not have to go back there. After seeing where we are going to live, that old apartment seems run-down; I'm going to be happy to be out of there."

"Sure," he replied. "I will ask Sheila."

Twenty minutes later, he got back a text stating that would be fine. She included the gate and house codes.

SUNDAY

Amelia set her alarm for 4:30 Sunday morning. They were both excited to get a jump-start on the move. As the beach house came furnished and their present furniture was cheap and self-assembled, typical of a struggling young couple's lifestyle, as in cheap and self-assembled, they only wanted to move out their clothes and personal items and start the next chapter of their lives in the beach house.

Reacting to the alarm Jack and Amelia took a moment to shake the cobwebs out of their heads. They silently dressed, got in their cars, and headed through crisp morning air to their apartment. They stuffed clothes and personal items into every suitcase, gym bag, and pillowcase they owned. Decisions were made quickly about things to keep or leave. The longer they were there, the less essential items became.

Inside of two hours, they had packed everything they thought they needed into their cars. They would call local charities to take everything else.

After the last trip, they stood in the apartment and looked around one last time. In the harsh lamplight of the dark morning, what had once seemed like the perfect love nest for a newlywed couple was dingy and drab. After nights at the Beverly Hills and Soho Grand Hotels and seeing their new beach house, the kitchen set, futon, and bedroom furniture from IKEA looked cheap. The only item of real value was the large flat-screen TV, which was now dwarfed by the size of the TVs at the beach house. Yet it was a sentimental moment, too. This was once their home. Where they had lived as a couple and intended to live once married. It was a little sad but exciting to walk out and lock the door for the last time.

They arrived at the beach house, drove into the garage, and quickly unloaded their bags. Excited to revisit all the wonderful things they remembered about the place, they went inside and wandered from room to room, eventually meeting outside by the pool as the sun rose into the morning sky.

"This place is truly incredible! It is even more beautiful than I remembered," Jack said.

Amelia nodded. Jack settled back in one of the plush lounge chairs. Amelia took a couple of towels from the box on the deck and covered them as she snuggled in close to him to gain extra warmth. Tired from the early morning start, they fell asleep and later woke with a start at the sound of a group of children yelling as they played on the beach.

"I needed that nap," murmured Amelia. "I aspire never to get up before eight a.m. again."

On the way back to the hotel, Amelia gave Kim a call. "Hey Kim, how is it going?"

"Oh, Amelia, I'm so glad you called. I have been thinking about you constantly since I heard the great news."

Amelia responded, "Well, it's true, and it's crazy. So much has happened already. We both bought cars, and we just purchased a house on the ocean in Malibu. Can you believe it?"

Kim replied, "That's such great news! You are so lucky. I'm so happy for you. So how does the house ownership work?"

"As it turns out, since we are not yet married, we each own half of the money and now half a house. Anyway, we haven't discussed it much. I guess what's mine is mine and his, his. At least until we get married…but, you know that's a good point. I should learn the ins and outs of the law on that. Maybe I will talk to Bill."

"Maybe you should talk to Bill about a lawyer who will look out for you and you alone. Bill is honest, but I don't know if he can separate himself from being Jack's best friend. Maybe that's unfair, but you know what I mean, right?"

Amelia thought a bit and said, "Yeah, I think that is pretty, pretty, pretty good advice."

Kim laughed, catching the reference to Larry David and Kim's favorite HBO series, *Curb Your Enthusiasm.*

"Listen, Kim, there's a reason I called. Since we've gotten new cars, I was wondering if you would like mine? You know, the Camry?"

"You mean…just give it to me?" responded Kim.

"Well, yes," Amelia said. "I would love for you to have it. You could sell yours and have enough money for gas for the next three or four years. Hey, I'll even pay the sales tax on the transfer."

"Amelia, that is so very generous. I accept. Thank you! Oh, I just wanted you to know that Connie gave out a bonus at work. She said it was from you."

"Great," said Amelia. "I'm happy to be able to share my good fortune."

"So, what's next for you two? What's going on with the wedding?"

"Well, with all of this going on, we put it off. Odd—before this all happened, it was the only thing we talked about frequently, and now it seems so distant. It's certainly not a pressing issue. We've canceled everything. Maybe we'll do something quiet and then have a celebration after, maybe even at the new house. You have to come to visit once we get settled. And bring your swimsuit."

Kim said, "Hmm. Well, you know best. I do look forward to seeing your new place. It sounds wonderful."

"It is pretty spectacular. Jack and I are looking forward to living there every day."

Jack and Amelia spent the rest of the day relaxing by the hotel pool, sipping drinks, eating from the room service menu, and having food delivered to their private cabana.

That evening they went for a drive up the coast on US 1 in the R8. Jack, who was into classic 60s and 70s rock and roll, turned on some old Eagles tunes. They grabbed sandwiches in a small roadside restaurant in Malibu, then decided to travel farther north and stay at a bed and breakfast in Santa Barbara for the night. Jack bought a six-pack, and they sat on their room's balcony and drank beer and munched on pretzel sticks while watching city lights come up as the sea turned black.

Amelia took her last sip and said, "I'm finished." Jack rose, put out his hand and said, "Come with me, my lady. Your Prince has plans for you tonight."

Amelia smiled and played along. "Oh, please, good sir, just be kind to an innocent maiden." They walked hand in hand back into the room.

MONDAY

In the morning they took a walk searching for sustenance, and found a small café just down the street to eat breakfast. Jack's phone rang precisely at 8:30 a.m. It was the banker, Clive Bultena.

"Good morning," he said. "Jack, I have good news; your home loan is approved. I have lined up home insurance on the property, and transaction documents are in progress of being produced and finalized. Would you and Amelia be able to come in early this afternoon so that we can sign those documents? The title company will be ready to close on the house any time after 1 p.m."

"Hey, great! We will be there at about 1:30."

"We will look forward to it," said Clive.

They would stay in the beach house that evening. To kill time before the closing, they spent hours walking and exploring the area around the hotel. Jack commented that they would have to do some grocery shopping and start living like ordinary people again.

Amelia laughed and said, "I would actually like that. As incredible a place as this hotel is, it is not my idea of a home. I'm wondering how we start getting back into being part of our group of friends. I mean, we are the same people, but now we are very different in so many ways. We won't want for anything for the rest of our lives. We don't have to worry about work or bills or whether we can do this or that. We can virtually do anything we please. How will our friends react to us? If we throw a party to celebrate with them, will they think that we're trying to show off or flaunt what we have versus the real truth, that we are just trying to share and maintain relationships with people we love? I'm afraid that we might lose the people we love and care about."

Jack said, "My take on it is that if they are truly our friends they will accept us for who we are, as we are, good or bad. We don't think differently about them. If they don't accept us now, then they were not true friends. I think our real friends will remain as steadfastly loyal and dear to us as we will be with them. I can see our friendship circle expanding, as we may likely end up mingling in a different crowd just based on where we'll be living and what we do with our lives going forward. I'm more concerned about those people, as they may try to get close to us not because they care, but because they want something from us."

He paused to think, then continued, "I think you hit on a great idea, though. Let's have a celebratory housewarming party! We could get settled in over the next couple of days and do it Friday night. What do you think?"

Amelia considered his idea then said, "You're right, let's have a party. I'll get to work getting it catered. We will have lots to do to get ready. I'll call Kim and have her start spreading the invites. Maybe Bill could help, too."

Amelia's phone rang. It was Grandma Kate.

"Hey, honey," she said, "they just delivered the car. It's beautiful! I'm so happy that you will have a safe new car to drive out west. I know how crazy those California drivers can be. So, when will I see you?"

"Gosh, I haven't thought that out," replied Amelia. "It's been a whirlwind out here. Did I tell you we bought a house? It is spectacular, and I can't wait for you to see it. We're moving in today, and it'll take us a little while to settle in. So maybe early next week? Have you looked up the route you would like to take?"

Kate replied, "I looked at the map, dear, and quite frankly, I'm not very good at planning trips. I haven't taken many. Then someone has to make decisions locking in where we want to go and see and where to sleep…and well…"

Amelia broke in, "I've been looking at the route, too."

"Well, good, my dear, then why don't you plan it and then let me know how long it will take so I can pack accordingly. Would that be okay?"

"Of course," said Amelia. "I will get it all worked out and get back to you with an itinerary,"

Kate replied, "I'll look forward to hearing again from you soon, dear. I know you are busy, and I don't want to keep you tied up. So, bye-bye." The line disconnected.

"Come on, it's time to check out," said Jack, getting up from the table.

"I'm pretty excited about the house," Amelia said. "It will be fun to live on the beach. We'll be able to enjoy the sun, surf and sand."

Jack nodded. "I'm excited, too. Let's go buy it!"

They dropped the Camry off at Kim's apartment and headed toward the bank. Once they arrived, they were escorted by the receptionist to Clive Bultena's office. Clive rose and shook hands with both of them, saying, "Welcome back to the First Premier Trust Bank. We hope that we can help make your dreams come true."

"They certainly have so far," said Jack.

"Excellent," said Mr. Bultena. "Please follow me to the conference room. We have it all set up for your closing. It should go smoothly and quickly."

They entered the conference room where Ms. Harris and the title company closer were waiting. The closer passed documents to them, and they kept signing, not fully understanding each document's full significance. Ms. Harris and Clive kept nodding, so neither of them felt they had to ask any specific questions.

When the paperwork was complete, Ms. Harris said, "Congratulations! You now own a spectacular home."

"Yes, congratulations," said Clive. "Now, just a bit of business." He passed a sheet of paper to them, stating, "This is your amortization schedule for your files, showing how much you will pay in interest and principal each year. Each month for the next thirty years, we will deduct the appropriate amount from each of your accounts. The interest rate is five percent."

Amelia looked at the sheet. She said, "Between us, we pay over $60,000 each month, $60,392.43 to be precise, and we pay a total of $21.7 million over the term of the loan. We pay in a month about what I used to earn in a year!"

Clive said, "First-time homebuyers are often taken aback when they see the actual payment totals."

Seeing Amelia's concern, Jack said, "It's an investment, Meels. We are paying off a loan. See here, year fifteen would be an average, and we're paying down over $300,000 that year. It's a great investment because the value of oceanfront property just keeps going up. Like Ms. Harris told us, they aren't making any more shoreline."

"Yeah, I get it. It's okay," Amelia said. "It just caught me by surprise. I'm not used to such big numbers being such a small issue."

Clive smiled, saying, "It happens all the time. Nothing to be concerned about!"

Ms. Harris handed them a homeowner's packet with warranty information and manuals for appliances and systems. Then she gave them the garage door opener, a list of entry codes, and the keys, and said, "Congratulations again, Jack and Amelia, I hope you enjoy your new home—well, honestly, how can you not? I put a couple of bottles of champagne in the fridge, just to save you from having to pick any up."

"Thanks, that is very kind and much appreciated, Ms. Harris," Amelia said as they rose from the table and shook hands.

Then they shook hands with the beaming banker and heard him say again with a large smile, "If there is anything, really, anything I can do, you just let me know."

Amelia and Jack left the bank and drove back north, heading toward their new home. Upon arrival, they offloaded their remaining personal items and agreed that they should first get everything put away and then find a grocery store and stock up on food.

Some hours later, Jack fired up the grill and put on a couple of chicken breasts while Amelia created fixings for a salad. They combined the food with a couple of Kona Longboards for a simple, relaxing meal. They sat on the pool deck, looked out over the Pacific, and enjoyed the view and warmth.

After they'd finished, Jack grabbed a couple of fresh bottles of beer and popped off the tops, saying, "This is the life. Want to go for a walk?"

Amelia smiled and said, "Absolutely, fiancé."

They walked on the white sand beach for several miles to the south, and by the time they returned to the house, the sun had passed below the horizon, leaving orange and purple against the darkening sky. They sat on the deck and held each other as the chilly ocean breeze wrapped around them. Amelia went inside and came back with a blanket. They lay in each other's arms until they both fell fast asleep.

TUESDAY

Jack's phone rang at about 10 a.m. the next day. It was Bill.

"Checking in to make sure all is well. Kim called last night and said you bought a house and were planning a party."

"Yep, Friday night, and you will be here," Jack replied.

"So, where is the new place?"

Jack gave him the address, and Bill entered it into Google Maps.

"Whoa, somebody's gone big time with the new crib! What a great location. What did it cost you?"

"Not saying," Jack said. "We look at it as a conservative investment! In addition, I will allow you to drool over my new Audi R8."

"Oh my God, are you kidding?" Bill exclaimed. "Am I going to get a test drive?"

Jack laughed. "Sure, come over a bit early on Friday night, and you can take it for a spin. But it will come at a cost. I'm putting you in charge of helping Kim with the party list and getting in touch with prospective guests."

"Perfect, no problem, happy to do that," Bill replied. "I can invite some of my newer female clients and have an excuse to spend time with them. So, thanks much for the invite!" Then Bill continued, "Hey, but that's not the reason I called. I know you're a smart guy, and I'm not trying to step on any toes. However, in my role as your attorney and advisor and all-around good guy, I want to introduce you two to a firm that handles investments for many of the top Hollywood clients my firm represents. I took the liberty of asking their top team if they would be willing to take on your account. They do very well for our clientele and are above reproach. What you don't want to do is invest money through the bank. That's fine for day-to-day money, but for ongoing, long-term investment and advice, these guys are in a whole different league."

"Well, thank you, Bill. I appreciate the guidance and advice. I knew we weren't going to leave the money in the bank, but we haven't started to explore our investment options yet. That might save us some time."

"Good. You have a lot of money sitting in the bank, not working for you, even as we speak. Do you want me to be there for the meeting?"

Jack thought and then said, "No, I think we can handle it. How do we connect with them?"

Bill said, "I'll send a text connecting you and Ben Otto. Then you can follow up with each other."

"Great, thanks, Bill. I'm glad we put you on retainer!"

Meanwhile, Amelia sat in the study in front of the large computer monitor working with Google Maps to lay out the trip. Amelia had calculated driving hours, located places where it would be logical to stay, and began booking rooms. Since room costs were not an issue, she could secure the rooms she needed when she wanted them. She also booked a one-way flight from LAX to MSP for that coming Sunday. Even though she had a choice of first-class, she picked a seat in coach and felt good about saving money. She called Grandma Kate and heard the voice recording asking her to leave a message. She left Grandma her flight information and told her that she would love to be picked up in the new Audi.

Amelia's phone buzzed with a text message from Bill saying that he was connecting her and Jack with a financial advisor he trusted. His next text said that he was always looking out for her best interests and that she could always rely on him. She considered it a lovely sentiment from a good friend.

Jack made an appointment with the advisor Bill recommended, Ben Otto, who would come by the house that afternoon with his team.

They spent the rest of the morning in the house, learning how its features worked and generally just poking around. The house was more digital than analog, from light sensors to the burglar alarm to the pool equipment to the garage doors and front gate. "This place sure has a lot of moving parts," commented Jack as he scanned the information on how to operate and maintain the spa, pushing buttons on an iPad used to control it.

"That is one high-tech washer and dryer," Amelia commented as she walked out of the laundry room. "Whatever happened to just putting the clothes in, adding soap and turning it on? There are so many settings; whichever one I picked is unlikely to be the right one. I guess we'll just have to practice."

The front gate security buzzer sounded at precisely 1 p.m. Ben Otto introduced himself and his team members as Gayle Matel and Ted Beeler. The temperature was moderate and the sky was partly cloudy, so Amelia invited them to come out on the deck and sit under the oversized umbrella. Ben brought salads, sandwiches, and fruit smoothies for all. They got to know each other as they ate. Ben asked about their story, and Jack obliged with the now oft-repeated details.

After lunch, they cleared the table. Ben began by saying, "Our firm represents high net-worth clients, and our single goal is to achieve your goals within your risk tolerance. Let's be honest here. There are hundreds of financial people like us here in the LA area. Some are bad, most are okay, and some are very good. We take pride in our performance record, which is among the best, year in, year out. The reason for that is because our research is better and we are large enough to offer investments that most other firms can't provide."

Gayle jumped into the conversation, saying, "Today, our goal is to get to know each other and understand what you want to accomplish with your money. We want to make you comfortable, and to trust that we are the right people to help you achieve your goals. If you're interested, we will talk more, and if not, we had a lovely lunch in a gorgeous location, and we will wish you the best of luck—no hard feelings."

To get the numbers straight, Jack quoted from a sheet of figures he made for the meeting. "Let's start with where we are now. We'll each get over $5.7 million after tax each year for the next thirty years. We each have a mortgage commitment of $30,000 per month, or $360,000 per year. That, plus real estate taxes at about $170,000 for each of us. So, what does that lead you to advise?"

Ben jotted numbers down and said, "So $530,000 each for the house payments. Then, living expenses of, what, maybe $175,000 each per year, or $350,000 total between you two? We will likely have about $5 million in free cash each year to invest or spend somehow. Of course, that would be double when you get married."

"Right," said Amelia.

Ben said, "I'm not trying to ruffle any feathers here; however, it might make a difference in how we approach this, so I have to ask: do you have a prenuptial agreement in place?"

The couple both shook their heads no.

"I see," he continued. "All right, do you have any other large assets, other than retirement plans from your work? Like investments or property?"

Jack and Amelia again shook their heads no.

Ben continued, "Okay, so the question becomes how much risk would you be willing to take with the assets? You see, some investments are higher risks and might yield well over twenty percent return; however, they also may end up with a loss of some or even all of the money you invested. And then there are investments like government bonds that will return a low interest rate but are safe. They are virtually guaranteed. We try to blend the assets in your holdings portfolio to provide a good return rate with controlled risk.

Imagine a pyramid where maybe fifteen percent of your investments are at the peak with relatively high risk and high potential return. Thirty percent are at the bottom, as the base is at low risk and lower return, and the rest sits somewhere in between."

He paused to give them both a reassuring smile and take a sip of his drink.

"Continuing, we also set up the portfolios to be countercyclical, meaning if one investment category is up, then historically the other is typically down. They offset each other. We try to have investments that complement each other, so if small companies are struggling, then international companies might be doing well, or when bonds are not returning well, large-cap dividend-paying companies might be up."

Ted chimed in, saying, "The bottom line is, how much risk are you willing to take? What will allow you to sleep at night? Are you willing to invest it all at high risk or no risk or somewhere in between? You have the luxury of knowing that for the next thirty years, even if there are rough patches in the market, you will receive an annual payment of more than most people could ever dream of saving in a lifetime."

"Further," Gayle said, "you also might want to think about what you might try to do with your money. Will you keep it for children? Or perhaps use it for philanthropic causes? We consider if there are industries in which you will not invest due to philosophical reasons, like coal or tobacco. Finally, we need to consider how your decisions might impact the investments we make in terms of income tax impact."

Ben patiently waited for Gayle to finish then started in again. "Let me give you a rough idea of what we could be talking about here. Based on similar clients' portfolios, if you were to invest $5 million for thirty years at an eight percent return on investment, meaning a four percent real return after tax…I'm guessing that could grow to as much as $290 million. Each."

Jack and Amelia were stunned into silence. The realistic potential sunk in. Together they could be worth well over half a billion dollars before they were sixty years old.

Jack asked, "Is that truly realistic?"

Ben replied, "In today's market, it is probably even too conservative. We achieve that kind of result on an ongoing basis. If we could hit a five percent after-tax return, we could be looking at $350 million each. There will be ups and downs, but on average that is very realistic. You have the advantage of a constant stream of money going into the calculation, and that makes it a lot less risky than trying to grow a retirement nest egg and having to live off of it at the same time." Ben took another swallow of his drink and said, "Quite honestly, I get it. There will be some partying and crazy spending and relatives asking for handouts. People will pitch investments and schemes to flatter and separate you from as much money as they can. No offense meant here. I was your age once too, and can only imagine what I would have done with this kind of windfall.

However, now being a bit more experienced in the real world, I would highly recommend that you two spend some time learning about estate and tax planning implications. It might not be exciting or something that interests you very much. Still, through good fortune, you are in a position where the decisions you make and actions you take will have implications in the millions of dollars over a long period of time. Frankly, and this is just me talking, it is improbable that you will be able to spend this money on you and your family in a lifetime. It could support your descendants for several generations and could impact causes you believe in, in a big way."

Ted Beeler broke into the conversation saying, "You are now in the top one-tenth of one percent of the United States' wealthiest people. You aren't at the Gates, Bezos, Musk, and Zuckerberg level; however, you are in a position to make a significant difference to the lives or causes of those you choose to support. You should have a financial team. Us if you so choose. Someone responsible for looking out for you on a full-time basis. You will also need to add some high-level accountants and estate tax lawyers who will help guide you. Laws and tax codes change and can be complicated and may require adjustments each year. There are advantages, which some would call loopholes, written into the tax code. They are legal for anyone to use but very valuable for people in your financial position. It requires an integrated and involved team to make the most of the assets you have. To be frank until you are married, you should each have separate legal representation."

"Okay," Amelia said. "We already have been working a little with an accountant. Do you know Leo Wessel?"

Ben said, "I know Leo well. He's a good guy. He's a friend of mine, and we golf together from time to time. Leo's a very competent accountant, but no offense to him, you are now in the major leagues. Even Leo would probably tell you that this will require a higher degree of sophistication than he could effectively provide with his staff. It will cost some money; this type of consulting service runs in the $500 to $1,000 per hour range. However, in the long run, that will be chicken feed compared to the value these services bring to you. Maybe it's not my place to advise you like this, but I believe in total transparency and truth, and I do want the best for you, as you seem like really decent kids."

There was silence around the table. Amelia and Jack were realizing that their financial affairs would be getting vastly more complicated and their decisions now could have serious future consequences. "Could you give us a minute?" Jack asked. "Feel free to stay here on the deck or explore the place a bit. We haven't been here very long, but it is an interesting house. A restroom is just off the kitchen."

Jack motioned to Amelia, and they walked down the steps onto the beach.

"I never really comprehended all this in terms of money and investment implications," said Amelia. "It has such great potential, but it's also going to be a challenge to handle it in the right way. Whereas I once saw us just traveling around the world and having people cater to our every whim, I see now that we have responsibilities too."

Jack nodded and said, "I certainly don't imagine saving everything for the grandkids or ending up with as much money as Ben said in his calculations, but I understand that we need to manage what we have. It is hard to fathom, isn't it—a half a billion dollars after taxes."

"What do you think of these guys?" she asked. "I like Ben. I think that he's a no-nonsense straight shooter, and I don't believe that Bill would send us to someone we couldn't trust. I suspect that several firms could help us. I don't know how we would even tell the difference between his and another firm if we talked to them. I propose starting with these guys, and if we like them, we stay, and if not, we look elsewhere once we know what we really want or need and how this could all work."

"I agree," said Jack. "I know our money is just sitting in a checking account doing nothing right now, so I want to get it working for us immediately. It's not earning much in the bank."

"Good by me," said Amelia. "Let's go back and let them know."

BILL HART

Bill Hart grew up in San Clemente, California. His family owned several apartment buildings and held half interest in a successful manufacturing company. These holdings more than provided for the family and helped build the family trust and charitable foundations.

He was an only child, an upper-class suburban white kid, his father's pride and joy. They enjoyed what Southern California had to offer a father and son: Disneyland, Lakers and Dodgers games, sport fishing, skiing at Bear Mountain, jet skis, and powerboats. Family trips to the Baja California were highlights of Bill's childhood. Despite his family's advantages, he was not spoiled. He understood and accepted that he must work hard to earn money to enable such a good life.

He was a good student, and although he did not give his education all his attention, he made an effort to do well at San Clemente High school. He was an excellent athlete, and while he may well have had the best skillset to be the quarterback on the football team, he chose to surf instead. In the winter, he played basketball and was the starting shooting guard. In the spring quarter of his senior year, he decided not to lead the boys' volleyball team to the State tournament again, as it gave him even more opportunities to surf.

His father wanted Bill to get a good education and follow him into the family business, where Bill worked during summers. But deep inside, Bill knew that he wanted to be involved in the Hollywood scene. He attended Pitzer College, one of the Claremont Colleges, near Riverside, California. His dual bachelor's degree in history and Spanish was the first step toward a law degree. He wanted the degree as a stepping stone to becoming an agent for Hollywood stars and California's professional athletes, so he enrolled at Loyola Marymount Law school, as alumni were well-connected throughout the entertainment industry, and the school was physically located in downtown LA.

He finished near the top of his class and earned the Order of the Coif. In his final year, he interned at AMF, one of the top agency firms, and after graduation was offered a junior position there, which he gladly accepted.

His father was disappointed that Bill would not take over the business. However, he was proud of his son. He enjoyed hearing the industry gossip which Bill picked up around the water cooler at the office—whatever Bill felt he could pass along without breaking confidentiality rules, anyway. Although Bill had chosen a different path than one his father had envisioned, he promised his father that he would assist when the family needed him to help with trusts, foundations, and investments down the line.

Bill worked hard to build his clientele. However, others hustled much harder and were able to land better talents. Bill was content dealing with B and C level players, networking with up-and-coming talent, and surfing on weekends and late summer afternoons.

Bill's relationships with women typically did not last long. The young women he met through work and his social circles were ambitious and always wanted to further their careers. Sometimes they thought that he was the means to accomplish this end. He did his share of social climbing, but deep in his heart, he was looking for a down-to-earth girl.

Bill saw what he wanted in Amelia. She was real, kind, sensible, and fun to be around. She was that prototypical down-to-earth girl of his dreams. That was hard to find in LA. He had backed away that first day when Jack said that he was interested in her. Looking back, he now regretted that decision. The more time Bill spent around her, the more enchanted he became. He found himself working covertly to try to win her affection. He questioned Jack's steadfast devotion to her. He was convinced that someday it would be found wanting.

THURSDAY MORNING

Jack was sitting on a lounge chair on the pool deck with his feet up when he called Bill. "Hey, buddy, the party is tomorrow. How are the invitations coming?"

"The usual suspects are all accounted for," Bill replied. "I tried not to make it too large a gathering, as people inevitably will invite others, and it could get to be a zoo. You don't want to alienate your new neighbors this early in the ballgame by accidentally throwing a rager. I also figured you didn't want a bunch of strangers showing up."

"Right," Jack said. "I just want to have a wonderful evening with my friends to celebrate and share our good fortune. I have enough stress without a bunch of strangers in my house adding to my list of concerns."

"Concerns? How could a guy in your position have concerns?"

Jack responded, "Well, maybe it doesn't sound like a big deal, but I keep getting calls and messages on the old number from my relatives, looking for handouts. It stresses me out. I want to do the right thing, but these people are like vultures. Besides the stress, I feel guilty that I might not be doing the right thing, and then it makes me mad because it isn't any of their business what I do with my money. I know if they had won the lottery, I would not be calling them. And the queen bee is my mom. She calls me every single damn day. It's driving me nuts."

"Hey, you were already nuts," said Bill.

"Yeah, you're right about that," Jack said. "Hey, changing the subject, do you remember the name of the guitar player you had at your office party for Christmas two years ago? He played that beautiful classic Spanish music?"

"Yes," Bill said. "His name is, uh…Ricardo Garcia. I think I still have his card because I was going to try to get him some work."

"I would love to hire him to stroll around and play for the evening. Can you try to line him up?"

"Sure, no problem. I'm sure he would love to come and play."

"Great, that will help make this a more memorable party. By the way, we met with those financial guys. We liked them and told them we would like to move ahead. They are a quality group, right?"

Bill said, "Yeah, they are tops in the field. I'm trying to hook my father up with them, too. Frankly, I wish I had enough money for them to take me on as a client. They only deal with high net-worth individuals. They can get a guy into special investment opportunities that we deplorables aren't able to access. Hey, why don't you make me part of the deal? So they have to manage my money along with yours? Hey, I'm serious."

Jack replied, "Sure, buddy. I'll try to remember to bring it up next time I talk with them. Okay, I'm going to continue working on party arrangements. I've got a party planner lined up. We are going to have bartenders and waiters to keep food and drinks flowing."

"Jack, that sounds like a perfect party. I will get Ricardo lined up. Oh, one more thing. Have you made any lunch dates recently?"

"Not yet," said Jack. "Please don't offer her an invitation to the celebration here. It would be awkward for all involved. Hey, I will catch you later, Bill." Jack hung up and found himself distracted and thinking about Londyn and imagined what it would be like being around her.

A short while later, Amelia found Jack still on the pool deck, reading something on his phone.

"Hey babe, what's up?" he said, raising his Oakley sunglasses.

She responded, "Ben Otto called. He will be coming over this afternoon to get papers signed, and he emailed a list of lawyers he suggested that we consider."

"Do you think we need separate lawyers?" he asked.

"Yeah, I think we do," replied Amelia. "I get the sense that it would be best that we both go into this with our eyes wide open, knowing the rules of the game. We are dealing with so much money. Nothing personal."

"Okay, just making sure," Jack replied.

She handed Jack the printout of Ben's email, which showed a listing of four attorneys. "Which one do you want to try?" Amelia asked.

Jack looked at the list and said, "Doesn't matter to me."

She looked at the paper and said, "I'll just call the first one on the list. You can take anyone except him."

"Sounds like a plan,"

"I'm going to try to set up a meeting soon. I hope to leave Sunday to fly to Minnesota and get Grandma, and I'd like not to have to deal with any of this legal and investment stuff again until after I get back."

"Sounds good to me," said Jack. "Hey, I've been looking at a trip to Italy once things settle down. Rome with the ruins, and the Vatican, Venice…"

Amelia lit up with a big smile. She sat down on the lounge chair next to Jack, saying, "That sounds fantastic. Could we include Florence? I remember reading about the Medici family and would love to see the Uffizi with Michelangelo's statue of David and the Duomo! Can we spend some time looking at that when we have time?"

Jack used his hand to make a pistol and shot her with it. "You got it, babe. One trip to Italia coming up." They gave each other a high five as she headed back into the house.

Amelia dialed the number at the top of the list and a receptionist answered, saying, "Good morning, Pierce and Emory. How may I direct your call?"

"I am calling for Bob Smith," she said.

"And who may I say is calling?"

Amelia said her name, and the voice on the other end of the line asked her to hold.

After twenty seconds, a male voice came on the line, "This is Bob."

"Yes, Bob, thanks for taking my call. Your name was given to me by Ben Otto as someone who could represent me. My name is Amelia Bauer. I think he might have communicated that I might call."

"Yes, I do remember that he did," Bob responded. "Thank you for calling, and congratulations on your recent good fortune. How may I be of service?"

Amelia said, "Well, Ben recently pointed out to me the importance of the legal aspects of our good fortune. My fiancé and I were to be married next weekend, but we put that off due to all of this, well, change. I don't know the law, but Ben said that we should both protect ourselves before and after we get married, and that we should have legal and tax advice as we move forward. He recommended several lawyers, and I thought that I would call you. So, there it is in a nutshell."

Bob responded, "That seems like very sound advice. Ben is very good at what he does and knows that putting a good team together is a solid strategy. When can we get together and discuss your situation?"

"I'm available most anytime, and I would like to get something started before next week, as I hope to travel for a week or two starting this Sunday."

"Hmm," Bob said. "Well, where are you right now? Perhaps I could free up some time this afternoon."

"We just bought a house in Malibu, and unfortunately, I don't have a car right now. That's a long story, but would you be able to come out to the house? We have someone coming at one o'clock for a meeting, but that shouldn't last more than an hour."

Bob said, "I can do that. What's your address?" Amelia gave it to him, and he said, "I will rearrange some of my appointments, and then why don't I pick you up at your house at two thirty, and we can find someplace quiet to talk?"

"That sounds great," Amelia said.

"Okay, good," said Bob. "I will look forward to meeting you then."

Meanwhile, Jack called the last name on the list, Justin Kruger, and made an appointment for Monday.

Ben Otto showed up right on time. Amelia rang him through the gate. He was punctual and efficient. Ben was not one to waste time, she thought. He introduced his young assistant, Phil Schneider, whom he brought along with him.

"I brought Phil for two reasons," Ben said. "One, he knows how to get the documents executed correctly, and two, if for any reason and at any time you can't get ahold of me, you should feel free to call Phil. He's on call twenty-four seven."

Phil handed each of them a copy of his card and said, "Truly any time, for any need."

Next, Ben produced a thick three-ring binder with tabs and numerous charts and graphs and said, "I can spend as much or as little time on these as you want. These are our recommendations for investments and our projections for what they could mean to you. The graphs show the results of 10,000 iterations of each asset's potential market conditions and performance in the portfolio and what a projected worst case and best case could mean to you over the next one, two, three, five, ten, twenty, twenty-five, thirty and six-ty years. As you two are significantly younger than most of our clients, we extended it out and asked about sixty years to get you into those twilight years, as we are planning for your entire lives. Sixty years is a long way out to project, but statistically, this is about as accurate as we can project today."

Amelia and Jack studied the binder's glossy contents. It all looked very professional.

"As you can see, the charts show what I was talking about during the last meeting. As promised, I was conservative in my projections. Even a conserva-tive estimate indicates that it is highly likely that if your spending budget is as we've projected, you would likely have over $750 million in assets after thirty years. In sixty years, you would be billionaires! Yes, that's right—billion with a B. You will have enough money, even under the worst-case scenarios, to live an extremely comfortable life. With proper management and planning, this asset will last for generations to come. I know it's a lot to take in, but do either of you have any questions at this juncture?"

Jack asked, "What investments are you putting us in?"

"Good question, Jack," Ben said. He opened the book to a section with a red divider tab. "Here is what we propose." The investment list went on for six pages. "We have you diversified over a wide range of investments. The intent is to provide an ongoing cash flow of at least $10,000 after tax per month. Now that's for each of you. If that is not enough, just let us know. I know that initially, it will take a while for you to settle into your lifestyle and figure out what you need. Comments, questions, concerns?"

The couple was silent until Jack said, "Sounds good to us. Let's get these signed."

Phil led them through the required signatures for the next twenty min-utes. Finally, he said, "These last two forms authorize the bank to fund these investments and also authorize automatic $10,000 dollar transfers from us back into your checking accounts each month. These are in addition to transfers covering the mortgage, real estate tax, insurance, and car payments which you are already making."

"Great," said Jack. They were happy to be done and felt optimistic and confident that they would be financially secure for the rest of their lives. Ben and Phil got up from the table, shook hands, and quietly left.

Looking at Amelia, Jack said, "I'm feeling excited about what we did there. They will do a good job for us."

LEGALITIES

Amelia looked at the time and realized that she only had five minutes before the lawyer was due to arrive. She exclaimed, "This is getting too busy! Just when one would think that we wouldn't have to deal with stress anymore. I can't wait to have a day when I have nothing to do!"

Ten minutes later, the gate intercom squawked: Bob Smith had arrived. Amelia hit the gate button to allow entry and headed outside where Bob got out of the car and walked slightly unevenly toward Amelia with his hand extended.

"Amelia, I am Bob Smith, and very pleased to meet you." He shook her hand.

"Yes, I am happy to make your acquaintance also," she said. As she walked to his vehicle, Bob opened the car door for her.

Once they were driving, he said, "I have reservations at a little place which I enjoy just up the road. I've been there for a few meetings, and if we sit at a little table outside in the back, we should have both comfort and privacy."

They reached the restaurant in about fifteen minutes. Bob politely held her chair as she sat down.

Bob said, "I know a little background about your situation. You are somewhat famous, and Ben Otto told me some things. However, I would love to hear your story."

Amelia recapped the last week and a half for him and included the just-completed financial planning session.

Bob took it all in and then said, "So, what are you looking for from me?"

Amelia described the team concept proposed by Ben Otto and also talked about protecting her interests until married. After a moment of thought, she said, "Now, since you know all about me, what can you tell me about yourself? I like to know and trust those from whom I get important advice."

Bob laughed. "Thanks for asking. I tend to be pretty straightforward and stick to business with clients as they do not pay me to talk about myself. Add that to the fact that I don't like to talk about myself very much. I just don't know how much people actually want to know. Are they just being polite by asking, or do they want to know?"

"I would like to know who you are and how you got here," said Amelia.

"Okay, here goes," he started. "I grew up in the projects in Oakland, California. Like too many other black kids in my neighborhood, I never knew my dad. He was into the whole gang banging and drug thing. He took off early, and the story is that he was killed in a drive-by shooting when I was two. It was pretty much just my mom and me. I'm sure you noticed my limp. I have a congenital disability, a deformity in my right leg. A prosthetic fitting allows me to walk normally."

Amelia said, "I'm sorry to hear that."

Bob nodded and continued. "Life deals you lemons; you get sour or make lemonade. I've learned to live with it. In some ways, it was a motivator for me to excel in non-physical challenges. But I'm lucky in other ways. Being a black kid, I knew at a young age that I was not going to make my way in athletics or hustling drugs and gang banging on the streets. My strict mother and stricter grandmother focused my attention on things that I did well. Learning came easy to me, and I did well in school. I was smart. I graduated from high school a year early, and by that time I had a year of college credits covered. I had scholarship offers from many schools and chose Stanford to be close to my mom. I graduated in two years with an economics degree and then went on to Stanford Law. I did well there, finished number two in my class, got offers from many firms, and chose to come down to LA. It seemed to be the right place for me to be. More sunshine and warmer than the foggy Bay Area, and frankly, I like the glitz and behind-the-scenes activity, even though I'm not exactly glitzy. There is so much money down here. I'm close enough to catch a flight or drive to visit my mom and grandmother back home, yet far enough away to have my own life. There you are: my whole life summarized in great accuracy and detail in what, forty-five seconds? Then you called, and here we are."

He smiled, and so did she.

They were about the same age, Amelia figured. She said, "Aren't you young to be one of the top lawyers in the field?"

Bob said, "I don't have much of a social life, and I'm single, so I am focused and work very hard. And even as I am trying to be as humble as humanly possible, I do know my stuff." He smiled again, and she laughed, looking down at her lap. He continued, "So, here we are, two introverts trying to have a conversation and not stare down at the tabletop to avoid eye contact."

"Yep, that's us," Amelia said.

"So, once again: what can I do for you?"

Amelia took a deep breath. "My fiancé and I were going to get married next weekend, and we postponed it. Winning the lottery has changed our lives. I need someone who can help steer me through the legal side of becoming wealthy. I feel like I don't know what a mine even looks like, and I am walking through a minefield. I don't have any real-world experience with having or managing money. I don't know how to protect myself from those who might harm me."

She told Bob about the projections that Ben Otto had put together. "My life now has so many more possibilities and very few constraints compared to before. Before, I just wanted to be married and work and be with friends, maybe have a family. You know, kind of the middle-class American dream. Now, that just doesn't fit into the vision of where I, we, might be going." She paused. "I'm so sorry. You didn't come here to hear me describe my life problems. I'm not complaining. I'm just adjusting to a new normal."

"I understand," said Bob. "You've hit on exactly what I believe you need to address. You need to be able to tell me your deepest and most confidential thoughts as to how you feel about yourself, your fiancé, your plans, and where you hope your life might lead. Only by doing that can our planning efforts provide results which address your real needs and intentions."

Bob continued, "Here's what you need to know in a nutshell. California is a 'Community Property' state. That means that in the case of divorce, *all* marital property is divided in an even fifty-fifty split, according to the court, *unless* agreed to otherwise by the divorcing spouses. All assets are in play, kind of lumped all together and distributed equally to each spouse. So, one may not necessarily get the assets one wants. It can be kind of a crapshoot. Now, since you are not yet married, everything you own by yourself is considered your separate personal property. That is to say that anything you have that you owned before you were married can be held out as your individual property and not part of the community property in case of divorce, that is, if you have both agreed to it previously. Sorry to toss around the word 'divorce' so casually. I know you are not even married yet."

"No, no, that's okay. I get it. It is what it is," Amelia said. "So theoretically, once we are married, if we put our lottery payments in a joint account, in the case of a divorce it would be split fifty-fifty regardless of how we each had spent or what our obligations or financial commitments were?"

"Basically, that is correct. All debts and liabilities are shouldered by both, even if taken on by only one of you. I have dealt with these types of scenarios many times, even though I am so young." He smiled to confirm that he was mocking Amelia's earlier attempt at humor. Continuing, he said, "It is common for wealthy individuals to sign a pre-nuptial agreement before marriage which defines what would happen in the event of a breakup. Both parties must agree, and it is best practice to renew the prenup every five to ten years so that the courts know that both parties still agree to the terms. In my opinion, with income from the lottery, neither of you will likely ever be destitute. Yours is a unique situation since the income is equal for both of you. So, when you marry, I see two ways for this to be equitably addressed. One, a pre-nuptial agreement regarding joint ownership after marriage, and everything becomes common property. You have to agree on the more significant issues. Two, maintain separate financial and legal holdings from the get-go. Either way, you will both have to agree to it in advance."

Bob took a sip of ice water. "My best legal advice is that since you are both relatively young, it would be better to separate your assets. You are unlikely to have the same vision, or visions, as to what will eventually happen to such a large sum of money. What if you want to invest in something, and he disagrees, or vice versa? For instance, I have one client who spends quite a bit of money on thoroughbred racehorses and participating in high stakes Texas hold 'em tournaments in Vegas, and the spouse thinks it is a foolish way to spend money. And yet she owns several costly jet airplanes which seem to leave the ground only occasionally, as well as rarely-used houses on three different continents. They have separate accounts and get along famously. In another case, the wife wanted to leave quite a bit of money in her will to her favorite non-profit charity, and the husband wanted to do something for his alma mater's football team. They were able to do this without having to negotiate permission from each other. I think that this strategy would work well for you as you both are coming into this union equally in terms of future earnings and have equal contributions to start."

Amelia thought for a while about everything Bob had said. Then she said, "We own a house together right now. How would that be resolved if we went our separate ways?"

"Well, you could agree now that you have to sell it, or agree on who would have the right to buy the other out at a fairly appraised price if you were to split up."

"That makes sense," she said. "Keeping our finances separate will take the pressure off us when we do get married. How do you think I should I describe this to Jack? I wouldn't want to offend him."

Bob said, "To prevent this from coming off as your idea, what I would suggest is to let Jack talk with his attorney and see what the attorney recommends. I'm guessing he will hear about the same issues, and then you two can decide together. Remember, it only becomes an issue when you marry or if you die. It would be best if you also thought about what you want to do with your estate sooner rather than later. That's what we call the assets left if one of you were to die. Do they go to Jack, or to your family? Or do they go to benefiting some philanthropic organization? After you two talk it over and come to an understanding and direction, it would make sense for us to meet and go over the outline of any agreement. Then his lawyer and I can hash out the details. You are in a position where if you buy everyday things in life, you can figure out how to pay them jointly. If you buy a big-ticket item like, let's say a Learjet or another house, you can agree on how to finance it in advance, so you are both comfortable with how you treat each other."

Amelia said, "Bob, this has been extremely helpful. After hearing from you, I believe that we should keep the money and assets separate."

"Okay," said Bob, "I am available if you have any questions at any time on any related subject or if you just want to bounce something off me. I am at your service." He fished a card out of his jacket pocket and gave it to her. "My cell number is on the card. Just call that. I usually always pick up, as I am usually always working. As I said, I don't have much of a social life."

As they drove back to the house, Amelia talked about her upcoming road trip, explaining that it might impact how quickly she would get back to him on what they might do. He told her again that she should be all right unless she got married or made a big-ticket investment.

As Bob dropped Amelia off at the front gate, he said, "Your fiancé is one lucky fellow."

She smiled and thanked him, then watched him drive away, thinking that he was undoubtedly a nice guy, smart, maybe even handsome, too.

Once inside, Amelia told Jack what she and Bob had talked about in general terms as Bob had recommended she do, and said that they'd need to have a serious discussion about it soon. However, that should wait until Jack had a chance to talk to his lawyer.

Jack said, "I already have the meeting set all up. We can talk about it again when you get finished traveling with your grandma."

FRIDAY

Jack and Amelia enjoyed spending time putting up strings of lights on the small trees and the ground within the deck area, to make the outside area twinkle like a fairyland after sunset. Both were excited, looking forward to seeing their friends and sharing their good fortune in their beautiful new home. By five p.m., caterers bustled in and out, setting up tables, serving dishes, and plates for heavy hors d'oeuvres. Bartenders had stocked both bars, set out ice buckets, and finished polishing wine glasses. By six, ice sculptures had arrived and were placed on serving tables.

The guests started to arrive. Early on, Jack and Amelia spent most of their time giving quick tours which usually ended with more guests arriving and Jack or Amelia just waving on the tour group, saying, "Go ahead and wander, the bar and food are outside, enjoy yourselves, we'll catch up to you later."

Jack soon found himself talking to his old boss, JP Hass. He always looks the same, Jack thought. Shirt not quite tucked in, potbelly hanging over his belt, cigar stub between two fingers, and in need of a haircut and eyebrow trim. "You're a lucky dog," said JP, slapping Jack on the back. "Hitting the lottery and not having to work for the rest of your life! Man oh man, what a life. I was thinking of firing you for not coming to work. But then I figured you would get unemployment, so I didn't have to do that when you quit. Hey, just kiddin'! So, tell me, what are the plans? Big and audacious?"

Jack responded, "No. We're taking things slow, getting expert advice, and not making any huge buys—except for this place and getting new cars. I will spend serious time working on my tan and having lots of playtime, and maybe travel a bit. There will be more parties; I hope to get on the Hollywood party list and wake up late and stay up later."

"I like it," said JP. "Yeah, I saw the new Audi in the driveway. Very nice. I can tell you what I would do in your shoes…I would disappear to an island in the South Pacific with a couple years' supply of Mai Tais, a couple dancing girls, and party, party, parteee…" Taking another gulp of his gin and tonic, he continued, "Yep, no reason to worry about anything ever again, Jack me boy."

Jack laughed. "Similar daydreams have crossed my mind. Something tells me that my fiancé might not appreciate the extra company, though. Maybe I should float the concept. I would have to tell her that it was your idea, of course."

JP said, "Right! No big plans, then?"

"I have been playing with some ideas, but nothing solid. I mean, Christ, we just hit the lottery, what, less than two weeks ago? Most of that time we've spent being interviewed, settling into this place, and just trying to get our lives normalized. I'm sure we'll do some interesting things. We just don't know what quite yet. We did talk about a trip to Italy."

"Well, you have my advice," said JP. "Dancing girls in the moonlight on an island where they can't get away, oh me, oh my."

Jack laughed and edged away, slapping his shoulder and saying, "Hey, JP, I will miss you. Don't forget to refill that drink and hit the buffet as often as you like. We have some great food here tonight."

JP looked at the bar, hitched up his belt, and raised his glass, saying, "On my way, me boy. Where are the beautiful women?" Then he made his way toward the bar, where he proceeded to drink himself into an Uber ride home.

Jack shook his head then located Bill standing with a group of friends. "Hey Bill, how was the test drive?"

Bill said, "Great, I love the car! Thanks for the gift to your best friend ever. I'll just keep the keys, and you can get a new one on Monday!"

"Tempting idea," said Jack. "Let me think about that a minute. Ah, no." He put his hands out for the keys.

"I'm hurt. After all these years of steadfast friendship, I would think that you could do a little, you know, somethin' somethin' for your best bud. The best man at your on-again, off-again wedding."

"Yeah, right," said Jack. "You're starting to sound like my mom."

Bill dropped the keys into Jack's outstretched hand and said, "Well, I never want to be in the same category as your mom, so here, take 'em back."

Jack continued to mingle and was approached by friends and their guests, all of whom congratulated him on his good fortune and thanked him for the invitation. "Please enjoy the house and the beach," he told them. "I'm told the cops in this area are pretty vigilant, as the other homeowners don't like drugs and wild parties to disrupt *their* drug use at *their* parties. If you are going to use anything, please head out onto the public beach, away from the house. There are gummies on the buffet table." Smiling and genuinely happy, he made sure all of the guests found the bar and the buffet.

He did notice that more than a few single women attached themselves to his arm. With hands adorned with long red fingernails, they pushed their bodies into his arm and moved their faces closer and longer to his than was socially appropriate. Their behavior left no doubt in his mind that they were sending silent but clear and open invitations to get much better acquainted. They laughed too loudly and too quickly at his weak attempts to be humorous. They told him that he was looking good and, touching his biceps and shoulders, asked if he worked out. Jack certainly enjoyed the attention and was amused by the attempts to encourage him to get into a setting where a more intimate conversation could take place. He mostly politely signaled that he was not interested.

However, there were two women whom Jack found very attractive. Though he made an effort to assure them that he was excited to be marrying his fiancé, his primal male instincts strongly signaled to him that he would like to get to know them much better. As they flirted with him, and as he had fun flirting back, he realized that he needed to be cautious. There were eyes and ears everywhere that could betray him to Amelia.

He drifted from guest to guest, After several drinks and a plate of food, he eventually found himself standing alone at the wall overlooking the beach and the ocean. Here, he shook his head to assure himself that he was not dreaming. Yes, this was all real, and it was his. He was indeed king of the world. Who had said that? He tried to remember. Oh yeah—Leonardo DiCaprio in *Titanic*. He thought about what could possibly make tonight better. The image of Londyn Bridges entered his consciousness. Her beautiful smile and remembering how her body felt pressed against him when they hugged woke up his emotions. Then he turned and saw Amelia talking to her old boss, and the vision vaporized.

"Really," Connie was saying, "Amelia, you should buy the company."

Amelia said, "Business investments are way over my head. I would have to be a lot more educated before I could ever consider anything like that. But one should never say never..." Then she smiled, wondering how Ben Otto would look at this opportunity.

She asked Connie about several coworkers whom she already genuinely missed seeing each day. Connie replied that she had invited them to the party, and Amelia responded that she hoped they would show. Sure, she wanted to show off the new house and their good fortune, but she also wanted to share all this with the people in her life.

Kim joined the discussion, saying hello to Connie and giving Amelia a big bear hug. They chatted a while longer, then Connie excused herself and headed toward food.

Kim guided Amelia toward a corner of the room where it was quieter. "First, I want to thank you for the car," she said. "That was so very kind and generous. You are my BFF!"

Amelia smiled and replied, "I was happy to be in a position to do it."

Kim told Amelia that it just wasn't the same at work without her there; she missed Amelia's smiling face and fun-loving attitude during the workday.

Then Kim asked, "What was Connie saying before I came over?"

"Oh, nothing of importance," Amelia replied. "She thinks I should buy the company."

"That would be so cool."

"Yeah, but, you know," Amelia said, "I don't know anything about business, and I don't think that Jack sees us working in our future, so I need to focus on things that really matter."

Kim responded, "Yeah? So tell me; what matters? Hey, how are the wedding plans reshaping?"

"They are not," Amelia said, without any hint of disappointment. "We are so busy and have a lot to do, which is a bit overwhelming. But we love each other, and it will happen when we decide it should. I'd guess that we'll do something simple and then have a party for others to celebrate with us. Jack has relatives asking him for money every day and to the thought of putting them all in the same place with us is a bit daunting. Maybe we will get married in Italy. We just talked about traveling there."

"So, you still are planning on getting married for sure?" Kim asked.

Amelia replied, "Well, sure, why wouldn't we be?"

"I just sensed that maybe it didn't matter anymore."

"Well, it certainly is more complicated with all this money involved."

Kim asked, "Have you talked to a lawyer about all of this? You know, like about a prenup or something to protect you? You just never know what the future might bring."

"Yeah, I have started the process, but Jack and I will be just fine. We are meant for each other. We'll work out the details. Like maybe we'll have twenty kids or maybe only twelve, or just six, or adopt several…and where we'll travel or how we'll do good things for people who need help. It will be clear as we go forward. I just know it." Wanting to stop talking about the subject, Amelia said, "Hey, let's go get another drink."

As they steered through other guests on their way to the bar, Kim asked, "What are you doing next week?"

Amelia said, "I'm going on that road trip. I thought I told you. I'm driving Grandma Kate to California from Minnesota, and we're taking in some sights as we travel. Ten or so days on the road. It might be a bit much, but I'm looking forward to it. After high school, I never spent all that much time with Grandma Kate, getting to know her as an adult. I always tried to avoid her as much as I could because she always got into my business. Now I realize how much I owe her and Grandpa for raising us. I mean, they gave up their golden years. They could have been traveling and enjoying themselves together. Instead, she spent time taking care of Henrik and me."

Kim said, "You're a good person, Amelia. I hope all of this doesn't change you."

"Thanks," said Amelia, "Me too."

The party had slowly migrated out onto the beach, and soon the bonfire lit up the area. Moonlight reflected off the quiet ocean. Music provided a catalyst. Many in the crowd were soon dancing on the beach.

Bill joined a couple of friends from his law firm around the fire and was light-headed from drinks he had consumed and the THC gummies which were being passed around. His mellow mood lowered his filters. "Yeah," he said to no one in particular, "I'm the guy responsible for these two being together. I stood aside when Jack told me that he wanted to date Amelia. I think that she might have liked me better in the beginning, but being the gentleman I am, I stayed away."

"You, a gentleman?" one of his friends commented. "Are we talking about you or your doppelganger?" The group laughed.

Bill replied indignantly, "Yeah, me. When they won the money, I was there for them, lining up TV appearances and investment, legal, and accounting help. Yeah, without me, they would have screwed up left and right."

He looked around and saw Amelia on the deck, talking with Kim. His voice dropped and he said, "I think Amelia could do a lot better than Jack. I don't think she should trust him. She had eyes for me at one point. I just know it. I really screwed up." Too out of it to realize that he was revealing his real emotions out loud and in public, he continued: "I guess I wasn't what she wanted. I'm sure she'll be pleased with Jack and all of this."

Bill waved his hand toward the house. He glanced at Amelia again, and then fully realizing what he had just said, he added, "I bet you guys bought all of that crap, didn't you?" He laughed. Some in the group joined in, unsure what to believe or what he was talking about. The people in the group quickly fell silent and sipped their drinks, looking out at the Pacific Ocean. Talk slowly turned to other girls at the party - who was hot and who might be available.

As the evening grew late, almost all the crowd was still on the beach, most standing by the bonfire, others danced. Bill spotted Amelia by the fire and walked over to stand next to her, carefully avoiding Kim.

She said, "Are you okay? You look a little shaky there. Have you had a few too many drinks?"

"Probably. Hey, Amelia, I'm just totally enjoying myself at your expense. I appreciate the gummies and the beer. I'm sure not sober, but I'm feeling as good as ever." Working hard to keep his balance, he said, "Great party, Meels, you have a beautiful house in a great location."

"Well, thanks. You helped us get here," she said. "You played a key role. Your guidance with lawyers, accountants, investment guys, and arranging for the hotel room was all so helpful." She gave him a quick hug, saying, "God bless you for that. I will never forget your kindness."

Bill joked, "So you must not have gotten my bill yet."

Amelia laughed, shook her head, and said, "We will gladly pay it when it comes, and please know that your help was worth far more to me than the money we will pay. You really showed that you cared about us."

"Thanks, Amelia. You guys are so important to me—my closest friends," Bill replied. At that moment guitarist Ricardo Garcia, wandered over to the bonfire, started singing Clapton's "You Look Wonderful Tonight." Bill asked, "May I have this dance?"

Amelia looked surprised, as they had never danced together, but recovered smoothly, and smiled saying, "Sure, why not."

As he took her lightly in his arms, he said, "I'm just so happy for you." She smiled at him and then looked out toward the ocean. "What are you concerned about?" he asked. "I can see from the worried look on your face that wheels are turning."

She said, "Oh, I don't know, nothing important." She paused. "Well, I am a bit anxious about spending ten days on the road with my grandma Kate. We haven't been together continuously for a long time, and I love her, but this might be a stretch. I also worry about her health. And lately, I am beginning to worry about Jack and me. I sense that we don't have the same goals. I think he's looking to party, surf, comb the beach every day, and work on his tan. I need more than that. Maybe I'm worried about nothing."

Bill spoke carefully. "I know that Jack is still a kid at heart and likely has not fully grown up and matured emotionally. Now he doesn't ever need to." Seeking to cast doubt and create opportunity, he said, "Maybe you should let this all percolate for quite a while before making any big decisions."

Amelia said, "Yeah, that's kind of where I am, too. No rush. See how this all changes us and maybe find out who we truly are down deep inside."

Bill said, "You are a smart girl, and if you ever need a shoulder to cry on or someone to bounce things off of, you just let me know. You can trust me to always look out for your best interests."

"I will count on you as my official provider of second opinions."

"I am your rock," he said. "Hey, what did the lawyer suggest you do?"

She described a condensed version of the conversation. Bill was pleased to hear that she would likely not combine her wealth with Jack's, at least in the short term. They swayed to the last half of the song, with Bill softly singing the words to her in Spanish. Bill was thrilled to hold her gently. Their bodies pressed lightly against one another. She felt light and moved in rhythm with his lead. Inhaling, he smelled the floral fragrance of her hair. Holding her, Bill felt happily lost in a dream come true.

As the music stopped, Bill stood back, bowed, and said, "Always at your service, Amelia."

Amelia thought that their dance had been a little too familiar. He had held her a little too tight, and singing in her ear made her feel very uncomfortable. But she chalked it up to Bill being overserved, and she appreciated his friendship too much to make an issue of it. She smiled and said, "I need to get back to the party, and I should find Jack."

"Of course," Bill said and turned back to the fire. The wonderful memory of holding her and moving with her without any resistance made him think that maybe someday there would be a chance. He would have to work behind the scenes to make sure Jack never had access to Amelia's money and to put himself in the right place at the right time. Right now, he felt optimistic that such a time would come.

Kim tapped his shoulder and said, "Dance with me, handsome?"

And they did. Bill closed his eyes and imagined that he was holding Amelia.

SATURDAY

It was late morning before Amelia opened her eyes. I love these blackout blinds, she thought. Thank you, previous owners. She rolled over and Jack's eyes fluttered open. "Hey, you," she said, "my name is Amelia. I'm your bed buddy this morning."

"Nice to meet you, bed buddy. I'm Jack. I seem to recall that we had a previous relationship of some type. However, I don't quite remember what it is."

She said, "Let me remind you," and moved in for a kiss.

By noon, they were spent. "We have to get up and get going," Amelia said. "The housekeepers will be here soon."

They both got out of bed, and both quickly washed in their separate showers. While she toweled off, Amelia asked, "Did you have a fun party?"

"Yeah, I did," he replied. "You know I love a party. I saw all of the old crew and met a couple of new people." He grinned and said, "I found out by some miracle, I have recently become a very desirable guy. I had women hanging on me constantly."

Amelia said, "Oh? Tell me their names so that I can arrange to have them roughed up."

Jack laughed. "I assure you, I remember nothing, no names, and now, thinking about it, their faces are fading from memory. I recollect that I only had eyes for you."

"You got that right, buster," Amelia said, raising her fists in a mock boxing pose.

"How about you? Did you have a fun night?"

"Sure! Like you, I got to catch up with everyone. I spent some time with Kim and Connie, and I had a dance with Bill. I think he was pretty stoned. I believe all had a good time."

Amelia headed out to the beach for a run. When she returned, she took a quick dip in the pool before kicking back to relax. Jack grabbed a Diet Coke and walked to the pool area to join her.

The sun was warm. It comfortably bathed Jack and Amelia as they lounged on the deck.

Jack said, "I'm getting excited thinking about traveling. I hope you're still good with the tentative plan to go to Italy? Maybe in a month or so? That will give you time to get back here and get Grandma Kate situated. By the way, you aren't thinking of having her live here at the house, are you? I'm sure she is very nice, and I understand that you sort of owe her for raising you, but I mean, I have never even met the woman. It would be awkward to have her live here with us."

"Oh no, Jack, don't worry," she replied. "I have Ms. Harris looking for a furnished month-to-month house to rent so she can stay here in LA for as long as she wants. I will pay for all costs, so no issues there. It won't be out of your pocket. So, now tell me more about the trip you have in mind."

Jack said, "Well, I did a little research and asked around. I figure that we could fly into Rome, then go down to Naples, then up to Venice, back over to Cortona. If we time it right, we could hit Sienna for the Palio di Siena. That's this crazy horse race I've read about and watched on YouTube, where the rules are that there are no rules and the riders try to win by any means. They do it twice a summer. Then Florence, as you requested, over to the coast to walk Cinque Terre, then up to Monaco, followed by a couple of days in Paris. Then we would fly home. And if we feel like it, we could even find a spot for a certain ceremony if our hearts desire!"

"That sounds just wonderful," she said. "Let's do it first-class all the way."

"Fantastic," replied Jack. "I'll call a travel agent—if there still are such people—and see what can be set up. It will be my treat, all expenses paid by Jack."

"That's sweet, Jack," she said. "Now to address something a little more basic. We have no food. I sent all the leftovers home with the guests. I'm afraid we might starve tonight, and I don't want sophisticated 'foo-foo' food."

"No problem," said Jack. "What can I provide?"

Amelia thought about it and said, "I'd like and an In-N-Out meal. Could you get me a protein-style?"

"Challenge accepted. I'll get an animal-style for me."

"While you're working on that, I will work diligently to address our grocery situation. My goal is to have a fully stocked fridge, freezer, pantry, and bar."

"You're just going to order all of the food, aren't you?" asked Jack, splashing pool water her way.

She splashed back. "Never you mind, it's simply an efficient division of labor." She smiled and said, "Just know I expect that the fridge will still be full and the house clean when Grandma Kate shows up. That's your job." She paused and said, "I do have an early flight tomorrow. So, can we float for a little while longer, then eat, take a walk on the beach and go to bed early? You have to get up and drive me to the airport, you know."

"You got it, Meels," said Jack.

SUNDAY

The couple rose to the alarm early Sunday morning and quietly got ready for very different days. It was still dark as they drove toward LAX. Amelia hoped to catch some sleep on the flight. She knew that she would have to keep her energy up over the coming days with so many hours of windshield time. She traveled light: a backpack with a couple of days' worth of clothes, toiletries, a laptop, and a swimsuit. She figured she could buy whatever else she needed on the route or have her clothes laundered where they stayed.

As they drove, they passed a city bus traveling the other direction. Both of them stared at the advertising sign mounted on the side of the bus. It was a picture of the two of them smiling and holding the check taken at the presentation ceremony. They both watched it go by and then looked at each other and laughed. Jack said, "Can you believe that? Our picture everywhere in LA. Talk about instant notoriety."

Jack stopped the car at Terminal 3. He got out of the car to give her a hug and goodbye kiss. He said he loved her, and that she should keep in touch and most importantly, to travel safely. She told him to behave, and that she would see him next week.

The terminal was relatively quiet. She breezed through security and caught the on-time flight to Minneapolis. She was lucky and had the entire row of seats to herself. Amelia stretched out, and slept almost the entire three and a half hours.

In Minneapolis, Grandma Kate waited in the baggage area. Amelia was surprised by how much older she looked than Amelia remembered. She had certainly lost weight and had become markedly more frail looking. However, the hug that Amelia received was strong and genuine.

"I've missed you so much, Meels."

"Me too, Grandma," Amelia responded.

"Did you have a good flight?"

"I did," Amelia replied. "I don't have any luggage. All I need is this back-pack."

"Wow," said Kate, "I have two suitcases packed. You certainly travel light."

They left the airport and went into the adjacent parking ramp. "Right over here," said Kate and pointed to the Audi. "I love the car," she said. "It is so luxurious."

She handed Amelia the key fob. Amelia walked around the car, taking a look at it. She had never had a new car of her own before. She liked the way the Audi looked and was excited to take a trip in it. Once inside, she quickly familiarized herself with the knobs and buttons and how the navigation screen worked, and soon, they exited the ramp and drove toward Stillwater.

Kate wanted to know the entire story about the events of the last couple weeks. Amelia dutifully recited the story, bringing her up to date. Arriving at the house that she remembered being so big, Amelia was surprised that it was relatively small. She and her brother were raised to be thrifty and conservative. The house reflected those attributes. Seeing it again, she felt somewhat apprehensive about bringing Kate to see where she now lived, in the opulent extravagance of her Malibu beach house. That old American expectation that you want your children to be better off than you might well be true, but Amelia could see that it could easily create hard feelings.

Inside, Kate served chili from the crockpot, and they ate and talked about Kate's daily activities and mundane goings-on in the neighborhood. By 8 p.m. Kate was ready for bed. She was tired and wanted to get a full night's rest before the big first day of travel in the morning. They said goodnight. Because Amelia was still on West Coast time, she called Jack, but got his

166

voicemail and figured he was out on the beach or partying with friends. She missed him already. Then she looked at her emails, caught up on the news of the day, and thought about lying in her childhood bed. She thought about the beautiful beach house and her life with Jack and the good luck which had assured them a comfortable and wonderful future, then drifted off to sleep.

JACK CALLS LONDYN

After he dropped Amelia off at the airport, Jack drove back to the house, laid down on the couch, and called Londyn Bridges.

"Hello," came her voice over the line. "This is Londyn."

"Hey, Londyn, this is Jack Lemke. I don't know if you remember me?"

She turned on her Southern belle accent: "Jack, you silly ol' boy, of course, I remember you. You that extremely handsome man who just became so incredibly rich. That combination is difficult for a li'l ol' girl like me to miss or fo'get."

"Well, thank you, Miss Sothern Dixie Belle," Jack replied, laughing. "Say, I have some openings in my schedule this week and was wondering if you would be available for lunch."

"Well, that might be doable," she replied. "Let's see, hmmm... how about Tuesday?"

"That works for me," said Jack. "Nothing too fancy. I can pick you up if you give me an address."

"I will be at the Twentieth Century Studios on the strip in the morning for a shoot. I finish around noon. After that, I'm free until about six. If you can pick me up and drop me off back at the studio, this girl would be so very grateful and forever in your debt."

Jack laughed, "You're laying it on a bit thick. However, I will be there with bells on." Then he thought that that was a stupid thing to say. What was I thinking?

"Okay! Sorry about the accent, just having some fun with you. I'll see you then," she said and clicked off the connection.

Jack spent the next few hours out by the pool, simply relaxing. He noticed a couple of kids having fun riding the beach on all-terrain fat-tire bikes. He called the local bike shop and asked if they could immediately deliver a men's and a women's bike. They said they could have them there in an hour, but they could not fit them properly unless the riders came into the shop.

Jack said, "I can set it up close enough," and gave them his credit card number. Two hours later, he was on the beach enjoying an excellent long-distance workout on his shiny new bike. He missed Amelia's call that afternoon, but when he came back from his ride he texted that he missed her and was glad she had arrived safely and was enjoying her trip.

PASSION PLAY

Kate and Amelia locked the house in Stillwater before the sun rose. Kate said, "I believe that I have heard that a long journey always begins with the first step. In our case, the first mile."

Amelia nodded, still trying to clear cobwebs from her head due to the time zone change. She said, "Yes, so the adventure begins."

They headed west toward South Dakota.

Even though they had covered it the night before, Amelia and Kate recounted some of Amelia's lottery ticket stories in more detail as they drove. Grandma said she was excited to see the new beach house and finally meet Jack in person. She had met him on video chats but never in person. Amelia looked forward to making the introduction. She loved Jack and was sure that Kate would love him too.

Amelia asked Kate about her day-to-day life and listened as she described a living that confirmed she was still involved with church functions, and from that came her circle of friends. She told Amelia that she was no longer as religious as she once was. Church members now served as her day-to-day contacts and support if she needed it. "It's lonely to be my age and alone," she explained. "If Grampa were still alive, maybe we would be taking senior cruises in the Caribbean or wintering in Florida."

After initial small talk, they traveled in silence for a while. The quiet made Amelia anxious; it seemed to prove that her concern about not having anything to talk about for the coming days was becoming a reality.

Several hours later as they traveled through southwestern Minnesota, Kate commented, "You know, some of our family on your great-grandfather's side came from this neck of the woods. Mainly from northwest Iowa, but some from southwest Minnesota, too. In fact, I was named after my great-aunt Kate, who grew up close to here. She was a twin. Her sister was my great-aunt Alice, whom I remember from pictures of us when I was very young. I never met great-aunt Kate, as she died in her early twenties."

Amelia looked over at Kate. "Oh, that's too bad. How did she die?"

Kate responded, "Asphyxiation." The word hung in the air.

"Huh? What happened?"

"Well, as I understand it, it was Christmas time, and those were the days when had no electric service so they still lit trees with candles. Somehow her long hair caught on fire from the candles, and that sucked the oxygen out of the air around her head, and she could not breathe, or inhaled smoke, and died. Very sudden and very sad."

"Oh, my God, Grandma," Amelia exclaimed. "That's terrible."

"Well, yes," replied Kate. "I don't know for a fact that it is true, but I don't understand why the family would make it up and keep telling the story if it wasn't. I know that she did die young, so I think something like that did happen."

"Why didn't you tell me about that before?"

Kate replied, "You were a young girl, and I never thought that telling you sad, terrible things was a good idea. Also, to be honest, it never crossed my mind to tell you. Our family has a number of odd coincidences, events, and stories. I can't think of any more right now, but I will tell you when they pop into my head from now on. We do have ten days together, and I'm sure something will remind me of a story from time to time. They might help you understand your heritage. I will probably drive you crazy with them before we get to California."

"I hope that they're not all sad stories," said Amelia.

"Well, there might be a few," replied Kate. "It is what it is."

Amelia was grateful that the conversation seemed to be picking up, and that they conversed in such a relaxed manner. From that point on in the trip, it did not seem like the silences were as loud or as long.

They stopped at the Corn Palace in Mitchell, South Dakota, where they ate lunch at the café and toured the building. Kate commented that it was interesting and that everyone should see it once.

Pushing on, they looped through the dramatic scenery of Badlands National Park. The canyons and dramatic red and tan sedimentary rock formations were nothing short of beautiful. Neither of them had ever seen such rock colors before.

They stopped in Wall, South Dakota to refresh themselves with the free cold water available to travelers at the world-renowned Wall Drug Store. An hour and a half later, they reached Mount Rushmore National Monument. They had both seen pictures of the sculpted rocks in books, but to see the four stone faces in person was awe-inspiring. The sheer size of the carving on the face of the mountain was most impressive. They reviewed the monument's history from storyboards in the Visitor Center. Amelia was impressed by the effort required over fourteen long years of construction. She looked at a display picturing the Crazy Horse Monument being constructed less than an hour's drive from where they were now. Amelia thought that these initiatives were indeed a national inspiration. She thought about what she would leave behind when she was no longer part of this world and knew she would like to be remembered for accomplishing something of value.

It had been a long day and would get longer, so Kate napped as they drove and headed north to Deadwood, South Dakota where they checked into their hotel. They needed to be twenty minutes north in Spearfish, South Dakota, by 7:30 p.m. Amelia had purchased two tickets for that evening's Passion Play performance. The Passion Play was a summer production depicting the last days of Jesus Christ. Kate had been told about it by a member of her church congregation. The friend had described a moving message delivered under a summer sky, and Kate had promised herself that if she could, someday she would see it.

The show was indeed dramatic. The stage was outside, underneath the deep black night sky. Yellow heat lightning flashed in the distance. At times it almost seemed choreographed to the action on stage. After the show ended, Kate asked if they could just sit for a while. Amelia was more than happy to sit with her in silence as seats slowly emptied.

Kate started to cry. "I'm sorry, Meels, I'm just a bit emotional right now. I am feeling so close to God and am so very thankful that I am here. Moreover, that I am here with you." Amelia put her arm around her, and Kate put her head on Amelia's shoulder.

"I have something I need to tell you," Kate said. "I should have told you much sooner. I'm sorry. It's my heart. It isn't working right. I take medications to help keep it beating regularly. The doctors tell me that it's failing and there is nothing much they can do for me. They can't tell me anything for certain; however, I likely don't have very long to live. I didn't want to burden you, you have your own life to lead, but now that we are going to be together for a while, I thought I would let you know."

Amelia started to cry. "Grandma, when we get to LA, I'm going to find the best darn heart doctor in town, maybe the world, and we're going to get you checked out. You can get another opinion."

"Meels, I've seen to the best docs in the Twin Cities. I even went down to the Mayo Clinic, and they all tell me that there's nothing they can do. Except maybe a transplant, which I don't want. Give the donor heart to someone younger or who needs it more than me. I've lived a good long life. Now I know that you are never going to want for anything and I know that you will take care of your brother if he needs it. I am content with my life. I can go when the good Lord calls my name. After seeing this play, for some reason I feel that much more comfortable with His love and plan for me."

They remained in each other's embrace. Minutes passed.

Finally, Kate said, "I suppose we should be getting back. It's been quite a day, but a good day. I'm bushed." They rose, made their way to the Audi, and returned in relative silence to Deadwood.

Amelia hugged Kate at the door to her room and said, "I will say a prayer for you and see you in the morning."

For the first time in more years than she could remember, she actually did say a prayer that night.

JACK ON HIS OWN

Around the same time that Amelia and Kate were at Mount Rushmore, Jack met with attorney Justin Williams, at Justin's office in Santa Monica. Justin was an experienced Trust and Estate planning lawyer and a sole practitioner simply because he liked it that way. Justin set his own schedule and was not accountable to anyone. His existing but limited client base of wealthy families and individuals allowed him to pick and choose for whom he decided to work. He valued his free time. He was still physically active in his early sixties and enjoyed biking, hiking, golfing, and spending time on and in the water. As he introduced himself, Jack noticed Justin had pictures of his boats (one power and one sail) hanging in his office.

They chatted for a while getting to know each other, and Jack asked about the boats. From that discussion and intriguing stories, Jack was soon convinced that he needed a boat to make his life complete.

Eventually, the conversation turned to Jack and his good fortune. Jack went through the story of the winning ticket. Justin listened, then asked a series of questions to help him clearly understand the issues at hand. His comments roughly mirrored what Jack had heard from Amelia.

At the end of the meeting, his concluding advice was that Jack and Amelia had to agree on executing a pre-nuptial agreement to guide financial and legal disputes if they got married. Since both had equal wealth and income expectations, it would be the best course of action. Jack could see the advantages of both options. However, he thought that it would be best to keep their finances separate for the time being so that they would not have to agree on every action that the other one might take—like buying a yacht, for example.

After leaving, Jack drove his Audi directly to the nearest marina and wandered up and down the docks looking at beautiful yachts. He stopped into the sales office and talked to the people there to get an idea of types and costs. He was excited about the prospect of enjoying the ocean as the captain of his yacht. He and Amelia could enjoy idyllic days on the open ocean. He wondered if Amelia would be willing to share the cost of one with him.

SACRED GROUND

After breakfast, Kate and Amelia headed out. On the way to Yellowstone National Park, they visited the upthrust of igneous rock known as Devils Tower. Kate remembered that she had seen the rock formation in a sci-fi movie called *Close Encounters of the Third Kind.*

They passed into the heart of Wyoming and through the Bighorn Mountains and pushed on. "I've always heard so much about this area," said Amelia.

"Me too," said Kate. "I'm sure this will be the highlight of the trip, although the Passion Play was quite memorable."

Five hours later, they had driven past the deep-blue waters of Yellowstone Lake, covering what was once a volcano caldera, and watched Old Faithful erupt for the first time.

They both had rooms at Old Faithful Inn. The clerk told them that the room that Kate was staying in had been used by Laura Bush, the President's wife, from time to time. The glass in the windows was so old that it had already started to deform and flow down. Yet there was a good view of the world-famous geyser right outside the panes.

That evening, they watched Old Faithful erupt skyward several times and then explored around the area. Historical signboards with information and markers described John Colter and Jim Bridger's explorations in the Yellowstone area and how it was a super caldera volcanic site. Amelia could not help but think about how bizarre this landscape must have seemed to those first pioneers and the indigenous peoples who had inhabited the area for thousands of years.

They walked the path around the Old Faithful basin, viewing smaller steam vents and bubbling pots. Upon return, they showered and went to eat at the main dining room. When finished, they each ordered a beer to go then sat outside and sipped their drinks. As the day drifted into night, they watched Old Faithful erupt one last time. Kate stood, saying, "See you in the morning, Meels. Thank you for another wonderful day. I appreciate you picking up the tab for this trip so far. If you want me to pay for anything you just let me know."

"Grandma, if you so much as take your pocketbook out before we get to Malibu, I will clonk you over the head with it! We are here mainly because of a lucky ticket. So let's enjoy good fortune."

Kate laughed. "Dear, I don't wish to get clonked, and I will likely say this more times; thank you for your generosity, from the bottom of my heart."

"Grandma, I am happy to share my good fortune. I'm just getting used to the fact that I can afford to travel and see these wonderful sights. You don't need to thank me again; it is my pleasure." said Amelia. "I'm going to finish my beer. I'll be in in just a little while. I will catch you in the morning. Sweet dreams."

Sitting on a rocking chair on the historic inn's veranda, Amelia watched the sky grow black. The crowd thinned out, and she felt the air grow cool. She considered the past several days. She was saddened by Kate's heart condition but pleased that the travel had been easy; she was enjoying herself, and it certainly was not the burden as she had initially feared it would be, though she did miss Jack.

IT'S JUST LUNCH

Jack was looking forward to his lunch meeting with Londyn. He picked her up at the studio. She was dressed in a tight pink sweatshirt with short white shorts and virtually no makeup. She did not look quite as stunning as she had in the green room at the Kimmel show. In a way, he was pleased about this, as he was concerned about becoming overly attracted to her. They made small talk as they drove to the beach, where they spread out a blanket. Jack provided salads, wraps, and several cans of Diet Coke on ice.

"A simple lunch," he said.

"Perfect for a couple of people getting to know each other," she said.

Jack brought up the *Jimmy Kimmel Show!* meeting in the green room and said she'd looked vivacious. He also told her that she was hilarious during the interview.

"I don't think Jimmy liked me very much," she replied. "He was not very complimentary of my movie or of me. I felt bad when I left. I asked Bill to talk to the producer about that. I was hoping that he could have me back on to make up for it, but I've heard nothing from them so far. So, what has been going on with you?" she asked.

"Well, we've been working on getting ourselves situated. We now have very nice a house on the beach, got a couple of cars, an investment advisor, and just yesterday, I think I decided to purchase a yacht."

"Oh, I love yachts!" exclaimed Londyn. "What will your fiancé say about that?"

"That's a good question. I don't know," said Jack. "We're keeping our money separate so that we can do what we want, so I guess I care, but then again, it doesn't matter what she thinks. It's my money, and I can do what I want with it."

"You go, boy," she said and gave him a high five. "And the wedding plans? Are they moving forward?"

Jack shook his head and deflected the question by saying. "Not exactly. We haven't talked about it much. We do have plans to go to Italy after she gets back from her trip. We might do something then."

Londyn's "opportunity antennae" perked up at the news of the delayed wedding.

"Oh? Amelia's on a trip?" she asked.

Jack said, "She's on a road trip, driving her grandmother from Minnesota to LA. It's a long way, but Grandma Kate raised her after her parents died, so I get it. She feels a real obligation to thank her for all of those years of child-rearing."

"How long will she be gone?"

Jack thought and said, "Let's see, over a week, maybe ten days."

Londyn put that piece of information away. "So, what are you going to do while she's gone?"

"I mentioned the yacht, and I might check into some golf clubs, try some recreational activities, and then, well, I don't have much planned, except for this lunch with you, of course."

"Of course," she said, and smiled a bright smile. "Jack, one reason I thought we should get together is that I liked you two. I thought you were a cute couple, and I wanted to become friends since Bill and I are buds. I thought we could be buds, too. I also have an idea that may interest you. I have an idea for a movie. It's a great story, and I thought that maybe you might be interested in producing it if we could get someone to write it."

"Really?" said Jack. "I do have a real interest in getting into that business. But I don't know anything about it."

"In that case, perhaps I can be of help," she said. "My idea is that you would be the producer and fund the production of the movie, and once done, you can sell it and make money. Of course, one of the stars of the movie would be…me." She pointed to herself in a sexy way and giggled. "I think I would be perfect for the lead."

"Tell me more," said Jack. "What's the plot?"

She said, "Okay, so you might think that this is off the wall, but the simple fact of the matter is that the story is about you. Think about it: a couple hits the lottery, and their lives are instantly changed. Both of them realize that they can have or do anything and everything they want. The story is about what happens. What do they do?"

Jack thought and said, "In my story, they settle down and get married."

"I know, I know," said Londyn, "but this story is about Hollywood, home of movie stars, wealthy society, Beverly and Hollywood Hills, the ocean, sex money, and intrigue. Anything can happen. In this story, the main character faces other choices, different options, and maybe he makes different decisions. We need to make it suspenseful and exciting." She continued, "I think that we should get back together sometime soon and brainstorm the story. In the meantime, I could talk with Bill about how you could produce it."

"I kind of like the idea," said Jack.

"I thought that you would. It is a compelling story, so human and emotional and open to plot twists and turns."

Jack started to see its potential more clearly and nodded his head. He said, "Yeah, let's take a look at it. How do we start?"

She said, "I think that we should plan on getting together in a couple of days and outlining the story, and then you could hire a writer to flesh it out, although it almost writes itself. So, let's see." She took out her phone. "I could make it Thursday night. Would that work for you?"

Jack didn't have to check his calendar. "Sure, he said, "We can meet at my house."

"Perfect," she said. "Hey, I need to be getting back. I have another shoot tonight. It takes a while and a lot of magic for this ugly duckling to be converted into a swan."

"Hey, that's not true," said Jack as they got up. "You are truly a beautiful woman."

"Oh, Jack," she said, "that's sweet. Do you really think so?"

"Yes, absolutely."

"Well then," she said, "you are a smart and handsome man," and she leaned in and kissed his cheek. Jack was flattered by what she said, and the kiss made him happy. It seemed harmless enough.

As they drove back to the studio, Londyn got Jack talking about his yacht purchase.

"Maybe you can include it in the movie, and you can write part of it off!" she said.

"Maybe," he replied. His mind started to wander, considering how that could all work. Soon, they arrived, and Londyn kissed his cheek again before stepping out of the Audi.

"I do like your car, Jack," she said, "and I like you. I'm glad that we are friends. I'm looking forward to Thursday already. See you."

HAZEL'S STORY

After breakfast the next morning, Amelia and Kate set off to explore Yellowstone Park. Kate said, "Let's go to up the Norris Geyer Basin. I want to look for something."

Upon arrival, Kate reached into her tote bag and pulled out a book titled *Yellowstone Place Names* by Lee H. Whittlesey. She opened it to a page which was marked by a yellow sticky note. She went to the area map sign and found what she was looking for. "Let's go this way," she said, pointing. After a fifteen-minute walk following the damp bed of a small stream, they stopped. Kate looked back and forth and then said, "This has to be it."

"Has to be what? I don't understand. What are we looking for?" asked Amelia.

"This is the main reason I wanted to come here," Kate replied. She pointed to an elevated spit of land with an upgrowth of trees on the South Fork of the Tantalus River. She walked to the center of the area. She took a container out of her tote bag and said, "I promised that I would do this one day. I was not certain that I would ever make it here."

She took the top off the jar and slowly spread its powdery grey white contents evenly onto the ground.

"That wore heavily on me," she said. "Now, I feel relieved and content. Those were ashes, Meels. More exactly, that was what remains of the ashes of your great-great-grandmother Hazel."

There was a long silence.

"Whoa, what? Really?" Amelia said. "I don't understand. Why here? Why now?" What's Hazel got to do with this place?

Pointing to a solitary bench oddly sitting in the middle of the little island, Kate said, "Let's sit on that bench while I try to explain. I will tell you a story. It might take a while, but it will be worth it."

"No one gets killed in this one, do they?" Amelia asked.

"No, no one is killed. Meels, this is a wonderful story. One I should have told you years ago. I guess the opportunity or need just never arose. You come from a long line of strong and resourceful women. Women who leave footprints on their own paths — often in the face of social norms. I hope, no, I just know, that you are going to continue that lineage."

They sat on the bench and made themselves comfortable. Kate looked up at the morning sun, took a deep breath, then began.

"Back in 1917, the United States was just getting involved in World War I. There was a strong patriotic movement among many of our confident young men to go 'over there' to quickly and easily end the war. The attitude was almost as if their very presence would cause the Germans to turn tail, run for home, and surrender. Your great-great-grandfather—his name was Arbor Fields, like Arbor Day—was going to an architectural school in Oregon at the time, and he decided to do his patriotic duty and go 'over there.' He traveled by troop train across the country to get back home to join his hometown friends in Ohio, so that they could all join up in the same unit."

"It was a practice, in those days, while traveling on troop trains, for young men to write their names and addresses on a piece of paper or whatever they could find and throw them out the train windows when they went through a town. The idea was that the young ladies in the town would pick up the notes and write letters as pen-pals, supporting the war effort while the boys were overseas. So, near Annawan, a small town in northwestern Illinois, Arbor wrote his information on a package of unsalted soda crackers—called 'hardtack' in those days—and threw it out the window of the train. A young woman picked it up and took it home. That girl was your great-great-grandmother, Hazel Mapes!"

Amelia absorbed the information and then exclaimed, "Wait a minute, you're kidding! I'm alive because of a package of crackers?"

"Yes, you and me both, Meels. Crackers and a French farmer," continued Aunt Kate. "This is a true story, and it has been a long time coming. Please relax and enjoy it. Don't get ahead of me. Well, they started writing while Arbor was fighting in the trenches in France, and they eventually exchanged photographs. Arbor kept her photo under his tunic jacket to keep it close to his heart. Unfortunately, during the battle, an enemy artillery shell exploded and killed everyone in his platoon except him. He was badly wounded and left for dead on the battlefield."

Amelia held her hand over her mouth. Obviously, if Arbor had died on the battlefield, she wouldn't exist, so the story had to end positively. Yet Kate was a good storyteller. Amelia hung on every word, and said, "That's terrible. So tell me, what happened next?"

"Fortunately for us, a French farmer found him, brought him into his home, and slowly nursed him back to health. He and that farmer became lifelong friends and visited each other several times throughout their lives. To his last day, Arbor still had German shrapnel in his shoulder."

"Now, I don't know any details as to exactly what happened from the time he recovered until after the war ended. But he did recover, and soon arrived on Hazel's doorstep back in Illinois to meet her in person for the first time. He proposed, and they were married in June 1919, just seven months after the end of the war."

"Wow. Not a very long courtship. Maybe things were different in those days, and they had been writing each other."

"Yes, evidently. Unfortunately, Arbor struggled with other demons. His father had beaten him as a child. I remember a story where he said that his father, a barber back in the early 1900s, had tasked him with the after-school chore of sweeping the barbershop floor. If he did not do it fast enough or to his father's satisfaction, his father hit him with a board. The board had a nail in one end. He told me that he bled many times. He also had PTSD from battle, back before they knew or acknowledged what it was, and had to spend time in the VA hospital back in Ohio, dealing with mental issues."

"Do you mind if I stand and listen, Grandma? I am anxious about this story and can't sit still." Amelia got up and began to pace.

"Arbor eventually returned to school and, after earning a Master's degree in education from Ohio State University, was hired the as superintendent schools for the Two Harbors, Minnesota school district."

"That's up on the north shore of Lake Superior, right Grandma?"

"Yes, that's right, Meels. They lived in a tiny white house along the shore of Superior. Arbor hand-built the house and several bridges over the small stream that ran past the house down to the lake. I remember that one even had a love seat swing. I drove up and found the house again about a year after you left for California. I was surprised it was so much smaller than I remembered as a child. It was like a white cracker box."

Kate smiled, remembering, then continued. "Arbor was a freemason and a conservative, stern father. He was a difficult man. Back in those days, the man of the house was king. What he said and wanted was what happened. The couple had three children, two boys and a girl, who was your great grandmother Beth. He made their lives very, very difficult. Arbor abused his children both mentally and not surprisingly, as cycles like this are common, physically."

"At some point, Hazel and Arbor got divorced. He moved out and ended up teaching school back in Ohio while getting remarried several times. He passed away at 103 years of age, so you have some longevity genes in you."

"Hey, me and you both. I did not know that. That's very nice to know. What a life."

Kate nodded. "Now, Hazel was a tough nut; she was born in 1897 and died at 75 years old in 1973. She stood under five feet tall, skinny as a rail. Not an ounce of fat on her. But she was very strong in body and spirit. She was a determined woman who could focus on what she wanted to accomplish."

"She was also an avid outdoorsman...or outdoorswoman? Hmm. I've never heard someone referred to as an outdoorswoman, but that is what she was. Anyway, now I always think of her as Teddy Roosevelt in a skirt! Bully! He was known for his love of the outdoors and nature's wild places, hunting, and fishing. Hazel fished the streams running into Lake Superior. She once told me she talked to the trout to get them to bite. She tied her own flies, and at one time, had a fly-fishing lure named after her."

Amelia asked, "Did you ever fish with her? It seems like it might have been interesting."

"No, I never did. When I was with her, she was just Grandma Hazel, and she doted on us kids and wanted us to understand science and to appreciate and respect nature. One vivid memory I have is that deer would come in and surround her house just after sunset most nights. I remember being woken up by my mother, your great-grandmother, during those visits. She'd say, 'Get up. The deer are in.' We would creep to the window, and in the bright moonlight, Hazel would slowly walk among the deer which crowded around her to eat apples right out of her hand. She would almost disappear in the herd of maybe up to fifty deer. I remember them actually jostling for position to get fed. She went out with a basket full of apples, and it always came back empty. I will never forget that sight."

"That must have been wonderful. She must have been in close touch with nature."

"Yes, that brings back so many wonderful memories for me. We would drive up there each summer when we were young, maybe until I was a teenager. We loved it up there. Exploring in the woods, 'hunting for bear' with homemade bows and arrows made of twine and sticks. If we heard so much as the slightest sound in the forest we ran back across the bridges and into the house as fast as we could, positive that a giant bear was chasing us and right on our heels!"

"We spent hours exploring the streams and woods and the lakeshore and watching huge iron ore ships steam by on Lake Superior. Some evenings we drove to the town dump and watched the black bears come out to forage for food amongst the waste. We would take the trail north from the main falls on the Gooseberry River and find the pool at the seventh waterfall, then swim in the cool, crystal-clear water. Yet, to my memory, we never stayed the whole week. Inevitably Hazel and your great-Grandma Beth would get into a loud argument, and we would have to leave early. We were always sad to leave. We visited Arbor in Florida years later. Beth and Arbor argued so severely that we also had to leave and find another place to stay. There was a trend there, I guess. Bad memories, too."

"I'm sorry to hear that. It sounds very sad."

"Well, they all were strong-willed and strong-minded. Anyway, after her divorce from Arbor, Hazel eventually remarried. When her second husband passed away in the early 1960s, she started coming out here to Yellowstone Park in the summers. Since she was so tiny, she could easily sleep in the back seat of her Buick sedan. She would set up her car camp probably out near where we just parked here in the Norris Geyser Basin parking lot, between Memorial and Labor Days."

"She was fascinated by Steamboat Geyser." Kate pointed to the geyser's location right above them. "She learned its sounds and tendencies. She would often tell park visitors when it was about to erupt. The geyser had gone dormant in 1911 and began to erupt again in 1961. Now, Steamboat wasn't like Old Faithful, going off every hour or so—it could be weeks or months between events. Hazel would take to sleeping on the ground for weeks on end near the geyser, and she would wake up hearing and feeling the geyser's rumblings and hisses. It literally shook the ground for hours before erupting and sometimes threw out large rocks along with tons of scalding hot water. I have a letter somewhere at home, sent by a high-ranking administrator with the US Department of the Interior asking her for any records and photographs she had for the National Park System archives!"

Amelia looked at the area around the geyser and tried to imagine where Hazel would bed down. The landscape and vegetation had likely changed over the past fifty years, but Amelia did not see a place that looked comfortable to sleep. She said, "Hazel must have been tough and determined."

"She was vigilant and would stay right on task," Kate agreed. "People got to know her, and frequent visitors came to look her up to visit with her year after year. She became a fixture here. She acted as the de facto hostess of the Norris geyser basin. From time to time, when the ranger cadre had too many visitors to handle, they would put a Smokey Bear ranger hat on her head and she would guide a group for them. I'm guessing that was strictly against the rules."

"That's really cool. I can totally envision this tough little woman tromping on these trails."

"She also became close to the park rangers, and they would pick up groceries for her in town. Some would even tell her when the rangers' shower room just happened to be open and would not be in use for a half-hour, to allow her to clean up. They let her park long-term in the parking lot, which was also strictly against Park rules. She paid them back with her energy and spirit."

"As I understand it, in July, 1967 a new geyser popped up, and she discovered it during her routine early morning walk. The rangers began to refer to it as 'Decker's Geyser,' and it was even in the guidebooks under that name. Unfortunately, there was a long-standing tradition of not naming any geyser after any individual, except for a United States president. So, in the early 1980s the Board of Governors met and renamed it Tantalus Geyser. The park rangers complained that it was not fair to Hazel. As a gesture of recognition, they named this little land area where we now stand, which Tantalus Creek flows around, 'Mrs. Decker Island.' As I understand it, the park rangers brought in this bench and put it in this shady spot for her. She used to sit right here for days on end and wait for Steamboat Geyser to erupt."

Amelia sat back down on the bench and tried to imagine Hazel patiently waiting for the next eruption and greeting familiar and new faces with excitement and her knowledge of the geyser. She smiled happily as the pleasant image formed in her mind's eye.

"The new geyser has long since burned out and no longer erupts," Kate went on. "However, this island remains. You can find information about Hazel on the internet. Just search for it. And that, my dear, is a roundabout story of why and how we are here today. In her will, she requested that her ashes be spread on this little island. I did not know if I was ever going to make it here, Meels. I feel so very much at peace for finally being able to bring Hazel home to rest in the place on earth which she loved so dearly." Kate wiped away her tears, and said, "Thank you, Amelia, for making it possible and allowing me to do this. Hazel has been waiting patiently in my closet for a long time. I made a vow that I would do this, and now I have. This little island is a good place for her to rest forever." She looked around and up at the bright morning sky and said, "It is so special here. I can understand why she loved this place. I can just feel it in my soul."

Amelia had tears running down her face. "That is an amazing story, Grandma. I'm glad that I got to hear it," she said. "Is it really all true?"

Kate replied, "Nothing but the truth, Meels. Nothing but the truth. Hazel was a smart, strong, independent woman at a time in our history when that was a challenging role."

As if to add its input, Steamboat Geyer puffed and popped a few times, then quieted. They sat in the silence of the morning and contemplated the little piece of ground that now meant so much to both of them and absolutely nothing to visitors walking past.

Kate said, "Isn't this the most peaceful place you've ever been? Yellowstone, I mean. It's kind of like nature's holy church. A magical volcanic wonderland out in the middle of nowhere. Who wouldn't want to rest here for eternity, given a choice?"

"I'm so glad we shared this, Grandma," Amelia said. "I'm thrilled to be alive right now, and to be here with you is truly a gift. Thank you so very much."

Amelia stood and walked about the small piece of land. Kate laid down on the bench, lost in her thoughts, watching clouds moving slowly overhead, white and fluffy against the deep blue sky. Amelia collected rocks and then built two cairns on the sand which now contained Hazel's ashes. A visitor's attention might now be drawn to the little memorial to her grandmother. She smiled. It was fitting.

After one last look at Mrs. Decker Island, they made their way back to the car and then to Grand Canyon of the Yellowstone River, where they walked along the trail on its banks.

"This is an incredible sight," said Kate. "Just feel all that power of the falls!" They watched the water pound down over the smaller upper falls and then the longer lower falls. The last several days of heavy rains caused a surge of water flowing from Yellowstone Lake to plunge to the canyon floor in a constant roar. The mist from the pounding water formed a continuous rainbow in the bright sunlight above them. It was a magical.

"Thank you for taking an old lady here, Meels," said Kate. "I'm glad I got to see it."

Moving on, they had lunch alongside the Gardiner River. They watched a trout fisherman work at casting his line, and Amelia imagined Hazel fishing the same stream years ago, tying her flies and talking to the trout. They watched the fisherman rush out of the water as a rattlesnake swam across the river near him. It was time to continue their journey west.

They left Yellowstone, headed north toward Montana, and then pushed a hard six hours west for Coeur d'Alene, Idaho. Kate was tired yet satisfied by her time in Yellowstone and slept part of the way. Amelia planned the schedule for a day of relaxation for tomorrow, and she was looking forward to it. They arrived at the Coeur D'Alene resort on the lake after nightfall, checked into their rooms, then met up for the evening meal. Both were tired, and the conversation was light. Amelia wanted to call Jack and check in with him; Kate just wanted to sleep.

Amelia got ready for bed and called Jack. He didn't have a lot to say initially, just that he missed her a lot and that he was excited about getting a yacht. She did not comment on the purchase, which he took to be silent but conditional approval. She meant it to be quite the opposite.

Amelia tried to describe the almost surreal experience she had that day at Yellowstone, but she was road-weary. She could not effectively get the emotional significance or impact of it across to Jack. She asked about the meeting he'd had with the attorney, and Jack said that they could talk about it when she got home and that there were no earthshaking revelations. He told her about his uneventful day: he hung around the house, watched Netflix, and rode his beach bike most of the day.

He asked what Kate and Amelia were going to do tomorrow and what it was like traveling with Grandma Kate. She told him that they would spend the day relaxing near the water and that Kate was much more easygoing now that she was older and not responsible for their welfare. She was not as strict or religious, but her faith still guided her.

The conversation wound down, and Amelia said she was tired and loved him and missed him and would call another time. Jack responded with the same sentiment and clicked off.

For Amelia, the emotional day had her thinking more about her new place in the world. She thought about Hazel and how determined and dedicated she was to make a difference by drawing attention to a geyser for others' enjoyment and excitement. Hazel found her own way to make a difference in the world. How could Amelia make her own mark? As she tried to come up with ideas, she faded to sleep.

BETH'S STORY

The sun rose and warmed the mountain air. Both Amelia and Kate were up early for breakfast. Amelia asked Kate what she wanted to do for the day.

Kate said, "For me, a great day would be to relax by the pool, maybe fish for a while, and then take that dinner cruise on the lake on that boat where they have that live, old-time brass band."

"That sounds perfect to me," said Amelia.

That afternoon, Amelia arranged to rent a large pontoon boat and paid for fishing licenses and equipment. She had never fished, which was odd given that she'd grown up in Minnesota, the Land of 10,000 Lakes. She remembered Jack's comments about getting a boat. She thought owning a boat like this might be nice. However, she didn't know how well it would do on the open ocean.

They headed out onto the lake. Kate baited their hooks, and they slowly trolled near the shore.

Amelia asked Kate, "Did you fish a lot growing up?"

"Not really," she said. "I told you that your great-great-grandmother Hazel did, and your great-grandmother Beth did too, when she was younger. Beth told me stories about when she was in her early teens: Arbor took the family up for fishing trips to Lake of the Woods in Minnesota, which creates part of the United States/Canada border. During the summer after school was out, they would camp for weeks at a time. She always said that she resented that Arbor and Hazel would make her and her brothers do all of the work around the campsite while the parents relaxed. But that's the way it was back then. Children carried their weight. Kind of different than today, I suppose."

"According to my mother, there weren't many people who fished the lake back in the 1930s. It was a long way for tourists from the Twin Cities to drive, and there weren't that many people who owned cars, which broke down quite often anyway, so long trips were risky and the local population was sparse. She told me a story about how, if you put your hand in the water you could see the wakes from the large muskies coming hard and fast to bite your hand. The hungry fish were easy to catch, and they would eat fish every day. Beth said that she once held a youth record for the largest muskie and her name was published in *Field and Stream* magazine. Pretty cool."

"What else can you tell me about Beth?' Amelia asked.

"Simply stated, your great-grandmother was quite something. Remember I told you that you come from a line of strong, intelligent women? Except for me, I suppose," she humbly mused. "Beth was brilliant—definitely a genius. She had a very high IQ and a photographic memory. She could recite whole pages out of books she read 50 years previously verbatim. Later in life, she could remember so many details about some obscure scientific thing. It never ceased to amaze and frustrate me."

"Wow, that is pretty impressive. What did she study in school?" Amelia asked.

"She went to the University of Minnesota. Now get this. She earned a nursing degree, a Master's degree in Zoology, and a Master's degree in Public Health. But once she had her first child, she never worked another day in her life. She never used that education. It seems like such a waste of potential."

Amelia said, "You are right, she certainly had a lot of potential. I just quit my job and I still feel guilty about it. I am growing more concerned about not being adequately educated or well prepared for the next chapter in my life. I would have loved to have had Beth's intelligence.

Kate replied, "She always struck me as extremely bitter about her lot in life. She wanted to go to medical school to be a doctor and was convinced that she could not get in just because she was a woman. Now I don't know if that's true or not. I don't know that she even applied. It was the time when World War II was just over, and there were millions of GIs coming back and using the GI bill to go to school, so competition in all academic disciplines was extremely fierce."

"Beth had a difficult time in her role as a postwar housewife. That was back in the day where a single-wage earner could support an upper-middle-class family. She wanted to be or do so much more. Beth needed a challenge but never found that opportunity."

"She could also be cruel at times, repeating some of her father's traits. There were many arguments. She used to hit my sister and me in anger. I believe that was part of the cycle of abuse started by Arbor's father. Thank my stars, it ended with me. Oddly, I remember that we had to eat a plateful of all of the foods that we absolutely hated on every Halloween, like spinach, asparagus, and sweet potato, before we could go out trick-or-treating. Odd, don't you think? A bit on the cruel side?"

Amelia replied, "Yeah, that is a bit mean and very weird. I can't imagine doing that to my kids one day. Must have been a different time, I guess."

"When we children were mostly grown, she and your great-grandfather got divorced, and she got a commercial pilot's license. That's a big deal; it took a lot of time and alimony money. It meant that she could fly passengers for hire and was instrument-rated for night flights. Not very common at that time for a private individual to attain that level and not be a professional pilot, and even less so for a female."

"When I was in high school, she left for Africa. Her goal was to join the 'Flying Doctors,' but she never did. You know she spent thirty years in Kenya. When she finally came back, she drifted from place to place in the Southwest United States, looking for warmth, love, and happiness."

"She was a loner. She did not fit in well socially. She never trusted people. They were 'always out to get her,' and by that, I mean to take advantage of a single woman with some financial means. Unfortunately, that fear turned out to be a reality. She got conned by at least two men proclaiming love and then scamming her out a good chunk of her cash. She did not want to re-marry and have a man tell her what to do or take advantage of her, as I just described. Sadly, I don't think she was ever very happy."

"So, whatever happened to her?" asked Amelia.

"Eventually, she came back to Minnesota. Her health was diminishing. She was so smart that she could live independently and hid her dementia from us for several years. Eventually, she had some other health problems, and we, as a family, saw too many instances of memory issues. She ended up in a memory care unit and questioned why she was there every time I visited. She passed away from cancer at 93 years old. On the day she died, she knew that she was about to die and told the facility staff just to leave her alone, closed the door to her room, and was gone within a couple of hours. I put her ashes into the seventh waterfall of Gooseberry River, where we used to swim. Brave, stubborn, but she left this life as she lived it, on her own terms."

"As I said, she was just never happy with her life, always wanted more, and believed others held her back. In today's more enlightened world, she would have been a doctor, or maybe a research scientist holed up in a med-ical research facility, where she could work with a few people and not have to socialize but focus on a cure for something. I know that she was driven to accomplish whatever task she set her mind to. She was an extremely strong, intelligent, independent woman and, like her mother, Hazel, ahead of her time. She had so much to offer, so much to give. If she were here today, I'm betting that she would say that she never had the opportunity. People don't typically hand you opportunities. You have to make an effort to get what you want. I think her life was wasted. So sad. Amelia, I hope that you can make a difference with what you now have. In my heart, I know you will be successful in whatever endeavor you undertake. Follow your intuition and use your intelligence. It will take you where you need to go."

"Thanks for telling me that story, Grandma. I guess I remembered hearing some of the things, but not all of them. It makes me sad to think that such a talented life was wasted. You are right; typically, one isn't merely handed opportunity, it has to be earned. On the other hand, I am one of the one in a billion people in the world who can say that I have had it handed to me. But I don't want to waste it. I have been thinking more and more about what I want to do with my life. I can't see myself living my life without a purpose. Jack might be able to, but I don't think that I can. I know that I don't have to work anymore, but I know I can use my good fortune to make a positive contribution. Honestly, I don't want to look back when I am much older and feel like I wasted my life. Hearing about Beth just makes me even more motivated to make a difference with what I have. I just have to figure out how to do it."

They managed to catch and release several Chinook salmon. Amelia enjoyed the excitement of watching her rod tip when a fish struck, setting the hook, and fighting fish on the line. Several hours later, they turned the boat around and headed back to the resort dock.

After Kate headed upstairs to take a nap so that she could stay awake for the cruise that night, Amelia relaxed under an umbrella by the pool and thought about her female forebears. Interesting stories, she thought. I wish Kate had told them long ago. But then, I might not have appreciated them as much as I do now.

She nodded off to sleep and was bumped awake by Kate, who was saying that the cruise was in an hour, and she better go and get ready.

They enjoyed the dinner and the music and the lights on the lake after a glowing gold red sunset in the west. They clinked their drink glasses, and Kate said, "More fun adventures to come!"

"Absolutely," responded Amelia.

CHANGE IN THE STORYLINE

Jack spent the day walking the beach and reviewing information on golf club memberships and yachts. He was looking forward to Londyn's visit and curious about what she had in mind.

She arrived right on time. She hugged him and kissed his cheek, then stepped back, looking at him, and exclaimed, "Handsome as ever!" She looked extremely attractive to Jack. She said, "I just got off the shoot and didn't have time to change."

"No problem," Jack said, "you look great." She was wearing a short low-cut silver party dress and matching silver spike high heels. She looked stunning.

He gave her a tour of the house, then they settled in on the pool deck where Jack provided sandwiches and drinks. They chatted about what Jack's life was like before and after the lottery and about her career.

Eventually, Jack said, "I'm excited to hear more about your film idea." As the sun set and the air temperature dipped, Londyn suggested that they move inside. They settled next to each other on the couch.

"Well, Jack, as I said last time we spoke, I think that it would be fascinating to tell your story and add some twists to make it interesting. You know, to add the human drama."

"Okay," he said. "Interesting. Again, how do you see the story going?"

"Just think about it," she said. "A handsome young guy is going to get married and follow that middle-class path just like everybody else. You know, job, spouse, house, mortgage, kids, mowing the lawn, getting older, kids grow up, college, claw your way up at work and save enough to retire. Then spend ten years trying to keep his aging body functioning on Medicare's dime while lying in the sun, golfing, drinking beer, and taking senior cruises near exotic islands. Most are constrained by society's conventions, money, family, the rules and norms of life here in the United States. But you, Jack, you are different. You hit a huge lottery. Now constraints and norms don't apply to you anymore. It has all changed. You have options you never considered before. Your horizons have expanded almost infinitely. You can do and get whatever, and I mean *whatever,* you want. Some would say you have 'screw you' money. That means that you have enough money that you can do whatever you want regardless of what anyone else or society tells or asks you to do."

Jack sat back, considering what she said. "So exactly how would my story go?" he asked.

Londyn said, "Keep in mind that this is just my take on it, and please, please, don't take any offense here. It's just a story, but an interesting one. You hit the lottery. Now you look at your life and see what it can be. You can make movies, learn how to fly a plane, join the yacht club, play in pro-am golf tournaments, travel, and own several houses—you know, the rich and famous lifestyle. You have unlimited options. Now: one day, you look at your fiancé and know that you care for her and love her. However, you now have choices that weren't available when you were working for the weekend. Now *any* woman might have an interest in you, so you postpone the wedding and say that you want to be sure and that you both can see other people for a while. You start hobnobbing with rich and famous Hollywood types. Soon, you are surrounded by young, talented, smart, and beautiful women. Your life becomes much fuller and more exciting. It would be like a fairy tale come true."

Londyn paused to give Jack a dazzling smile.

"I was even thinking that you could have a parallel story running with another lottery-winning couple, older, maybe in their late forties with kids just out of the house, and they win a large lottery prize. They are faced with the same kinds of decisions. With money no longer being an issue, do they want to stay together? What are their dreams for the years of life they have left? They might have been staying together because of the kids, or one feels trapped because the other is the breadwinner, or one is not confident they could have made it alone without more income and now has a chance to live a different life."

"It's compelling stuff, Jack. Relationships, trust, love, values, and affording one's lifestyle with mind-blowing amounts of cash." She gave him a quick wink and an alluring smile.

Jack sat forward on the couch, not knowing what to say. He was thinking hard about what she'd said, particularly the storyline that did not include his marrying Amelia. He was uncomfortable just hearing about the option.

Londyn sensed that she had Jack thinking about possibilities that he had not considered before. Now was the time to see if she could move the relationship forward.

She said, "I'm sorry, Jack. I've been under the bright lights all day, and my eyes could use a bit less light intensity. Can you turn down your lights a little? I'll make us another drink."

When she returned with the drinks, she sat down very close to him and did not adjust her already short skirt, which had hiked up her thigh. Jack felt her presence, smelled her perfume, and quickly gulped down several swallows of his drink. His head buzzed.

He said, "It would be a compelling story, wouldn't it? It goes to how people get into a rhythm of life and get swept along, accepting their lot in life. We don't have the time, energy, assets, or opportunity to explore or make other choices. Then in this situation, one finds they do have those choices to make. Yeah. So, what part would you play?"

Londyn smoothly replied, "That would be up to the producer and director, I suppose, but I think that I would be great for the female lead—the girl our hero finally chooses to be with." She paused, turned to face him, and looked directly into his eyes. "I could play that part with genuine and real passion. Someone who is very attracted to the real Jack."

It quickly dawned on Jack that what she just said could have two meanings. As he turned toward her and looked into her eyes, he could see her full lips parting. They both leaned forward. In a moment, her lips were upon his.

Their lovemaking was urgent, spontaneous, and passionate.

Afterward, Jack was content and happy. He was uncertain as to exactly how what had just happened had occurred; and yet it seemed so very right. He felt such a strong physical attraction to Londyn. With her warm and sensual body lying next to him, thoughts of Amelia were very far away.

He now clearly understood that the storyline of the movie Londyn had described it was right on. He'd based his past choices and life on conditions that existed before. He *was* a different person now, a man of means, of great potential. His position was different, and so were his options. He had moved from being one of the invisible among the masses to the upper half of the upper one percent. He was now extraordinary, the master of his own life and surroundings. The rules were now different.

His past promises were made under old conditions and situations. They no longer applied, as he and his conditions had changed. Jack decided he liked where he was right now. It was exciting, stimulating, and satisfying. He turned to Londyn and said, "I think your story idea is perfect."

Londyn smiled, and her lips found his once more. They made love again.

Later, Jack texted Amelia saying that he was turning in as he was exhausted, and that he hoped she was safe and well.

Londyn stayed the night. She had no new clothes for the morning, so she put her silver dress back on after a quick shower. She acted like the night before was natural and meant to be. He was just about to make breakfast when she came into the kitchen and put her arms around his waist, kissed his neck, and said, "Good morning, handsome."

Jack felt slightly awkward in this situation. He was uncertain how he should act. It felt good and exciting, and yet when he turned toward Londyn, part of him was about to say that last night had been a mistake. But she kissed him before he could get a word out. He succumbed to passion and, aroused, returned the kiss. They were soon back in the bedroom.

Later, back in the kitchen, she took over making breakfast. As they finished up the meal, she brought up the movie idea again. "Jack, did you mean it when you said that the story would make a good movie?"

He replied, "It might be a little personal for me. I'm a little uncomfortable with that."

"Maybe, but I still think it's a compelling story. It would be fun to make. If not, I know many writers who have other scripts that they would love to have independently produced. I can definitely help you get into the movie business."

"I am very interested," he replied. "We should continue the conversation."

"Great, I'm free tomorrow night. Can I stop by?"

He stammered. "Well, I…"

She reached out and touched his face, saying, "I'll be back here at seven, but right now, I gotta run." She kissed him and quickly walked out of the house.

GUMMIES

The Spokane Valley gave way to the Cascade Mountains and their lush green forests, which evolved into ocean coastline as they approached Seattle and Puget Sound. Using the GPS on the Audi, Amelia and Kate easily negotiated the streets into downtown Seattle. They visited the famous Pike Place Market and watched fishmongers throw fish as part show and part sales tactic. At Kate's request they went to the Museum of Pop Culture, dedicated to rock and roll.

After they'd spent their fill at in the museum, Kate said, "Meels, I have always minded the rules, but now that I am older and closer to the, well...end, I have come to realize that God may not have intended some of the rules that society has made. For that matter, God may not have intended many rules my church has made either. Maybe I've just become cynical. Anyway, I read that marijuana is legal in Washington, and I would like to try it before I go."

"Grandma!" Amelia said. "Two things. One, you aren't going anywhere for a long time, and two, well, two, hey, why not?" Amelia used her phone to search for the nearest dispensary. It wasn't far, so they walked over and Kate made a purchase. Then they headed back to the car for the next leg of the trip.

Kate did not hesitate to sample a gummy immediately. Heading north, they drove an hour and a half to get to the Anacortes Ferry Terminal. By the time they got there, Kate was feeling the full effect of the THC. She asked Amelia if marijuana was legal in California.

Amelia said, "It's legal there, Oregon, and I think Canada, too. You can get more at any time if you like it."

Kate said, "Good. I like the way I feel. I'm very relaxed, but it feels like my head is buzzing. Really, it is actually vibrating."

Amelia laughed. "I suppose next you'll tell me you have the munchies! Next time, try a little less."

They waited in line to drive the car onto the ferry deck. Once safely on board, they proceeded to the upper deck to view Puget Sound and watch the San Juan Islands come and go. The ferry eventually docked in Friday Harbor, on San Juan Island. The town was relatively small, so they quickly found their hotel.

Amelia and Kate found a rustic hotel and bar just up the block, where they had fish baskets and a beer apiece for an early dinner. Afterward, they drove back down the steep slope to the harbor. Seagulls were raucous, swirling over the fishing boats as they returned to shore with their daily catch. Kate and Amelia walked the docks and looked at the large beautiful boats. They stopped by a small building with a sign in the window that read "Boat Sales" and looked at pictures of boats for sale. Amelia looked at boats under the yacht column and was surprised to see the prices. There was nothing priced under $3,500,000. Was this what Jack had in mind? If so, it wasn't going to be a purchase in which she was all that interested. She did not love the water enough to invest in such an expensive toy.

As dusk arrived, they drove back up the steep harbor hill to the hotel. Once back at the hotel, Kate wanted to turn in and try another dose of her new "medicine."

Amelia said, "Okay, but only take five milligrams of those gummies. I will meet you for breakfast in the morning."

UNSCRIPTED

Londyn arrived an hour late and rang the gate bell. Before she arrived, Jack had become increasingly uncertain as to whether he should go through with meeting her again. He liked the idea of making a movie and thought that the concept and storyline which Londyn had presented was indeed exciting. However, the relationship had taken a new direction — a direction which, in some ways, he had hoped for. A direction that was, he knew, fraught with potential consequences. He was undoubtedly very attracted to Londyn, but he also had a fiancé. His conscience and male instincts were fighting an intense battle. As the hour of her arrival approached, he became increasingly agitated and began to tell himself that he should call Londyn and cancel the appointment. He should leave the gate locked. But he knew that he was unable to resist temptation and the desire she represented. When she finally arrived, he buzzed her right in.

Londyn breezed into the house like she owned it, gave Jack a hug and a quick peck on the lips, and said, "I had a long, hot, miserable day, and I need to cool down. Can you make us a drink?" Her confidence struck Jack. He admired that she knew what she wanted to do and just did it. He nodded his head and gawked as she strode through his house, shed her clothes, and dove naked into the pool.

At that moment, Jack knew he was lost. He was thankful that Amelia had decided to make the long road trip with her grandmother. He was captivated by Londyn's sensuality and her self-assured personality; he wanted to be with her. He quickly made his way to the bar, poured two large vodka-and-7-Ups on ice, and headed out to the pool.

She swam slowly toward him as he walked out and pulled herself up on the edge of the deck, resting her head on her hands. "Hey, handsome," she said. "I hope your day was better than mine."

Jack said, "Since I don't have to work or do anything, I'm betting that it was. Would you like your drink?"

"Yes, I would," she said. "Could you get a girl a towel?"

He pulled one out of the large towel storage box and held it for her as she climbed up the ladder. He tried to look only directly at her eyes but could not help looking at her body as he wrapped the towel around her. She wriggled into his arms for warmth. She raised her face to receive his gentle kiss on her lips.

Jack invited her to sit on one of the double-wide chaise lounges next to the low table which now held their drinks. She laid down, still wrapped in the oversized white towel.

"So, what was so bad about work today?" he asked.

"The director is a twit. He was in a snit about everything: the lighting, wardrobe, the camera angles. Everything ran late, and production is way over budget. Lots of name-calling, yelling, accusations, and putting people down—and it's only a music video. I just kept my head down. Oh, it's so nice to be here with you, catching some sun."

They relaxed a while, enjoying the bright, soothing sunshine, letting vodka adjust their moods.

Breaking the silence, Jack asked, "Did you talk to anyone about the script yet?"

Londyn stretched and sat up, saying, "Oh, yeah, right. During my lunch break, I talked to a guy I know who says he's looking for work. I asked him if he was available to work up a screenplay of a story outline, and he said he would do the first draft for $10,000 and rewrite for an hourly rate of $150. I thought that was competitive."

Jack nodded his head, appreciating the scope of Londyn's effort but not knowing if the price was fair or not.

She asked, "Have you thought any further about the storyline?"

He said, "Yes, I have. I can see the storyline going either way. I have not yet made up my mind as to which ending I prefer."

"You know, Jack," she said, "I had an idea for the ending. Maybe it's dumb, but here goes: What if you were to dream about one option and then wake up to the real one? Meaning the one you actually picked."

"Hmm," he mused. "That would be interesting."

"Yeah, I thought so too," she cooed. She downed the remainder of her drink and asked for a refill. He left and came back with refills for both of them. She took a long sip from her tumbler and said, "Thanks, you don't know how much I needed that." She opened her towel to expose her naked body, stretched back on the chaise lounge, and said, "Ah, that feels so much better."

Jack could not help but stare at her shapely form through his sunglasses. He took another large draw on his drink.

She said, "You could help me stay warm, Jack."

Jack did not move. He knew that this was a crucial moment. Whatever action he took through a simple choice right now, could well impact the direction of his life and take it out of his control.

"Please come keep me warm, baby." She raised her arms toward him.

He removed his swim trunks as he laid down next to her. She snuggled into his body and her lips soon found his. Her hand found proof of his willing excitement.

Afterward, they lay in each other's arms, holding each other as the ocean slowly consumed the sun in the west.

As darkness fell and the air chilled, Jack stated that he was hungry, and she concurred. She slipped some of her clothes back on and walked into the kitchen. Jack made spaghetti for dinner. The wine they drank, in combination with the heavy pasta made them both very relaxed.

After dinner, they returned to the chaise lounge, wrapped themselves in blankets, and watched stars come out. Londyn focused the conversation on Jack and his life's history. After an hour of cuddling, Jack stood, held out his hand, and said, "Come with me." She took his hand, and he led her into the master bedroom, to the bed that Jack and Amelia shared. She kissed him deeply while her hands ran through his hair. He broke the kiss and softly pushed her onto the bed where they entertained each other throughout the night.

In the morning, Jack's phone rang. It was Bill. "Hey, Jack, what's going on? Any big plans for the day?"

Jack said, "Hey, Bill, no, nothing specific, I'm free."

To his dismay, Londyn called out, "Hey, hi Bill, what's up?"

Bill was silent for a moment and then asked, "Is that Londyn?"

Jack jumped out of bed, rapidly padded into the study and closed the door. "Um, yeah, she came over last night to work on a movie script we're working on together. We had way too much to drink and I wouldn't let her drive home."

"Oh, yeah, right," Bill said.

"Seriously, nothing is going on. We have a great outline for a movie. But I can see where this could look awkward. So, Bill, not a word of this to anybody, ever, right? It's the bro code."

"No issue here," said Bill. "I would love to see the script outline sometime. I might even have some clients who could fill the roles."

"Right," said Jack. "Hey, why don't I meet you at the beach restaurant at about noon? I think the Brewers are playing. You can bill a couple of hours to my account. I'm buying."

"Okay, buddy," said Bill. "I'll see you there."

Jack was frustrated as he came back into the bedroom and said to Londyn, "Why did you say something? Why did you do that?"

Knowing full well that she had done it on purpose to try to force Jack's hand, she replied. "Hey, Bill and I are good buds. Didn't he hook us up? I'm sorry. His lips are sealed, as are mine. Don't worry about it. Can I make you some breakfast?"

Jack sat down on the bed, frustrated and angry, with his head in his hands and said, "Sure, thanks."

Jack was quiet while eating. Londyn fully realized that this was a critical moment in her efforts not only to get an inside track on a role and production of a movie but also to have a serious romantic relationship with Jack. She would not mind being near Jack's money, and she did like Jack. He was a nice and attractive guy. He was fun to be around. Who knows where it could lead?

She said, "Jack, I'm sorry that I said hello to Bill. It was a mistake. I was trying to be funny, but I do trust Bill. He's my friend too. It'll be fine, don't worry. I'll talk to him later this morning to square that away."

After more silence, Londyn asked, "Have you thought any more at all about the movie script?"

Jack picked at his scrambled eggs and said, "No, not really haven't had any time to think about it. You were distracting me."

Londyn grinned and replied, "I'm happy to be your distraction!"

Jack nodded, then said, "I guess, just thinking out loud now, I do like the idea of making his dream about his options, and then wakes up to find that he's already made his decision."

"Can I have my writer friend work up an outline for a draft script?" she asked. There was a long pause. Jack did not reply. She said, "Jack, the roads are full of flattened squirrels that could not make up their minds. To make it in Hollywood you have to be bold and take action."

He said, "Okay, okay, I guess so. Yeah, let's do it. I really would like to get into the movie business. It could be fun, and I could meet some famous and influential people." And, he thought, he might meet even more attractive actresses.

"Well, great!" she said, "I'll give him a call today and get him started. This is a bit awkward, but…could you make a payment to him so he can start?"

Jack said, "Sure. Of course."

"Great," said Londyn. "I think this will be a great success. You won't be disappointed."

She got up and started clearing dishes. Jack sat at the kitchen table, thinking and going over messages on his phone.

When she finished cleaning up, she said, "I need to be off. I had a great time. I like you, Jack. You are a great guy. This movie is just the start of a fun career and a whole new lifestyle for you." With that, Londyn bent over and kissed him. "Have a nice day, sweetie. See you soon."

SATURDAY

Kate and Amelia were back at the docks early the next morning. Amelia had scheduled an orca-watching tour.

The tour only had ten total people that day, so the boat was loaded quickly. As it headed out from the harbor, it picked up speed, heading northwest into the Sound. The guide pointed out points of interest and described how orca pods formed family units around the alpha female and how they hunted together in organized packs.

Amelia was surprised and interested to learn that family units formed around an alpha female. The guide explained that the whales are apex predators with no natural enemies and that they are known to kill some species of whales and even great white sharks.

The captain accelerated, turning hard to the west. After twenty minutes of running hard, the boat slowed. The guide told the passengers to watch off the boat's left side. Soon tall black fins became visible. The pod swam at the water's surface in a slow up and down motion, breathing and swimming. The guide said that the pod looked like it was merely traveling and not hunting at this time. He described how the mammals slept with half of their brains "shut down" and the other half managing their swimming and breathing functions, and vice versa. Amelia stated that it was interesting how the whales had evolved to allow them to do this. All the tourists, including Kate and Amelia, took pictures and videos. The guide was able to put names to the four orcas.

After another hour of searching, the captain turned the boat back toward the harbor. On the return trip, they observed one more orca pod. Kate and

Amelia were happy to arrive at the harbor and warm up, as it was frigid out on the Sound.

As the boat docked, Kate said, "I never expected to witness orcas in the wild. Again, I am in your debt, Meels. Thank you."

Amelia just hugged her and said, "No, it is I who owe you so much, Grandma. It's my pleasure. I enjoyed it too, except for the cold."

After lunch, they drove back down the slope, joined a short car lineup for the ferry, and soon crawled onto the lower deck. After securing the Audi they climbed the stairs up to the upper deck to view the Salish Sea.

The ferry docked at Sidney on Vancouver Island, British Columbia. They offloaded, passed through customs, and proceeded to Victoria, a half-hour away, and their hotel on the waterfront. After checking in, they walked to the harbor and wandered the docks, looking at boats and taking in seabirds, playful seals, and port sounds. They found the Cary Mews Tea House, for a spot of afternoon tea. Kate was excited to be in a genuine tea room, where they were seated at a heavy oak table. The décor was dark, with floor-to-ceiling red velvet curtains covering the windows. The air seemed heavy and still.

Holding her pinky finger out as she held the teacup, Kate joked that all of her years training in manners and etiquette and finally came in handy. Smiling, Kate knocked on the table top with her knuckles and said, "You know, this table reminds me of another story."

"Oh my," said Amelia, "Is this one going to be sad?"

Kate replied, "Well, yes and no. It happened so many years ago. It is about another one of your great-great-grandmothers. Her name was Edith. She was actually the second Edith born to the family who lived in a sod house on North Dakota's plains. The first child they named Edith died in infancy, so in her honor, they named their next girl Edith, too. Kind of odd, but that is the fact. Anyway, when Edith was a very young girl, maybe five or so, they moved to St Paul, Minnesota. After living there a while her older sister was about to get married. As I understand it, on the day of the wedding a jilted ex-suitor came over to the house, burst in with a pistol, and started shooting."

Amelia gasped. "Grandma!"

"He was not going to let the woman of his dreams get married to another man," Kate continued, undeterred. "Sadly, the bride-to-be was killed right there in the dining room, but Edith escaped unharmed because she had the good fortune and good sense to quickly hide beneath the heavy dining room table, a table just like this one. I'm guessing that the tablecloth hid her, and the heavy wood protected her from the shots."

"Oh, Grandma, that's another terrible story!"

"Well, yes, I guess so," said Kate. "But the point is that for you to be here, Edith had to live, and her quick thinking probably saved her life. Life is not all duckies and bunnies."

"I suppose," said Amelia. "All your stories relate so much sorrow."

Kate replied, "Kid, life is full of sorrow. Some people call our short dance on this earth a veil of tears. Humans live and die. It's been going on for hundreds of thousands of years. We all have so many forefathers already buried, and all of us will join them soon enough. I believe that the important part for us is to live as full a life as we can, while we can. Spend your time making life better for those you love. If you do that, I believe that you will die happy and fulfilled. Hopefully, you will be old and physically spent but content in the knowledge of what you have given back and accomplished. One thing I have come to believe is that there isn't any secret meaning to life. It is what we make it. Nothing more."

Thinking about those words, they sipped their tea in silence and ate tea cakes.

Kate asked about the schedule for the next day.

"Well," Amelia replied, "we will spend some time in the morning here in Victoria, and then we catch a ferry to the Washington mainland and drive south to Olympia."

"I'm excited already," Kate said. "I can already feel California in my bones, now that they have thawed from that orca excursion this morning. This trip has gone fast. We have been swamped and seen so many beautiful and interesting things. But there is much more to see."

ENJOY THE DAY

Jack and Bill spent the afternoon on the beach and enjoyed activities they used to do every Saturday when they were roommates. That meant beer, volleyball, surfing, and hanging out with good friends and new acquaintances. Jack bought rounds of beer for everybody he knew and some he did not. He enjoyed himself. He flirted with a couple of girls and noticed the positive reaction he got once they discovered who he was — the big-time lottery winner. Jack seemed to be the most popular man in LA.

Late in the afternoon, tired and having had enough sand, sun, and beer, he told Bill that he was heading out. Bill told him to take care and turned back to an attractive girl he was trying to impress.

Jack couldn't help but notice that Bill had not mentioned the phone conversation from that morning. Jack would expect Bill to give him grief in such a situation. Considering this, Jack became more confident that his friend would either let the whole thing go or that he had believed Jack's phony story. He was relieved and much more relaxed about the incident. Maybe Londyn had spoken with Bill earlier that morning.

Jack rationalized his actions. He was single. He and Amelia were not married, so he reasoned that he was not really cheating on her. He was free to do as he pleased. He was a man of means. The guilt he felt inside that morning diminished until it was gone.

Once home, he mixed a drink and sat back in a chaise lounge and thought about making films. He saw himself becoming a famous producer, a mover and shaker in Hollywood. His films would be legendary. Jack imagined walking down the red carpet on Oscar night to the sparkle of flashing cameras. Of course, he would often win the coveted award. He could see it all so clearly in his mind's eye. He imagined people hanging on to every word he said and exclusive parties at the beach house with the rich and famous from Hollywood. Yes, it was going to be Greeeaat!

His phone rang. The call from Amelia snapped him back to the present.

"Hello, Meels!" he said. "How is the trip?"

"It's good," she said. "But I'm glad that the end is in sight. Kate has been great, and I'm enjoying the sights, but I just want to be home in your arms in our beautiful new house. I want to get on with our new life. We will be in Sacramento tomorrow and will stay there overnight. It'll be long hard push south. I like that the nose of the car is at least pointing toward home."

"How's Kate doing?"

"She's napping more each day. Not a lot of energy today. She has discovered marijuana! I'm learning a lot about her and my ancestors. Some interesting stories, to be sure."

"What's after Sacramento?" he asked.

"We head to Yosemite, then back over to Frisco, and after that, home. Three more nights."

"That will be great," said Jack. Then she asked how his day had been, so he told her about the afternoon on the beach, then said, "Now I'm just going to relax and maybe spend more time on the beach. Possibly look for some fun activities to keep me entertained until you get back."

"I miss you," she said.

He replied, "I miss you too. See you in a couple of days."

"Love you. Behave." And then she disconnected the call.

Jack thought about Amelia and Londyn. He was uncertain about his true feelings. He knew that he loved Amelia. And yet was not looking forward to her return as much as he had been when she first left. Maybe it was that Grandma Kate would be with her, or perhaps it was that he was enjoying his extended alone time with his new buddy Londyn, and wanted more. He thought of the old saying, "Absence makes the heart grow fonder," but now he realized that it might not be true, as part of him wanted Amelia to add a few more days to her trip. At the moment, Amelia felt very far away.

Londyn was by contrast very present, vivid, and real. He desired her. It was as if he could still feel her warm body next to his. It felt very sensual and arousing. She brought out a different part of him. She talked about what he could be and what he could accomplish with her support. She tapped his potential and was gently guiding him forward; he was grateful for her encouragement.

With Londyn's motivation, Jack had decided that he should enjoy his new-found wealth. He sat down in front of the computer and Googled "fun and adventure in Los Angeles." He found appealing ideas and formulated plans for experiences in the air, on the water, and on the golf links. It was time to start living it up. Amelia was gone. He was not responsible for anyone else; he was responsible only for his own entertainment. Life was going to get... *fun*.

Jack made reservations for three activities in the San Diego area: tee-time at Torrey Pines, a reservation to skydive, and another to take a flying lesson. He was a man of means—and a risk-taking adventurer. He was excited about his growing feeling of empowerment.

He walked out onto the pool deck and decided to take a short nap. He closed his eyes and soon slept in the warm late afternoon sun, the bike ride forgotten.

The gate buzzer startled him awake. He went to the console and saw Londyn at the gate. He buzzed her in. As he opened the front door, she held out a bottle of very expensive handmade tequila and asked, "Apology accepted? I'm sorry. I want to make it up to you."

It took him a moment, but then he smiled, accepted the bottle of tequila, and let her inside, saying, "Of course. I'll mix up some margaritas for us."

"I'll volunteer to taste-test," she laughed and slipped off her high heels. She wore a dress that showed off her figure.

She walked to the window walls and looked out at the ocean. "How did you find this place?" she asked.

"Our banker knew the agent, who knew what we were looking for and hooked us up."

"Can I ask how much it cost?

"Now, I know that it might sound like a lot, but it's worth every penny," Jack replied. "$12.5 million."

"Good God," she said. "Are you kidding me? That's nuts."

"I only own half," he said. "So, I'm only half nuts. It did come fully decorated and furnished."

"Yeah, kind of. It is a fabulous home in an even more fabulous location."

The blender roared, then Jack poured large drinks into frozen, salted glasses and added bottled lime juice. He walked to the window next to her and handed her a glass. "To friends," he said, and they clinked their glasses together. They each took a couple of sips; Londyn sighed and slowly leaned into him. As he felt her warm body, he knew he could not resist her. He put his arm around her shoulders drawing her close.

Jack considered his relationship with Londyn to be a fling. Nothing serious. Something he could cut off at any time. They were simply two friends talking about a movie project, and she could assist him and be involved while having a bit of fun on the side. When she was not around, he felt pangs of guilt when he thought of Amelia. Yet when Londyn was near him, he found that he could not resist her feminine allure. It was as if she could put him under an intoxicating spell with her body, face, and charisma.

She spent the night. When his phone rang in the morning, Jack made certain that he did not answer the call.

HEADING SOUTH

On their fine morning in Victoria, the girls got lucky. There was only a short line waiting to get seated at the famous Jam Café for breakfast. Afterward, they leisurely walked Chinatown, including Fan Tan Alley, then visited many of the gardens within Butchart Gardens. They saw floating homes at Fisherman's Wharf and relaxed on a bench, appreciating the inner harbor's beauty. It was soon time to continue their journey, so they took the ferry across the Strait of Juan de Fuca to Port Angeles, Washington and arrived in the United States, where they reentered through customs.

They drove south through the Olympic National Forest toward Olympia. It took about three and a half hours, longer than Amelia had planned, as they stopped several times to take short walks on different trails surrounded by the thick, heavy, green jungle of vegetation found in the Pacific coastal rainforest. Moss hanging from enormous trees, fern-like plants and forest sounds made it almost seem like they had time-traveled back to prehistoric times. While driving, Amelia wondered why Jack had not answered her call that morning. In her wildest dreams, she would not have guessed the truth.

They continued their trek and spent the evening at the southern end of Puget Sound in Olympia, ending another memorable day. Although it would be a long haul, Amelia and Kate looked forward to crossing into California sometime the following day. Amelia was excited to show Grandma Kate her house. Then Amelia would finally sleep with Jack again in their bed. She felt that her life had been on hold since the night of the house party. Amelia wanted to be with Jack and her friends. She missed her old, predictable life.

PLAYTIME

Early Sunday morning, Jack headed south. Three hours later he stood on the first tee box of Torrey Pines South Course. Jack was an accomplished golfer, as he had played on the golf team in high school. He played from the back tees and shot an 86. He thought that wasn't bad for a guy who hadn't played a round in over nine months. Jack enjoyed watching the military aircraft which regularly flew over course.

After golf, he headed to the airstrip and met the instructor assigned to him. For the next three hours, he learned about how the aircraft worked, how to do preflight checks, and what to think about during takeoffs, cruising, and landing. They talked about safety while in the air and on the ground, and went over emergency procedures. That was all before starting the airplane engine.

Once they were airborne, the pilot instructed Jack to work on straight and level flight, smooth turns, climbs, and descents, and eventually, with some assistance, two takeoffs and two landings. Jack loved it right away and asked how many hours of training it took before he could solo. The instructor told him it would likely take forty hours of instruction before he could solo, and then perhaps five hours of solo flight to get a pilot's license.

Jack knew right then that he wanted to fly. Before he left the airplane, he got the name of an instructor closer to home in Long Beach with whom he could continue his training. Just another opportunity afforded him by his new position in life. He more clearly understood how narrow his view of life had been before he won the lottery. There were so many exciting things to do and experience. He felt expansive. He wanted to share his happiness. He thought of Londyn.

After the flight lesson, Jack went into an office two doors down, filled out a liability waiver, and watched a video to prepare for his first skydive. After training and lessons on how to pack a parachute, he donned a jumpsuit and diving goggles then strapped on a harness and parachute. Jack learned how to get his head, arms, and legs into the proper jumping and landing positions. Soon he was on the plane with the jumpmaster, climbing to 10,500 feet.

They were going 200 miles per hour when Jack crossed his arms, bent his knees, put his head back, yelled "Geronimo!" and jumped. His chest tightened, and his eyes went wide. The exhilarating feeling of heightened senses offset his fear of potential death. This was truly understanding what it felt to be alive. Freefalling was like nothing Jack had ever experienced. Jack relaxed, controlled his emotions, and enjoyed speeding through the rushing air as he plummeted unbound toward the unforgiving earth.

The jumpmaster was attached in tandem and allowed them to freefall for ninety seconds to reach terminal velocity. When signaled to do so, Jack pulled the ripcord and felt the parachute abruptly stop their descent by crisply snapping open, jerking them upward. They maneuvered the chute in sweeping turns for seven minutes while they descended toward the enormous white cross target in the landing area. After bending his legs for a smooth landing, they were safely back on the ground. They rolled up the parachute and were ready to head back to the hanger.

The jumpmaster asked Jack what he thought.

Jack replied, "Awesome. That freefall feeling was an incredible rush." As he vowed to do it again, he wondered if Amelia would be interested in joining him. Would she be too afraid to take the risk? He concluded she might join him because as she was not usually afraid to take chances. That was one of the reasons he loved her.

He was pumped about his day. He headed back home in the Audi with the Rolling Stones blaring on its Bang & Olufsen speakers. It had been a good day with new experiences which he would likely never have tried had he not hit the lottery. This is what his life would be about from now on, excitement, no worries, and living life to the fullest.

When he arrived home, Londyn's car was parked outside the gate of the house.

CHECKING IN

The next morning, Jack answered Amelia's call. "Hey, babe, where are you?"

"We drove through Oregon and are now in California on the way to Sacramento."

"Good to hear that you're making headway," Jack replied, holding a finger to his lips to warn Londyn to be quiet. She nodded as she lay naked on top of the sheets. He left the room and went into the study.

"Sorry I didn't get ahold of you last night. I was just exhausted. I had a great day and want to tell you all about it when you get home. I flew a plane, jumped out of a plane, and played golf on a great golf course. I also left my phone in the car when I came into the house," he lied.

"Whoa! That does sound like an interesting and busy day. I'd love to hear more about it when I get home."

"I'll tell you everything when I see you," he said. "Hey, before I forget to mention it, I have a surprise for you when you get home!"

"Oh really? Did you get me something? Does it sparkle?"

"Nope, but it matches mine, and we will enjoy using them together," said Jack.

"You didn't get me a surfboard, did you?"

"No, but you do use it on the beach near the water. You will see it when you get home, and I know you will love it. How's Kate?"

"Enjoying her gummies! It is pretty wild," responded Amelia. "Okay, I'm going to focus on my driving and being safe. I love you. I miss you. Do you miss me?"

Londyn stood patiently and silently outside of the study, where Jack couldn't see her, listening.

"Of course, miss you. I love you, too."

Amelia asked, "What are you doing now?"

Oh, nothing. Oh, my look at the time. I've got to get going. I've got an appointment at the marina to check out the yachts. So, can I catch you later? Love you," said Jack, and hung up. He felt guilty for lying. His mood brightened though, as he thought it through a little more. It wasn't a real lie. He was going to the marina this morning. He went back toward the bedroom.

Londyn silently returned to the bedroom and slid under the sheets when she heard Jack saying goodbye. Clearly, she was in competition for Jack's affection; she intended to win. When Jack returned, she held the sheet open and said, "Come back to bed."

"I want to get going. I'm looking forward to yacht shopping this morning."

"You will have plenty of time for that a little later. Right now, why don't you spend a little more quality time with me? I'm worth it."

As continued to hold the sheet open to receive him, Jack did not need any more convincing.

YOSEMITE

From Sacramento, the women headed south, then east into the sun. By noon they were in Yosemite National Park. They parked at a spot with a full view Half Dome, sat on a cluster of rocks, and ate the picnic lunch Amelia bought at Yosemite Valley Lodge. The view of the Sierra Nevada Mountains was simply nature at its best.

After lunch, they followed a path through a meadow, ending up at the base of El Capitan. Several climbers carefully worked their way up and down the sheer face. Amelia saw camp locations where sleeping hammocks hung on the side of the mountain. She could only think, no, not me, not ever, but I'm glad that someone has the fortitude to challenge that face. She remembered a documentary about a man who'd free-climbed it with no safety ropes. Incredible, she thought.

At the Yosemite Museum visitor center, Kate seemed to be looking for something specific. Finally, she found a wall of photographs: all of the past superintendents of Yosemite Park.

"Amelia, come over here," she said and beckoned her over to where she stood. "Your grandfather played basketball in high school with a man named Merriam. Once, before your grandpa died, we were visiting with him and he mentioned that they were having a family reunion at Yosemite. The story came out that his grandfather was a superintendent here at Yosemite and that he had met FDR—that's President Franklin Roosevelt—during his visit to the park." She pointed to one of the pictures. "Look! Here is his picture. It says superintendent from 1937 to 1941. Here is another picture with him and FDR at the park. It says July 15, 1938. Pretty cool, huh?"

Amelia nodded, although she thought that any event that old was almost ancient history. But she was pleased Kate had connected with a memory of her husband, Amelia's grandfather.

After dinner that evening, they walked to a location where they could watch Yosemite Falls until dusk.

Kate said, "I'm just so tired. Don't get me wrong, it's been a great trip, and I've enjoyed it immensely. However, I'm glad that the trip is almost complete. I'm worn out."

"Just one more night on the road!" Amelia said, sensing Grandma's waning energy.

MARINA

After Londyn left that morning, Jack took the Audi out for a drive and ended up in La Jolla, where he stopped at the marina.

He looked at the "For Sale" pictures of boats in the sales shop and walked the docks looking at yachts. He had convinced himself that he needed a yacht to make his life complete. Making movies would be fun and rewarding, but for weekends and late summer afternoons, a yacht might just be the answer. He vowed to investigate more thoroughly.

He walked by a group of people standing in line waiting at a shop with a sign that said "Snorkel Diving Trips." Jack asked at the front desk what the trip entailed. The clerk described the snorkel tour, and Jack decided to do it. He bought a pair of swim trunks, paid his fee, and joined the line.

A dive boat took them out into the harbor; after brief instructions, they donned masks and fins and soon observed fish and seals.

After two hours, the group headed back to the marina, chilled but pleased with the experience. Jack had enjoyed the underwater views. Seeing seals dance and the different colors of the fish was entertaining. Jack made it a point to talk to salespeople about scuba lessons.

Jack also saw a sign that there were wave runners for rent and sale. After enjoying a two-hour rental, he bought two units with trailers to be delivered to his house. Jack handed the clerk his credit card to finalize the purchase then left the shop.

While he walked to his car, Amelia called. Jack told her of his day and asked about hers. She said, "I'm glad that the trip's coming to an end. Kate's energy appears to be fading fast. Have you ever been to Yosemite?"

"No, but I hear it's beautiful."

"That is an understatement. It truly takes your breath away. You can watch crazy people climbing El Capitan. I get dizzy just thinking about it! So, what did you do today?"

"I looked at yachts again. I snorkeled. I'm going to take scuba lessons. I've also been looking at country clubs for golf, and maybe we can take up tennis. I'll look into that more tomorrow."

"Well, it sounds like you're having fun!" she said. "I'm happy for you, Jack. Just be careful."

FRISCO

Amelia and Kate were excited at the prospect of seeing the Golden Gate Bridge and Fisherman's Wharf for the first time.

Along the route toward San Francisco, Amelia said, "Grandma, I have to tell you something. Before we left Minnesota, I was apprehensive that this trip was going to be hard. I was afraid that we would not have anything to talk about or get into an argument that would make us both miserable. Now I feel awful for thinking that, because it has been totally opposite of that. I have had so much fun, and we've seen some amazing sights. I've gotten to know you on an adult basis, and I think that I have grown. I know we have grown closer. I've learned about my family through the stories you have told me, especially Hazel and Beth. Most of all, I'm beginning to feel more strongly about the direction I want to take my life. I can see the potential that a woman of strength can bring forth, and I now have money behind me to do something of importance. I know I can make a difference in the world. With you, as my witness I make that promise."

"Oh, my dear, I wasn't worried a bit. I think that besides my honeymoon, this has been the best week or so in my life. Well, come to think of it, this was actually better." They both laughed.

They were silent for a minute, then Kate spoke. "Meels, I have to tell you something, but first I am asking you to promise not to get mad at me."

Amelia could not think of anything she could get mad about. She said, "I promise. Just not another sad story, please."

"It's not a story, Meels. This trip has been one of the true highlights of my life. Kind of sad to say that my life has been so mundane. However, spending this time with you and seeing what kind of young woman you are and the kind of woman I know you will become has been gratifying. I'm glad we got a chance to do it, and I can't thank you enough."

Amelia was about to respond, but Kate held up her hand so as not to be interrupted.

"When we get to LA, I would like just to spend a couple of days seeing where you live and taking in the beach and then fly back home to Minnesota. I would love to spend more time out here with you, even though I know that I would be a burden at some level. But the real reason is my health. You know my heart is weak, and so I don't have a lot of energy. The doctors did not want me to go on this trip, and they also ordered me to return home soon to monitor me. So that's it. That is my wish, and I don't want to argue with you about it. Will you accept that?"

Amelia felt tears welling up in her eyes. "You're asking me to do something that is so hard to do. I was hoping to have you out here and find a house, and…but if this is what you need to do, I will help you make arrangements. I love you, Grandma." And then tears spilled.

She pulled off the road until she could compose herself. Kate put her hand on her shoulder and soothed her as best she could, saying, "It is okay, my dear. We have had a wonderful trip so far. Just think of all that we have seen—the Passion Play, the Black Hills, Mount Rushmore, and Orcas. I have fulfilled my promise to Hazel, and now you need to get on with your life. You have made all the arrangements and paid for everything. You've been the perfect trip host and guide. I can only say that I am grateful and deeply in your debt. If you want me to pay for anything, you just say the word."

"Okay. I'm good to go. Now, let's enjoy the rest of the trip and not talk about you leaving or paying."

"Ditto," said Kate. Ten minutes later, she was snoring lightly, fast asleep in the passenger seat.

As she drove, Amelia considered what Kate had told her. She now understood the full extent of the risk that Kate had taken to make this trip with her and be able to see her grandchildren, perhaps for the last time. She considered Kate's self-control, knowing that she was at high risk and kept this stressful secret to herself up to this point.

Amelia appreciated her drive to fulfill her promise and obligation to Hazel, and she could sense that her grandmother was now at peace in her life. She had checked the boxes and could exhale. When Amelia turned to look at Kate and saw that she had nodded off again, she softly said, "I love you, Grandma." She watched her sleep for a few seconds and then turned her attention back to the road. She felt the same calm serenity that Kate did.

At last, they reached San Francisco where Amelia had arranged for a guided tour of the city. A guide took them over the Golden Gate Bridge and back while explaining its history. They experienced curvy Lombard Street, took a cable-car ride, saw parrots near Telegraph Hill, and visited Fisherman's Wharf. Later in the afternoon, they took a cruise of the bay, passing under the famous bridge again, and viewed Alcatraz Island from the boat's deck. Afterward in Chinatown they had a simple meal, then wandered along the streets looking at shops, and finally caught an Uber back to the hotel.

Kate was tired and went to bed right away, but Amelia couldn't sleep. She was saddened by Kate's desire to go home to Minnesota and held out hope that maybe once they got to LA, they could find medical support and Kate could stay for a while longer. Knowing that she could not sleep anytime soon, Amelia left the hotel to wander the streets for a couple of hours and absorb the city's noise and energy before she felt tired enough to turn in for the evening.

CLUB MEMBER

Jack reviewed information about country clubs over the last couple of days. He decided on a specific club for two reasons; First, he knew that he qualified for membership financially, and the website indicated that there were openings for new members. Jack loaded his golf clubs, drove to the club, parked, and walked into the clubhouse lobby. He asked the receptionist if he could meet the club manager. After a fifteen minute wait, Mac Zelinski the manager approached and introduced himself. Jack told him that he was interested in becoming a member.

Mac silently looked him over and said, "Are you sure you have the right club?"

"Well, yes," Jack said. "I am quite certain."

"You know that our stock buy-in is $350,000, and, of course all dues and restaurant minimums are on top of that."

The answer triggered Jack's fight or flight instinct. He resisted the impulse to fight by tossing a smart remark back at Mac, but he was not going to turn away, either. After a pause which Mac interpreted as time Jack needed to understand he was way out of his league, Jack responded, "Oh, that's a little less than I expected. Can I write a personal check today, or will I need to wire transfer funds?"

Mac was taken aback. He responded, "Why don't we step into my office?"

Once they'd settled in, Mac held out a membership application. When he'd completed it, Jack handed it back. Mac reviewed it and said, "You didn't fill out your occupation."

"I don't work," Jack replied.

"Oh?" Mac smiled. "Family money, eh?"

"No," said Jack. "My family is poor; dad died years ago, and my mom's a drug addict."

Mac sat back in his chair, thinking that maybe this guy was yanking his chain, and said, "Well, I don't know…"

Jack said, "Type my name into Google."

Mac looked at him suspiciously, then tapped on his keyboard. The search engine brought up Jack's story, and now Mac understood. He sat back in his chair, looked at the screen again, then stood and offered to shake Jack's hand saying, "Well, Mr. Lemke, we do have a membership process. However, I'm quite certain that there won't be any problems with your application."

"Great," said Jack. "Would it be possible to get in a round today?"

"Yes, Mr. Lemke, we could certainly accommodate a complimentary round today."

"Good," replied Jack, "My clubs are in my car. I will play with those today. However, before I tee off, I'd like to stop into your pro shop and order twelve dozen monogrammed balls and two new sets of clubs, one to leave here and one to keep in the trunk of my car."

"Absolutely, Mr. Lemke. I will ask the pro to take care of your request, and you can let the caddy master know which car your clubs are in, we will get you set up. And welcome! Unofficially, though, as I don't have official approval yet."

Later, Mac met Jack as he came off the 18th green. "Mr. Lemke, how was your round?" he asked.

"Two things, Mac," Jack responded. "One, I shot a 79, but I can do better. I haven't played much recently. And two, Mr. Lemke was my father, so please, call me Jack."

Mac smiled. "Hey, we might have gotten off on the wrong foot. We get a lot of people coming in here who think that they can afford to be members. Most are young guys like you who think that they have the world by the tail and find out that they haven't quite got what is needed to be a member here. You, of course, do. Can I buy you a drink at the bar?"

"Sure," Jack responded. "That would be great."

Once settled into a booth and sipping a cool drink, Mac asked, "So, what does a young guy who has all the money in the world do to occupy his time?"

Jack replied, "As of today, golf!" Then he smiled. "I'm looking at several ventures right now. I have a movie project in the works. I might be producing on that one, or perhaps just investing and developing it."

"Really." Turning his head, Mac said, "Do you see those two guys at the far end of the bar?"

"Yeah," said Jack, looking in their direction.

"Have you ever heard of Ralph Gottstein and Leland Gentile?"

"You mean the big-time Hollywood producers? Of course, who hasn't?"

Mac nodded. "Yes, that's them. They can't golf to save their lives, and they'll cheat every time they can, so watch out for that. But I know they do a lot of big deals sitting in this bar."

"Wow," said Jack, keeping his voice low. "I would love to meet them."

Mac said, "Sure, finish your drink and I'll take you over. That's what clubs like this are for: bringing together like-minded people of means. But, just a word of caution on these two. They are said to have, how should I say it, connections to certain…families. Families who take their work and money very seriously, and take losing very badly."

"You mean the Mafia?" asked Jack.

"That's the rumor. I advise caution when dealing with those two. Crossing them could cost a guy his knees, if you catch my drift."

"I still would like to meet them," said Jack, and he quickly swallowed the last of his drink.

Mac walked up to Ralph and Leland and shook their hands as he greeted them. He said, "I want to introduce our newest member, Jack Lemke."

Jack stepped forward and shook their hands and saying, "Pleased to meet you."

Mac continued, "Jack's a pretty good stick, so watch your wagers with him out on the course! He also tells me that he has a film project that he is developing and which he may produce. I just thought since you two are in the business, there might be some mutual interest in business opportunities. Maybe even help develop his project."

Leland asked, "You ever develop and produce a picture before, kid?"

"No, sir," said Jack. "It's just that we have a good story, and we think that it can be shot cost-effectively and be profitable."

"What's your background, kid?" asked Ralph.

Jack replied, "Well, um, I was in marketing. However, I recently came into some money and want to invest it and grow a reputation here in Hollywood."

Mac stepped in, saying, "Jack was the guy who won that huge lottery a couple of weeks back."

"Oh," said Leland, perking up a bit. "How much was that again?"

"Six hundred eighty-five million dollars," Jack replied.

"Nice," said Ralph, "Congratulations. A guy might be able to live on that for a while, I guess. Any investment plans for the money?"

"Nothing right now, except, of course, the film, although I'm looking at a yacht and maybe an airplane, too."

Ralph continued, "Well, tell you what—Jack, was it?"

Jack nodded.

"Jack, it's kind of like buying the first year of a new model car or software. You know that there will be issues and bugs, and you don't want to deal with those issues. We see it as the same with first-time producers. It usually ends up being a disaster. After you get your first picture under your belt and make some money, come look us up. But good luck, kid! You'll need that and more. This is a tough dog-eat-dog business." Then, he dismissively turned away from Mac and Jack and continued his conversation with Leland.

Upon arriving home, Jack checked his phone and saw that his mom and brother had called again, leaving messages about sending them money. "I'm getting tired of this," he said out loud to himself.

Reluctantly, he called his mother, "Hey, Mom. It's Jack."

"Oh honey, I'm glad you called. I know I said that I would pay back what you sent me last time. But I'm sorry, times are tough, and I just don't have the money right now. I feel bad about that. I guess what I really wanted to say is that I could use a little more cash to tide me over until I'm a bit more caught up."

"Mom, I sent you $10,000 just days ago. Where did that money go?"

"You know, Jack, I am not as young as I once was, and I can't remember everything. I just don't know."

"Mom, are you using again?"

"Oh Jack, don't be silly. It's just that I hurt all the time, and I have doctor bills, and I have to take a cab wherever I go. I guess I also owe some money to the IRS for back taxes."

"Mom, I can't just keep giving you money. I am not sure how it is being used."

"Jackie, I know that rich children give money to their parents all the time. It's in all of the magazines. But I'm not one of those people. If you send me $10,000 more, I will never ask for another nickel! Promise."

"Mom, I will do that, and we will never have this discussion again. Right?"

"Yes, Jackie. Even though I think you are cheap, I will leave you and Emily alone from now on. Thanks, bye."

Jack shook his head. What a mess.

Next, he dialed his brother. Jack told him that he was going to send more money to their mom. That was not well received. "Don't send her money," his brother said. "She just uses. Send the cash to us, and we will decide what to do with it."

Jack did not trust his brother any more than his mother. Jack said, "I won't send her any more money. She knows that."

"Have you made any decisions about what to do with family members? You know, in terms of giving out any cash. We are all excited about your fortune and success and would love to be involved in your happiness."

"I have not made any decisions, and please don't ask me again."

"Well, we are anxious. We can put any amount to good use."

"I'm sure. Later, bro." And Jack disconnected. "What a pain," he said aloud. "I hate this."

LAST LEG

Amelia and Kate were scheduled to visit the San Francisco Aquarium on their last day of the trip, but over breakfast Kate said, "You know Meels, I've been to the aquarium at the Mall of America a couple of times. We're just six hours from LA. Why don't we just take a nice leisurely drive down the coast and have an easy, short day? I'm still feeling low on energy. This trip has been fun, but long."

Amelia was disappointed but said, "Okay, as long as we get to stop at Hearst Castle. Then the next stop will be my house in Malibu."

As they drove, Kate asked Amelia, "Can I ask a question?"

"Sure, anything. Shoot."

"First, I am not questioning or complaining; we have stayed in nice places and ate nice meals. However, we did not go to the best restaurants or stay in premium rooms. You can stay anywhere you want to, eat at any place, have any service rendered. But you don't. It's not that you have been cheap—we have had everything we wanted on this wonderful trip. I'm just curious how someone with the millions you have decides how to spend money."

"I understand the question, and I take no offense. I wonder that myself sometimes. First, I believe in saving it until I have a plan on how and why to invest or spend it. Living day to day, it seems prudent that I consider if there is any real value in spending more. It's like a hotel room. You want something clean and safe. But is it worth fifty or a hundred and fifty dollars more for one on the top floor or one with marble countertops in the bathroom or roses in a vase? I don't think so. I get in the room and sleep eight hours, shower, then I'm up and out. Money saved and ready to be used for something else— to have fun or support good causes, to buy nice things like clothes or gifts, or to address a real need. But I'm not going to spend money just because or to show that I have it. I think that is foolish. But I realize now that money is a powerful tool, and if you don't respect it, it will slowly dissipate. The pull to spend is strong, a little here and a little there, like a slow leak in a tire. I am afraid that Jack may not value it as much as I do. I am concerned about how to address this once we get married. He tends to be pretty loose with his money. He will give it away, big tips, wanting to be involved with huge risky projects, trying to impress people because to him, it seems it's easy come easy go. I'm glad that it's his money he is spending. I can imagine potential conflicts once we are married as I have a feeling that he will want to have us combine our money. I don't want to do that. I'm sorry I'm babbling on; I guess you can see that the question has been on my mind. An easy answer to your specific question is I like nice things too, but I will ask myself if I need it or just want it because I can afford it. I want my money to make a difference in the world. That is my goal."

"Marriage is a game of give and take." Kate said, "I'm sure that you will learn to negotiate. This whole being rich thing is new to both of you. Who is really ready to deal with that? I'm sure I would not know how to work through it. But you will figure it out. You're young and smart. And again, thanks for bankrolling this trip, I've truly loved the time we have spent together. I'm looking forward to seeing LA and seeing Henrik. I do hope that you can find a happy medium with Jack."

"Yeah, me too. This trip has been my pleasure, even though I am anxious to get back to the beach house. And Grandma, I will likely never spend all of the lottery money; however, if this trip and car were all I got out of it, it still would have been worth it!"

Five hours later, they finished the Grand Rooms tour at Hearst Castle which focused on the building design and decor. It was nothing less than impressive. Kate got tired quickly, so they decided that one tour would be enough.

Back in the Audi, they both looked forward to getting to LA. The Pacific Coast Highway was a beautiful drive, the kind that one should take at least once in a lifetime. Kate enjoyed the ocean views from the cliffside road. The sun was bright and reflected off the waves. "Isn't this just beautiful?" said Amelia. "It's a good day to be alive."

Kate said to Amelia, "I would like to tell you something. It may just be the ramblings of an old lady, but I would like to share them with you. I've been thinking about representing how life works over the past couple of years. I know that I have fewer tomorrows, and can share it with you, someone who is looking forward to many more. Maybe it will make sense to you, perhaps not. Ok, here goes. My analogy is that one's lifeline is like a thin sewing thread that moves slowly forward through a series of life tasks, which are like sewing needle eyes. The first eye is when you are born. It is enormous, like the size of a car. At that time, your thread is short and strong and can fit through easily. All you had to do is eat and breathe. As your life passes, your thread spools out becoming longer. It becomes heavier gets frayed and weakened. It takes more energy to move forward, and it is harder to steer through the needle eyes which are staggered along the route of life. The needle eyes continue to get smaller, making them harder to thread, each taking more energy and effort."

"As I said, at first your thread is strong and you can easily thread through the eyes of growing up and going to school, getting a job, and maybe raising a family or accomplishing specific challenges. As you get older, there are some needle eyes which you just can't get through, so you miss out on those opportunities and have to move on to the next. Other people's threads intertwine with yours and thread common needle eyes, supporting your thread to make it lighter, creating a web and making it easier to move forward, but also pulling you in one direction or another. When you get to my age, your thread is stretched out. It is very long, and it has become fragile, and it is heavier, harder to support. It takes more strength and energy to push it forward, much less thread another eye. The thread has become more frayed and is now begins to unravel; the needle eyes get smaller and smaller. It gets darker, hard to see, your friends pass away and family spreads out, there are fewer threads in your web. Finally, you reach a point where it's too much. You can't push or pull the thread anymore. It is too worn and frayed. Then it snaps, and it's over, broken forever, and you're adrift and gone, not connected to anyone or anything. And you die. That thin thread and the needle eyes through which you've threaded—that's your legacy, what you have accomplished, and your web is your network of human connections. The contact points are memories others have of you. It's your path through life. I'm just a crazy old woman, but that kind of makes sense to me. It's how I see my life and that of others." Then Kate fell silent, thinking of her thread, her web, her legacy.

Amelia said, "That is an interesting way to present it. I think I understand. It emphasizes the importance of having your support network in place. It also makes me think of challenges we face and pick the right needle eyes, or challenges, to thread. That's what I am struggling with right now. What do I want to do with my life? How can Jack and I, or at least I, make a difference? I will remember your story and see where my thread takes me. In any event, you're not crazy." Kate did not notice tears running down Amelia's face.

They continued south. Amelia was excited to be close to home, where her new house and fiancé awaited. Kate stayed awake for a while but eventually nodded off.

Outside of Mussel Shoals, about an hour from home, Amelia reached over and touched Kate's shoulder to wake her up and see the view of the ocean. Kate's body felt heavy, and she did not respond. Amelia pushed her again a little harder and called her name. Again, there was no response.

Amelia swerved to the side of the road and pushed her shoulder again. Kate was lifeless.

Amelia got out, ran around to the other side of the car, and opened the door. Kate's body slumped toward her. "No! Kate!" she cried out. "Oh, God, somebody help me!" She pushed her grandmother's body back into the car and felt Kate's neck for a pulse. There was none. She cried out, "No, Kate, we're almost home. Please."

She pulled out her phone and dialed 911. The operator came on the line, and Amelia told her what happened. The operator calmly said, "There is an ambulance en route. How long has she been in this condition? Have you tried CPR?"

Amelia cried out, "I don't know CPR, and I don't know how long." Thinking back as best she could, she said, "Maybe five minutes, maybe fifteen."

"Is she warm"?

"Yes, kind of."

The operator said, "I'll talk you through it. Get her out of the car and on flat ground."

Through her tears, Amelia unbuckled the seat belt. As she was about to try to lift her out of the car, a California Highway Patrol car with flashing lights pulled in behind the Audi, braking to a hard stop. An officer rushed toward her, asking, "Are you the 911 call?"

Amelia cried, "Yes, please help me get her out. I think she's dead. I thought she was just sleeping. Please help me! Do you know CPR?"

He said that he did. After they got Kate out of the car, he quickly cleared her airway and started compressing her chest. He worked on her for at least ten minutes before they heard the wailing siren of the approaching ambulance.

The EMT team worked on her for ten minutes more, then looked up at the patrolman and Amelia and shook their heads. The patrolman put his arm around Amelia's shoulders and moved her away from the car.

"You said you thought she was sleeping?" he asked.

Amelia was sobbing. "Yes, she had a weak heart, and we were on a road trip from Minnesota and almost home to Malibu, and I tried to wake her up, and I couldn't. I didn't know her heart was that weak—that close to failing."

The EMT crew loaded Kate's body onto the gurney and then into the ambulance; the ambulance pulled out with its siren off.

The officer said, "Why don't you follow me. Can you do that?"

Amelia slowly took a deep breath, composed herself, and nodded yes.

At the hospital, she went over her story with the patrolman again and provided Kate's identification. He escorted her into the ER. One of the EMTs from the ambulance guided her into a sitting room off the ER to wait. Five minutes later, a doctor came in.

The doctor looked at his chart. "Kate was your mother?"

"No, grandmother," she replied.

"Oh yes, sorry, of course," he said. Looking at Amelia, he said, "You look familiar. Have we met before?"

"No, I don't believe so."

The doctor paused and said, "We couldn't do anything for her. I'm sorry for your loss. Will the family want an autopsy? We don't do one in these types of circumstances unless the family requests it."

Amelia had not thought about an autopsy yet. She responded, "No, she had a weak heart. In retrospect, she did seem to be growing weaker, with less energy over the past several days. I just did not recognize the signs."

The doctor nodded. "Lack of energy, falling asleep, maybe shortness of breath?"

"Well, yes. I'm not sure about the shortness of breath, but the other two signs were there for sure."

"Again, I'm sorry. I know that this is a shock. But have you thought about what to do about funeral arrangements? If not, we have staff here who can help."

She replied, "That would be very nice."

The doctor nodded. "Sorry again. I will get those people to come to see you."

After about ten minutes, a young woman and a chaplain walked into the room. They introduced themselves, offered condolences, and asked if they could be of service.

"We can call the funeral home," the woman said. "They will handle all the paperwork and tasks. They will want to know about financial arrangements."

Amelia said, "I can handle that."

"Okay," said the woman as she handed Amelia a printed form. "They will come to get her and give you a call as to specifics. If you give me your information, they will be in touch."

"Thank you. Can I see her one last time?"

The chaplain nodded his head and said, "Follow me."

They went to the hospital morgue and viewed Kate's body. The chaplain asked if Amelia wanted to pray.

"Kate would like it if we did," Amelia said.

He said the Lord's Prayer.

"Do you need more time with her?" he asked.

Amelia bent and kissed her grandmother's forehead and said, "This one is from Henrik" and kissed her cheek. She covered Kate's face with the sheet.

"No," she said. "I want to remember her as she was when alive."

"I understand," he said.

When she got to the parking lot, the CHP car was gone. She had wanted to thank the officer for his assistance. She thought that law enforcement got beat up so badly in the press, yet they provided such an essential service.

She got into the Audi and started it, then sat. Her brain was numb. What had just happened? Was it real? She had not had a chance to say goodbye, an opportunity to thank Kate for raising her and Henrik. On TV shows and in movies, people always seemed to get one last chance to say goodbye. It did not seem fair. She broke into sobs. Slowly, she gained control. Then she cried some more.

Amelia felt like she had lost more than her grandmother. Kate was her connection to her family's past. With her parents long gone, there was no one else left to represent the lineage. Except for Henrik and Jack, she was alone in the world. Amelia and Kate had gotten close on the road trip. It seemed that she had gained a new confidante and cheerleader and then lost her in a matter of ten days.

Wiping her eyes, Amelia challenged herself to find something positive to hold on to. She realized that if Kate had passed away ten days earlier, she would never have heard the stories about Hazel and Beth. She would have lost the valuable motivation and insights into her ancestry which she gained from learning of the lives and challenges of her forebearers through Kate's stories.

When she finished crying, she called Jack. She managed to tell him where she was and what had happened. She said, "There just wasn't anything I could do."

"I'll come and get you. Where are you?

"No, I can drive home. I've got a car full of dirty clothes and stuff. I don't want to leave that here and then have to deal with it again later. I just want to be home with you."

"Are you sure? I can leave right now."

"Yes. I'm sure. I just want to be home, in your arms."

On the drive home, she called Henrik and told him what had happened. It was a hard conversation; however, between tears, they agreed that Kate wanted to be cremated, and they would talk again about what to do next. She needed to get home and get her mind settled before any more decisions.

HOME

Amelia pulled past the gate into the driveway. She turned off the Audi and breathed a sigh of relief. Jack had been watching for her and rushed out of the house to open her car door.

"I'm so sorry," he said. "That must have been terrible." Amelia got out, and he took her in his arms, saying, "If there's anything, I can do..."

She burst into tears. Jack simply held her firm and close. Then he led her inside the house.

Jack asked, "Want to talk about it?"

"I'm not sure," she said. "It's just such shock. You reach over to jostle someone awake, and find you're touching a dead body."

He put his hand in the small of her back to direct her and said, "Come on out to the pool deck, and we can talk."

They lay down beside each other on the same double-wide chaise lounges—the same ones that Londyn and Jack had used several nights before. As that thought drifted through his memory, Jack felt a pang of guilt to now occupy the same position with Amelia. He resolved to better focus his attention on Amelia. Jack wrapped his arms around her and asked, "What can I do to help?"

"Just support me," she replied. "There is a lot that needs my attention. I've got to figure out what to do with her body and then plan a funeral and take care of her estate. It means I have to go back to Minnesota again, very soon. I need time to unwind and think." She lay in his arms for a while and let the sound of the ocean waves soothe her mind and allow the sadness to recede slowly.

Finally, Jack spoke, "I'm sorry she is gone. I was looking forward to meeting her. It might not have been enough, but at least you two were able to share this trip before she died."

"She was looking forward to meeting you. It was such a great trip, really. We saw so much and talked about everything. I heard some wonderful family stories, some good, some very sad. They inspired me. I now know that I have to accomplish something with my life. I'm not sure what yet, but I have some ideas."

"Like what?"

"Well, I want to make a difference for people, but I'm not yet sure how," she said. "I think I want to use our good fortune to make a difference for people like Hazel and certainly Beth. Women who had a lot to offer and would probably have done better in this world if they'd had support and a different social environment to showcase their talents. Maybe I can financially support or get involved with a women's group."

Jack thought that such efforts might just be a waste of time and money and knew he would not want to be deeply involved. On the other hand, he knew that if Amelia was busy with other interests, it would free up his time to do what he wanted, so he said, "Oh, that sounds noble and worthy. I want to hear more as you figure that out."

"I know that I can't just play all the time. Last, I know that I want to have children around the house. I want a family around me all the time. It seems like that is all that matters in the long run."

Jack laughed. "If they are anything like my family, we might have to live in separate houses." He was not in any hurry to have children. In fact, he was not sure that he even wanted children. Domestic responsibilities would hamper playing in the sun, traveling, climbing social ladders—basically, they'd be an obstacle for anything he considered fun and exciting.

She snuggled deeper into his arms. "I will be so happy to be home with you when this is all over. I missed you so much, and I just want to get back to being normal, whatever that might turn out to be. I always thought that rich people were never stressed out. If you have enough money, you can simply make your problems just go away. I guess that is not true. One will always have problems that won't go away."

"Yeah. I hear you. Again, I'm so sorry about Kate and what you had to go through. That had to be such a shock."

"It was. I think I missed the warning signs. She kept getting so tired and slept a lot. Her heart was giving out. I just did not see it. I had hoped to get her some help here in LA. It's just so sad. Oh, hey, speaking of people who need help, how's your mom?"

"What a mess. I sent her some more money. I think it was a mistake, but she keeps calling and driving me nuts. My brother said I should give the money to him and he will take care of her. The problem is, I don't trust him either. In a way, having this money is a curse."

"Sorry you have to deal with that. I'm glad I don't have to, even though the only reason is that I've got basically no family left. Oh, I have missed you so much. I missed your strong arms and your warm body holding me in bed, hearing your voice, and listening to what you have to say, even if it's goofy. So how much have you missed me?"

As he considered the question, Jack realized that the close bond that he had with her had been weakened. His devotion to her was not the same as before they had won the lottery. He thought of Londyn. He felt that he was now a man of means and many options in life. However, he responded, "Lots, Meels. It was so lonely here while you were gone. I've tried to keep myself busy. I bought some toys, you know, the bikes and wave runners, so we can play. I puttered around, golfed, and tried my hand at diving, both ocean, and sky and think that I am going to get my pilot's license. But I also spent time looking at a couple of investments. So, it has not been all play for me. Mostly I waited around for you to come back. I'm looking forward to settling in with you, my best buddy."

"Please," she said, "just hold me tight."

He did.

ARRANGEMENTS

Later that afternoon, Amelia got a call from Baltanery Mortuary. She closed her eyes, gathered her thoughts, and answered. After listening to condolences and a pitch for a higher-priced cremation package, she explained that she did not need anything fancy. She ordered the least expensive set, comprised of a plastic cremation urn in a wooden box, and confirmed that Kate's remains could be picked up on Monday morning. "That will do," Amelia said.

Overhearing the conversation, Jack asked if she might have picked out a more expensive cremation set. She responded that it would have been a waste of money; Kate would have wanted something simple. Jack swallowed his response.

Henrik called later, and Amelia reviewed the day's events in detail. Henrik asked, "So what do we need to do next?"

"We have to get her remains back to Minnesota and arrange to have her buried next to Grandpa and our parents."

"Hey, sis. First, I'm sorry that you had to deal with this on your own so far. It must be very hard. Thanks for being so strong. I don't know that I could have done what you did. Second, I am underwater with a rewrite deadline on a documentary, and the producer is all over me to finish so that the production schedule stays on track. Is there any way we can hold off on the trip to Minnesota? I just can't lose three or four days right now. I could get away in a couple of weeks, though. Since she was cremated, and no one else back home knows about her passing, I don't think we are in any rush."

After considering his comments, Amelia said, "Henrik, I'm the one with the time to deal with this. I also feel obligated to do it. I was much closer to her than you were, and that is okay. I propose that we have a celebration of life for her on the beach here at our place, and then I can take her back to Minnesota and deal with the issues there. I'm totally, and I mean totally, okay with that. She knows you loved her. Let's plan on you coming down on Monday, late afternoon. You can see our new place, we can have some food, and I will arrange a ceremony to say goodbye to her."

After hanging up with Henrik, Amelia booked a flight back to Minnesota for Tuesday, then went outside to the pool deck where she found Jack looking out over the beach.

"Jack," she said, "I'm flying back north on Tuesday morning to take care of Kate's affairs. I don't know how long I'll be gone. Do you want to come with me?

"Meels, do you actually need me there? You'll be busy, and I think I will just get in your way. So, I would rather not. I have plenty to do here to clear the decks for us to spend time together when you get back.

"Oh. Well, are you at least going to miss me when I'm gone?"

"Of course," he said. "I'll be happy when you can finally settle back in here. It's lonely when you are gone."

YACHTS

The next morning, Jack made pancakes for breakfast. They sat at the kitchen counter without speaking, engrossed in their thoughts. Suddenly, Amelia noticed a brochure from the marina on the kitchen counter. She said, "So, you said something about a boat?"

Jack replied, "Yeah, I've been looking at some models. And by the way, we call them yachts. Can't you just imagine being out on the open water, free to travel up and down the coast, have parties, hobnob with the rich and famous?"

"I see. So, how much is a yacht?" Amelia asked, although she already had a pretty good idea.

"Um, well," he said. "I haven't asked for a quote from the broker yet. We've just talked in generalities."

"Yeah, but surely you have a ballpark number, right?" she asked.

"I'm thinking probably $2.5 to $3.5 million. The dock slip is also an investment; you buy it and then can sell it just like a piece of real estate if you don't need it anymore, so that's a good deal as values keep going up."

"Jack," she said, "I love you, but I don't know if I'm interested in spending that kind of money on a boat—sorry, a yacht."

"Well, I guess I could just buy it with my money."

"You sure could, and you should, Jack, if that is what you want to do."

"I might not let you on board, then," he said sarcastically.

"Maybe I don't want to!" she kidded him.

"Of course I want you with me," he said. "But that said, I will get a financial model put together before asking you again. Agreed, I will be solely financially responsible should I buy a yacht."

"Deal."

"Hey. You saw the surprises I had for you in the garage, right?"

"Do you mean the wave runners and the bikes?" she asked. "Yes, I like them. They look like fun! Thank you."

"Good. While you were away, I joined the golf club, signed up for more flying lessons, and am planning on scuba diving lessons. I would love it if we could do those things together."

"Wow, you have been a busy boy," she stated. "I think I might be interested in some of those activities. Can I let you know after I get settled back in after the funeral?"

"Sure, I can wait. I would have told you about all this before, but you were gone for such a long time, and I wanted to start enjoying the advantages of our newfound good fortune. I have also taken some early steps to get into movie production. The ideas are still in the brainstorming stage, but it is exciting. I'll keep you posted as it develops."

"Sounds kind of interesting," she said.

"Through the golf club, I've already met some big-time Hollywood producers. They asked me to keep them informed."

"That sounds very promising," said Amelia.

The subject of discussion changed back to the highlights of the trip interspersed with memories of Grandma Kate. Jack tried to be attentive but found it difficult to focus on listening to Amelia as she rambled on about her journey. Amelia, though, was content to have someone she loved to hear her thoughts.

GOODBYE KATE

Henrik arrived the evening of the celebration. Amelia gave him a big hug when he got out of his car. The hug felt good. "Hey, big brother," she said, smiling.

"Good to see you too, Meels."

They went into the house and Jack gave him a bro hug, complete with back slaps.

"What's new?" Jack asked.

"Compared to you guys, nothing," Henrik said. "Work has me buried. I told them I was going to my grandmother's funeral just to get away from their phone calls this afternoon. I love my work. I'm excited to get up every day, but it is a tough world out there. Oh, and congratulations to you two on the big lottery win. It couldn't have happened to better people. I'm very happy for you."

Amelia brought him over to the dining room table and pointed to the wooden box. "That's her," she said.

"A life condensed down to its most basic chemical elements." Henrik nodded.

After a tour of the house, they stepped outside to enjoy the view of the beach and ocean.

Henrik said, "Wow, Meels, this is just incredible. Have you got an extra room for a guy to move into?"

"Feel free to visit any time," she said. "You living here would serve as an open invitation to some of Jack's family, though, who are best appreciated when kept at much more than arm's length."

Henrik nodded. "I get it. The big brush-off!"

"You know what I mean," she said.

Henrik laughed and nodded. "Of course I do, Meels. Just giving you the needle."

Amelia said, "Speaking of needles, I have a 'Grandma Kate theory on life' to share with you someday. I learned a little more about her on our trip." She continued, "I'm not looking forward to this journey, though. I hope that I find some legal documents at the house; the minister or maybe the neighbors can fill me in on her personal life. You know she never talked much about herself, on the phone or even on the whole trip. She was always talking about you and me, family, but never about herself. To be honest, now I realize that I don't know enough about her personal life at all."

"Same here," he replied. "A mystery surrounded by an enigma. Sorry, not trying to be funny, but it's the truth."

"Did she ever mention a will or anything like that to you?" she asked.

"No, never, but she had that small portable safe where I think she may have kept important stuff."

"Oh yeah," she replied. "I remember it. I never saw inside it. Wonder where the key to it is? I do remember that she once told me the house was paid off."

The minister arrived at the house about the same time as Kim and Bill. After introductions, they went onto the beach. The minister began the ceremony by talking about the mystery and circle of life. He asked that they all pray for Kate, then asked if anyone had any words. Henrik spoke of the kind woman who took in two orphaned kids and spent years of her life making sure they were safe and prospering. Amelia spoke of a strong woman and promised that she would someday tell her children how their great-grand-mother had given up many good years to raise her and Henrik.

When the ceremony was over, Amelia said, "Kim and Bill, thanks for coming and sharing with us. We appreciate your friendship. We have food and drinks. No sad talk; this is a celebration of a good life."

Jack, Kim, and Bill went inside to tend to the meal, and the minister talked with Amelia and Henrik. They shared fond memories of their time with Kate.

After dinner and a round of hugs, the minister, Kim and Bill left. Henrik and Amelia walked to the beach.

"Well, Meels," Henrik said, "tell me about it."

She described the trip it's tragic ending.

"That must have been tough," he said. "I would not wish that on anybody."

"Thanks," she said. She asked Henrik if there was anything he wanted from Kate's house back in Stillwater.

He said, "No, I have all that I need."

She said, "I will donate the furniture, then get a service to come in and clean out everything. You know, there may be some pictures and stuff that we might want. I'll call you once I've had a chance to look around. As for the house, I think we'll get a real estate agent to list it. You can have the proceeds."

"Oh no," he said. "It's half yours."

"Seriously, Henrik—you see where I live, right? I have all that I will ever need and more, brother. I won't hear of it. Maybe you can use the money to get your own apartment or put a down payment on a house out here. Someday I would like to do something more, just for you."

He looked at her and said, "I don't want you to feel obligated to give me anything. I'm doing okay."

She nodded, then looked out over the ocean and started to cry. "I already miss her so much!"

Henrik put his arms around her and said, "We both do."

NORTH STAR STATE, AGAIN

As Jack drove Amelia to the airport the next morning, he said, "Seems like déjà vu all over again. Didn't we just do this?"

She smiled. "Yeah. Seems like just yesterday. When I get back, I'm not leaving for a long time unless I'm with you. I do wish you were coming with me. You could still get a ticket."

Jack said, "I just know I'd be in the way. If you go alone you won't have to babysit me, and you can focus on getting your tasks done, maybe connect with some old friends and then get back here to me. I never even met Kate, and I certainly don't know anyone back there."

"I know, but you would be supporting me," she said.

"Sorry, babe, it doesn't make any sense to me."

After several minutes of silence, Jack said, "Maybe when you get back, we can get back into planning that Italy trip."

Deep inside, Jack was excited about the opportunity to spend more time with Londyn. When he heard Amelia talk about her plans to take Grandma Kate's remains back up north, he had decided that if his choice was between going to a funeral and having to clean out an old house full of family junk versus five more nights playing with Londyn, it was a no-brainer for him to stay in LA.

Upon arrival at the terminal, she said, "I will miss you."

Jack nodded. "You'd better. I'll miss you, too."

They kissed goodbye on the sidewalk, and she headed into the LAX terminal, determined that she would to get back here as soon as possible and into the rhythm of her new life.

STILLWATER

Standing in Kate's house, Amelia felt like an intruder in the quiet old structure. She had made a to-do list on the plane. Her first task was to find any legal documents and contact the church. Then, in no particular order, deal with personal effects and get a realtor to sell the house.

After searching for a short time, she found the small black sheet metal safe bolted to the basement floor and then the key in Kate's jewelry box—the only place of value besides the safe. She said out loud, "Not very secure, Grandma! Any self-respecting burglar could have done the same in maybe fifteen minutes."

Inside the safe box, there were several envelopes: the car's title, a document stating that the house loan had been paid off, and an envelope titled *Last Will and Testament*. The final envelope contained a whole life insurance policy for $50,000 on the life of Katherine Bauer. There was also a man's gold wedding band and a man's wristwatch. Amelia's guess was that they were been her grandfather's. She quickly scanned the will. Everything was split equally between her and her brother.

As she walked through the house, she took a mental inventory. She determined that there was nothing in the house in terms of furniture that she or Henrik would want.

With her new appreciation of family history, she put aside some individual pictures and photo albums. Her favorite family photo was on the mantel over the fireplace: her parents, grandparents, and brother smiling happily at the camera when everyone was so very young. She smiled, remembering that they had a water balloon fight just before the picture was taken. They were all laughing and soaking wet. It was a happy day. Her parents died less than a month later. She remembered Grandpa Gerald looking at this photo and saying, "Every picture tells a story, don't it?" then sadly shaking his head. She added it to her collection.

There were bills for the phone, water, gas, electricity, and a credit card on the floor beneath the mail slot in the front door. There were monthly statements from the bank for Kate's checking account and an investment account.

She wondered about the proper way to handle these items. She decided to call Bob Smith for advice.

Bob said he was pleased to hear from her. She quickly told him the story of Kate's passing, and informed him that she was now standing in Kate's house and unsure of how to go about whatever legal and financial steps to manage Kate's estate. Bob commiserated with her over her loss and told her that one often brought in an attorney and possibly an accountant to help manage the legal and tax tasks in general.

He said, "I would be happy to help, but you would be far better off with local representation as I can't practice in Minnesota." He asked her what specific items most concerned her, and as she described the documents she had discovered, he immediately confirmed that he was way too expensive for this project. He told her that for any estate under a million dollars, someone local should be fine. However, he did give his advice as to how to handle each item she described.

Amelia said, "I'm pretty sure that all totaled, it will be well under that amount. I think I know a local attorney I can call. I'll call back if I need help. Thank you, Bob. I will talk to you again soon. I think I have some ideas to review with you."

"Great, looking forward to it already," said Bob. "Amelia, again, I'm sorry about your grandmother."

She could tell from his tone that he meant it.

As she hung up, she decided to visit the cemetery to get a visual reminder of what was in place and then proceed to the church to make funeral arrangements.

First, she visited the graves of her grandfather and parents. She was slightly surprised to find that there was already a matching grave marker for Kate, with the date of death not yet filled in, resting next to her grandfather. Then she entered the church and waited in the lobby for help. She noticed a posting for a church fundraiser to help repair the leaking roof with a total goal of $20,000. A couple of mop buckets set out to collect drips emphasized the need. Soon she was directed to Reverend Michael's office.

Amelia told him about Kate's passing. He said, "I'm truly sorry for her passing and your loss. Kate was a regular at church every Sunday morning."

Amelia nodded and asked, "Reverend, did Kate have many friends? She never talked about any with me specifically, and I am in the dark as to who I should be informing of her passing."

"Oh yes," he replied, "she was a quiet one, but she knew a great number of people and was always active in the congregation. She lived in Stillwater for so many years, and it is a relatively small town. So, I'm assuming she knew many others here. Oh, and by the way, congratulations on your good fortune. Kate mentioned it to several of our congregation, and there was a small article in the local newspaper. She was so proud of you and your brother."

Amelia was caught off guard by his knowledge of her family but said, "Thanks, it truly is a stroke of luck. I know it may seem like I'm rushing here, so please don't think poorly of me; however, when is the soonest that we can have a service? There are no close relatives, except for my brother and me, and we had a celebration of life service in LA earlier this week."

After considering the question, he responded, "The day after tomorrow. Thursday is the earliest possible day."

"That would be fine. I will plan on that," she said. "What about flowers, memorial cards, food, obituary, reception, music, vocalist, updating the gravestone marking? I'm sure I'm forgetting things. I am truly grateful for any assistance and guidance you could provide."

He said, "Don't worry. Kerri, one of the staff here at the church, is excellent and experienced at making the required arrangements."

Amelia met with Kerri immediately afterward, and for the next hour they worked on the service details. When done, Kerri said, "We can get all of this arranged and set up in time."

"How much will I owe for this?" Amelia asked. Kerri gave her a figure, and Amelia took out her checkbook, added $20,000 to the number, and signed the check.

Kerri looked at the check Amelia handed to her and said, "Oh, no, that's not right."

Amelia said, "Oh, I assure you it is. Kate was dedicated to this church. Her life revolved around it. It's simply her and my way of saying thanks for keeping her soul shining for all to see."

After a moment, Kerri said, "Well, thank you very much. This is very generous."

On her way home, Amelia stopped at the hardware store and bought duct tape and a small padlock shaped like a heart. She also had a couple keys made for the house.

Once back at the house, Amelia stopped by some of the neighboring homes, many of which were still occupied by the same families she had known growing up. Most everyone already knew of her good fortune with the lottery, as Kate had told them about it or they had read the article in the paper, and they all were excited to see her, inviting her in to talk. On each doorstep, she politely said she would like to; however, she had sad news to share and many other stops to make. She told them all of Kate's passing and the details of the service, and asked them to share the information with anyone else whom they thought should be informed. She continued until she had covered all the neighbors she knew.

She arranged for the home to be listed for sale and the disposal of Kate's personal property, including all of the furniture to a non-profit liquidator who would clean it all out, donate useable items, and then clean the house for selling. She looked in Kate's jewelry box again and did not find any valuable jewelry. Then she lifted out the top tray.

In the base of the box, there was a small envelope. She opened it and found a small, handmade book. Amelia remembered Kate telling her something else about Hazel Decker years before. Kate said that Hazel made her grandchildren little illustrated children's books about a squirrel named Sooty and his cute interactions with Kate and her siblings. Kate told her that she remembered one about catching a falling star and one about skating on a pond. She thought that Hazel had made nine or ten of them, and that she wished she knew where they all went, she knew there was one at home in her jewelry box for sure.

Amelia opened the little book, read it, and smiled at the story's simple beauty and her great-grandmother's hand drawings. She wrapped it in a heavy brown paper bag and placed it carefully into her backpack.

Amelia felt like she had stepped back in time when she went into her bedroom. She had avoided entering it earlier as she was reluctant to face her emotions and memories. It looked almost exactly the way she left it when she left for California. This was the house where she'd grown up, and now that seemed like a long time ago. Even though it had only been a few years, Amelia felt like it was much longer. So much had happened, her life was changing, and it was as if she had stepped back in time to see the trappings of a naïve younger girl.

Alone in the room, she thought of her parents and that terrible accident so long ago. The grandparents who had raised her were now gone. Her father's parents, whom she had rarely seen since they lived in Vermont, had both passed several years after her parents.

She laid down in her old bed and stared at the ceiling, still covered with glow-in-the-dark star constellations she had put up as a child. In the center, there was a happy face glowing down at her. It used to make her happy. Now it was just a reminder that this was no longer where she belonged. This was just a place where she had spent all of her formative nights. She felt dark loneliness.

The house was silent. It was as if its soul had gone away along with Kate, and it was now hollow and lifeless. She thought of what she knew of Kate's life and her existence here in this old house. Life had occurred here, but it seemed that it was without great joy; more like a simple base existence. It appeared to Amelia that Kate had just lived day to day. She repeated the same routine without an expectation of anything exciting or positive. She simply pushed her thread forward through smaller and fewer needle eyes. Amelia could see no evidence of human inclination to accomplish, build, explore, or be deeply attached to other people. Kate's faith and devotion kept her going.

Amelia did not think that she was a special person. She was not a genius, someone upon whom fate had bestowed great intellectual gifts or talents. And yet had been given an opportunity to test who she could be. Could she leave an imprint on the world? The money she had won was a responsibility. Something inside of her, maybe the strong and independent traits inherited from Hazel and Beth, told her that she could make her life and luck count. She had something to offer. She was more determined to make a difference with what she had. She thought more about working for a foundation or non-profit that could use her time and financial support. Jack did not want her to work, and she did not have to work a nine-to-five job, but did want to maintain her self-esteem and provide value to the world.

She texted Jack to say goodnight. She was in a far too melancholy a mood to talk and was disappointed that he had chosen to not be there with her.

LAZY DAY

As Jack drove home from the airport after kissing Amelia goodbye, he resisted the temptation to call Londyn immediately. He got all the way home and was out walking on the beach before dialing her number.

After spending the last several days with Amelia and supporting her in dealing with her grandmother's death, he now felt guilty about not going north with her and uneasy about his relationship with Londyn, so he made an effort to keep their conversation focused only on their business relationship and asked how the script was coming. She said, "I will call the writer and see how he's progressing." Then she asked, "How are you doing? What's new?"

He told her about Kate's passing and Amelia going back to Minnesota to settle affairs. Londyn said she was sorry to hear of Kate's death and asked if he and Amelia were okay. Jack assured her that all was well.

There was a pause in the conversation. Londyn was intentionally not going to say the next words. She wanted to gauge where Jack was in their relationship.

Jack was struggling, feeling pulled hard in opposite directions while trying to understand his feelings clearly. He desired to be with Londyn physically yet did not know if he wanted to be involved with her in a long-term relationship. Jack had not considered breaking off his engagement and leaving Amelia. He saw Londyn as a friend with benefits, or perhaps even his mistress. Yet it seemed that he increasingly fell deeper under her spell. He was aroused whenever she was near him, whenever he heard her voice, and whenever he thought of her. He had stayed in LA to be able to spend more time with Londyn. He was weak. He physically needed to be with her.

Jack finally succumbed to his desire. Words just tumbled out of his mouth. "Hey, I'm going to look at yachts today. Do you want to come along?

"I would love to," she responded and smiled. She knew she'd won a battle in Jack's conscience. "However, this girl has to work to eat, and I have a modeling gig today which will probably shoot until three or so."

"That might work. Marina Del Rey is only forty minutes away, and the sales office is open until nine p.m. Why don't you come to my place after work, and we'll go down there together? Maybe grab some food after?"

Londyn hesitated, then said, "That would work. But Jack, you know, I would rather spend time with just you. You know, quality alone time."

"Well, that's nice to hear. I could go to the marina and look around, then meet you back at the house. I can pick up some food to go on the way home?"

"That sounds much better to me," said Londyn. "These photoshoots take far more energy than a person might think. How about Chinese? Maybe some lemon chicken, sweet and sour pork, and fried rice?"

As usual, Londyn knew exactly what she wanted.

"That sounds very nice," he said. "I will see you at the house."

"Okay, great, looking forward to it! Gotta go," she said and hung up.

Jack was invigorated. He was excited that they would be together tonight. His physical desire for her was overwhelming. He honestly did not remember if he ever felt the same way for Amelia. He knew that Amelia filled his needs as a life companion, a cerebral equal, best friend and buddy. However, he found Londyn physically exciting and irresistible in a way that Amelia was not.

Londyn arrived at about five p.m., and Jack served the food he had picked up. They ate out on the deck and watched the late afternoon slowly turn into evening.

Londyn said, "I talked to the writer. He has an outline completed and wants to meet to discuss the storyline and interview both you and Amelia to get personal color to add as he flushes out the story. When could we arrange the meeting?

"Amelia will be back within the week. I'll let you know after I have had a chance to confirm this with her. But he can interview me any time. Why don't you have him stop by tomorrow night?"

To Londyn, it was strange to talk to Jack about Amelia so casually. However, she put aside her competitive nature and stayed calm and cool, appearing to support Jack's relationship with Amelia as she simultaneously used her assets and ingenuity to align Jack's affections toward her with the long-term goal of winning the grand prize. Jack, seemed to be able to separate the two relationships and not feel conflicted.

They each drank a beer and relaxed as they watched the ocean waves rhythmically break on the beach in front of the house.

She asked, "How was your yacht shopping this afternoon?"

"Interesting," he replied. "I think I identified the yacht I want, but when I got to talking to the salesman, I came up with an idea. They rent yachts to wealthy clients who don't want to own one. He was probably trying to imply that I should consider renting as the best option to start. But then I started thinking about it and flipped it all around. What if *I owned* the yacht and they rented it out for me? I asked him how often people were looking to rent, and he said all of the time. I got the brochure they handed out, and it has prices on it. I don't know how much commission they get on a rental and how many rentals they get each year for each yacht, but once I know that, I will start a business and buy several yachts for my rental fleet. Do you think you have any friends that would want to party on a nice yacht?"

"My friends are the original party animals," she replied. "But most are poor and needy like li'l old me. But that sounds like an interesting opportunity." Londyn seemed genuinely interested. She asked questions about the yachts and wanted him to keep her informed about the progress of his potential business venture. Jack appreciated her interest, in contrast to Amelia's disinterest.

Inevitably, Londyn finally said, "I'm hot and sweaty from my photoshoot today. I need to cool off." She quickly removed her clothes, stepped down the pool steps into the water, and waded in. Turning to Jack, she beckoned him with her fingers to join her. He rose and accepted her invitation. They spent the rest of the night accepting each other's invitations.

TOUCHING BASE

The next morning, Amelia spent two more hours carefully going through the main and second floors, ensuring that she had not missed anything of value. She packed all the items that she wanted to keep into boxes and loaded them into the car.

She contacted Henrik over Facetime, apologizing for the timing of the early morning call, and provided him a video tour through the house to ensure that he agreed with her decisions about what to keep and what to get rid of. Henrik again apologized for not being there and said that he appreciated her managing Kate's affairs.

Next, she headed to the UPS store, where she shipped the boxes back to LA. After that, she went to a coffee shop, purchased a roll and a latte, and used their wireless internet to book her ticket for a flight back out west late the next evening.

Amelia looked out the large window at the street activity and thought about her little hometown. She saw her reflection, her face gazing back at her. Did that face belong here, in this small town? Her history was here, but no— she knew in that very instant that this town could never be her home again. With her assets, she needed to live in a place with a much larger stage; she was now too big for Stillwater. However, as long as she was here, she wanted to reconnect with old friends.

Amelia sent a group text to several members of her old crowd and said that if anyone was available, she was buying beer and food from the food truck that evening, starting at 6:00 at Maple Island Brewery. From their responses, within ten minutes she knew to reserve the largest room. She was happy that she wouldn't have to spend the entire night alone in the old house.

She drove Kate's car to two car dealers and finally negotiated a sale. She was disappointed in the result as she knew that they did not give her the best price. She was frustrated that she did not have other viable options with her limited time in town. She thought back to when Jack bought their cars and realized that he had never even asked how much they cost, just that he got a five percent discount off list price. Yet another reason to keep their accounts separate, she thought. There were too many needs in the world to waste money.

She spent the afternoon back at the house, rummaging through the last boxes in the basement and garage to make sure she had not missed anything.

When it seemed there was nothing left to pack or sort, she walked down the hill past Main Street and slowly followed the St. Croix Riverwalk. The river flowed under the iconic old lift bridge heading south, eventually entering the Gulf of Mexico.

Amelia's small hometown was proclaimed "The Birthplace of Minnesota." French settlers had established fur-trapping and logging operations here and used the St. Croix River to ship products downstream. With no industry to speak of now, Stillwater depended on touristy, eclectic restaurants, and candy and antique shops, as well as river paddleboat cruises. It featured inns and bed and breakfasts in houses once owned by wealthy families whose forebears owned the lumber mills and packet-steamers on the river.

She walked over the bridge and back, watching for bald eagles which had made the river valley a nesting area over the last forty years. She wondered if she missed anything at the house and looked forward to getting back to LA and getting on with life with Jack. She called him and got his voicemail, so she left a message saying that she missed him and would be meeting up with old girlfriends in an hour. She had enough time to stop at the Valley Book Seller shop on Main Street and peruse the packed shelves, eventually selecting two easy reading historical fiction books to read on the flight home.

The brewery was just off the end of the bridge. By 6:15, the sound of laughter and conversation was loud, as fifteen young women enjoyed their impromptu get-together. Amelia recounted the lottery story and discovering that she was a multi-millionaire. She showed pictures of her new house, and justified the wedding delay to her friends. That discussion evolved to the glory days of high school, and they talked of the boys, now men, they knew and girlfriends not present and what had become of them.

Loud laughter filled the air as beer flowed. Amelia noted that each of her friends was currently working. If they had children, they were in daycare or with grandparents. There was a general lament that the world was challenging and put significant pressure on time and family. However, on average her old friends seemed content with their lot in life—like all of their efforts were worth it.

Amelia asked what would make their lives better. She blended the responses she heard into common themes: less work, and that more time with family and friends would make the biggest difference. At the same time, several others talked about the lack of real opportunity and the difficulty of moving ahead in a world that still seemed to be controlled and built by and seemingly for men. One described an idea for a new business she had, but lamented that with three children not yet in school and no money to spare, there was no realistic way to start and fund the small startup.

When they asked Amelia what she was going to do with her newfound wealth, she said she was still working on figuring that out. However, she promised to make a difference in the world, even if it was small, which brought nods and smiles.

It was close to 10 p.m. before the gathering broke up. For all but Amelia, there was work and family in the morning. As they left the bar, her friends gave Amelia hugs and condolences on her grandmother's passing, apologizing for not attending the funeral due to short notice and work constraints. All made promises, likely to be broken, to keep in touch.

Amelia felt emotionally charged and excited, yet drained. Seeing them had brought back so many good memories; however, Amelia realized that she was different now. Without the lottery win, she would likely have been fated to go down the same path—not that it a was terrible path, just different from the path she walked now. With her unlimited future, she was destined never to be like them again. Her good fortune had elevated her to a level where life operated differently. She would never be stressed about tomorrow; she provide care for children and still provide income to the household. Her expectations for her life going forward would certainly sound very foreign to these girls who were once so close to her, of that she was sure.

There was no going back. It was time to make decisions and move on. The only way forward was to proceed with the plans which she was now envisioned more clearly.

As she walked back to Kate's house, she thought back on her time here in Stillwater and how its people and her friends made all the difference in her life. She already missed them, and they had only been out of sight for ten minutes. These were the types of relationships that mattered. She wanted to be close to people she loved, to people who made her smile and laugh; she did not want to be attached to the material things that would tie her down in the long term. She considered how many friends she had in California and realized that almost of her friends were those she'd met through Jack. She determined that she would change that.

She was looking forward to tomorrow being over. She wanted to be home and start her exciting new life.

Back at the Kate's house, she called Jack and told him about her day.

He responded, "Sounds like a good time. See? I would have been in the way. Anyway, I generally took it easy here in LA. I did look at yachts again today. But I mainly missed you, my best friend."

Other than that, he did not have much to add.

She said, "Well, I'm heading out tomorrow. I will be home soon!"

As she hung up, she realized how much she missed him. How lonely she was for him and the warmth of his body next to hers. It seemed like months since they were happy in New York, spending time with each other, talking and enjoying each other's company. With the events that had transpired since, it seemed like there hadn't been any time to settle in and be together.

She was pleased though, to hear that Jack was looking at investments and developing interests in other activities which could give his life meaning. She was less concerned now about him occupying his time with only leisure activities than about his impetuousness and lack of understanding about his investments. She wondered if there was a way to assist and support his endeavors.

YACHTS

As Amelia packed in Minnesota, Jack drove to the marina and asked to speak to the manager. When Randy Whitehand arrived in the sales office, Jack got right to the point. "I'm thinking about adding to your marina's rental fleet," he said. "I was thinking of buying three, maybe four yachts, docking them here at your marina, of course, and then renting them out through your rental management service."

That certainly got the manager's attention.

"So," Jack went on, "what can you tell me about how you manage and price the rentals and what you would sell me the units for, based on that plan?"

The manager got out a sheet of paper and started scribbling out his figures and tapping on the calculator.

Finally, he said, "Okay, here you go. This is the cost of the units and the slips. Here are estimated operating costs per year, what we can charge for rent, and what we charge for our commissions. I also included a cost for insurance. We rent by the day with a captain and a mate, while fuel and cleaning are extra. Additional crew, like a deckhand and perhaps a cook, are provided as needed. If we determine that the renter has enough experience, they can put down a larger deposit, insure it, and captain it themselves."

Jack looked at the numbers, knowing he would have to put together a plan to see if this made sense. He asked, "How many rentals days per year can I expect?"

The manager thought for a while and said, "We could target maybe 150 to 200 days per year. Lots of rentals are by the week. I can't say for sure. You just don't know. We don't track that statistic. It also depends on the weather, the economy, any number of factors. However, there is usually no affordability issue with our clients, as they have oodles of money. It's more about them having the time and the inclination to go out, and the ocean cooperating, as high seas can be a strong deterrent."

They talked for another half hour, with Jack making every effort to glean information that would help him better understand the business.

Jack took the information sheet home and tried to set up a spreadsheet. He quickly realized that he did not know enough about accounting, business modeling, or the business itself, for that matter, to make sense of the information, so he emailed everything to Ben Otto and requested that someone at his firm build it into a business model for review.

That evening, Londyn arrived thirty minutes after Paul Miller, the scriptwriter. Jack and Paul were already on the pool deck, discussing what Paul had written so far. She joined them and occasionally engaged with their discussion to assure she would be well suited to play the role of Amelia.

After Paul left, Londyn and Jack talked for another hour about the ideas for the film. Jack appreciated her insight and thanked her for helping him understand how detailed scripts and dialogue actually had to be to shoot a movie.

By then, dusk had settled over the coast, and stars were out. After pointing out planets and other constellations he knew, he asked, "Are you hungry?

"Only for your lips, baby," she replied.

Jack laughed and said, "You are full of it sometimes. Quite the actress, aren't you? But I love it."

"I'm good at what I do. I work hard every day to become better at my craft," she said. "But I'm not acting now, Jack. I'm enjoying our time together, and you are fun to be with. I think we have a chance at a rewarding relationship. I think you're a great guy who has all the potential in the world. I would love to be part of achieving that potential. We are going to make a great movie and have a good time making it, and I hope someday you see me as more than a good friend."

Jack kissed her and said, "You are good at what you do. I can attest to that. You support me and make me feel positive about myself, and I want to thank you for that. You are very, very special to me."

FUNERAL

Amelia found her disposition surprisingly upbeat for the day of her grandmother's funeral. As she and Henrik had already said their private goodbyes, her grief, it seemed, was left on the beach in Malibu. She also felt happy that she could provide this final celebration to honor Kate, though she was sad about losing her grandmother and wanted to preserve her legacy. The upcoming funeral now seemed more like a formality versus a day of mourning and sorrow.

She put on the black dress she brought from California. The funeral wasn't until late morning, so she drove through Dunn Brothers and got a coffee, then spent an hour driving up and down streets, remembering her youth. Riding bikes, walking with Grandma and Grandpa, playing at the park, going to school, athletic competitions, friends.

As she greeted the line of mourners that day, she saw the pain of loss on their faces, confirmed by their consoling words. The service went smoothly. Following the luncheon and thanking the staff for their service, she returned to the gravesite. Next to Grandpa Gerald's marker, Kate's gravesite was still open. The burial box still rested on a green velvet cloth. The heart lock, still in place, in the clasp in front.

Amelia spoke. "Mom, Dad, I'm doing okay. I have been fortunate and am excited about my life. I'm sorry you aren't here to share that with me. Henrik is doing okay, too. We both love you. Grandpa and Grandma, we love you very much also. We will work to make you proud of us." She stood silent in contemplation for several minutes, deciding something; then she made up her mind.

As she walked away from the gravesite, she said, "Sorry, Grandpa, I know you loved her, but I'm sure she would have wanted it this way. You will just have to share her."

Back at the house, Amelia quickly changed clothes, packed her backpack, and walked through the house one last time, closing the drapes and checking the thermostat. The realtor would manage the property until the house sold.

At the door, she turned and looked back one last time and said, "Goodbye, house. Hope you get a new family that loves you."

Then she went outside, locked the door behind her, and waited on the steps for the Uber driver to take her to the airport.

Amelia had a ticket back to LA, but she decided that she had an important stop to make first. She had to take care of something. As she waited, she sent a text to Jack to update him on her revised plans.

A PLAN

Londyn was gone by the time Jack woke up. He had the day to himself.

After showering, he called Ben Otto, who'd emailed Jack asking for him to call. Ben answered on the second ring. After assuring each other that they were well and doing fine, Ben asked what Jack was looking for regarding his "Rent-A-Yacht" business plan. Jack described his idea: buying a small fleet of yachts and renting them out. Would the program make money?

Ben said, "Well, I'm not going to speculate on what we might find here, but we can model it up on a spreadsheet for you to take a look at and then go over it with you."

"Sounds great," Jack responded. "I'm looking forward to hearing from you soon."

Next, Jack headed to the beach for his morning bike ride in the sand. He was excited about the rental business idea. He also thought that the movie script could be successful and a substantial investment. He was hoped that Amelia would come to see the value in both ideas and invest with him.

Even as he mentally made plans to pitch these ideas to Amelia, his memory went back to Londyn. Last night had been even more enjoyable than the previous nights they had spent together. He genuinely enjoyed spending time with her. She was smart, and funny, and so sexy and beautiful. He was not sure what his long-term intentions were, yet his physical desire was strong.

Amelia would be home in a couple of days, and he knew he would have to decide how to handle both relationships. Right now, he did not know what to do. He felt the weight of his dilemma. He truly enjoyed being with both women. He felt love for each of them. As he was a man of means, he wanted to keep both relationships going until he could understand his true feelings and figure out the best course of action for himself.

As he thought about the movie, it occurred to him that working on the project could provide a cover for seeing Londyn, at least a while. He smiled. Yes, as long as they were careful, that should do the trick. It would work just as long as no one spilled the beans. He couldn't let Amelia find out before he could decide which woman he wanted going forward.

When he got back to the house, Jack called the golf club and made a tee time for that morning. Then he called the airport and scheduled his next pilot's license training session for that afternoon. Londyn planned to come over after her video shoot was complete. It was going to be a Greeeaaaat day!

PERFECT TIMING

Londyn drove away from Jack's house that morning deep in thought. Jack was a nice enough guy; she liked him, and he was fun to be around. He was ungodly rich, reasonably handsome, young, and the sex was good. She did not know Amelia well. The meeting in the green room during *The Jimmy Kimmel Show*! had been brief. Her takeaway was: nice girl, not very worldly, relatively attractive by Midwest standards but not categorized as LA model/actress beautiful.

She was intent on accomplishing two things. One, getting the movie off the ground and making sure she would have a prime role in it, and two, getting herself into Jack's life for the long term. She did not know yet if she loved him. She certainly liked him a great deal. That kind of money could make anyone handsome and loveable. It could be a win-win. While a movie role was an acceptable outcome, ending up with Jack would be hitting her personal lottery jackpot.

She smiled to herself. Things were coming along nicely either way. She thought about how to keep the relationship with Jack going strong once Amelia arrived back home. Londyn knew that it would be tricky and that she would have to be careful, but she was confident that she could pull it off. She believed that Jack would be as interested as she was in keeping up their liaison. But she would have to come across as formal and strictly business when around Amelia. She could be friendly when moving the movie forward, but Londyn knew that they could not become close. She could never be a "social girlfriend."

She arrived at the studio and went into makeup for her role in a music video. It was not the type of role she truly wanted, but bills needed to be paid. While in wardrobe, she slid into a skimpy, tight, slinky outfit that

285

emphasized her breasts. As she looked in the mirror, she concluded that she had intelligence, ability, and skills enough to earn Jack's devotion. She just needed the time.

She decided to wear the outfit to Jack's house that night.

She called Jack after the shoot while driving toward his beach house. "Hey, Jack," she said, "I have a surprise for you."

"Oh?" he said. "What's that?"

"If I told you, then it wouldn't be a surprise, would it now? See you in thirty minutes."

When she got to his and Amalia's house, Jack was on the deck, watching the ocean and drinking his third margarita.

"Hey, Jackie boy," she called out from inside the house, "come on in here." She took his hand as he entered the house, and led him to the couch. She said, "I was in a music video today and snuck out with this costume so I could dance for you. So, sit back and enjoy."

She started the music. The dance was seductive and, in combination with the outfit, emphasized her sexuality. Jack was mesmerized and slightly intoxicated.

When the music stopped, she stopped asked, "Well, what do you think?"

After a moment, Jack got his voice back enough to say, "Wow, that was incredible. I love the way you move. It's so provocative and sexy."

She walked to the couch and sat on his lap. "Maybe we should write a dance like that into the movie script," she said. "It could be followed by a sex scene. Do you want to rehearse the scene right now?"

"Yes, definitely," he said.

Her skimpy costume was off before they got to the bedroom.

In the morning, Jack told Londyn that Amelia would be home the day after tomorrow.

She replied, "So, are you saying that I should not stay over tonight?"

"That might be best," he said. "It will give me a chance to get my strength back up and tidy up the place." Then he told her that he was glad they would get to work on the movie together, but he wanted them to have more of a relationship than just that. He said, "Londyn, I would still like to see you, both on a professional and well, um, an intimate basis. Are you interested?"

Londyn had been prepared for the moment. She knew precisely what to say. She had rehearsed her lines in front of the bathroom mirror more than once.

She said, "Yes, Jack, I want to be with you, too. I'm so happy that you really care about me. You are a wonderful guy. I think that I am in love with you, Jack. I don't want you to ever forget about me."

"Forget you?" he said. "Never. Can we make that plan work? You know, so you and I can spend time together? I really enjoy being with you, too."

She nodded her head and smiled. "That sounds wonderful to me."

"I'm so happy to hear you say that," Jack said. "I am going to miss you until we see each other again, though. I hope that that time is soon."

"I'll miss you more," she said as she bent over and kissed him. "Stay in touch, baby." Then she walked out the door and she got into her car. As she drove away, Pink Floyd's *Money* started playing on Spotify.

Londyn just smiled.

FRIDAY

Amelia awoke, rose, dressed quickly, then ate breakfast in the dining room. She ordered two turkey sandwiches and three cans of Diet Coke to go. She put ice in a plastic bag, added the cans of soda and sandwiches, stuffed them into her backpack, checked out of her room, and headed out. She was excited and looking forward to the day.

When she arrived at the parking lot, there weren't any other cars. She headed out onto the trail and was glad that she remembered enough to walk directly to where she wanted to go. The cairns still stood where she left them. She sat on the bench, popped open a can of soda and sat back, enjoying the still and quiet of early morning.

Then she spoke out loud. "Hey, Great-Grandma Hazel, it's Amelia. I'm back. You don't know me that well, but I wanted to visit with you again. I also brought someone to keep you company."

She opened her backpack and took out the plastic urn. Carefully, she took off the duct tape that sealed it shut. Kneeling on the soft sand, she poured out and then used her hands carefully spread what remained of Kate's ashes, blending them into the sandy soil.

"I hope you aren't upset with me, Grandma Kate," Amelia continued. "But when we were here last, it seemed to me that a part of you wanted to be here. I asked Grandpa to understand. Some of you is back there with him. Maybe someday I or others will join you. Until then, thank you for all you did for Henrik and me. I know we did not thank you enough while you were alive. We were too naïve to understand the burden you took on and the sacrifices you made. I still can't comprehend what it takes to raise a child, although I hope I get the chance one day. Thank you for our trip together and

288

the memories you shared with me. You have inspired me, and I vow as I kneel here, in the presence of you and Hazel, to stand tall and make a difference. I will tell my children about you. I love you now and always will. God Bless."

With that, she rubbed her hands together to knock off the sand, opened the ice bag, and used a couple of ice cubes to wash off the remaining soil. There were no tears, just appreciation and strong determination, and a sense of deep inner peace.

She settled back onto the bench, letting the soft morning sunlight bathe her face. After a few minutes, she picked up her phone. She was surprised and delighted that she had two bars of reception and called Jack to check in.

"Hey," she said. "I'm in Yellowstone! But I plan to be home tomorrow. Can you come to LAX and pick me up?"

He replied, "Sure, just text me the flight info. Did you get it all done?"

"Yes, I did," she said. "I feel very, very good about it all. I know that Kate would feel right at home here. I feel at peace with what I have done. It's a wonderful feeling."

"I'm proud of you," he said. "That was a beautiful and fitting thing to do. So, what are you going to do with the rest of your day?"

"I'm just going to focus on enjoying the beauty and peaceful serenity of this amazing place and keep thinking about what I want to do with my life." She paused, then changed the subject. "Hey, have you made any Italy plans yet?"

He responded, "I've done more online research, but haven't booked anything yet. We can do it when you get back."

Amelia was a little disappointed by his inaction on the Italy trip; it had been his job to plan it, and she'd been completely busy with everything she had to do. "So, what has been occupying your time?" she asked.

Unable to tell her the whole truth, he said, "Enjoying the house and the beach, flying, and golf. I am making progress on the movie script development planning, and—well, I think I picked out a yacht. I'm sure I can build a good business out of owning a fleet of them."

After a pause, Amelia replied, "I'm sure we will talk about all that when I'm back. I will see you at the airport, okay?"

Happy to end the call, he said, "Sure kid, I'll pick you up. Miss you, bye."

Her immediate tasks now complete, Amelia settled back on the bench and closed her eyes, letting the morning sun wash over her face and warm her and the earth on Mrs. Decker's Island. She took a deep breath and exhaled slowly. Cleansed. Okay, she thought. You are done. What is past is past. It is time to move forward.

Vacationing tourists hiking by eyed her; she must have seemed out of place, sitting on the bench relaxing on the little spit of land in the middle of Yellowstone National Park so early in the morning.

A tour group approached. A woman in a Winona State University sweatshirt, carrying a bright orange flag labeled GUIDE in white block letters, conversed with two young women who were explaining that they were taking a break from their medical residencies at Johns Hopkins University, where they were doing research using CRISPER to change the impact of disease and abnormalities by making human DNA changes.

The guide stated that she didn't understand much about what the two were telling her, but that she appreciated their work and passion and wished them success. She said, "I'm a math professor at Winona State University, and I do this volunteer guide work in the summer because I simply love it here in the Park. I do hope you both find treatments to help the world someday."

She raised her orange flag and turned back to pull the group into closer ranks. She pointed toward where Amelia sat and, to Amelia's amazement, told Hazel Decker's story and how she had gained notoriety in this very spot.

Amelia could only smile to herself, thinking that this had to be more than a coincidence. It was providence. What were the odds? Though she guessed that they were probably more than winning a $685 million lottery, she took it as a sign she was making the right choices and that her ancestors, now passed, were blessing her new direction.

Leaving her sacred spot on Mrs. Decker's island, she hiked the surrounding trails for almost two hours, enjoying the bubbling pots' beauty and the shouts of children pointing at the oddities of nature. These shouts were often quickly followed by sharp words of warning from worried parents, telling their offspring to be careful.

Amelia's focus was introspective. She was soon so lost in her thoughts that other hikers' voices were tuned entirely out. She stopped walking and stared into a bubbling brown mud pot. The ideas that had been percolating in her brain the past several weeks finally congealed into a solid plan.

She returned to Mrs. Decker's Island and was pleased that no one had bothered her little campsite. She had made a decision. It was time to carry it out.

She was excited about her plans. Now, having made her final farewell to Hazel and Kate, Amelia promised that she would not return to this place until she had accomplished her goals.

Amelia made her way back to the Grand Canyon of the Yellowstone for a final look at the majestic falls. After watching and listening to its magnificent thundering, it was time to hit the road again for the two-hour return trip back to the hotel in Bozeman, Montana, for an overnight rest and then an early morning flight to LA. After checking into the hotel, she left a message with Jack confirming her flight information. She called Ben Otto to ask questions. Later she called the admissions office at UCLA to enter the Anderson School of Management MBA program.

THE BOYS

Jack spent the morning going carefully from room to room to ensure there was no evidence of Londyn left in the house and was pleased with his thoroughness when he found a silver barrette, she dropped on the master bathroom floor. He buried the barrette deep in the garbage, never to be found. Then he cleaned out the refrigerator, made a shopping list, and sent it to the new grocery delivery service that he'd discovered.

Ben Otto called later that morning and said that his assistant had worked up a business model for Jack's review. He said it was in an Excel workbook and asked if Jack knew how to work with one. Jack said he did, even though he knew that his skills were rudimentary at best. Ben told him to look it over and get back to him. At his convenience, they could go through the model and look for results. Jack now wished that they had taught Excel and databases in high school instead of calculus or trigonometry, both of which he knew he would never use in real life.

Jack went for a run on the beach. After he returned, he swam in the pool to cool down, rinsed off in the outdoor shower, then headed into the kitchen for lunch. He noted that the food delivery service had arrived and put the food away. He looked at the spreadsheet, and although he thought he understood how to make changes and look at "what if" scenarios, he didn't want to screw it up or make a mistake.

He thought of Bill. He knew that Bill understood the program.

Jack sent him a text: "Dinner tonight, my place? Need a bit of your help."

Bill responded: "What time"

Jack texted back: "6:30" and got thumbs-up emoji in response.

Having several hours to kill before Bill arrived, Jack got in a quick round of golf at the club. He ran into Leland and Ralph, and they asked about progress on his film project. He told them he was making headway and that it was looking better every day. Leland's reaction was one of open skepticism. "Yeah, well, kid, you got to keep your chin up when it gets smacked. There are always a couple of bumps in the road."

Jack made it home just before Bill arrived, half an hour early.

Bill said, "Hey buddy! I was done working and figured I'd rather spend that extra half-hour here at the beach with you, versus sitting in the office waiting to leave."

"Hey, no problem," said Jack. "You're always welcome here! What can I get you to drink?"

"I'd love a beer. You got a cold one?"

Jack popped the tops off a couple of Harps and handed one to Bill. "Hey, before we go outside, do you know much about spreadsheets?"

"Yeah, I'm competent."

They went into the study, and Bill looked over the workbook Ben Otto had sent. After a few minutes, Bill said, "Hmmm. It would take a while for me to really understand how everything they're doing here is flowing back and forth. They've set it up showing the number of units, meaning yachts, as a variable input. It is set up with three. Then the other key variable is the number of days each unit is rented. The operational expenses and revenue revolve around those numbers. Then that data pours over into the profit and loss and cash flow tab. So, let's see. If you enter 200 days per year rented at the rental rate set, you can break even. Below that, you lose money, and above that, you profit. To get a good return on your investment, it looks like you need to be renting at least 250 days per year. I wonder if that's realistic."

As Bill moved about within the spreadsheet, Jack watched closely. Soon, he felt that he had seen enough to manipulate the data. Bill suggested that he save the original and create a couple of copies to answer "what if" questions. Jack nodded and said, "Great, thanks, buddy. Let's hit the beach. I have a pizza coming."

They walked and talked while drinking their second beers. Jack described the movie that he and Londyn were creating. Bill inquired, "Who is advising you on the project?"

"Londyn is getting that all lined up."

Bill swallowed a response related to his lack of faith in that approach and instead changed the subject, asking, "So, you and Londyn...what's going on there?"

Jack replied, "Oh, I like her. She's quite a girl. Smart and sexy all in one package. We flirt with each other all the time. But it's all in good fun. There's nothing serious going on."

Bill looked at him, and Jack looked away. "Look, she's just a good friend who is helping me out, and I'm sure she expects a part in the film."

"More likely, she is trying to help you out of your money, too," said Bill.

"No, no," said Jack. "We're going to make a movie. I have a partial script back at the house. In fact, you are in it! Well, not you personally, of course, but your character has a big role as we tell the story of Jack, Amelia, and the winning ticket. The writer has done an excellent job with the banter back and forth between our characters. The dialogue is pretty funny. You'll look good, I promise."

"I better, Jack," Bill said. Then he continued, "Listen, Londyn is one of those girls who, once she sets her sights on something, is very tenacious. I know that she can focus her efforts on attaining what she wants. She will get her claws in you. She has built her career with hard work and effort while playing the game hard by 'Hollywood Rules.' She is very sharp, nobody's fool. I know she's beautiful, but you have to be very careful with her."

Jack just nodded and said, "Nothing going on there, man, I swear. Nothing."

They turned around, headed back to the house for a pepperoni and sausage pizza, and talked of other things.

AMELIA AND JACK

Jack waited by the car at the curb when Amelia exited the terminal. He took her backpack and tossed it into the trunk of the Audi. They hugged each other tightly and then kissed hello.

Amelia felt a wave of relief to be back in her home environment. She sat with her head back in the Audi's reclined passenger seat and closed her eyes. The lottery win, a long road trip, Kate's passing, and then the last several days with Kate's funeral and handling her affairs had come at her like a continuous tidal wave of emotion and challenges that swept all other issues in her life in front of it as it came ashore. Now the tide had receded, and what was left was her life and future. She was ready to relax and gather her energy and then get on with Amelia's life, *Part Deux*, now that so many obstacles were behind her. She took a deep breath, held it, and then exhaled slowly. She looked forward to finally enjoying an afternoon at her new house in the sun with no responsibilities.

Upon arriving home, she asked if she could quickly shower and clean up before they had lunch. Jack nodded. With his best French accent, he said, "Of course, mademoiselle, lunch is served in thirty minutes. What would mademoiselle like to drink?"

She thought for just a moment then said, "An icy cold beer, please."

"Oui, bien, mademoiselle," he replied and went to the kitchen to make preparations.

Amelia had washed her hair and was simply enjoying the hard stream of hot water when Jack joined her in the shower. He certainly proved that he missed her. Amelia reciprocated, proving that she missed him too.

After lunch, they sat on the pool deck and took in the sun. After an hour and a half, she felt recharged and fully ready to take on her life.

She asked, "So, what is all of this about a boat and a movie?"

Jack described his idea about leasing yachts and said that he had a financial model built and was just beginning to evaluate the concept.

He said, "I know that other outfits are doing this, so it must be viable at some level. I need to learn more. I have work to do on that one. And I'm still working on that movie. The script is right here." He picked it up from the patio end table and handed it to her. "It's basically our story, babe. The writer wants to interview you and get your insights. It's a great story. The more I think about it, the more I like it. Do you remember Londyn Bridges? We met her on the Kimmel show. You know—Bill's friend? Well, anyway, it was her idea. She went through Bill to contact me, and I invested in a writer to provide a silver screen script. I thought that we could finance it, or at least invest in it, and make some money. Hollywood, here comes the Lemkes! Prepare a star on the Walk of Fame!"

Amelia paged through the script. "Do you really think people would be interested in our story?" she said.

"Yeah, I think they would. It is partly fiction, so the writer will add other storylines to make it exciting and maybe twist up the plot, but yeah, I do. You know—a real American, feel-good, happy-ending story."

"Well, if it's what you want, I am willing to talk to the writer for you."

"Great," Jack said, "I'll let him know right away. He's a sharp guy, really talented. You'll like him. So, what's on your mind now that you've been back home for, what, all of three whole hours?"

Amelia exhaled slowly, then sat up and said, "Jack, I did a lot of thinking while I was gone. I have decided to go back to school to get an MBA. I called yesterday, and admissions already told me I will be admitted. They didn't even ask for my transcript. I talked to Bob Smith and Ben Otto about it yesterday, and I have a feeling one of them might have made a call and greased the skids for me. I'm also thinking that the school figures my attendance will benefit them in the long run, like by getting a donation for a new building wing or a computer lab. Anyway, bottom line, with the kind of wealth we have, I want to be able to make educated investment and money decisions."

"Hmmm. Don't you think that our advisors can guide us on our investments and business activities?"

Amelia responded, "Sure, yes, I depend on it, but I don't want to feel like a fool, helpless and reliant on others. I want to understand the ins and outs of any business ventures we might take on, like your rental business concept or movie production. I want to understand the risks and rewards and what financial statements mean. I don't want to be solely dependent on any advisor. I don't want anyone to ever take advantage of us, either. I know that there are people out there who will try. I want to use my money to make a difference in this world, and I have other ideas on that, but I'm not yet quite ready to share them. I have a lot more to learn."

Jack considered what she'd said. "If you're going to school, won't you be gone a lot? How are we going to travel and enjoy our good fortune?"

"I can take many classes online. I can be done in a year, but I can also take more time than that, so maybe up to two years. That being said, I don't even have to finish the coursework to get what I want out of it. I plan on finishing, but I don't feel compelled to graduate. I am not necessarily looking for a degree, and even if I end up getting it, I'm not looking for the degree to get me a job like other students are. I am looking for education, knowledge, and skills. I want to be competent in business matters. Even if I were to skip some classes and never actually graduate, I'm still getting where I need to go. Make sense?"

"Yeah, I understand," said Jack. "The more I think about it, the more I like the idea. We have to know what we are doing, or as you said, we will likely get taken advantage of at some point by someone."

Jack thought that if Amelia was tied up doing schoolwork, he'd have free time to do other things.

Changing the subject, Jack said, "Well, every one of my sisters and brothers has called and hinted that they would like to see some money. Some were very blunt, saying if they had won that much money, they would have already given me a check for at least a million dollars. They say that's virtually nothing compared to what we've won. They tell me to think of my nieces and nephews and what that money could do for them. They don't understand the impact of taxes and that we are getting paid out over thirty years and don't have a huge pot of money to disperse right now."

Jack sighed. "I tried to tell my brother Ed how things work, and he's a smart enough guy, but he proposed that I borrow to make the payouts. That turned me off. I can see doing something for them. But geez, come on. Then there is my mom. The woman who doesn't even try to get your name right, Amelia. Ed said the money I sent her has already been spent. I'm guessing what I sent to her has already been shot into her arm or squandered on alcohol. Uncle Howard has been calling daily. I finally blocked his number, and he went and got another phone. He has some great real estate deals for me, and evidently, they are so good that the world will end if I dare to pass them up. He did mention a house on a lake in northern Wisconsin near where I went to summer camp once as a kid. That might be a nice place to go in the summer with our kids someday."

"Anyway, I talked to my attorney about how I might handle this, and bottom line, what do you think of this idea? I'd set up a 529 college saving plan account for each niece and nephew and put $60,000 in each account. Knowing my brother Ken, he will have more kids just to get the cash into his control. Crazy and frustrating at the same time, for sure. What do you think?"

Amelia looked at him and said, "First, I think it is absolutely your call. It's your money. That said, I love the idea of funding education. It is a win-win in my book and truly benefits others in the long term, compared to, let's say, buying a fancy car for the same price. You just described how windfalls of money get squandered as people don't know how to manage it, so your plan makes long-term sense to me. I think that if we don't make our money work to accomplish something positive, that at some point we'll feel like we've just indulgently squandered it selfishly on ourselves."

She continued, "I also think that beyond education and instead of gifts to our families, we should look to support larger organizations and initiatives. Kind of like Bill and Melinda Gates, but of course not on their scale. Maybe we should do some research on that."

"Yeah, maybe. I like that," said Jack. He certainly did not want to spend any more time worrying about his family. "Oh, one more thing. The script-writer would like to meet with you as soon as possible. I know you just got back, but would you be willing to meet with him tonight? He's anxious to complete the script so he can get paid."

Amelia considered the request. She felt that the relaxing afternoon ahead would give her the time to rejuvenate. "Tell me again what he will be looking for?"

Jack replied, "The main story is about us. What do two young people do when they hit the lottery? He wants to know how you felt and what you did and thought. I told him that he has a license to embellish to add drama and humor."

"Yeah, okay, sure," she said. "Let's do it."

"Great," he said.

FLESH OUT THE SCRIPT

Amelia and Paul Miller met at the beach house that evening to go over the script. She told him about the events of the day they learned that they were winners and the timeline of what transpired afterward. She described her thoughts, actions, and feelings in the moments after the ticket was confirmed. She also told him of her childhood, losing her parents, the road trip with Kate, and finally Kate's passing. She even related some of the family stories which Kate had told her.

All the while, Paul eagerly took notes and nodded his head as he saw how he could weave these events into his script. As he listened, he gained insights into Amelia's transformation. From her comments, he perceived how she had personally grown over the past weeks. So much had happened in her life. He realized that winning the lottery had changed her life, and she was preparing herself to use the windfall as a means of benefiting others' lives. She was determined to do something other than play on the beach and shop. He did not see the same maturation in Jack.

After three hours, Amelia was talked out and ready to call it a night. She agreed that Paul could contact her in the following days with questions, and he told her that she could send a note or give him a call if she had any other thoughts. They shook hands as he headed out the front door.

Jack had wandered in and out of the discussion area and heard much of what Amelia told Paul. He thought that her plans to "help others" would fade in time. They would travel, spend their money, and have children, and this do-gooder talk would fade as rapidly as it came. Then he thought about the script, which led to thinking about Londyn and wondering what she was doing tonight.

"You know," Jack said to Amelia, "the more I hear, the more I think this is going to be a great script. I can't wait to see what he writes into the story."

NEXT MORNING

The next morning, Jack asked Amelia if she was interested in investing in his yacht rental fleet. Amelia asked to see his model. He opened the spreadsheet on the computer, and she sat down and looked at it. She asked if he could please not hover over her shoulder, so he left to walk the beach.

Amelia spent some time with the workbook. As she had taken a spreadsheet class in high school, she felt that she had a good idea about what the model results were telling her. However, she was not comfortable enough to make a big decision with what she saw without outside help, so she called Ben Otto, who summarized the results. The main thing she gathered was that the yachts would need to be rented out at least 250 days a year for the venture to turn a reasonable profit. Before she hung up, she thanked Ben for his time and told him that she had been accepted into the UCLA MBA program. For some reason, he was not surprised.

When Jack returned, she said, "Hey, Captain Jack, let's go down to the marina. I'd like to talk with the marina rental agent and see the yachts you have in mind."

Jack was excited to have her involved. He wanted them to be a team committed to the same projects and investments both emotionally and financially. It was what real partners did.

Upon arrival, they walked out on the docks, and Jack showed Amelia the yacht model he'd selected. They boarded the unit that was for sale, and Jack showed her around.

"This is very nice," she said. "You're right that it would be fun to be out on one of these from time to time."

"That's what I'm thinking," Jack said. "Let's go talk to Randy."

After introductions and some chit-chat in Randy's office, Jack and Amelia started asking questions about the boat. Jack said, "Randy, I think the bottom line for us is, how many days per year are these units typically rented out?"

Randy said, "Well, I think we touched on this before. We don't keep records as to the specifics, and there are variables to consider, like size of unit, weather, and the economy. I think I told you that 150 to 200 days a year was my best guess."

Amelia was surprised. She was also immediately suspicious. Why wouldn't they have accurate data when this was what they did for a good part of their business? Also, at those rental levels, this investment would never work. Why was Jack looking at this investment?

"The numbers I quoted," Randy continued, "could be higher than that, but I get very uneasy putting out numbers and then having people like yourselves depending on them for investments. I don't want to be responsible for that. The yacht rental business is risky, and the players in it are usually very well off."

"I understand," Jack said. "But for all, you know, the real number could be 225 or 250 days, right? You don't think that, let's say, 300 days a year would be realistic?"

Randy leaned back in his chair and said, "I do not think that 300 days is realistic at all, but I suppose 250 days or so is possible, in an outstanding year. I just don't have the data."

As they continued talking about the boat business, Amelia realized that it was far more complicated than renting out a pontoon fishing boat at the Coeur D'Alene marina.

Eventually the conversation wound down, and the couple thanked Randy and departed the office.

Jack was excited. "Aren't those yachts beautiful?" he asked.

Amelia nodded her head and said, "Yes, they are, but they are so expensive."

"Yeah," said Jack. "But if we get the rentals, then someone else is paying for them, and on occasion, when they're not rented, we can use them ourselves."

"That would be nice," she said. "We will have to look at that spreadsheet model in more detail."

Upon arriving home, Jack went straight to the den. He pulled up the spreadsheet, put in 250 days of rental, and looked at the results. He called out to Amelia, and when she joined him, he pointed at the spreadsheet cells showing the profit dollars and percentages, saying, "See, this is an excellent investment!"

She reached past his shoulder and entered 200 days into the program: the profit immediately went to zero.

Jack said, "Yeah, I know, but I think Randy is just protecting himself, and the real number is more like 250 days."

"I just think this is pretty risky," Amelia said. "These yachts you're looking at are close to $4 million each, so with three of them, you're talking $12 million on a risky investment."

"Well, yeah, but we would get to use them, too. And think of the people we would meet! The yachting set! It would be so much fun."

"That's all true, but we could also be the customer and rent them only when we need to go out. I don't even know how often that would be."

"I want to do it," said Jack. "You will have to decide whether you want to be included or not."

"I'll think about it, Jack. I'll let you know," she said.

Amelia thought for a while, then called Ben Otto to review what she knew about the yacht fleet investment along with the recent information she heard from Randy.

Ben brought up the model on his computer as they spoke and said, "Using the numbers you gave me, this is not something I would advise as a good investment for either of you. Also, why risk starting with three units instead of going one at a time? It's your call, of course. However, I would advise both of you to stay far away from it. There are better investments out there."

"That's where I was, too," she said. "I think that Jack might still be thinking that he wants to proceed, though."

"Well," said Ben, "I will try my best to convince him otherwise when we next talk."

Amelia remained at the computer. She remembered that first meeting with Ben Otto, when he'd suggested that she and Jack check out the fates of prior lottery winners. She thought about Jack's yacht business plan and his intention to get into the movie game.

She was curious to find information about how other lottery winners had fared. After searching and compiling a wealth of information, she printed it out and took it to show Jack, who she found in the kitchen making sandwiches for lunch.

She set the sheaf of papers down on the counter and said, "Hey, remember when Ben Otto suggested that we check out the fates of other lottery winners?" Jack nodded. "Well, I spent some time researching, and I know that not everything on the internet is necessarily true, but I printed these quotes verbatim just now. I think that it will provide us some insight."

She started to read:

"'According to CNBC, lottery winners are more likely to go bankrupt within three to five years than the average American. Studies found that instead of getting people out of financial trouble, winning the lottery got people into more trouble. The lowest income earners buy fifty percent of lottery tickets. When these types of people win, they often have no idea how to handle money, and don't know that money can make money just by existing. So, after a couple of years of spending extravagantly, loaning money to friends and family that will never pay it back, and poor investments, they find themselves right back where they started.'"

Amelia continued: "And other studies have found that winning the lottery generally didn't help financially distressed people escape their troubles. Instead, it only postponed the inevitable bankruptcy. One study I came across found that a third of lottery winners go bankrupt. It's the curse of the lottery. It made their lives worse instead of improving them."

She put the papers down. "My point in doing this, Jack, is to look for insights and learn from others who may have been in our situation. Ben Otto was right. We must have guidance and professional support. We did spend some money on cars and a house—granted, more money than we would have spent if we hadn't won—but still, those are things we would have invested in at some point anyway. We did the right things so far; we have advisors, and they will watch out for us. We should look carefully at any investments—I guess you more than me right now—and we should not do crazy things. That's a big reason why I'm going back to school, which I think is a step quite counter to the norm of most of the stories I just read."

Jack responded, "Exactly. I agree. We are doing the right things. We have the accounting and legal team in place. We aren't spending money foolishly. I have a great business plan for my yacht business, and I'm sure that the movie will succeed. And now, with you in school to learn the finer points, we are in great shape for years to come."

Amelia considered what he just said. She instinctively nodded her head as she thought about it, but she was actually bewildered. Jack's idea to invest in a yacht fleet and produce a movie sounded a lot more in line with the stories she had just read than he seemed capable of seeing, much less admitting. How could he not see this?

She did not wish to argue with him. He was strong-willed, and she coud tell that he genuinely believed in what he was doing. She hoped that he would eventually get good advice on the risky investments he was contemplating and back off. On the other hand, it was his money, and even though a failure would impact their relationship, she would wish him well and support her husband to be.

Amelia let Jack know that, at this time, she was not interested in the yacht investment and that Ben Otto would like to talk with Jack regarding it. But she said that she would love to rent a yacht some weekend with friends and have a party cruise.

Jack was very disappointed. He was convinced that the investment was a good one, and besides that, he was insulted that Amelia did not believe in his skills as an entrepreneur. He said, "I mean, I guess we could rent one, but I know my plan is going to prove to be a great investment. You are going to miss out. I wish you could see the value in the plan. It's so obvious, can't you see it?"

"Sorry, Jack, it just isn't what I want to do with my money. Again, I would be happy to rent one for a weekend. Heck, I'll even pay for it. It would be fun. But I just don't see investing in a yacht rental venture. If you want to, go for it."

"It seems that you don't trust my judgment."

"Jack, you are investing millions of dollars that could be invested in any number of ventures. What are the returns for the amount of risk being taken?

I just don't think that this one is the best for me. Again, I love you and wish you well. You will make a fine and handsome captain."

Jack felt betrayed and disappointed. He knew that he could make this work. It was evident that Amelia did not believe in his business skills.

Later, Ben Otto called Jack and asked if he had any questions for which he could be of assistance as to the yacht rental venture.

Jack said, "I've thought about it, and I think that I can make it work."

Ben replied, "I would strongly advise you against that, Jack. The lack of information about past performance by the marina rental staff makes this a precarious investment. I am stunned that they don't have good data on this. That's a huge red flag for me. I'm confident that there are better investments out there that could provide better returns with less risk."

But Jack was cocky and sure of his business acumen. "I think that I'll take that chance," he said. He was imagining himself associating with jet-setters; he desperately wanted to be included in that group. "So, what I am asking for now is that you look at my income flow and figure out how to best finance this venture. I want to buy three yachts."

"Jack, are you sure?"

Jack was confident that he had a gift for business. "Yes. Positively. Let's get it done. Call me when you have it put together." Then Jack hung up.

He found Amelia in the kitchen, cleaning up. "I'm going to do it," he said. "It's going to be a great investment."

Amelia replied, "Jack, I would agree with you but then we would both be wrong. However, that said, good luck."

MOVIE SCRIPT

Several days later, Paul Miller and Londyn Bridges were due to stop over to go over the movie script.

Jack was nervous, filled with trepidation about having Londyn and Amelia together in the same space. He begged Londyn not to give Amelia any reason to be suspicious of their relationship. Jack was concerned that his or Londyn's words might slip, or that his attraction to Londyn would be transparent and Amelia would see right through him. Londyn assured him that he had no reason to worry. She said, "I got this, no worries. I like what we have going and am not going to risk it." Londyn understood what she had at stake—both Jack and the movie.

After Londyn and Paul arrived, Jack made it a point to generally avoid direct eye contact with Londyn. Her skills as an actress became more apparent to him as she was calmly ingratiated herself to Amelia by asking for a house tour. She complimented the house and praised Amelia for her excellent decorating skills while knowing full well that the house had come fully furnished. She provided no clue to the fact that she had ever been in the place before. In the master bedroom, Londyn ran her hand over the smooth cover spread on the oversized California king-size bed, winked at Amelia, and said, "Oh, what a great bedroom—you're able to listen to the ocean waves at night. I bet you two have some fun in here."

Amelia, caught off guard, stammered, "Yeah, thanks, yes, it is a great room. I'm glad you like it."

"I do indeed, and maybe someday I will be able to stay in a place with a bedroom just like this or even own something like it." Outside of Amelia's line of vision, Jack shot Londyn an angry look. Londyn's face did not change a bit as she continued, saying, "And what a nice walk-in closet."

In the kitchen, Londyn noticed the yacht brochure on the counter. She said, "Oh, I like yachts. They are so much fun. Are you two going to rent one, maybe have a party?"

"No," said Amelia, "Jack is thinking about buying several for others to rent."

"Well, that sounds nice. Sounds like a smart plan. Jack is such a great guy. You two are so fortunate. Oh, my goodness, I didn't notice your engagement ring at first—why, it's huge! Where did you pick it up?"

"New York, when we were out there for a TV show."

"Oh, of course, you mentioned that on the Kimmel show. Oh, and Jack mentioned to me that you just lost your grandmother. I'm so sorry. Were you close?"

"Thank you. We were at the end. I'm going to miss her very much."

"Certainly. Again, my condolences."

They finished the interior tour and walked out onto the pool deck. Londyn said to Amelia, "Oh, this is glorious. What a great view, and it's a perfect place for skinny dipping, not that I ever have, of course."

Hearing that comment, Jack quickly wheeled around and headed back into the house, worried that he was about to explode at Londyn for what she was doing. Why did she insist on playing these games? Damn it, why was she taking these risks? It might be funny to her, but it certainly wasn't to him. It was just like that morning when Bill was on the phone. This isn't a game, he thought. It's my life; please stop screwing around. On the other hand, part of him found it was kind of exciting to have her pull off innocent innuendos, causing him to remember their times in the bedroom and skinny dipping in the pool.

After coming back outside, and when no one else was looking, he quickly drew his finger across his throat as a signal to Londyn to stop her shenanigans. Londyn gave him a slight nod, smiled, and turned away.

The four of them settled in chairs under the oversized umbrella, and Jack made sure to sit opposite Londyn to keep his distance and avoid any possible physical contact.

Paul took the scripts out of his bag, saying, "I provided the main script and two endings. One ending is printed on pink paper, and one is printed on blue paper. Both would make a good story. The pink one is what I would call the happily-ever-after version. It's the path I'm sure you two are on," he said, smiling at Jack and Amelia. "It's where you two lovebirds spend the rest of your lives together: do philanthropic work, raise a family, and enjoy a wonderful life. The blue one depicts a nasty split-up where your lives take much different trajectories. In this version, one of you does very well; the other has several slips and hiccups and has a much more difficult life. I had to pick one of you, so I decided that Jack's character would slip. Please pardon the choice, Jack. No offense intended."

"None taken," said Jack. He was being careful not to spend much time looking in Londyn's direction.

"Why did you pick the guy to be the screwup?" asked Amelia. "It seems that either one could run amok. We live in an equal opportunity world."

Paul replied, "I took a quick inaccurate and informal poll amongst some other writers that I trusted, and they all said that it has to be the guy. We are dealing with forty thousand years of human history of men philandering and being narcissistic, and some things in human nature just don't change much. It has to be the guy."

Amelia smiled and nodded. She was happy that the real Jack was devoted to her, but she understood and agreed that having a more antagonistic ending would probably make a better story.

Paul continued, "I've never done this type of ending before, but I suggest that you keep both endings in place if you try to market this script, even to the point of shooting both endings. Then you can let the test screening feedback tell you which way to go. Also, and I know that this technique has been used before on soap opera-type TV shows, you could show one ending and then show that it was actually a dream sequence of one of the main characters from which they wake up and then are relieved that the nightmare is not true, and continue with the alternative ending. I don't know how well the audience would receive that approach in a feature film. But who knows? I suggest that you read the work and let me know if there's anything you might want to change. Remember, this work is 'based on a true story,' but I've taken creative license to make it more humorous and dramatic. I love the story about how the ticket was purchased and what you guys did immediately afterward, the road trip stories about Amelia's family history and how it impacted her life, and the reality of Kate's passing. We might have to spice it up in terms of sex, nudity, or language to get the R-rating that sells well at the box office. But I think you have a solid story that is as good or even better than many picked up recently by studios."

There was a lull in the conversation, and Amelia asked Londyn, "What do you think?"

Londyn had not put on any makeup that day and had her hair pulled back into a ponytail. She wore non-corrective glasses, a loose-fitting Cal Berkley sweatshirt, and baggy pants in an effective effort to make herself look somewhat dowdy and plain for the meeting. She responded, "I agree one hundred percent. I'm excited about this project. I can work with Bill and others to help connect you with producers and people in the industry to give the project some wheels and momentum. We'll need someone who can do film budgeting. Typically, this is done by a unit production manager, a line producer, or an accountant. Once the production and marketing costs are established, you can look for financing. You would likely look for a studio or private investors. I even think that you two might get involved in that respect. That's none of my business, of course."

She continued, "I also know that product placement advertising is putting more and more money into films these days. These can significantly defray production costs, because with online streaming movies being so prevalent today, advertisers see that placements are a great way to get their products in front of consumers at a low cost per viewer over a long period of time."

Paul chimed in, "Yeah, with this story, we could look to car companies, fast food outlets, beer…any number of things could be easily written in."

Amelia thought about the risk and cost of such an undertaking and said, "What does a film like this cost?"

Londyn answered, "The average cost of a film is $70 million to $90 million. Just a warning, most films lose money. Maybe eighty percent of them don't get their money back. Maybe seven hundred films get made each year, and only two hundred get a decent release, and not all of those earn money. However, the whole industry is changing with the demand for online content. I'm not saying that to scare you all off. I'm just providing facts in an area where I have some level of experience. That said, since the career life span of an actresses in Hollywood is very short, I've been paying close attention and learning as I work so that someday I can be on the other side of the camera, either directing or producing. I believe that this particular film could be made for less than average costs. It will not need elaborate sets or a huge cast, or a big music score. I'm not sure that it even requires known stars in the leading roles. We can use B-level talent, or look for up-and-coming new faces and pay them to scale. You could also use this house as a set and write off some of the cost that way. If you bought the yachts you are thinking about and used those for a scene, you could even put some of that into the budget. Any beach shots are relatively inexpensive, as you could use your beach; talk show sets are already in place, and networks would probably like the publicity of being in a film."

She bent forward and made eye contact with Jack and Amelia, "Most importantly, guys, I agree with Paul that it is a good story. It's a human-interest story, a Hollywood love story. Plus, the audience already knows some of it, as you were on talk shows and in the papers. Heck, you are even on the side of the city busses. That is free publicity in advance if the movie can get shot soon. People will want to know how it will all turn out. It is a winner."

Paul nodded his head and concurred.

Then Londyn excused herself to visit the restroom. Amelia said, "It is just off the main room to the right."

"Thanks, I know exactly where it is." Then realizing that this might be misunderstood as previous knowledge of the house, she called out, "I remember from the tour!"

Amelia did not seem to catch the gaffe, and Jack breathed a sigh of relief.

When Londyn returned, Jack poured drinks, and they all made a toast to success as they continued discussing the project. They talked about production costs and the potential for each ending, and laughed about other ideas well into the night.

As Paul and Londyn left, they all exchanged hugs. Jack was impressed with how Londyn made the hug between them stiff and short-lived, holding him at greater than normal distance, as if she did not want to get too close to any guy. He smiled inside thinking this gal is sharp and can play any role.

After Londyn and Paul left, Jack and Amelia took a late-night, moonlight stroll down the beach. "So, what do you think?" he asked.

"It is more exciting than I previously thought," she replied. "Paul seems to be a talented writer, and I want to read the script closely tomorrow. I don't know if anyone out there is still interested in our story. However, since we got on a couple of TV shows and the side of the buses and I have even seen some posters, there must be some human interest and notoriety remaining. I have to say that even though I really appreciate Londyn stepping in and helping us, I'm not quite certain as to what her role is in this. But she certainly is a smart girl and so nice and energetic, and I'm sure she can help us develop the project with her knowledge of the business. I was a bit surprised, though—in the green room she was so glamourous, and tonight she kind of looked, well, I don't know…frumpy."

Jack replied, "Well, I guess movie stars are just normal people too. I'm pretty sure that she's angling for a role in the movie, maybe playing you as the female lead. She is Bill's friend, so she felt comfortable coming to us with the whole idea. I'm guessing she might see this as a role that could take her out of the B-movie queen genre she told Bill she was stuck in." He took Amelia's hand and said, "Yes, it's exciting."

Jack was already looking forward to the project, not least of all because he knew it would allow him to spend more time with Londyn. He was glad the night was over and happy with the outcome. He made a mental note to keep Amelia and Londyn as far apart as possible in the future.

SURPRISE VISITORS

Several days later, the gate buzzer sounded. Jack asked Amelia if she was expecting anyone. She shook her head no. Thinking that it might be a friend, or perhaps a neighbor dropping by to welcome them belatedly, Jack hit the intercom button and asked who was there.

The voice on the other end of the intercom said, "It's your mother, Jack— Alice. I brought your brother Ed with me!"

Jack was stunned and groaned. Amelia's eyes opened wide.

"Oh no. What do I do?" he asked.

"Well, you have to let them in, Jack. They know you are here."

"Damn, this is a nightmare." Jack continued to get calls from his mother and relatives. Someone must have also given out his number to people he didn't know who kept calling with "investment ideas." But he was certainly did not expect this pair of visitors.

He pushed the gate button to let them in, and he and Amelia greeted Alice and Ed at the front door. His mother pushed into the house and hugged him, saying, "Jackie, my favorite child, I'm so glad I get to see you" Then, stepping back and looking at Amelia, whom she had never met in person before, she said, "And this must be the beautiful Emily. How are you, my dear?"

"Mom, her name is Amelia. I keep telling you that."

"Oh sure, that's right. I'm just an old lady who can't remember much."

Jack introduced Amelia to his mother and brother, but he did not want them to come inside. He cringed inside when Amelia graciously invited her future mother-in-law into the house while offering refreshment. Both asked for a beer. Jack gave them a tour and finished on the back deck looking at the ocean.

Alice proclaimed that the house was beautiful and asked how much it had cost. Jack told her that they loved it too, and ignored the question about its price.

"So, what brings you two out to California?" Jack asked. "It's kind of a surprise to see you here. We did not get any notice that you were coming."

Alice responded, "Well, Jack, the family met and decided that your brother and I should come out and have a talk with you about what we call 'family responsibility.'"

Amelia and Jack exchanged knowing glances. They both knew what was coming next. Jack said, "Why don't we go inside and talk?"

Once inside, Alice started, "As I said, we want to talk about your responsibility to your family. You have had wonderful good luck, and we back home have all agreed that you should help your family. It's just the right thing to do. We know that if we'd won money, we would have shared it with you. So, we are here to get checks to take home with us."

Jack's anger rose quickly; he struggled to control his emotions. "Mom, I have told you before that I am not giving you any more money. I have already given you two checks, and I suspect you did not use the money properly. Ed, you do not understand that the money is paid out over time, and they take taxes out, and half of it is Amelia's, not mine. The money we have has either already been spent or is committed to investments. Regardless of what the family decided, I'm not giving you a goddamn penny at this time. Amelia knows that I have been working on setting up 529 education plans for the nieces and nephews, but nothing for the adults. And Mom, you have blown through more money in the past two months than you usually get as income over a whole year. Where did it go?"

Alice did not respond, but Ed jumped in and said, "Jack, you should know better than to give her money; she has a drug habit." Alice looked down at the floor and would not meet Jack's gaze. "You should give the money to me," Ed continued, "and I will dole it out for her benefit when it is needed for a legitimate expense."

"The problem with that, Ed," Jack said, "is that I don't trust you either. Sorry, that's the truth. Tell you what I am going to do. If you two leave right now and never darken my door again, I will continue with my plan to fund 529 education plans for the nieces and nephews. Ed, that means all three of your kids have a guaranteed college education. If you two are still on my property in sixty seconds, you can tell those kids that you were the ones that screwed them out of a free ride to school. Your call."

Alice looked at Ed and said, "Would he do that?"

"I don't know, Mom. Everyone back home is going to be really disappointed if we flew all the way out here and aren't bringing home the money they expected."

"I did not invite you. Forty-five seconds," said Jack.

Ed saw the anger in Jack's eyes. He had seen that look when they fought growing up and knew that Jack was serious. Ed also believed that Jack would fund his children's education, for which he had not put away any money. Besides, he did not want to be responsible for meting out cash to Alice, if Jack even gave him any. Damn, coming out here to confront Jack was a stupid idea and a waste of time and money. How had he let his mother talk him into it?

"Thirty seconds," said Jack.

"Come on, Mom," said Ed as he pulled her to her feet. "This is not going to work."

"But I want my money," said Alice, stamping her foot for emphasis. "All rich people take care of their moms. You read about it all the time. Dammit, I'm entitled."

"Let's go, Mom," Ed said.

"Maybe Emily will give us some money, son."

Amelia shook her head no.

"Fifteen seconds."

Pulling Alice firmly through the door which Amelia had opened to assist in their departure, Ed exited the house. Looking back at Jack, who stood in a defiant posture with his feet apart and hands crossed, blocking the doorway, Ed said, "You better come through with that college funding."

"I will if you never come back or call me for money again. Time's up."

Amelia pulled him away from the door then, closed and locked it. "I'm sorry you had to deal with that, Jack. I can't believe that they showed up here."

"I can't either."

"I admired the way you stood up to them."

"Thanks, Emily," he said with a smile. "I hope this is the end of it. But I know my mom will be back at it soon, and I probably will give her more. But for now, let's not think of it."

PINK OR BLUE

Over the next several months, Amelia faced increasing demands on her time as she took on the MBA curriculum. She was happy that Jack had found something gainful to do with his time; the film project was gaining traction as Jack had financed a production budget put together by a producer Londyn knew.

Occasionally, Londyn and Jack met at the beach house to go over the project. Those meetings were all business. Amelia sat in on several to keep apprised of the project's advancement. However, most of his and Londyn's sessions were held away from the house—according to Jack—at the office of someone who could help move the project forward. Unbeknownst to Amelia, they were usually at Londyn's apartment; the project was not always the primary focus of attention.

Fortunately for Londyn, she was savvy. She understood how business was done in Hollywood and could help keep the project moving forward. They were close to being ready to pitch to studios. Londyn reinforced Jack's confidence with her own.

Jack found that he was increasingly attracted to Londyn and more conflicted about his relationship with Amelia. Both women appealed to him in different ways. Amelia was the girl you wanted to introduce to your parents, but Londyn was the one you wanted to spend the night. Other women might have been suspicious of the amount of time he spent with Londyn, but Amelia was naïve to the signs which may have been apparent to others and trusted Londyn and Jack. She never dreamed that Jack could betray and be unfaithful to her.

ITALY

After a long day working on the movie project, Jack arrived home in a good mood. Besides working on several online classes, Amelia had prepared a large salad for dinner. They sat, ate, and related their activities.

Jack said, "Well, I did it."

"Did what?"

"Booked our Italy trip."

Amelia jumped up and gave him a hug, saying, "Tell me more!"

He brought out a file folder and showed her the trip vouchers he'd printed out. "We'll fly from here to New York, then to Rome. Three days in Rome and three in Naples, then north to Florence, Sienna, and then Cinque Terra. Then an overnight train to Paris for two days, then a direct flight home. We leave in just under two months. Now, just in the interest of full disclosure, I bought fully refundable and reschedulable tickets and hotel bookings, so if the movie project or your school schedule gets in the way, we can move the dates around indefinitely. The important thing is that I booked it, paid for it, and we can go when it works for our schedules. Just pick the dates."

"I'm stoked," said Amelia. "I'm going to get to see Michelangelo's *David* and his *Pieta*, and then there is the Duomo…Thanks, Jack, for taking care of this."

"No problem, Meels," he said. "I'm excited, too."

YACHT DAY

Jack and Amelia scheduled the maiden voyage on his first of three new yachts for the next weekend. Aptly named *Lucky Ticket,* the boat was now his. Jack hired a captain and crew so he could enjoy himself. He also stayed sober so that he could learn more about how to operate the big boat. To share their good fortune, they invited a number of couples to come along, including Bill and Kim. The event was catered, and the bar had plenty of activity on a sunny, hot Saturday afternoon. There was no destination, so Jack had the captain stop running their course parallel with the shoreline, about a half-mile, out so that Jack could lower his wave runners to allow attendees the thrill of zipping over the water.

Several paddleboarders between the ship and shore slowly made their leisurely ways down the beach on the smooth ocean surface. While Jack and Bill were on the jet skis doing donuts on the smooth water surface. The girls talked of Kim's work, Amelia's new lifestyle, and her upcoming classes.

The whining of a drone caught everyone's attention. As it came into sight, it was evident that the drone was being controlled by someone aboard a 25-foot runabout that closely tracked the drone's progress. It was moving toward them. At one point, the drone buzzed them, coming in over Jack and Bill's heads where they sitting simply floating on their machines, talking and laughing. It continued toward the paddleboarders and then suddenly wheeled back and dipped and hovered near a young girl on a paddleboard.

Suddenly the runabout surged forward, honking its horn. The boy with the drone controls in his hand sat in the bow of the boat and started screaming, "Shark, shark!" pointing at the water near the drone. Bill and Jack saw the grey dorsal fin of a large shark cut through the water very close to the girl's paddleboard. It slowly turned back, bumped her board, then moved slowly away. The girl dropped to her knees to keep her balance and called for help.

Jack immediately throttled forward accelerating toward the girl. The shark, curious if the paddleboard represented food, slowly circled back. Picking up speed, the shark approached the board bumping it firmly as it swam by. The girl lost her balance and partially fell off the board. She thrashed and kicked her legs in the water desperately pulling with her arms to get back on the board. Jack approached fast, slid off his wave runner, grabbed the girl by the waist, and threw her up and forward onto the safety of his machine. As the shark turned back again, Bill drove his wave runner on a path between it and Jack. The big fish turned away for several seconds to avoid Bill's speeding machine, then turned its attention back toward its new potential prey, Jack's thrashing legs. Bill's maneuver gave Jack just enough time to pull back up onto his machine. The shark passed them and rammed the paddle board hard, lifting it clear of the water and flipping it over. Finally, its curiosity satisfied, but hunger not, the shark swam down the shoreline. The runabout tracked it, calling out warnings to those at risk.

Bill maneuvered over to the paddleboard and grabbed its tow line, while Jack and the girl collected the paddle. Jack asked if she wanted a ride to shore or wanted to paddle back. Shaking and obviously very scared, she whispered, "Shore." Jack and Bill delivered her and the paddleboard to the beach, where the girl's father, who had seen the encounter, met her with open arms. It wasn't until after Jack and Bill were headed back toward the yacht, that they looked to thank their rescuers. Upon arriving back at *Lucky Ticket* they were met by the applause and admiring shouts of admiration and congratulation from all of those onboard the vessel.

As Jack came aboard, Amelia ran and jumped into his arms, and they held each other close. "That was so brave, Jack. You risked your life for someone else. Most people would not have that courage," she said. "I'm so proud of you." She kissed him and held him tightly. "I was so scared for you. I never want to lose you! I need you. Don't ever take a chance like that again."

Jack was rattled. "I don't even know why I did it. I just reacted. I was thinking about that girl and how scared she must be. And then she fell in—she was panicked and needed help. You could see it in her face. I just had to act. I'm not a hero. I was just trying to do the right thing and help her. It was scary, man, really scary. Once I was in the water and got her up on the machine, I realized that I was now the one with legs hanging down, and I saw the shark turn back toward me. If Bill hadn't distracted it while I got back up, I don't know what I would have done. That thing was big, and it swam right past us. It was Bill's quick thinking that saved me. The last thing I want do is to become a snack for a shark. Bill, did you see what kind it was?"

"It looked like a hammerhead to me," said Bill, who was as cool, calm, and collected as he had been throughout the whole ordeal. Having grown up surfing in the area, he had been near and encountered sharks and knew that actual attacks along that coastline were relatively rare. "They've been following their food into warmer waters for the last several years. However, that was a little too close for comfort. It had to be at least ten feet long. Buddy, I've got to hand it to you—that was pretty heroic. I'm impressed. I take back some of the things I said about you!"

Jack laughed gave Bill's shoulder a playful push.

Amelia asked, "So what did they say to you onshore?"

Jack replied, "Nothing. The poor girl was still shaking like a leaf, and I think that her father was so happy to hold his daughter that nothing else mattered right then. I never thought much about what it might be like to have a child, but I couldn't imagine losing one that way."

Kim took the opportunity to give Bill a big hug and a kiss to tell him she was happy he was safe and that his quick thinking had saved Jack. Bill felt awkward and responded somewhat stiffly; he did not want to show affection to Kim in front of Amelia.

The two couples stood at the deck railing and looked toward the beach. The girls were impressed with their men. Jack and Bill slowly came down from their adrenaline highs.

Amelia remembered a story that Kate had told her about sharks. When she was eleven years old, her family had gone to Florida to enjoy spring break and visit Beth's father, Arbor, where he wintered with his second wife at Riviera Beach. They had also witnessed a shark encounter.

"Hey guys, I just remembered something; listen to this," she said, "when I was with Kate, she told me this story about sharks."

"Tell us," said Bill, hoping that Kim would stop clinging to him.

"One day, they were at a beach in Florida and people started shouting and piling out of the water, exactly like what we just saw. Three sharks were swimming up the beach in shallow water. People who knew later said they were a hammerhead and two lemon sharks. Anyway, there was a guy, maybe in his late teens, out on the water, sitting on a blow-up float raft with his legs hanging down. He was either out too far to get to shore or didn't hear the warnings. As the sharks came near him, one of the sharks bit his leg and pulled him into the water, and there was some thrashing and splashing. Then a group of brave people went charging out from shore to help him. The sharks swam off, continuing up the beach. The people pulled him out of the surf, and someone called for an ambulance. The young man had bite marks on his legs that were bleeding profusely and he was in great pain, but fortunately, the sharks did not take out any large chunks of flesh."

"Kim said, "Oh my God, that is so terrible. So what happened?

"Well, people helped slow the bleeding, and an ambulance arrived shortly after to take him to the hospital. Kate said after that, she was always afraid of sharks. Then, when *Jaws* came out, that sealed the deal for her, and she was quite happy to live in a landlocked state. Anyway, here is the amazing coincidence part of the story. My great-grandfather was on that very same beach maybe ten years later. I don't know why he was there, but he struck up a conversation with a young man sitting on the beach, and mentioned that he'd witnessed a shark attack on that very beach. He described it to some extent. The young man looked at him knowingly, nodded his head, and said, 'Yeah, I know all about it. I was here that day too.' Then he paused and continued, 'Because that person was me.' He showed his scars, and they talked about the attack and how the young man had recovered and still came to the beach now and again to spend time in the surf with his children. Now you tell me what the odds are of that meeting and conversation. Pretty incredible, huh? What are the odds? It's kind of like hitting the lottery. I suppose every family has these types of stories. It just seems like the ones Grandma Kate told me were on the 'That's pretty incredible' side. However, I don't think that compares to what you guys just did. That was incredible too. I'm so happy you guys are safe."

Amelia took Jack's hand and said, "That's enough fun and games in the water, Captain. Let's spend some time with your adoring fans."

They mingled with their friends, who were pleased to shake Jack's hand and slap his back. Amelia was proud of her brave fiancé. Jack said, "Maybe I'll name my next yacht, 'Just Missed!'"

Kim kept her arms around Bill's waist since he'd reboarded. She was not going to let him go. After Amelia and Jack disappeared, she whispered in his ear that heroes usually get rewarded and that she knew just how to do that. They ducked into one of the staterooms and locked the door.

As they drove home that evening, Amelia said, "Jack, I almost lost you today. I am still reliving seeing that fin go right past your jet ski a second after you got up on it. You could be dead right now."

"Yeah, it was close. But it didn't happen. Got to admit, though, I was scared until I got back on that machine and headed toward shore."

"Well, it got me thinking—maybe we should get married. I realize that that is more important to me than I thought. I want us to get old together and have a family. Why wait any longer? I'm thinking that we can fly to Vegas and get married and then do a party later. Almost losing you made me see what is important, and I want us always to have each other. We could do it tomorrow. What do you think?"

Jack was immediately panic-stricken. He was not ready to make that commitment; he had genuinely strong feelings for both Amelia and Londyn. He was struggling to come up with an answer that would buy him time, for he knew he could not say no. Then he thought of the trip to Italy. After almost too long a silence, he said, "That sounds nice, but wouldn't getting married in Italy be more romantic? I've got the tickets booked. We just have to schedule it in with the movie project and your schoolwork."

"Well, that would be nice too. I guess it would be a better story to tell our friends and children. Yeah, a wedding at an Italian villa or on a cliffside overlooking the sea. Or maybe in Florence. That would be very nice, too. Okay, let's try to schedule that. Soon."

Jack said, "You got it. I'll look into options. It will be Greeeaaaat." He reached over and squeezed her hand reassuringly. Inside his head, though, an alarm clanged loudly. Amelia had unwittingly closed the window of opportunity for his decision. He knew that her schoolwork was flexible enough that it would not present an obstacle. He quickly concluded he would have to find a way to make the movie production allow him to string along both women long enough to suit his needs. In any event, a decision would be in the offing.

The next day there was a small article in the paper about the shark attack. No names were mentioned, just the heroic deeds of unknown men on wave runners.

PILLOW TALK

Kim was still fascinated with Bill. They had continued to date occasionally since they first met on the volleyball court. They were in a relationship that could best be defined as "friends with benefits." On this particular evening, both had enjoyed marijuana gummies, several glasses of wine, and physical pleasure. Lying in bed, feeling relaxed from chemicals and lovemaking, their pillow talk turned to Jack and Amelia.

Kim asked if Bill had heard any more about the movie script. He said he had read it, and that although he was not an expert, he found it entertaining. He thought it was good enough to be a hit movie.

Bill was also involved in trying to put the production financing together while maneuvering several of his clients into position to perform in the film. He knew that as an unknown, first-time producer, Jack would eventually have to borrow against his lottery income to finance the production himself. No one wanted to trust a first-time producer in this town. It also appeared that Londyn was going to end up with the part of the female lead.

Kim said, "It seems like Londyn has put herself in a good position."

Bill had promised Jack that he would never tell Amelia about his suspicions about Jack and Londyn's relationship. However, now he suddenly had an idea. If he were to imply this information to Kim, he could be relatively confident that it would get to Amelia in due course.

As if he was absentmindedly musing, Bill said, "Yeah, Londyn has set herself up well. Not only a part in a movie, but maybe ending up with the producer, too."

Kim missed the meaning initially. Then she said, "Wait. The producer? Hey, I thought you said that Jack was going to be the producer?" She sat up in bed and turned toward Bill. "Are you saying that Jack and Londyn are sleeping together?"

Bill said, "Um, well, what? I don't know anything for sure. I was just speculating based on the fact pattern. Hey, just forget that I said anything. Please?" He turned toward her, pushed her down on the bed, and kissed her to silence her next question. They made love again then faded into a deep slumber.

When he awoke, he smelled bacon and eggs coming from the kitchen. He quickly showered and went into the room. Kim served him and then sat down. She told him, as she always did, that she'd enjoyed last night and that they should spend more time together. He nodded, confirming that he enjoyed it without committing to anything more.

She said, "Say, Bill, last night you said something, and I just want to make sure I understood. Did you say that Londyn and Jack are sleeping together?"

"Did I?" he replied, "Kim, I was pretty stoned last night. What did I say?"

"You said that Londyn might end up with the movie's producer."

He was silent as he thought about how to answer. "Look, Kim, I don't know anything for certain. It seems that they spend a lot of time together on the project, and it just seems to me like they are pretty friendly. Besides, I know how Londyn's mind works. She can be aggressive and tenacious when she is going after something she wants. But this is between you and me, okay? No further, right? Someone could get badly hurt."

Kim nodded. But Bill knew full well that Kim would eventually find a way to warn her friend. Feeling uncomfortable with the situation he had created, yet pleased that he had, he gulped down his food and said, "Hey beautiful, I'm late, I gotta run. This has been fun. Thanks."

"Bye. Call me," said Kim, knowing full well that she would have to call him.

After Bill left, she felt the unbearable weight of possibly knowing something of real importance to her closest friend. She could damage her relationship with Bill due to her betrayal of his confidence. And between Amelia and Jack, she faced a double-edged sword: if the accusation was false, she could damage her relationship with her best friend and her significant other. If true, she would destroy Jack and Amelia's relationship. She was not even confident that this was any of her business.

KIM'S VISIT

Kim could not stand it anymore. For three days, she wrestled with her conscience. She finally decided she could not stand by and let Jack and Londyn's deceit hurt her best friend. She simply had to let Amelia know. So she called Amelia and asked if she was available for a walk, and they agreed to meet up at Amelia's place later that afternoon.

When Kim arrived, she casually asked, "Is Jack home?"

Amelia said, "No, he's with Londyn and the writer, working on the script to get it ready for a second production costing. I'll grab my sandals, and we can head out to the beach."

Kim looked at her and burst into tears.

Amelia was surprised and asked, "What's wrong?"

"I'm so sorry," said Kim, "I thought I could be an adult about this. Let's go sit down on the couch."

Kim collected herself and said, "Meels, I don't quite know how to say this, so I'll just say it. Bill and I were together the other night, and he accidentally let it slip that he thought that Jack and Londyn might be having an affair. There. I said it."

Amelia was stunned. She felt like her world had collapsed and gone black. Her heart squeezed in her chest. She could barely breathe.

Then she rejected the possibility. "Why...why...why would Bill think that?" she asked.

Kim replied, "This is so hard. He said that he was putting facts together, and I guess, you know, two plus two equals four. He wouldn't talk more about it, and I promised him that I wouldn't say anything to either of you, but I just could not sit idly by and not say anything."

Amelia was silent, her head spinning. She was devasted just to think it could be true. Then she said, "So you don't know for sure? I thought Londyn was only in this movie for the part."

"I can only tell you what I heard. I truly hope I'm wrong."

Amelia said, "Kim, I need to be alone right now. I need time to digest this and figure it out. I know that you're only doing what you think is right and protecting me. I love you for that."

Amelia stood and opened her arms for a hug, which Kim stood to receive. "You are my best friend. Thank you again. Can you find your way out?"

As Kim left, Amelia covered her head with her hands and burst into tears.

After a time, she laid down on the couch, deep in thought. She was horrified to think that Jack would be unfaithful to her. She was crushed to consider that she might not be able to trust him. Trust was everything to her. Was it possible that the man to whom she had dedicated her love for the last two and a half years and whom she had intended to marry had betrayed her and was being unfaithful? They weren't yet married, but that did not matter. They had promised to be faithful and loyal to each other.

Was it true? In some ways, it made sense: Jack was gone a lot, and the meetings on the movie project were seldom at their house. He had lately been preoccupied and distant in some ways, yet he was also attentive to her needs, kind and loving. The more she thought about it, the more she was in denial. She thought Kim had to be wrong. But she had to confirm the truth. She knew what she had to do.

When Bill saw Amelia's name on his phone screen, he knew what the question would be even before she spoke.

"Hello, Amelia," he said. "How are you?"

"I'm not very good," she replied. "Can you come over?"

He immediately said, "Sure, anything I can bring?"

"No, I just need to talk. The gate and front door will be open."

When Bill arrived, he knocked on the door as he entered, saying, "Hello?"

She walked over to meet him, they exchanged hugs, and she said, "I think you know why I called you."

They sat on the couch.

He started the conversation. "First of all, I think the world of you, Amelia, and I would do anything to keep you from being hurt." He took a deep breath and continued. "This is so hard. Jack is my closest and best friend. Please don't hate me for this, but well, I will just say it. I'm pretty sure that Jack and Londyn are having an affair. There. I said it. I've been holding that in for far too long. It's probably been going on for a long time, at least since you went on your road trip with your grandma, I think. I never wanted to be a rat. But I'm also sorry. I should have said something sooner."

Amelia was silent, then said, "Are you sure?"

Bill looked away and said, "I think so. I've suspected for a long time. When you were gone, I called here early one morning, and I think I woke them both up. Londyn said hi to me in the background. They said that they were working on the movie and had fallen asleep. But I thought it might have been a one-night thing. Then, last week, after a meeting with a potential investor, Londyn told me flat out that it was true. She told me that she and Jack are in love. She wants to marry him, Amelia. I don't know why she would lie to me. I'm so sorry. I just had to tell you. I had to protect you because I care about you."

Amelia burst into tears. Bill moved closer and put his arm around her, holding her while she sobbed. He cherished the feeling of holding her, knowing he was helping her grieve and knowing that there now would be a good chance that Jack would likely no longer be in her life.

When her crying stopped, he said, "I'm so sorry, but I am glad that you know what I know. Is there anything I can do?"

She shook her head, "No, but thanks for telling me. Would you please be so kind as to leave me alone now? I need to digest all of this."

Bill nodded, gave her another hug, kissed her forehead, and said, "I'm so sorry. I'm here if you need someone to talk to."

He left quietly and drove away, muttering, "Jack deserves what's coming to him. What a fool."

PREPARING TO DEAL WITH LOST TRUST

Amelia spent the next day thinking about how she would deal with Jack and doing schoolwork. She focused on avoiding her natural fight or flight response and trying to reason out her next steps. She agonizingly considered several options: first, allow Jack to stay with a promise never to see Londyn again. Second, seek a conversation to understand his position better and take a time out in their relationship until they could sort out their feelings. Or third, terminate the relationship.

A year ago, she knew that she would have let him come back. But today she was a different woman. She had means. The road trip had challenged her to think more about being strong, capable, and independent. She had a legacy to uphold. She felt that she was growing quickly in that respect. Her expanding life knowledge and academic education were preparing her to take the path best suited. She was being tested. Was she ready?

Later afternoon, she contacted Bob Smith to ask for advice. He told her that his thoughts went to the legal protection of her interests in the house and her financial assets should she split from Jack.

Her conversations with Jack that day were cordial but short. For Jack, it was business as usual. He golfed in the morning and said he had meetings related to the movie project that afternoon. He had assumed that Amelia was simply swamped with schoolwork, and her focus on that effort freed him up to do other things. Amelia now interpreted the phrase "movie project" as code for time with Londyn.

She intentionally fell asleep on the couch that night surrounded by her textbooks and notes. Jack did not interrupt her slumber.

When she got off the couch the next morning, Jack said that he was going golfing with Ralph and Leland. He enjoyed their company, as they were interesting guys, and he was also picking up film production tips, but they cheated badly during games. Later he was meeting with a group about investing in high-end gym/workout facilities, which they promised should make an excellent investment. It was a guaranteed profit maker. He commented that it looked like a great opportunity, upsides all the way. He kissed her cheek and said, "See you later, have a nice day," and left. She cringed wiped the kiss off.

As his Audi pulled out of the garage, she realized that he'd probably lied about some of his planned activities and that she simply did not trust him anymore. More importantly, she probably never would.

At that moment, she made her decision.

CONFRONTATION

When Jack arrived home from his long day out, Amelia was sitting on the deck, a textbook in hand. He popped open a beer and came out to sit down beside her.

He asked, "How was your day?"

"Terrible," she replied. She looked directly at him and said, "Jack, tell me the truth. Are you screwing Londyn?"

Jack was stunned. His face turned ashen.

He finally said, "What? No, no, of course not. We are just working on the project. Why would you say that?"

"So, you are trying to tell me that you've never had sex with her? Ever? Not while I was on the road trip with Grandma and not over the last several months?"

Jack was silent. His heart raced. Then he asked, "Why are you accusing me of this?"

She looked him in the eye and said with conviction and a calm, hard force in her voice, "Just answer the damn question, honestly."

Jack asked again, "Why are you accusing me of this? This is crazy."

She responded, "Jack, you are a liar. Londyn told Bill about you and her. He wouldn't lie about that. You owe me the truth."

Jack put his head down, angry at his friend for ratting him out but knowing he was guilty. He did not know yet how much Amelia knew. What else had Bill told her? Had she noticed some comment or telling glance when Londyn was over? Jack did not want his world to change. He enjoyed having the option of both women, but now he was tangled in his own web, and the outcome was out of his control.

Finally, he said, "We did sleep together, but only once or twice, and it didn't mean anything. I was lonely while you were gone. I was tempted. We aren't married, and it was a harmless little fling."

"But you kept it up once I was back?" she shot back.

Jack put his hands on his head and started to cry, dropping to his knees on the concrete pool deck. "I'm sorry, so sorry, I love you, Amelia. Oh, God, I didn't mean to hurt you. She doesn't mean anything to me. I made a big mistake."

Amelia looked at him and angrily said, "She told Bill that you two were in love and she was planning on getting married."

Amelia stood up and pointed toward the front door. She said, "You need to leave now. We are so done. Your freshness date has expired, you slimy bastard. We had everything, the perfect life in front of us, and you couldn't keep your zipper up. Now I can never trust you again. Go, get what you need from your closet, get the hell out of this house and my life, and go be with her. I'll find another place to live. I will be out in thirty days. I'll sell my portion of the house to you if you want it, or we can sell it. I don't care. I won't stay in a house where you cheated on me with her and who knows who else. You betrayed me, Jack. You betrayed your friends, too. Who does that? I—hell, we—deserved so much better. Just get the hell out!"

Jack stuffed some personal items and clothes into a suitcase, then stormed out of the house, slamming the front door. The sound of peeling tires signaled his angry departure.

As he drove off, he tried to calm himself. He had to control his speed and temper as he sorted out what had just happened and what he should do next. He called Londyn and told her that he was staying the night and would explain later. First, he had a stop to make.

SMACKDOWN

Arriving at Bill's place, Jack knocked on the door. When Bill opened it, Jack told him that he had a surprise in the car for him. Bill followed him outside and was only just able to duck to avoid Jack's first punch, which was aimed at his face. The second punch caught him in the chest, but Bill grabbed Jack's arm and pulled him into a clinch, then used his weight and size to take them both to the ground. They wrestled, rolling over each other down an incline and threw punches, none of which did any damage.

Bill was finally able say, "What are you doing?"

"You ratted me out!"

"I never told her anything!"

"Liar!"

"No, but you deserve what you've got coming!"

"It doesn't concern you."

Bill pushed away from the smaller-framed Jack. Both were exhausted and panting, unable to continue. Bill said, "Yes, it does. Because I love her too!"

"What?"

"Yeah, but I never told her and I never told you. I held back. I respected your relationship. But now it's different. You don't deserve her. You don't deserve to walk on the same ground that she does. You're just slime."

Jack burst out, saying, "I thought you were my friend."

"I was. Your best friend. Someone who helped you and always had your back."

"You promised me that you would never say anything about Londyn."

"I kept that promise. I did not tell Amelia. But I did confirm the truth when she asked me. This is on you, not me. Now get your cheating ass the hell out of here before I call the cops and have them charge you with assault."

Jack said, "Don't you ever speak to me again." He flipped him the finger as he limped towards his Audi.

"Done. No problem there," said Bill.

SCORN

After Jack left, Amelia sat down on the couch and cried. She was crushed to know that Jack had betrayed her. She felt miserable and defeated. She felt alone in the world. The instant wealth had destroyed her vision of where her life was going. Her future was dark now and uncertain.

She felt anger rising in her body. How dare he do this? How could he live a double life and cheat on her with that woman? How could she have missed the signs? Then she started to recall some things that Londyn had said and done in her house. Amelia now understood how she'd known her way around. She remembered Londyn touching *her bed,* no doubt laughing silently at naïve Amelia and remembering the nights she and Jack had spent there. Amelia was sickened by the thought of Londyn in that bed with Jack. She was sure that Londyn had been mocking her with many things she'd said that night. Amelia's anger at Jack was now doubled by her distaste for Londyn.

She jumped to her feet and stomped to the bedroom. She tore off the bedspread and sheets and stuffed them in the garbage bin. She gathered all of the spare sheets and towels and added them to the container. She tossed the mattress off the box spring. She would never lie on that bed again.

She exhausted and vindicated by her actions. She laid on the couch and cried herself to sleep, angry, betrayed, frustrated, and lost.

LOST CONTROL

Londyn was alarmed by Jack's appearance when he arrived at her apartment dirty and bruised. "What happened to you?" she asked.

Jack went to the freezer, pulled out the bottle of vodka, and poured himself a glass.

"She knows. She kicked me out. I think Bill told her, otherwise I don't know how she found out. Bill and I had a little rumble. I messed him up pretty good, the bastard."

Jack was angry that someone had ratted him out. He had lost control of his freedom of choice. He sat on the couch taking gulps of his drink and talking to himself. At this time, not being able to have Amelia made him want her back. Who he decided to be with should have been his call, not hers. How could he get back into Amelia's life and control his destiny?

Londyn knew that this was a pivotal moment in their relationship and that her best course of action was to say nothing, just listen and let him be angry and vent. She wanted Jack to set the path forward.

Jack sat with his head in his hands and was lost in thought when Londyn said, "Jack, I have an early morning shoot tomorrow. Why don't you sleep in the bedroom, and I'll sleep out here on the couch so I won't wake you in the morning?"

Without bothering to answer, Jack took the vodka into the bedroom, closed the door, and thinking of Amelia, drank himself to sleep.

JACK'S MORNING AFTER

When Jack awoke to a splitting headache, Londyn was already gone. Jack's memory of the previous night returned, and he moaned. He decided that if he could just get an opportunity to talk to Amelia, he could gauge her disposition and maybe talk his way out of this mess. Yeah, he could do that. He was still unsure if he wanted to marry her or stay with Londyn, but he wanted to have that choice. If she truly loved him, surely she would give him another chance.

He dialed. Her phone went right to voicemail. He left a message saying in a pleasant, sincere voice, that he loved her and he was truly sorry and wanted to talk. He assured her that they had too great a relationship to throw it all away.

He tried Facetime: no answer.

He sent a text: no answer.

He sent flowers and dictated a message to be written in the card asking for forgiveness and a chance to talk.

He waited to hear back.

Several hours later, he received the last text Amelia would ever send to him. It read, *"Never contact me again, ever."*

He was sad and felt guilty due to the loss of their relationship. They were so close to being married. Then the lottery and a chance to live any life they wished —and now all of this chaos. He realized that his situation was a result of his actions, but he rationalized that if Amelia hadn't taken the road trip, all would likely have ended up differently. Kate might not have died due to the stress of the journey. Amelia would have been around. They would have been having fun, and Londyn would not have seduced him. So, in a way, Amelia had brought it on herself. Her absence made him vulnerable and lonely. He did not ask her to go. Undoubtedly, she shared some of the blame in this.

Londyn texted him, asking how he was doing. He responded that he was sad but okay and that he missed her.

When she arrived home, she did everything that she could think of to distract him. She knew that if he was focused on other things, Amelia could continue to fade from his life from that time forward. Keeping his focus on his businesses and her sensuality would be just the ticket.

AMELIA'S MORNING AFTER

Amelia woke early and sat up on the couch. Then the memory of last night's developments crashed down on her.

But she was not going to let Jack dictate or destroy the rest of her life. She took a deep breath and said, "Okay, this is the first day of your new life. Are you going to mope or be proactive?"

She put on her running outfit and ran on the beach for an hour. When she returned, she showered in the guest bathroom and dressed.

She phoned the housekeeping service and requested an emergency deep house cleaning. Then she put in a call to Henrik and explained that she and Jack had broken up and she just wanted him to know. She promised to give him details at a later date.

Kim answered her phone and commiserated with Amelia. Amelia said that Kim knew the story, so there was not that much to tell except that she and Jack had split. Kim asked if there was any chance that Amelia might take Jack back. Amelia, trying to add a bit of levity to the conversation, said that that was as likely as the Minnesota Vikings winning a Super Bowl. Kim asked if there was anything she could do. Amelia asked only that she let Bill know.

Next, Amelia contacted Ben Otto. She explained that she and Jack were parting ways and that their finances were to remain totally separate. Ben said he'd never mixed their finances before and certainly would not now. He told her if there was anything he could do for her, just ask, and that he was there for her if she needed assistance.

Finally, she rang Bob Smith and informed him of her decision. She asked him to handle her future contacts with Jack in terms of the house or legal issues. She said that she did not want to speak to Jack personally ever again. Bob understood.

Her phone rang: it was Jack. She declined the call and did not listen to the voicemail. She also ignored the Facetime call and the text.

She grabbed her purse and keys, left the house, and took a long drive up the Pacific Coast Highway. She stopped for lunch at a burger place, and while eating, realized that she simply had to get away from LA for a while. She didn't have many friends here, and when the news got out to them that she and Jack had split, Jack would likely be the one getting sympathy and attention, as they were mostly his friends. He would spin the story and they would believe him. She thought of where she might like to go as she drove back to the house. Before she went anywhere, though, she needed to find her own place in LA right away and leave the beach house behind.

When she arrived home, a florist delivery truck was just turning around to leave. She thanked the driver and promptly tossed the flowers next to the overflowing garbage bin without venturing a glance at the enclosed card.

Inside, she called Ms. Harris, the real estate agent, and told her that she and Jack were parting ways and she would be looking for another place. Maybe someplace quieter, more remote, not on the beach. Ms. Harris promised to look into it.

As she sat at the kitchen counter, still considering where she could go to get away, she noticed Jack's folder on the countertop—the one marked "Italy". She opened it and looked at the vouchers. She thought, Thanks, Jack, I deserve this as a reward for you being unfaithful.

She texted Jack and told him never to contact her again.

She changed the dates but used the vouchers and flew to Italy the next day.

FLORENCE ENCOUNTER

Amelia waited in line for an hour to get tickets to the Uffizi to see Michelangelo's statue of David in the Accademia Gallery. The tall, white marble statue was beautifully flawless. She sat and admired it, memorizing its shape and form. Then she explored the Piazza Della Signoria, casually walked the Ponte del Vecchio over and back several times, enjoying its old-world charm.

She found a small café for an early lunch, sat under an umbrella, and enjoyed a salad, a small pizza, and a glass of wine. She kept up with her MBA courses online while she enjoyed her Italian itinerary. She took out her laptop and asked the proprietress and owner, Sofia for the café's wireless password. It turned out that Sofia, owned the restaurant and spoke English. After finishing her meal, Amelia ordered a glass of wine and worked on an assignment. As she was the only patron at that time, Sofia was curious and paid close attention to Amelia.

Eventually, Sofia asked if she needed more wine. Amelia shook her head no. "I won't be long. I just have a little bit more to do on this assignment."

Sofia asked what the class was, and Amelia told her it was an accounting class and that she was working on her MBA. Sofia was interested and asked what Amelia intended to do with her degree. She said she had spent ten years in the United States as a child before her parents moved the family back to Florence. That accounted for her excellent English. Amelia responded that she wanted to work with finance and to support women-owned businesses at some point.

Sofia cocked her head and said, "That is interesting. I am involved with a group of women who pool their investment money and make equity capital contributions to finance start-up businesses for local women who have good

347

business plans and have what it takes to succeed. I don't do any business analysis because a lot of that is over my head, although I am learning. I am an investor, yes, but I also research the person. I talk to neighbors, friends, and relatives to get a sense of who the person really is. You can tell a lot by what people think about a person. When we have the information, we decide whether to invest or not and how much ownership we get, or whether we simply offer a loan. I've seen United States TV shows where a panel of rich people invest in business ideas pitched by the owners. We kind of do a similar small-scale local thing for women. So far, we have invested in six businesses and five are doing very well. We have gotten most of our money back. One still needs to do better, but I am hopeful."

"Wow, that is cool. How many women are in your group?"

"About thirty. They come from a variety of backgrounds, and they are all really smart, dedicated, and work hard. It's invigorating to be around them."

"I hope that I could do something like that someday. I want to make a difference with my life and am looking for avenues to do so."

Sofia thought and then said, "How long are you in Florence?"

"Another two days."

"Would you like to meet some of the women and talk with them?"

"Would I? Oh, yes, absolutely."

"Come back tomorrow at the same time, and I will see what I can do."

"Deal." Amelia rose, shook Sofia's hand, and left. She spent the rest of the day wandering the old city and thinking about what Sofia had said.

The next day Amelia met with five women and, with Sofia translating, understood the process and concepts behind the women's group. They were excited by the success that they had experienced. Amelia was impressed by their energy and determination. By the time Amelia left the meeting, she knew exactly what she wanted to do with her money. She just needed to get fully prepared.

While wandering the streets of Paris on the last afternoon of her trip, Amelia saw couples walking arm in arm on the promenade along the Seine River. That could have been us, she thought. She still hurt badly from Jack's betrayal. She knew it would take a while for the sting of past events to subside. She still could not fully understand how or why he had turned on her, why he'd made the decision to cheat. She rationalized that their love was not meant to be, and the impact of money was simply the fuel that drove the process and quickened it. She came to realize that he did not deserve her. She knew that she certainly did not want him back, but it made her wonder if she was inadequate as a partner. She was ready to move on and see what her future love life would have in store. How would she recognize real love when it was in front of her?

Amelia considered what she would face when she returned to LA. She planned to stay in a hotel until she could find a house. She only had to move her personal items; the furniture had to stay with the beach house. Ms. Harris had several homes for her to consider. The listing of one particular property she reviewed in Topanga Canyon was exciting.

What would old acquaintances say? Would she be accepted within her friend groups? Would people talk behind her back? Would friends side with Jack instead of her? Would she be shunned? She decided that if that was who they are, she is better off without them.

She looked forward to school and developing her business skills. However, it kind of felt like she was going away to the first year of college again. She didn't know anyone well, except Kim and Bill.

But this was her new life. She was comfortable going it alone if need be. She was strong, wealthy, and independent. She resolved to make her plan work and positively impact the lives of women who needed her support.

INVINCIBLE

Jack and Amelia had not spoken to each other in the four months since she kicked him out of the house. Bob Smith, acting on Amelia's behalf, negotiated the transfer of her ownership of the beach house to Jack.

Jack had given up trying to contact Amelia and realized that he had made his choice by being caught in his dalliance with Londyn. The guilt and anger were gone. Jack still thought about Amelia from time to time. He knew that he had made a mistake trying to burn the candle on both ends. He also knew it was over. Even if he went back to her and begged for forgiveness, he was quite sure that she would toss him out the door or even worse.

Londyn wisely made sure that she satisfied Jack's emotional and physical needs. If Jack was distracted thinking about work or her, there would not be time to reconsider what might have been with Amelia. She did not need a despondent Jack to slow down their relationship or her career. He kept the focus of his attention on business. The movie production took most of his energy and time. He golfed twice in four months and had not flown an hour.

Londyn quickly replaced Amelia and moved into the beach house. Londyn loved living in the house by the ocean with Jack and sharing his life. She learned to control Jack's emotions and effectively cater to his needs. She had confidence that now that Jack had Amelia's engagement ring back, she would wear one soon.

Jack borrowed against his future lottery income stream, against Ben Otto's most strenuous cautions, to finance his purchase of three yachts. The rentals were coming in continuously but at a much lower rate than needed to break even. Jack just knew in his gut that there should be more rentals. He made a mental note to talk with Randy about increasing the number of rental days.

He suspected that Randy did not like him and was shunting rentals to other owners on purpose. What else could it possibly be?

Jack and Londyn were deeply involved in the movie project. He was learning more every day, usually the hard and expensive way. He had borrowed against his future lottery income and invested a substantial sum to finance and independently produce *The Ticket*. The projected cost was now $60 million. Londyn was proving to be wise and insightful with her advice about working inside the Hollywood infrastructure. She could find talented and work hungry actors and pay them far less than known Hollywood stars. She also made sure that they used the beach house and a yacht as sets and then charged those costs to the movie's production budget.

They intentionally leaked the news that Londyn would star as "Amelia" in the movie. The Hollywood publicity over her playing the part of the woman she had "stolen" from the real-life-fiancé who won the lottery caused quite a stir in the tabloids. The paparazzi had a field day. Many pointed out that it seemed ironic that city buses still had Jack and Amelia's enlarged publicity photos mounted on their sides. When the press tried to get a comment from Amelia, they received none.

Londyn told Jack, "Out here, any publicity is good publicity!" She made sure that the paparazzi got as many photos as they wanted, many with her arms around Jack and her lips upon his. Because of the hype and publicity, he and Londyn received immediate firm commitments from several well-respected companies to distribute and promote the film. Its scheduled release date was four months away.

Financing the project was a huge gamble for Jack. He was relieved that shooting had wrapped and money stopped pouring out. He was excited for the movie to be released. He had listened to Londyn and others when they said that the script was solid and the story was good, and marketing screen tests had all gone very well.

The distributors decided that the film's premiere was to be held at Grauman's Chinese Theatre. Jack and Londyn arrived in a stretch limousine to loud applause and slashing lights. Jack looked dashing in his black tuxedo, and Londyn was nothing short of dazzling in a skin-tight black formal gown that accentuated all her curves. They waved to the applauding crowd as they walked on the red carpet. They stopped for an interview, where Jack thanked everyone who worked so hard on the project to make it a success. When asked if the film's story was real, he responded that, for the most part, it did follow the real lottery story. He said he'd financed it himself, so he hoped that it would be a great success; otherwise, he might be flipping burgers next week. The crowd laughed. They cheered when Londyn showed off her new engagement ring and told them how excited they were about the film, and assured them that it would be a smash hit. They hugged and kissed for the onlookers and paparazzi. The interviewer asked if the real Amelia would be attending. Jack responded, "You would have to ask her." Jack found himself wondering what Amelia was doing that night.

He was ready for his next success. He was invincible.

DONE WITH JACK

As she signed title transfer papers selling her ownership portion of the beach house to Jack and releasing her from bank debt, Amelia contemplated the end of what was their life together. Once intent on fulfilling the plan of being together until "death do us part," she now knew that the plan was conclusively over.

Because of the ticket they'd bought anticipating a life together, they had been blessed with the gift of relatively unlimited monetary resources. She now clearly saw how the possession of money had so negatively changed their lives. Instead of providing a fantastic future and growth of their love, it caused them to be driven apart. Had they not hit the lottery, they would likely have been very happy spending the first years of their marriage acting like typical newlyweds, planning their future, and earning money to fund their dreams. It saddened her to think of what was.

Winning the lottery was like a hot, bright spotlight, exposing different sides of both of their characters, whether for bad or good, flawed or not. The betrayal Amelia felt was overridden by her determination to live her life positively. She wanted to be the victor and not the victim. She was moving on from Jack's infidelity and failure to be faithful and love her, and looking introspectively at who she was. She considered the possibility that shortcomings and flaws in her character could have caused Jack's betrayal. Had she contributed to the events that transpired, not because of what she did, but because of who she was deep inside? After considerable introspection, she concluded that it was Jack who'd chosen to betray her. She would have been happy to spend her life with him had he decided to be with her.

In hindsight, she thought, perhaps it was human nature that their outlooks on life and internal values would not remain the same after winning the lottery. They were happy when they worked for a paycheck, living day-to-day, enjoying the simple happiness of loving each other. The changes in the range of choices for each of them had instantly become vast. In their relationship, the paradigm shift was greater than their—or, more accurately, his—love could absorb. Perhaps that theory she once heard was correct. Females are biologically programmed to look for security and protection to maximize their children's survival and prospects in a relationship, which she felt when she was with Jack. Men were more driven by sexual desire, looking for young, beautiful, and fertile mates, a theory which Jack seemed to have proven by his actions. The breakup showed that Jack simply did not genuinely need and love her enough to commit to her. And so, with her signatures on the sale documents, she moved on.

Subsequently, Amelia purchased a lovely home in Topanga Canyon. She became fond of the quiet. She felt at peace when viewing the winding, green canyon with its lights at night and from the back deck a view of the ocean in the distance and found that she preferred it to the constant sound of ocean waves and activity on the beach. She found great peace, knowing that this would be a wonderful place to live and hopefully, someday raise a family.

Amelia worked hard with a heavy class load on her MBA curriculum. The work was exciting and motivating. She truly enjoyed learning accounting, finance, organizational theory, and marketing. She spent much of her spare time at Ben Otto's office, pestering his staff with questions about investments and entrepreneurship. She focused on mastering the nature of business and how to analyze financial documents and strove to understand how well a company was performed, and more importantly, how to help it perform better.

Since the breakup, she'd seen Bill from time to time to eat or walk together, sharing their close friendship. She was approached by any number of men, even friends of Jack's, looking for dates, and turned them down, stating that she was not ready for any romantic entanglements.

BILL

Bill had made every effort to make himself available to support Amelia. When she needed a shoulder to cry on, he was there. He took her out for simple meals on some evenings. They walked and hiked when they had more time. He kept telling her that everything would be all right and to just keep breathing, live, and focus on her studies and future. He helped convince her that she would get through this and that she had a wonderful life ahead of her. He never spoke of his altercation with Jack.

Sometimes Bill put his arm around her shoulders as they walked when she needed comfort. Bill saw it as the beginning of a solid romantic relationship, and he was thrilled.

Amelia looked forward to her time with Bill, as most of her friends in LA were made through Jack. She found that they seemed reticent to align with her and potentially offend their wealthy movie mogul friend, who was making an exciting splash in Hollywood with his sexy movie star fiancé. At times Bill and Amelia found it challenging to talk about their past and friends because they were all entwined in Jack and Londyn.

After one walk, they sat on a cliffside overlooking the ocean and watched the stars come out. Bill decided to tell her how he felt. He turned to her and said, Amelia, "I have a confession to make. I have wanted to say this to you since just about the first day we met. I was very attracted to you, but with Jack there, I had to stand back. I have been in love with you since that first day on the beach. You are kind, thoughtful, caring, smart, and beautiful. You are everything I could ever ask for or could ever need. Amelia, I have dreamed of being more than just friends. Do you have any romantic feelings toward me?"

Amelia initially looked confused. Then she thought that he was joking and trying to make her laugh. As Bill spoke though, it dawned on her that he was honestly romantically attracted to her.

But she had never looked at Bill in that way. She saw him as a friend, a confidante, more a brother than a potential lover. She knew that she had not ever felt romantically attracted to him and never would be. However, past comments and actions, including that dance on the beach, now made a lot more sense.

"Oh, Bill," she said. "I'm so sorry. I know that was very difficult for you to say, to put yourself out there where you could get hurt. I just don't see us together as a couple. Right now, you are my best guy friend. You mean the world to me. I don't want to lose that. Can you see a way that we can remain just best friends?"

Bill felt deflated. He longed for at least an answer that would give him cause for hope. "Meels, I will always be your friend. That will never change. The love and dedication I feel for you will always be strong. You can depend on me and trust me all the days of our lives. I just wish that you saw me differently. I really do."

Amelia stood and held her arms out; he rose and entered her embrace. She said, "I see you as a dear, devoted friend, and I love you for it." She kissed him on his cheek and backed away.

"Now, this is a bit awkward," he said.

"Yeah, a little, but it's okay," she said. "We should probably go."

They walked toward their cars. As Bill held her door open, she asked, "Could I buy you dinner tomorrow night and celebrate being friends?"

Bill smiled and replied, "I would love that." He watched her drive away slowly into the night through his tears.

They would remain friends. Bill would never find true love.

SIX YEARS LATER

Amelia had set up her staff of fifteen in offices within her building. She had used some of her own money and raised matching funds from other foundations to set up the Yellowstone Women's Foundation. The YWF's sole mission was to finance and support sustainable, wholly women-owned small businesses. She remembered telling one of her earliest startup clients, "I've learned that what matters in life and what I enjoy most is being with family and being able to do things that help other people." She had also set up an investment fund to be offered to Ben Otto's investment brokerage clients who focused only on investing in women-run businesses.

She had looked at investing in her old company, West Coast Advertising, and determined that it wasn't a good risk. She showed Connie what she saw, and Connie pointed out several other hidden negative issues that she might have missed. As a result, Amelia hired Connie to manage the YWF enterprise on a day-to-day basis. She also hired Kim, who had just finished her own MBA and married a handsome tech entrepreneur she met in class. She relished her role as Amelia's executive assistant.

Amelia found that she increasingly relied on Bob Smith for legal, business, and personal advice. As they got to know more about each other over time, she found him funny, kind, and extremely smart, and always remembered that he had been very supportive during her breakup with Jack.

They spent time together working on YWF business issues, and she became aware that she was drawn to him and genuinely liked him. They thoroughly enjoyed the time they spent together. Bob was the consummate professional and never let on that he also admired and respected Amelia. He felt that it would be improper to express his feelings for her due to his professional role.

One evening, about a year after starting YWF, Amelia invited Bob to a working dinner at the Topanga Canyon house with two female start-up entrepreneurs pursuing funding. Amelia wanted to discuss the potential of combining their businesses into a larger and more robust enterprise. After dinner and the guests left, she asked Bob to join her on the deck for a drink. They shared several glasses of wine while watching dusk settle in over the ocean and canyon.

She asked, "Bob, what do you think of the two women we just met with?"

He thought for a moment and said, "Honestly, I thought that Marilynne was impressive and will knock it out of the park. I think YWF's investors would be well served to invest in her business. I'm confident that she will be successful. I think Julie is a much different story. My grandmother used to say, 'It's better to have people think you are a fool than open your mouth and prove it.' I'm just saying she said some things which were flat-out wrong. Then she doubled down on them when we probed a bit. I also believe that she showed that she doesn't understand what we are trying to accomplish, and that she does not have the business acumen you deserve when you invest in a venture. I don't think that she saw the value in merging the two businesses. Lastly, I think that she believes she was the smartest one in the room, which in this case is dangerous."

Amelia nodded her head in agreement and then was silent, thinking. Then she smiled and said, "Enough work for one day." She turned to him and said, "Bob, this might be entirely improper of me, with our working relationship being what it is." She paused. "However, would you ever consider taking me out on a non-work date sometime?"

Bob's face lit up the night like a Christmas tree, smiling ear to ear. "I would like nothing better. It would be an honor and most definitely a pleasure."

The wine had lowered her filters. She had been considering this for the last several months. She continued, "Well then, let's just say that the dinner we just had was our first date. Do you think that we should kiss on the first date?"

He laughed and said, "Yes, I do believe that there is a requirement in California State Law that requires that anyone on a first date and sitting on a deck in Topanga Canyon is absolutely required to kiss on the said date."

"I see," said Amelia. "And as my lawyer, can you advise me as to who kisses who? According to the law, of course."

Bob said, "If I recollect, wait, just need to think this through clearly, yes, I clearly remember now, the guest is obligated to initiate the first kiss, that is, if the moon is at least half full."

She glanced at the beautiful, bright yellow, full moon which had risen over the canyon lit up the sky and valley.

"I see," she said. "Is there a penalty for not performing to the letter of the law?"

He stood and said, "There probably is a substantial fine and perhaps jail time. However, I'm not going to let my favorite client run afoul of the law." He put out his hands and, taking hers pulled her to her feet and kissed her. She kissed him back. After several minutes of holding and kissing, she looked up into his eyes and smiled, then asked, "Is there a law against making love on a first date?"

He replied, "I'm quite sure that there isn't, but I'm willing to break the law and do hard time if there is."

They dated for six more months. Bob was dedicated to Amelia both in and out of the office. She worked hard on the business. Bob would provide his advice when appropriate, and they found that their values were aligned and well-matched. Amelia loved him deeply. She knew his soul. It was kind, giving, and pure of heart. She knew that this man would never betray her love or trust. She knew that this man could make her world whole. She understood now that she'd never truly felt that from Jack.

Then one day, while hiking on Big Bear Mountain, Bob cited a dubious California legal code that required that anyone who had increased their elevation to over 5,000 feet on foot to request the hand of his or her hiking partner in marriage.

Amelia laughed and said, "That sounds extremely bogus, counselor."

Bob laughed, awkwardly got down on a knee, and said, "Well, if the said hiker has a ring and asks the question on his knee, then it's real. Amelia, I love you with all of my heart. You make me a better person and inspire me to be my best every day. You would make me the happiest man in the world if you were to spend the rest of your life with me. Would you do me the honor of marrying me?"

Amelia put her hand over her mouth and then said, "Bob, if I'm legally required to provide you with a verdict, my answer is yes. I'm found guilty on all counts of loving you and would love to spend the rest of my life with you."

He rose, and they kissed.

Bob said, "I know that you had a bad experience with an unnamed someone in the past. That man was a fool. I love you, Amelia, with all my heart and soul. I will never let you down or betray you. I will always be here for you. You can always put your trust in me."

She nodded, "I believe you, Bob, and you can always expect the same from me."

They kissed again to seal their promises.

Two weeks later, they were married in Oakland, California, in a small ceremony in the church where Bob's mother and grandmother attended services. Henrik was present to give the bride away. They honeymooned at a rented beach house in Bora Bora, soaking up sun, snorkeling, and sipping cold refreshments served on the beach during the day while enjoying each other at night. When they returned to LA, they surprised the office staff with their newlywed news and catered a luau party for the YWF staff.

Several months after the wedding, Amelia called Ben Otto and Clive Bultena and asked that her accounts be retitled to both her and Bob's names. They asked if she was sure about this action, and she assured them that she was.

That night she asked Bob to come sit out on the deck and share a drink with her.

She said, "I've taken some actions and would like to take several more. They concern you and your family, and I want to discuss them with you."

"Okay," Bob said, settling back into the deck chair, not knowing what to expect.

She started, "One, Henrik has money from Grandma Kate's estate. I want to give him enough money to buy a house, help fund the real estate taxes, and be assured that he can keep the cash he got from Grandma for other purposes. Two, I want to buy your mom a house in a safer neighborhood, with enough room in it that your grandmother could stay there, should she need or want to. I know she will protest about leaving her friends, but I worry about her so."

"As do I," Bob said. "I've often asked her to move, but she refuses."

"Okay, bear with me," Amelia continued. "Three, you will tell her that the grandmother of our child cannot live in a dangerous neighborhood when her grandchild is going to come and visit." She paused, waiting for Bob to connect the dots.

His eyes lit up as the light bulb turned on. "You mean we're having a baby."

Amelia smiled and said, "Yes. I tested positive again this morning."

Bob jumped up and pulled her to her feet. They hugged and kissed while he said, "That is such great news. I'm so excited. Oh, I have to tell my mom! She will be so thrilled. A baby! Wow."

"Hold on, buddy. There is one more thing I need to tell you."

"What's that?" asked Bob.

"I called Otto and Bultena today, and they are sending out paperwork to move all of my assets, except for YWF, into joint accounts. I want YWF to be wholly women-owned and directed."

Bob was stunned. He said, "Did you talk to anyone about this? Do you realize what that means? Only a fool would give up control of all of that money."

"Well, I am that fool," she said, "and this fool is in love with you. You were the one who told me about the laws regarding this, and I understand exactly what I'm doing. I trust you, and I love you. We are now a family, and I don't want to hold anything back."

"Well then," said Bob, holding back tears welling up in his eyes, "that is an amazing, loving, and selfless gesture. I'm without words, and for a lawyer, that's pretty rare." After a moment of reflection, he smiled and said, "I suppose it's okay if I keep my accounts all separate?"

Amelia responded, "Not if you want to keep your head on your shoulders. It's all for one, one for all for this family."

Bob laughed. "You know I was just yanking your chain, right?"

"You better be."

"Can we get back to the 'We're going to be parents' thing? I gotta call my mom and grandma."

"Oh, you go ahead. I'll catch up with them later," she said. "I'll just stay here and enjoy my drink."

"Do you want more wine when I come back?"

"Hey, dad-to-be, I'm pregnant. Do you think I should be drinking wine? However, another Diet Coke with a bit of lime juice would be very nice."

He smiled, kissed her and said, "I'll be back soon, and we can discuss nursery plans."

PARENTS

Bob and Amelia were loving parents. The house in Topanga Canyon was always noisy with the joyful sound of kids being kids. The twins, Hazel and Kate, were their biological children. As Amelia and her brother had been orphaned as children, Amelia had long harbored aspirations to help other children in need, so, to further grow their family, she and Bob adopted two more: Beth, who came from Mali, and Gerald, from Haiti. Amelia had been correct, the Topanga Canyon house was an excellent place to raise a family with her husband.

At bedtime, Amelia read Hazel Decker's little book about Sooty the Squirrel once a week to the children and made up "Once upon a time" stories about Hazel and the family living on the shores of Lake Superior and Yellowstone Park. The fireplace mantel held several family pictures. The children always pointed to the photo of Amelia's family soaked by water balloons as their favorite, and mimicked what Amelia had told them, that every picture tells a story. While yet not entirely understanding what that phrase meant.

Bob had become selective about accepting outside work as he now spent most of his time working alongside Amelia to support the women's startups. YWF became a rising force in the Southern California venture capital market. Investors, especially female investors, put their risk capital into Amelia's hands to be invested in promising startups. Not all succeeded; however, overall the investments paid off well, and the reputation and brand grew. Several of the more powerful and savvy investors served with Amelia on the YWF board. Amelia had worked to surround herself with friends and business colleagues whose loyalties were to her.

They were happy, and their life was as she had hoped it would be. Her time with Jack was a real, yet sad and distant memory.

She traveled back to Stillwater, Minnesota every year to award four full scholarships at the high school to female seniors who might not have the best grades but showed great independence and potential. Whenever she came to Stillwater, she and her friends always gathered at the brewery to catch up. Their promises to keep in touch were taken more seriously.

This summer, Bob's mother and the nanny would watch the children, and Amelia and Bob were going to take a trip to Italy. Amelia was excited to show Bob Florence, and try to touch base with Sofia.

Next summer, the family would travel to Yellowstone National Park for the first time. Amelia looked forward to a chance to tell Kate her thread was strong and was heavily webbed. She thought about the needles she had threaded.

JACK

Jack's movie production company, Hammerhead Films, had one success under its belt. *The Ticket* made $75 million in the first six months, which made Jack confident that he had skills and street cred to produce other profitable projects. Some in Hollywood called him "The Wunderkind." He was the twenty-six-year-old producer who could make a hit show out of his own life story. Who does that?

Londyn convinced Jack that she could make his life complete. They loved each other, or at least said so. They were married shortly after *The Ticket* became a box office hit and honeymooned in Italy that summer, replicating the trip he had planned to take with Amelia.

While in France, they attended the Cannes Film Festival where they received royal treatment and were widely congratulated on their monumental success. Matt Damon even stopped by their room to congratulate the new stars. Londyn relished the attention, and Jack showered her with new clothing and precious stone adornments and baubles. Jack was approached to produce any number of independent film projects, but he had to turn down those opportunities as he had his own new project in the works.

Londyn was thrilled with the success of her role in the film playing Amelia. There was speculation in the press about an Oscar nomination, and she received offers for roles that she could have only dreamed about a year earlier. She no longer had to remove her clothes to get parts. Jimmy Kimmel had even invited her back on his show and was gracious and seemingly overly polite.

A year after his inaugural production success, Jack made Londyn the star of his next project, *The Witches Stix*. The project did not have any of the same magical success as his first film. In Hollywood terms, it "bombed" and lost a net $40 million.

Fortunately, Ben Otto had convinced him to diversify his risk on this Hammerhead Films production, and Jack had invited Ralph and Leland to invest. Based on *The Ticket*'s success, they had been more than willing to invest personal funds along with money from other silent investors whom they represented. They now owned eighty percent of the losses from *The Witches Stix*. As a result, the investors voiced loud complaints and public allegations of blatant financial mismanagement and possible fraud on the part of Hammerhead Films.

With their Hollywood connections and substantial influence, Ralph and Leland quickly made Jack a persona non grata in Hollywood. He would not be able to produce any more movies. No one would touch him. They also told him in no uncertain terms that he owed them and their close personal friends "from back East" who had invested. These friends wanted their money back, with, as they called it, "a little vig."

Jack was convinced that several men were following him, and after an attempted break-in at the beach house, Jack hired several ex-Navy Seals as bodyguards to provide security for the next several years. Even with their presence, Jack never quite felt safe from the possibility of reprisals.

After *The Witches Stix* disaster, it became clear that Jack's marriage to Londyn was negatively impacting her ability to get work. His reputation tainted her, and they were both viewed with the same jaundiced eye. This created a rift, leading to an expensive divorce a year after the second film's release. Even with the prenuptial agreement, Londyn got enough of Jack's money to either stop acting forever or be selective about accepting roles and focus her efforts on producing or directing films. She always told people that *The Ticket* was her idea and that her efforts made it a success, while *The Witches Stix* was one hundred percent that idiot Jack's project and she had reluctantly just acted in it; she claimed she told him it would be a failure from day one. Londyn would become one of Hollywood's most successful producers and she married a plastic surgeon who kept her looking young.

Before his and Londyn's divorce, Jack met Amanda Higgins at a party at the Playboy Mansion when Londyn was invited to be the guest of honor celebrating her acting accomplishments and the anniversary of being Miss February several years before. Amanda was a beautiful brunette whom he had quickly and personally cast as one of the sexy witches in *The Witches Stix*. They started dating soon after the movie was released, which hastened the divorce with Londyn.

Immediately after the divorce was finalized, Amanda and Jack were married in a Las Vegas chapel. Amanda knew a golden goose when she saw one. Even though she swore that she was physically incapable of having children and promised Jack that she used birth control as an additional precaution, she was six months pregnant by the time they got married. Amanda made his life tolerable at best, reminding him often about his obligations to her and his daughter.

After *The Witches Stix* debacle and the realization that Amanda wasn't the key to a happy life, Jack turned to recreational pharmaceuticals to ease the pain of his failures. Amanda cared about Jack and his cash flow just enough to check him into the Betty Ford Clinic, where he went through successful drug rehabilitation. After leaving, the treatment stuck: Jack no longer used any drugs or alcohol.

Jack now looked more like fifty than just over thirty. He had developed a significantly larger midsection. Due to increasing stress levels, Jack needed to comb in coloring to hide his prematurely graying hair.

After just nine months of marriage when their daughter was not yet twelve months old, he traded in Amanda for another up-and-coming Hollywood starlet who also mistakenly thought Jack could help her career. His third marriage to former Miss Oregon Maureen Milne came after a short courtship. She quickly ascertained that Jack was a wealthy man and that she could secure her future as the mother of his children. She bore two sons. Jack and Maureen put up with each other for six months after his second son's birth before she found him in bed with a pair of attractive twins, and she booted him out of the beach house and filed for what would eventually be a lucrative divorce.

The settlements from his three divorces cost Jack a large portion of his annual income. The alimony going to "those gold-diggers" was a source of much irritation and anger.

His first child, his daughter, had been born prematurely. Jack had spent many hours walking the hospital halls and worrying. While there, Jack became acquainted with a foundation that raised money for terminally ill children to pay for their dream vacations. Jack was touched by the beauty of this undertaking and personally donated a substantial amount. He also raised funds for the foundation at charity events and even by simply knocking on doors.

After his daughter was out of danger, he raised money for more hospital treatment space, without any fanfare or publicity. He matched it with personal funds to build a new hospital wing to house premature children's critical care operations.

Through his children, he slowly learned how to make a positive difference in the world.

Jack genuinely loved his daughter and sons. It came as a surprise that where he once thought that children would hamper the life of a father who wanted to enjoy a life of leisure, he looked forward to every opportunity to spend time with them. Even though they were a handful when they were all together, Jack felt that they were the best part of his life.

He tried to get full custody of the children, but his past indiscretions made claims that he was a better parent than the children's mothers weak and did not sway the court. Even when Maureen was arrested on drug charges and eventually acquitted when Jack paid for high-powered lawyers, the judge felt the boys were better off in her care. He was pleased that at least some proportion of his alimony payments went to help raise his children.

He was a good father, and his children looked forward to being with him. He would haul all of them to the park or beach every other weekend and play with them as if he were a child, too. They almost always came home tired, happy, dirty from play, and full of fun foods and treats. Their mothers were rarely pleased by this, but Jack and the kids were. It was one of his few pleasures. In his spare time, he wrote and self-published several children's books about a loveable, flying purple dragon named Griffy who befriended Jack's children. They demanded that he read it to them before bed each weekend they were together.

Sadly *The Lucky Ticket* sunk near Catalina Island one night. Wife number two, Amanda, was drunk and heard the bilge pumps running; she mistakenly thought that the ship was taking on water and sinking. She fired off a flare to call for help. Unfortunately, she discharged the gun downwards through an open hatchway and into the lower cabin area, which started a fire and sank the vessel. Fortunately, all on board made it to onto life rafts and were plucked from the ocean by the Coast Guard. The insurance company refused to pay for the loss, stating that an owner had intentionally caused the fire.

Newspapers found the entire episode scandalous, as the passengers included several underage young women and two men well-known in Hollywood. According to the article, Ralph Gottstein and Leland Gentile (whom Jack had invited on board to help alleviate their continued demands for repayment of their investment) were held in the LA County jail under suspicion of having illegal relationships with underage females. Rumor also had it that a large amount of cash was delivered to the teens, for they refused to press charges or testify. Charges were dropped when the girls left the country with their parents.

Jack was concerned about severe retribution from Ralph and Leland. With losses caused by *The Witches Stix*'s failure and incarceration as the result of the sex charges, Jack was afraid that one of these days he might end up, as *The Godfather* film put it, "sleeping with the fishes."

To add to his maritime misery, the insurance company canceled the policies on his remaining two yachts after the fire. When Jack tried to insure through other carriers, they quoted him their highest risk rates due to his loss experience and reputation. His inability to get affordable insurance grounded the ships. Under the stern direction of Ben Otto, Jack decided to sell the remaining two yachts and stop hemorrhaging cash.

He kept up with flying lessons, obtained his pilot's license, and earned a commercial rating. He purchased a Beechcraft King Air 350i for $3 million after he sold the yachts. He enjoyed his time in the air. It was quiet, and he could think while he soared above the beauty of the California coastline.

Since his marriage to Londyn, his philandering outside of wedlock had led to additional suffering. Jack had settled two paternity suits. He found out that it was rather hard to say you did not father a child when DNA testing was involved. Again, "gold-digger" was his standard response to many of the judge's questions. He cared about his children but believed that he had been taken advantage of by their mothers and resented it.

Against Ben Otto's advice, to reduce the impact of the alimony and paternity settlements, Jack tried to hide a significant amount of his money into offshore accounts in the Cayman Islands. When Leland Gentile got in deep audit trouble with the IRS, he gave up his personal knowledge of other offshore investing participants, including Jack, as part of his plea bargain. Jack was still negotiating to get some of the money back.

Unfortunately, when the FBI raided his beach house looking for evidence of the offshore accounts, they found a stash of drugs, which unbeknownst to him, were hidden by Maureen. As a result, he was engaged in an ongoing court battle with the DEA and their attempts to use civil forfeiture laws to confiscate the beach house. It was obvious to him that pending Health and Safety Code 11366 charges should be against her, and not him, because he was not aware of the drugs, nor was he using any drugs; he was rehabilitated and continued to test clean.

His mother had since passed away from a drug overdose. The family continued to accuse Jack of causing her death, claiming it was his fault for giving her money, not providing it to those who could have monitored her spending. He attended and paid for her funeral. The family treated him like a pariah while he was home, yet they never ceased to call him, asking for money. They were rarely successful in getting anything from Jack. He funded 529 college education investment plans for each of his nieces and nephews, some of which were already in use. He was proud to provide for their educations and was especially proud to pay tuition for one niece to attend medical school.

The lottery money continued to come in, and Jack still had a comfortable life, simply because of the size of his yearly payments and the fact that he had the right advisors —when he listened to them. Yet, he lived in a world of female money-sucking leeches, and they were all firmly attached.

He was depressed about his state of affairs and wondered how things might have gone differently had he not taken the path he did, which led to so much sadness in his life. He had three ex-wives and five children to whom he was a four-day-a-month father.

Hammerhead Films was closed, his yacht business sunk and gone. He was currently dealing with the IRS, FBI, and DEA. His lawyers told him that he might serve jail time if he was unlucky. Hell, "unlucky" was his middle name. It seemed that, besides his children, Jack had never failed to fail at everything after the first film.

Jack did not believe he was a bad person. The lottery money had altered the trajectory of his life; it should have been a good thing. He realized how immature and destructive his past actions had been. He thought back to

when Amelia had researched the fates of previous lottery winners on the internet. For a long time, he remained firm in his belief that he had not fallen into the same traps as the others. It had finally become apparent to him that he had. Perhaps money really was a curse.

When he thought about the past, he eventually come back to that first script for *The Ticket*, with the pink and blue endings. He knew that he should have lived the other one. Sometimes he thought of finding Amelia's phone number to call and apologize. But he did not know if he would be able to come up with enough words to express his feelings.

CHANCE MEETING

"Mommy, can I please have ice cream?" "Yes, yes, can we please? "Please?" everyone chimed in.

"Okay, okay," Amelia said. "You can each have only one scoop; we have a cookout at Uncle Henrik's new house tonight."

As they walked into the ice cream shop, Amelia recognized Jack standing at the counter. She wanted to turn and run and not face him.

But Jack turned at that moment and recognized her. He slowly smiled and approached. "Hi, Amelia. It's been a long time."

She nodded and said, "Yeah, six years or so." She calmed her instinct to flee, and introduced her husband.

Jack and Bob shook hands politely. Jack introduced the young woman he was with as Peggy MacIntarry. She might have been all of legal drinking age and wore a skimpy outfit that showed off her figure, which seemed to have silicon in every body part that could be enhanced. Jack said he was sure Amelia and Bob had heard of Peggy. She was an up-and-coming actress/songstress with the best classical training.

Amelia, thinking that nothing had changed with this guy, shook Peggy's hand, saying the obligatory, "Pleased to meet you." Peggy nodded and backed away.

They asked how each other was doing. Jack lied, "Greeeaaaat, never better."

"We are doing fine, too," said Amelia.

"Are all those your children?" asked Jack, nodding toward the four children who jumped up and down happily asking the nanny to help get them their ice cream.

"Yeah," said Amelia. "They are all ours. They look happy, don't they?"

Bob said, "Anytime they get ice cream, they're happy," and limped over to bail out their nanny.

"We adopted the younger two after having the twins," she said.

Jack turned to Peggy and said, "Please excuse us for just a moment, sweetie." Turning back to Amelia, he asked, "Can we talk for a minute?"

He gently touched Amelia's elbow and guided her out of the shop and into the parking lot, where he leaned against the side of an older Dodge minivan.

"Careful not to scratch the car," she said.

"No worries," he said. "It's mine. Wife number two totaled the R8 and one of the yachts, and I decided I didn't need anything that fancy anymore. I also have to tote around five kids. But I loved that car. Remember when we got it?"

She nodded. "I do."

"Those were the best days." He looked at her and asked, "How are you really doing? Are you happy?"

She looked at him and calmly said, "Yes, very happy. My life is good. I love Bob and the kids. I'm doing what I want to be doing and I'm helping people. I think, no, strike that, I know that I make a difference in many people's lives. I'm content but always trying to do more."

She paused then continued, "This is a difficult and uncomfortable conversation, isn't it? Jack, you know that you hurt me deeply. It took me a long time to trust anyone again. But now, I have so much to live for, and I am contributing. I'm not living in the past. I've moved on from you. I come from a line of strong, individualistic people, mainly women, and I hope to pass that heritage to my children."

She took a deep breath, exhaling slowly while Jack patiently waited for her to go on. Then she said, "I've begun to wonder if all of this happened for a reason—if it was fate. Could we have been put on this earth to do exactly what we have done? I think about it every day. It drives me on. It is not that we are special people, just people who were put into a special situation and tested. Then what happened to us was cause and effect. Isn't it less about just having a stroke of good fortune or an event that changes your life, and more about having the determination and vision to use it for the good of yourself *and* others?"

She waited for him to speak. He looked at her in dejected silence. She didn't want to but asked anyway, "What about you?"

Jack looked directly into her eyes, then looked down at his shoes finding himself unable to hold her gaze. "Well, I have made a few mistakes, as you might well know. Otherwise, I guess I'm doing okay. What I wanted to say is that I've often thought about looking you up to tell you how bad and horribly guilty I felt. How guilty I still feel. I just could not think of how to start the conversation or what words would come next. Would you please give me that chance now?"

She shrugged, then nodded, saying, "Sure. Go ahead"

"If I had to do it over again, I would have picked the pink story. The one the scriptwriter printed on the pink pages."

Amelia looked momentarily confused. Jack continued, "Remember when we had the script for the first movie, the one about the lottery? We had two endings based on how our lives could go in two different ways. Well, anyway, it did well at the box office because of the human-interest side appeal. It was the story of you and me. But the critics didn't warm to it. They said it was hokey and make-believe, yet most of it was the real story. You probably never saw the picture."

Amelia said, "I saw it in real life. I didn't need to watch a movie about my reality."

"Sorry. Yeah. Anyway," Jack continued, "don't you remember that one choice, the one on the pink paper which was to be happy ever after together with you? The other was on blue paper, and that one took a different path, which I guess in many ways I did follow. You know, chasing other women and having my money taken by gold-diggers. In the movie, I had picked the blue one and it was a terrible nightmare, but then I wake up from the dream, and you're there sleeping next to me, and I'm so relieved that I had actually picked the pink one. Then you and I, live happily ever after."

"Amelia, I admit I have had a lot of fun and some good times in my life, but in truth, I have not been really happy since you and I split up. I can't change the actions I decided to take. I own that, but I can freely admit that I'm certain that I made the wrong choice back then. It is a mistake that I can't change, and I'm so very sorry I hurt you. I apologize. Do you think that you could ever forgive me?"

"Forgive you?" Amelia glanced at Peggy, who stood by the building, obviously fuming that Jack was talking to her. Then she looked over at her children, sitting at the outdoor picnic table, happily eating ice cream and spilling quite a bit. Then she looked back to Jack.

She said, "Jack, I loved you once with all of my heart. I would have gone to the ends of the earth for you. I was more than willing to spend my life with you. But you betrayed me and lost my trust. Your actions were selfish, arrogant, and narcissistic. You satisfied yourself with no regard for others. You had no values, boundaries, or self-control. It took a lot to get over you, Jack. But I did get over you, and today I am so very happy and content. I'm sorry that your life has been difficult; however, it is the life you chose. I can forgive you for following your heart and for being you, even though it hurt me. I can forgive other transgressions too, and maybe someday I will find a way to turn the other cheek, but as we stand here today, I can't forgive the betrayal of the trust I bestowed in you, Jack."

Jack asked, "Would you ever have taken me back?

She replied, "Jack, if you were the last male human being on earth and I was the last female, the human race would end with us."

"I guess I wouldn't forgive me either," said Jack. "I don't know how, but maybe someday I can earn your trust back. In retrospect, from my perspective, I think it would have been better to donate every penny we won from that ticket to a charity. Just give it away and continue to live the lives that we lived. We might have struggled or fought like cats and dogs, but it would have worked out. I know I would have been happier. I know I would have made you happy, too. I guess I am no different than all of those other lottery winners you read about after we had just won. Maybe if we had stayed together, we would have shared the meaningful life that you have built for yourself. I must admit I am envious. I am trying to do the right thing for my children, and I have become a better person and vow to be an even better one in the future. Amelia, I know I made the wrong choice. I should have picked the pink ending. I should have chosen you."

Amelia looked him directly in the eye and said, "Yes. Yes, you should have."

She then turned toward her young family at the picnic table, who were finishing their ice cream. Before she walked away, she said, "You still have the opportunity to make a difference in this world. I sincerely hope you do." She smiled tightly at Peggy, then as she walked a few steps away, called over her shoulder, she called out, "Good luck, Jack."

The author has previously published two children's books.
He splits time between Arizona and Minnesota.

Made in the USA
Monee, IL
20 August 2022

11912497R00225